D1098126

THE LAST HUNT

HOUGHTON MIFFLIN
LITERARY FELLOWSHIP AWARDS

To E. P. O'Donnell for *Green Margins*
To Jenny Ballou for *Spanish Prelude*
To Robert Penn Warren for *Night Rider*
To Clelie Benton Huggins for *Point Noir*
To Dorothy Baker for *Young Man with a Horn*
To David Cornel DeJong for *Old Haven*
To Maurine Whipple for *The Giant Joshua*
To Mary King O'Donnell for *Quincie Bolliver*
To Helen Todd for *A Man Named Grant*
To A. Fleming MacLeish for *Cone of Silence*
To Donald MacRae for *Dwight Craig*
To Joseph Wechsberg for *Looking for a Bluebird*
To Ann Petry for *The Street*
To Beatrice Griffith for *American Me*
To Elizabeth Bishop for *North & South*
To Helen Mears for *Mirror for Americans, Japan*
To Arthur Mizener for *The Far Side of Paradise:* A Biography of
F. Scott Fitzgerald
To Anthony West for *The Vintage*
To Fred Ross for *Jackson Mahaffey*
To Rebecca C. Patterson for *The Riddle of Emily Dickinson*
To Madison A. Cooper, Jr., for *Sironia, Texas*
To Charles Bracelen Flood for *Love Is a Bridge*
To Siegel Fleisher for *The Lion and the Honeycomb*
To Harold Livingston for *The Coasts of the Earth*
To Milton Lott for *The Last Hunt*

❖ ❖ ❖

THE

HOUGHTON MIFFLIN COMPANY BOSTON

The Riverside Press Cambridge

1 9 5 4

LAST HUNT

BY MILTON LOTT

Western
Americana
PS
3500
L 884
L 3

Library of Congress catalogue card number: 54–8695

DECORATIONS
BY WALTER LORRAINE

The Riverside Press
Cambridge · Massachusetts
PRINTED IN THE U.S.A.

CONTENTS

PART I
SPRING 1882

CHAPTER

1

CROSSING THE LAST STRETCH OF PRAIRIE THAT
sloped off to the valley of Sand River was, Sandy thought, like
coming home — the river, a grey metallic band curving off southwest; the lines of rimrock that enclosed the valley following the
river, converging where it came out of the hills; the valley itself
flat, covered richly with the grey-green mat of buffalo grass and
spotted dark with buffalo; the white spots of the Medicine Rocks
to the north; all — the whole configuration of the land — as well
remembered and familiar as the face of a friend. Yet he had seen it
only once before, ten years ago in the early seventies when he had
been through as a hunter for a reconnaissance unit of the Army
Engineers, exploring northwestern Montana. They had followed
Sand River up from the Missouri a hundred miles or so, finding
the valley thick with game, then had turned off southwest and
crossed over to the Yellowstone. It had not changed much since
then.

The lead bulls, as if feeling the lift of his own spirits, raised their heads and stepped out faster, and the wagon surged close to the heels of the wheelers.

Clouds were moving in from the southwest with the look of rain, dark clouds swelled and palpable as the prairie hills. Below them, beyond the river, the hills were clouded black with buffalo, moving in patches as the clouds moved, but rich and solid-looking as the earth. Only a part of the herd had crossed to the flats on the near side.

He came down the last hill and moved in among the scattered herds, causing hardly a stir. The buffalo drew off on either side to let him pass, keeping a distance of two or three hundred yards, but not running. Ragged-looking, half-furred bulls with their winter shedding clinging still in tatters turned to stare and bawl, curving up scoops of dirt that, falling, left the air hung with dust. The cows, some with little buff-colored calves at their heels, moved on beyond the bulls, out of sight.

He was traveling west now, toward a grove of cottonwoods on the riverbank where he would make camp and begin the hunt. The rain had started, spring rain with the iciness of winter, needling his face under the drive of the wind. His horse swung sideways, bowing his neck, but straightened out with a touch of the rein.

The grove stood at the mouth of a creek — Greasewood Creek, the engineers had called it — that came out of the butte country northeast. It was running heavy with mud, forming a bar out into the river. Swells coming in off deep water broke choppy where they struck the bar.

Buffalo were watering in the open space between the grove and the mouth of the creek. Seeing the wagon coming up on them from the rear, a few of them threw up their tails and charged into the herd, starting a small stampede that fanned out around him and spent itself as the last ones passed. Looking back he saw that all the animals on his side of the river had bunched into one solid herd looking after him, milling some at the edges, the guttural bawling of calves and cows rising with the storm. There were several hundred of them, but they acted as if they felt lonesome, cut off from the main herd.

He stopped in the shelter of the trees, dismounted and unyoked the teams, keeping his eye on the buffalo. They were uneasy — the storm, maybe, he thought, conscious of the blue knives of light dropping from the far edge of the storm cloud and the quick crashing thunder above the noise of the buffalo.

He mounted and drove his cattle to the watering place, glancing nervously back to the east as his horse drank. The rain stopped. The clouds coming off the mountains thinned, showing a red stain of sunset, but east they blackened over the low hills.

While the cattle drank, he swung his horse around and scanned the herd for every movement, feeling a growing tension, noticing the long pause between lightnings. As he watched, over a far hill a gigantic shining blade stabbed downward. In the brilliant light he saw a sudden stirring on the far edge of the herd, a surge inward, even before the thunder reached him.

As the noise died he was whipping the slow cattle away from the watering place, cursing and yelling and hardly hearing his own voice. Without looking up, he knew the buffalo were funneling toward him into the V formed by the grove and the stream where it ran down to the river. The sound of hooves came like a whisper above the other noise, swelling to a vibrating roar.

A trap, he thought, a damn-fool trap to get into. He knew suddenly it was too late to save the cattle. He kneed his horse to a run and gained the trees, grazed by the first line of buffalo. Turning he saw his cattle struck by the first crest, thrown ahead and down, the grey gone under the black; saw the leaders rear back at the river's edge, hesitate just an instant and hurtle outward from the great, blind force behind and drop in a wall of water to flounder in the bar of mud and go down under the hooves of those that followed.

The herd moved out in a black fan from the bank, forced on by the drive of those behind, held to the surface by those gone under, till it reached the edge of the bar and moved on swimming, released.

He felt his strained muscles relax and heard himself exhale a long breath.

Buffalo were running within a few feet of him, grazing the trees, leaving a steaming wake of gamy scent — of mud and breath and trampled sage and willows and the green smell of manure. His horse was backing into the trees, head bobbing, rearing now and then as the edge of the herd came closer.

He sat his horse and watched, fascinated, knowing the bridge that crossed the bar to be alive and struggling, but seeing only the steady column moving over with only a few dropping off at the edges and plunging and going down in the oily muck.

In the thickening dark he saw the leaders reach the far bank, scramble out and gallop into the night. Along the near bank he seemed to detect a line of hesitation, a galvanic line of rebellion that swept out and back in waves, but stayed roughly at the river's edge; as if each animal reaching the jump-off suddenly came to its senses and stopped, only to be carried on by those unseeing ones behind, who would see also and themselves be carried on.

The sound of running faded. Looking east he saw the last of the herd funneling into the river, running with that curious bowing gait of buffalo, heads low, beards flicking the ground with each jump. A few calves, lost by the herd, stopped at the bank, then one by one plunged in, their heads dotting the black water.

He stayed watching till the last buffalo had climbed the far bank; then returned to the wagon, unsaddled and hobbled his horse and rolled his bed out on the ground. He built a fire to dry his clothes and broiled a strip of hump meat while he waited. Afterwards, hearing wolves snarling and fighting, he walked down to the watering place.

The sky was clearing. A full moon sailed high over the white flying scud. Across the river, the valley lay black as new-turned earth. Waves moving toward him on the river struck a shower of light off the surface.

Some of the mired buffalo had struggled back to the bank, there to be pulled down by the wolves as they climbed out. One old bull had come clear out, though he seemed unable to use his hind legs. He was drawn up on his forelegs hooking at the wolves when they came too near. The wolves, having other meat, avoided him. Out from the bank a few shaggy heads still rose above the moonlit water, swaying like snags in a current.

He turned away and walked back to camp. A long while he lay awake, listening, remembering the stampede.

Buffalo were grazing at the edge of the grove when he awoke, moving down river. He brought his horse back into the grove, and, after breakfast, set about making a permanent camp. He cut a few poles from the straightest cottonwoods and carried them to the spot he had chosen to set up a shelter. He stopped then and walked to the edge of the grove and just stood feeling the friendly presence of the valley, thinking that he could stand like this for hours and not be tired of it.

The sun struck warm through the cold air; mist like steam hung over the herd. Eagles and a few early crows sailed in the clear air, now and then slipping down shadowlike into the mist. The herd was quieter now, grazing, though always overhead the nasal bawling of calves and cows hung like the mist, muted, many-voiced as the hum of insects. Buffalo covered nearly all of the flat now; a few files were moving up through breaks in the rimrock onto the hills, east. He watched them scatter out and begin grazing.

Beyond them he saw a rider top a slope and start down, following, probably, his wagon tracks of the day before. Automatically he moved to the tree where his gun belt hung, buckled it on and picked up his rifle. Back at the edge of the trees, he searched long and carefully for other riders. Seeing none, he leaned his gun against a tree and waited.

The rider came on at an unhurried jog, headed for the grove. Ahead of him the herd parted wide and closed again slowly behind him, as the animals went on grazing. He was a large man, riding straight and easy in the saddle, keeping his eyes fixed on the grove. At about five hundred yards he stopped and studied the grove carefully.

Sandy walked out away from the trees and waved, and the rider came on. He was a young man, Sandy thought, but not a kid — maybe thirty. He sat his horse with an easy, confident style. The horse he rode was a big, rangy, long-headed bay, with a lot of white showing in the eyes and a tough, indestructible look.

The rider dismounted and led his horse the last few yards, holding out a slim, tapering hand.

"Charley Gilson, they call me. Buffalo hunter with no outfit. Lost it."

Sandy shook his hand. "Sandy McKenzie. And damned if we

ain't in about the same boat. Like a fool I lost all my cattle in a little old stampede last night — got nothin left but a saddle horse and wagon. If you ain't in a hurry come on and set while I rustle you up some chuck."

"Thanks. To tell you the truth, I followed those tracks a good long way for just that. I ain't et in a hell of while."

He followed Sandy into the trees. "You got a good spot here, Sandy. You can do your killin within walking range. And for a good long while to come, from the looks of this herd."

"I aim to. I figger it'll move north slow, and this is just the head end. I'll have to git some more stock to haul with, though."

"Lost em in a run, huh?"

"Yeah, I was just waterin. Damn buffalo come down to the river hell-bent. Lightning scared em I guess. I couldn't git the cattle out and come near waitin too long myself. Damnedest thing I ever saw. They crossed at a bar of quicksand, used the leaders and my cattle for fill, and went right on over. Damnedest thing I ever saw."

"Yeah. Ain't nothin stupider than a buffalo. I swear, I've handled a slew of cattle and they ain't no ways as dumb as a buffalo. Beats me how they live to make so many more."

"I don't know as it's that," Sandy said. "It's just there's so many they can't see what's goin on around em. No little bunch'd do what those done last night. They'd stop. But the ones behind keep pushin without seein, and somethin's gotta give. Maybe they're dumb, like you say. Maybe a little dumber than men. But damned if a bunch of men won't do the same thing sometimes."

Charley laughed but declined to argue further.

There was a derisive quality to his laughter he didn't bother to hide; a cocksureness that was maybe all right, Sandy thought, and maybe not. He tossed the stranger a piece of hump meat to cook, watching the quick sure movement of the hand that with no waiting attitude plucked the meat out of the air.

Good with a gun, too, Sandy thought.

He set a pot of coffee to the fire and brought a pan of cold biscuits.

"Ain't much," he said. "You can shave the biscuits if there's too much buffalo hair to suit."

Charley smiled at him curiously, but did not laugh. He had a lean, bony face that contrasted strangely with his strong, full set of shoulders. He had a hungry look, Sandy thought, then laughed at himself. Damn it, he is hungry.

"I'll tell you what," Charley said, finishing. "I like this place. I ain't flush, but I got enough for a team and wagon. I was thinkin maybe we could team up, hire some skinners and make this thing pay. Dog it all, I hate to skin buffalo. Nigger work."

"Maybe," Sandy said, offhand. He got up and walked away from the fire. "Come on around and I'll show you where those damn fools crossed."

Charley followed reluctantly. "Dog it," he said. "You're worrying a lot about a little stampede, for an old-timer, ain't you?"

"Maybe so. But there's somethin about it I can't quite lay my mind to. Gittin old, I guess." Still he led the way.

Some carcasses lay along the bank, partly eaten. Half a dozen wolves were lying in the sun licking their fur. When they saw the men they walked slowly toward the trees.

Charley drew his gun. "Nothin like wolves to practice on."

"Cut it out," Sandy said sharply. "No use scarin the herd."

Charley shrugged, but holstered his gun. He picked a bone out of the hoofed-up dirt and shied it at the wolves. It came close; but instead of running, the wolves chased after the bone, slapping at it with their paws like awkward pups. They went on into the trees and turned to watch.

"Doggone," Charley exclaimed. "Will you look at that! Ain't scared of nothin. Hell, I hate a wolf."

The old bull Sandy had seen the night before was stretched out at the bank, apparently dead, though there were no wolf marks on him.

"Hell, there's a start already," Charley said, "if he was skinned. He don't look like much, but hell, he'll make leather."

Sandy walked slower. "Look out. That son-of-a-gun maybe ain't dead."

"Aw," Charley snorted. Nevertheless, Sandy noticed, he swung off to the side, though he walked on ahead. He picked up another bone and tossed it at the bull.

The buffalo came up like a steel spring and seeing Sandy directly ahead, came at him, tail in the air, roaring. His hind legs seemed weak but he started fast.

In the same instant, before he touched his own gun, Sandy saw, rather than heard, the shots from Charley's, coming from the side. The buffalo drew up in the middle, blew out a spray of blood and uncoupled not ten feet away. Charley turned toward the trees, looking for the wolves, but they were gone.

"Damn!" Sandy said. "Three holes you could cover with your hand, and him moving. Much obliged."

Charley blew the smoke out of his gun and reloaded, smiling.

"Well, we got us a start. How about it?"

Sandy nodded, turning abruptly back to camp. "Let's git started. I'll get some knives."

Charley followed, trotting to catch up. "Hell," he explained, "That was just a way of talkin. We better head into town for an outfit. One damn buffalo ain't gonna make us. There's plenty more."

"No, by God," Sandy said. "We'll skin him. Plenty of time to go to town afterwards." He tossed a knife to Charley and started back, walking fast.

CHAPTER

2

JIMMY STOOD UP IN THE WAGON AS THE MULE skinner turned into the hide yard behind Black's store, ready to get off.

"You keep your eyes open, boy," the skinner said, pulling up. "Old Black's a nice feller — but he's a businessman too, and you got some nice pelts there."

Jimmy nodded. "Thanks for the ride." He dragged his pack of furs from under the canvas and climbed down, stepping aside as the wagon rolled on into the yard.

A flight of geese swept low overhead, clear and sharp against the evening sky; but he could not hear them for the noises of the town — wagons jolting along the rutted street, dogs barking, mule skinners and bullwhackers yelling and swearing as they pulled into the wagon yard down the street. A bunch of cowboys came along the boardwalk, yelling as if they were hazing a herd of cattle. They were dressed in tight-fitting new clothes and all of them had revolvers slung on their hips. He stepped back off the walk to let them by and watched them go on down the street and turn in at Ed's saloon.

He shouldered his pack then and went into the store, feeling strange and bewildered — as he always did in a white man's town — though he had been here before. Black was the only one in the store and he shook hands in a friendly way, even remembering Jimmy's name.

They sorted the furs out and agreed finally on a price.

"Where's your sidekick?" Black asked. "This is the first time I ever saw you alone."

"He's dead."

Black made a clucking sound with his tongue. "It's too bad. He was a hard case though for just a kid. Pure Injun . . . Well," he went on, changing his tone, "what do you want to take back to the reservation with you?"

"I ain't goin back."

"No? What'll you do?"

Jimmy shrugged. "Try to find a job, I guess."

He walked over to the gun counter and selected a .45 Colt revolver and belt. "I'll take this for a start," he said, buckling the belt around him. He tried the action and stood running his hand over the grip.

"Well," Black told him. "If you're not going back, I'll tell you what you'd better do. Get rid of those damn black reservation clothes and dress like a white man. Get yourself a haircut, and with that red hair, no one'll ever take you for an Injun — or a half-breed either. You'll get along better."

While he talked he worked with a pencil and paper figuring the account.

"I don't know what you want the gun for, but even with that, you still got some left for clothes. And I can fit you." He looked toward the door and Jimmy turned to see two men entering. The one in the lead — a tall, square-shouldered, gaunt-faced man — walked immediately up to Black, stepping in front of Jimmy, bumping him.

Jimmy stepped back patiently, expecting a long wait as the stranger talked to Black. He dropped his hand unconsciously to

the revolver, exploring the newness of it with his fingers. The
stranger turned toward him suddenly — and there was a gun in his
hand. Jimmy had not seen him draw — it was just there. He was
too amazed and puzzled to be scared.

"Keep your hand away from that gun, kid," the man growled.
"You just had a close call, in case you don't know it."

Jimmy said nothing, still marveling at the man's handling of the
gun.

"Put the damn gun away, Charley," the other man said. "This
boy wasn't out to trouble us."

"How the hell do you know he wasn't?" Charley demanded.
"And how was I to know?"

The other, a big slope-shouldered, clean-shaven man, winked at
Jimmy as he spoke. "Well, I tell you," he said slowly, "he just
ain't got a troublous look."

Charley snorted but said nothing.

"Sandy's right, Charley," Black put in, "this is a good kid —
just bought the gun. Probably doesn't know one end of it from
the other."

"How the hell could I tell that from the look of him?" Charley
complained.

"Just by lookin," Sandy said, "but not along the barrel of a gun."

"Well, forget it," Black said. "What can I do for you two?"

"The boy was first," Sandy said. "Go ahead and wait on him."

"He's in no hurry," Black said, "are you?"

Jimmy shook his head.

"Here," Black went on, "give me that gun and I'll keep it till you
get ready to leave town. Damn it, I'd hate to see you get hurt."

Jimmy unbuckled the belt and handed it over. He had been a
little bit resentful of the men at first, but not now. He liked Sandy,
and Black was genuinely friendly. He could only marvel at
Charley; Charley might have killed him, he knew, and yet he felt
no real hostility in the man. He did not dislike him.

He stood around listening with interest as the two men made their
purchases. They were buffalo hunters, he found, getting together
an outfit, buying in what seemed to him enormous quantities — a
hundred pounds of lead, a hundred and fifty pounds of powder,

several cases of primers and a case of knives. They bought a wagon and eight head of mules and a whole slew of camp supplies and — except for the wagon which Charley bought on credit — paid for it all in cash.

After they had gone, Black fitted Jimmy out with a suit of clothes — a grey felt hat, tight-fitting blue pants, a red checked flannel shirt and a leather coat with big patch pockets on the sides. The shoes Black tried to sell him hurt his feet so he kept his moccasins.

"You want the old clothes?"

"Burn em," Jimmy told him emphatically.

"You get those braids chopped off now," Black laughed, "and you won't know yourself."

They settled up then and Jimmy started out.

"If you don't find anything to do, maybe I can put you on — it wouldn't be much, but something to keep you going."

Jimmy nodded and went on, feeling strange in his new clothes. He found the barbershop but it took him a long time to make up his mind to go in. He had been in jail once at the reservation and they had cut his hair; and for months, until it grew long again, he had been ashamed to be seen. Now he was doing it voluntarily and it was hard — a kind of surrender. He went in, though, and sat stiffly in the chair, not talking to the barber, hardly hearing what he said, retreating afterwards to the street in a confusion of feeling.

Moonlight lay bright along the side of the street, divided from the zigzag solid shadows of the buildings by the roof lines. Patches of yellow lamplight flattened from the windows fanlike on the shadow side where he walked.

It was quieter, with no wagons on the street and only a few horsemen and now and then a buggy. He could hear music from down the street and followed it, feeling alone and strange, but curious too. Two women passed him, clattering along the boardwalk with their hard shoes, trailing a disturbing scent of flowers and musk. They paused, looking in the window of Ed's saloon, then went up the stairs that led to the floor above. He was tempted to follow, knowing this to be a whorehouse; but changed his mind. They did not take Indians and he was not sure his new clothing changed him so much.

He went on slowly, still hearing the music, drawn by it, locating it finally in the gambling hall farther along the street.

He stood in the shadow of the building listening, finding it hard to enter the lamplight that poured out over the swing doors.

As he stood, a buggy rattled along the street and pulled up in front of the hall, drawn by a pair of high stepping greys that stood fidgeting nervously while a girl climbed out on the side next to the walk. She was just stepping down between the wheels, holding her skirts with one hand, when someone burst through the swinging doors going in and sent a flashing patch of light under the feet of the horses. They reared up together against the pull of the lines and came down moving. The girl stepped out from between the wheels, but her skirt had caught on the foot iron. It jerked her backward and she sat down hard and was dragged a few steps, sitting, before the hind wheel ran up on her skirt and pulled it loose. Jimmy had stepped out into the street when the team started, but he was too far back to do any good.

He helped the girl up now, knowing she was not hurt, amused at the anger flashing in her face as she turned and stamped her foot after the departing buggy.

She remembered Jimmy then and thanked him, looking up at him, her face in the light, her eyes still sparkling, her lips pouting. He could not help laughing, drawing her indignation on himself.

"I don't see anything so funny," she snapped. She bent over and started brushing herself, twisting around to reach the back of her voluminous skirt.

"Does it hurt?" Jimmy asked, still grinning.

"What?" she asked, then added quickly, "Oh, shut up."

He stepped close to her then to help, and saw that her skirt and the petticoat underneath had both pulled loose at the waist. The gathered cloth had sagged down in back revealing a patch of dusty ruffled underpants.

"No use brushin the dress," he told her. "It's hardly dusty except where the wheel ran over it. This is where the dust is." He reached through the hole, hardly controlling his laughter, and slapped her behind. She flirted it away from him, gasping, and reached back with both hands to explore the tear, her eyes growing wide with dismay.

He heard someone behind him then and started to turn, but something struck him on the head, dropping him into darkness . . .

He moved upward toward the light till his eyes opened and he saw the moonlit buildings. There was pain in his head like needles and before his open eyes little points of light exploding as from the stroked fur of a cat. Someone was bending over him, a man whose bulk was outlined black against the silvered wall across the alley.

He struggled to his feet, fumbling for the knife at his belt.

"Easy, boy. Ain't nobody gonna hurt you. Looks like somebody slugged you."

He relaxed, knowing he could trust the voice. He rubbed the back of his head and brought his hand away stained and sticky.

"Seems so. I don't guess that's paint. I thought for a minute somebody'd got my hair."

The stranger handed him his new hat. "I figgered at first you'd had too much to drink, but I couldn't smell it on you. Well, come on. I'll buy you a drink."

He put his hat on carefully and followed, into the warm air and light and noise of the saloon.

The man was big, he saw now, no taller than himself, but broad. His shoulders sloped, his walk was a bearlike amble. He ordered two drinks and turned, extending a big rough hand, and Jimmy recognized him as one of the men he had seen at Black's.

"Call me Sandy. Sandy McKenzie." He paused, then smiled. "You're the boy we saw at Black's ain't you?"

Jimmy nodded. "Jimmy O'Brien. I'm obliged to you."

"For little." He paid for the drinks and drank his with obvious relish.

Jimmy imitated, though his throat rebelled. But he knew that no one watching could have known.

Sandy was looking at him. "You take your whiskey all right, sonny. But I can't help feelin you ain't very old. Not that I see any fuzz on you," he added quickly.

Jimmy hesitated.

"That's all right. Don't tell me. It don't matter a damn. Too old to suck and too young to die, I can see that. How come you got mixed up in that fracas? Somethin tells me a woman."

Jimmy nodded ruefully, feeling his head.

It occurred to him then that his purse was gone. He felt for it quickly.

Sandy laughed. "I see. The money too. Well — a few years and you'll learn to take your women like your whiskey — slow and easy."

"I'm sorry I can't buy the drinks."

"Forget it. What'll you do for eats?"

"Get me a job, I guess."

"You ain't been workin up to now."

"No, but I have before. I trapped this winter."

"I know that," Sandy said. "I'll tell you what. I'm lookin for a skinner. Buffalo. Sixty and found."

"Summer hide?"

"Sure. It pays as good as prime now. They use it for leather. You on?"

Jimmy nodded.

A girl had come out on a stage at the back of the hall and was singing, her brown hair shining in the warm light. With a shock he recognized her, knowing her not by her voice or her hair but by the shape of her face as he had seen it in the street outside. He watched her till he realized that Sandy was leaving, and followed reluctantly out of the hall and down the moonlit street. He was remembering her face and the patch of light from the doors flashing on the street. He felt his head ruefully and smiled, feeling at the same time a puzzled sadness.

CHAPTER

3

Woodfoot awoke suddenly, hearing the rattle of hobble chains as the mules circled the camp, crossing to the other side of the draw below. They were moving fast in a stiff-legged gallop, raising their hobbled front feet together and high with every jump. When they reached the side of the draw they whirled in a bunch, stopped, and pointed their big ears back the way they had come. They were maybe three hundred yards down the draw and he could hardly see them in the muddy half-light.

He raised up on his elbow and scanned their back trail to see what had scared them. He saw nothing, but he could hear the snarl of wolves close in.

He glanced around at the other men, finding them still asleep. Charley, who had rolled out his bed under the wagon box, was snoring, blowing out his breath in a long rasp, like the snarling of the wolves, only regular. He was directly upwind and Woodfoot caught the sour smell of whiskey in little gusts. Sandy and the kid, Jimmy, were away from the wagon, their beds rolled out to-

gether. They were both sleeping with their buffalo robes drawn
up over their heads.

Woodfoot dropped down into bed, cutting off the wind that was
flowing around him cold as water. But he could not sleep. He was
curious about the wolves.

Finally he sat up quietly and dressed. He put on his shoe and
strapped his leg on, admiring the painted, round-bottomed wooden
foot he had carved himself. He remembered with a smile the awe
of the Indians who had nicknamed him. Once a chief had thrown
him out of the lodge when he took his leg off. He had to hop back
in on one foot to get the leg because the Indian would not touch it.

He got his old needle gun, eased around the wagon and looked
up the draw. In a little depression about fifty yards from camp the
wolves were working on a yearling buffalo they had pulled down.
The hind legs were still kicking, keeping the space around the
belly clear of wolves. He saw the head lift up once above the grey
bodies and drop back with finality.

He stood watching a while, curious. There were half a dozen
wolves, big ones, slashing and tearing at the meat. Once when
they all pulled together they moved the carcass. Then they jumped
back, hackling up like dogs, finally coming stiff-legged back to the
meat to continue their meal. He smiled unconsciously. Then remembering the mules, he selected a big wolf across the carcass from
him, drew a bead quickly and fired. At the same time he yelled
for all he was worth, a long-drawn-out whoop, laughing to see the
wolves scatter.

The one he shot dropped over on its side, galloping with its legs
and yipping. Suddenly it came to its feet and began running a
spiral toward the camp.

Out of the corner of his eye he saw Charley rear up out of bed,
bump his head on the wagon box and drop back, swearing. Woodfoot tried to get a bead on the wolf coming in, but he was laughing
too hard. Instead he hollered, "He's comin in, boys!" Charley
came up again bumping his head, but crawling out still tangled in
his robes. He stood there clawing at his hip for the revolver which
was lying on the ground under the wagon. When he saw the wolf
he turned to run but hit the wagon and bounced back.

The wolf, on the next loop, missed the wagon and ran between Sandy and the kid who were both up now. They danced back gingerly on their bare feet and the kid cut down on the wolf with his new revolver, but Woodfoot could see he was not hitting within a mile.

A little way down the draw the wolf keeled over, still kicking.

"I golly," Sandy said, "we ain't that hard to wake up." He walked over to his bed and sat down, rubbing his chin. He was grinning. "I didn't figger it was less than a hull damn tribe on the warpath, the way you was yellin."

Woodfoot stopped laughing and wiped the tears out of his eyes. "Doggone, I forgot about you guys for a minute. Those damn wolves chased a buffalo down the draw and scared the mules, and if there's anything I hate, it's peggin around the country after a bunch of mules."

Jimmy tried a couple more practice shots that missed and put his gun away. Charley shot once, taking the wolf through the head, then found his boots and sat down on the wagon tongue to put them on. He looked a little pale and he was scowling. Mad, Woodfoot thought.

Sandy said, "Hey Charley, you didn't knock any holes in the wagon box, did you?"

"Aw," Charley snorted. "What a crazy damn trick." He ran his fingers over the bump on his head, looking at Woodfoot with a half-smile. "That barkeep told me this was a crazy son-of-a-bitch when I hired him. I believe it."

Woodfoot shrugged and rolled up his bed and threw it into the wagon. He was still amused, having a hard time to keep it from showing on his face.

Jimmy left to rustle wood for the fire while Woodfoot got his pans out of the chuck box on the back of the wagon and started breakfast. He was still smiling to himself.

Charley was sitting across the fire with a plate full of food but he was not eating. He stared at the fire with a long, mournful expression that was peculiarly out of keeping with his square-shouldered, powerful body. Comical, Woodfoot thought, sizing him up, comical but maybe a little dangerous.

The other two were eating their stewed dried apples and biscuits with great concentration. When Sandy finished he noticed Charley and smiled.

"Hell's fires, man," he said, "you can't live on whiskey. You better eat."

Charley grinned sheepishly and tried a bite of meat, but again stopped.

"Have a drink," Sandy advised. "It'll take the edge off."

"I can't. I'm out."

Sandy went to the wagon and came back with a bottle. He poured out Charley's coffee and filled the cup half full of red-looking whiskey.

Charley drank with a shudder, but he finished his breakfast.

They were on the way soon after breakfast, Woodfoot skinning, the extra mules strung out behind on lead ropes. Charley was in the wagon with his bed rolled out on top of the load, trying to sleep it off. Sandy and Jimmy were riding ahead, Jimmy on Charley's horse.

The mules were hard-mouthed and eager, glad to be rid of the hobbles and allowed to stretch their legs and warm up. When they passed the dead buffalo leaving camp, they swung wide and tried to run but he held them to a trot, seesawing on the lines. There was no road, though now and then he saw the tracks of Sandy's wagon between the curly brown patches of buffalo grass. He was following in general a deeply cut buffalo trail, cutting across where it curved too sharply. When he crossed at an angle the wagon tongue whipped back and forth, jerking the wheelers roughly. The big grey on the off side nipped fiercely at the neck yoke when it whipped or sometimes tried to reach his mate, the crazy jenny. The mules were an assorted bunch — none had been teamed before, so they worked together awkwardly. But he liked to make his own teams. The wheelers, for instance — Charley had laughed at what he called the mismatch, the extra-heavy grey and the crazy jenny. They would be all right — and it was the only way he could use the crazy one.

He eased up on the lines and let them trot, thinking of Charley and wondering how he was making out. He was fascinated by Charley — it was half of why he had taken the job. That and being broke. He hated the thought of skinning buffalo again, but there was no use thinking about it. Skinning mules, now, he thought wasn't so bad.

Wind thrust cold in his face and, overhead, moved a wide stream of muddy-looking cloud that promised snow. The clinking of the butt chains took on a steady rhythm as the teams settled down, ringing coldly above the chuckle of the hubs and the jar of bed on bolster.

Since leaving Sand River they had traveled plains country, gently rolling hills, cut occasionally by small streams. Now the hills became steeper, moving up toward what Sandy called the Antelope Creek Divide. From the tops of the hills he could see the high country ahead to the west, high bare hills, timbered sparsely with jack pine and scrub cedar, and off to the south and higher still, a rugged-looking butte country.

Soon after leaving camp, they crossed a creek that was running high and muddy and it took some doing to get the mules into the water. The wagon about capsized on a boulder under the water and Charley came crawling out from under the canvas looking scared and cursing a blue streak. He went back though as soon as they got lined out again.

They traveled along the creek upstream for a way — the hills were too steep to climb — then where it forked, followed one of its tributaries that came down from the east. The creek was small but the draw it followed was flat and fairly wide, and it was not such bad going. There were a lot of big sandstone boulders along it though, so it kept him busy driving. There was a scattering of greasewood and sagebrush along the sides of the draw and up the ridges, and along the creek little clumps of leafless bushes, buffalo berries mostly and chokecherry.

Sandy and Jimmy were riding on ahead to pick the trail. He followed them at a few hundred yards but for the most part picked his own trail, amusing himself by cutting close to the rocks. He was getting the feel of the teams and growing a little reckless. The danger of breaking a wheel on the rocks occurred to him, but he was sure of himself now — he knew the wagon and the mules — and the danger only gave him a sense of exhilaration. He was warming up now. He laughed aloud remembering the incident with the wolves.

There were long ridges on either side broken now and then by side draws in which he saw small bands of deer or antelope, or sometimes a few elk. When they saw the wagon they scattered up over the hills.

It was nearly noon when, nearing one of these side draws, he heard the sound of hooves running. Just as he passed the mouth of a draw a small herd of buffalo swung out behind the wagon and started by him on the left. He heard the snap of rope as the led mules broke loose and stampeded past him. The teams smelled the buffalo and saw them at about the same time. They reared and plunged in panic getting started, then settled down to a scared run. He sawed on the lines with all his strength, but there was no holding them.

The buffalo were off to the side, running upwind. The leaders stayed about even with the wagon, apparently paying no attention to it. The loose mules were on ahead. He caught a glimpse of Sandy and Jimmy trying to stop them.

His arms became tired from hauling on the lines and he was getting annoyed. He had his feet braced on the foot board, laying all his weight on the lines, easing up on one or the other to miss the rocks. The mules were not so scared, he thought, but what they still minded. Whenever the wagon hit a bump his wooden leg slipped, spoiling his balance.

Charley crawled out from under the canvas hollering something Woodfoot could not understand. He glanced back and nodded, grinning. Charley was crouched down behind the seat holding on with both hands. When Woodfoot nodded, he started hollering again. The creek cut across the draw ahead, but was shallow with a natural ford. He crossed it and was drenched with a spray of water kicked up by the mules. It shut Charley up for a minute, but he started in again as soon as he got the water out of his mouth.

Woodfoot's arms felt like they were coming out at the shoulders now. His foot kept slipping and Charley kept hollering.

"The hell with it," he said aloud. "I'll be damned if I lose an argument with a bunch of damn mules." He dropped down onto the seat and shook out the lines, letting go with a long wild whoop. "Run, damn you, if it's run you want!"

The old grey wheeler turned his head in surprise but did not break his stride. He had his speed and he didn't change it. The crazy mule was weaving and jumping but she had to stay with the tongue. She twisted like a snake and bucked whenever the line slack touched her back. When she crowded too close, the grey reached over and nipped her.

Sandy and Jimmy had ridden alongside of the leaders trying to stop them. When Woodfoot yelled, they pulled off to the side.

"Get outta my way," he yelled, and let out a whole string of high-pitched yips. He was skinning mules now and going good. He could feel the blood swelling into his throat as he yelled. He felt a little drunk and giddy as the recklessness swept over him in a wave. He was not scared. There was no time for it. He had the feel of the teams and the strength of control in his arms, and under him the wagon bounding and swinging exactly as he knew it would, watching the ground ahead.

The rocks were thicker with the speed. He had to hit some, but he was missing the big ones, picking his road, curving back and forth. He could feel the hind end whip on the turns. In the clear spots he slapped the line-slack on the backs of the wheelers, yelling and cussing in a steady singsong.

The draw was narrowing, crowding the buffalo in closer to the middle. Some were ahead of the wagon now, some behind. He could hear them grunting and blowing as they ran.

He was cutting close to the rocks, driving as straight as he could to keep the rear wheels from skidding. If they hit going sideways it was a busted wheel sure.

Charley was standing up behind him now, hollering Whoa. He kept trying to reach around and get hold of the lines but Woodfoot knocked the hands aside with his elbows. Finally he leaned ahead, then reared back suddenly. He struck Charley solid with his head and shoulders and heard him hit the canvas and go down.

He did not have time to look back. The near wheeler was going crazy now with the buffalo crowding in close. She kept trying to climb over the tongue. The old grey was nipping her almost every jump but holding steady. Woodfoot felt a sudden affection for the ugly old iron-jaw.

Then, suddenly the crazy mule got a foot over the tongue and went down. The wagon veered to the left just a second, then straightened as the old grey threw his weight against the pull of the tongue. The lead chain snapped tight in the guide ring and they went on, dragging the downed mule. She slid along on her side for a way, then hit a rock and came to her feet. She settled down after that, though she still bucked when the lines touched her back.

The mules were willing to stop now, but he kept pushing them.

Charley was up behind the seat again. He made another grab for the lines and this time got hold of the two on the right and hauled away. Woodfoot saw the surprised white of the old grey's eye as the mules swung to the right, barely missing a big boulder. The front hub grazed it; the rear wheel, skidding with the turn, struck it slanting and collapsed with a crunching sound. He felt the axle hit the ground and heard the reach break. Then the front running gears came out from under the box and the lines jerked him out of the seat. He fell face first onto the swinging bolster and went out still hanging to the lines . . .

CHAPTER
4

CHARLEY LET GO OF THE LINES WHEN HE SAW
the crash coming. He grabbed the back of the seat with both hands
just as Woodfoot was jerked into the air and the box went down.
The sudden stop threw him belly-boost across the seat, knocking
the wind out of him, but he was still aware of Woodfoot face down
across the front bolster, riding a few rods, then slipping backward
and down to catch on the hounds and drag, then unhook and stop
without rolling, like a bundle of rags.

The mules ran on, slowing, still dodging the rocks, the bolster
swinging crazily, the hounds bobbing up and down on the hinge
of the tongue. The buffalo were on ahead now, gaining fast.

When his breath came he climbed out of the wagon box and
walked toward Woodfoot, but Sandy and the kid were there ahead
of him. He could not remember seeing them pass or even remember
them riding with the wagon. He had been dozing when the runaway started, and trying now to remember, it was as if he had not
awakened but had only dreamed the hazy, crowded time.

He vaguely remembered crawling out from under the canvas, trying to stand against the crazy lurching of the wagon, falling and finally pulling himself up by the sideboard and getting hold of the seat. After that all he could remember was his own fascinated concentration on that crazy son-of-a-bitch, Woodfoot. It wasn't the runaway had scared him, it was Woodfoot, yelling like a damn Comanche and shaking out the lines over the mules and laughing, by God. Thinking of it now he wondered why he hadn't hit the damn fool on the head. His hand felt automatically for his gun and dropped away.

Woodfoot was still out. Sandy had turned him over and was getting the canteen from his saddle. Standing now, watching, not thinking of anything to do, Charley felt sick again, as if from the whiskey. It seemed impossible that the little shrunken-cheeked man crumpled on the ground before him — blood running from a cut above his eyebrow back over his pale bald head, his peg-leg cocked off at an angle — was the same as the one of minutes before. Then — with his hat on and his hands full of lines, red-faced and swearing — he had seemed bigger and stronger and somehow dangerous. Now he looked small and, with the scars on his face and his leg bent off to the side, breakable.

Sandy poured water on Woodfoot's face, smearing it around with a rough hand, and he stirred and sat up, rubbing his head. He pulled up his pants leg, restrapped the wooden leg and suddenly was on his feet looking for his hat as unconcerned, Charley thought, as if he were just getting up from a nap.

"Go easy," Sandy said. "You're apt to keel over again."

"Hell, just a knot on the head." He walked back toward the wagon box and picked up his hat, then turned and looked the way the teams had gone. Following his glance, Charley saw the mules stopped and standing quietly at the side of the draw — unconcerned, he thought resentfully, like Woodfoot.

Woodfoot limped off toward the mules with Jimmy, and Charley turned and with Sandy walked back to what was left of the wagon. Looking at the smashed wheel and remembering Woodfoot and the mules, he was suddenly angry.

"By God that is a crazy bastard," he said. "Did you see him

hazin those mules? Like he wanted to kill himself and me too.
Loco son-of-a-bitch, I had a notion to plug him. And now look
at that wheel."

He was aware that Sandy was looking at him curiously, his eyes
wrinkling.

"You sure you had nothin to do with that?" Sandy asked.

He felt himself flushing but he was somehow too confused to
answer.

Sandy shrugged. "No offense," he said. "I was too far back to
see anything. But he was goin so good I figured he was all right if
nothin interfered."

Charley said nothing. He was remembering now, hazily, trying
to stop the mules. Then he was mad again but holding himself in.

"By God," he said, "you oughtta try ridin a runaway with a
damn loon."

Sandy was examining the broken wheel. "We'll get along," he
said. "There's a few good spokes left. We can either tie the wheel
together with rawhide or hoist this end of the axle up on a pole
runner and drag it on in. What do you think?"

"Suit yourself," Charley said. "I don't give a damn myself."

"All right, I'll tell you," Sandy went on. "We gotta round up
those loose mules and we'll need some green hide. If you and the
boy'll go after the mules and bring in a bull hide, I'll rustle up some
sticks — the chokecherry'll be all right — and me and Woodfoot'll
make some false spokes and a new coupling pole."

Charley assented reluctantly, not understanding his own re-
sistance. He'd just as soon not face Woodfoot at the moment, but
at the same time, he didn't like to be told what to do. It was his
outfit that was broke down and here was Sandy telling him how to
fix it and maybe even blaming him for breaking it. He liked the
big red-faced bull-necked man, but he didn't like playing second
fiddle and he did feel himself to be the injured party. Well, the
hell with it.

Woodfoot was coming back, walking out to the side, driving the
mules, the kid beside him leading the two saddle horses. Charley
got his rifle and some shells out of the wagon and mounted. The
kid took Sandy's horse.

Woodfoot swung the front wheels around in front of the wagon box and stopped. He stepped back, still holding the lines, and stood close to Charley's horse.

"Careful they don't get away from you again," Sandy laughed.

"Not a chance," Woodfoot said, looking up at Charley. "I got all the lines now."

Again Charley felt the blood rising in his face and could think of no answer. Instead he raised the bay onto his hind feet, swung him over Woodfoot's head and set him down facing the other way, up the draw, and rode away without looking back. His throat was dry and his blood was pumping in excitement that was not fear, nor anger either, nor even exultation as he had first thought.

He was seeing Woodfoot in that instant looking up past the bay's big sharp-shod hooves that waved loosely over him, showing the whites of his eyes in that crazy shining look, but with no fear and not moving a muscle of his face or even raising his hands.

Charley kicked his horse to a lope and the kid fell in beside him.

It was an old trick, rearing your horse over a man's head, but with a big, mean-looking horse it was enough to scare the daylights out of almost anyone. But not Woodfoot.

There was something cockeyed about the whole thing, a puzzle he could not solve, remembering Woodfoot lying like a bunged-up tin soldier after the runaway and then up as pert as you please and not scared of, by God, anything.

The puzzle is, Charley thought, that the damn fool's lived as long as he has.

They found the loose mules about a mile up the draw where they had evidently tired and let the buffalo pass. Charley headed them back down the draw and with his revolver dropped a few shots close to their heels to hurry them along; then rode on looking for the buffalo.

The kid was a quiet sort. He was tall and skinny with an awkward look that had nothing to do with the way he rode a horse. He rode hunched over in the saddle, the reins dangling loosely from his hand. He was studying the ground, and the horse, with no touch of the bridle, was moving from side to side across the trail, slowing and starting up in an unaccountable eagerness. He rides like a damn Indian, Charley thought. He had never looked that closely before, but suddenly he decided that the kid probably was part Indian. He remembered him then as the kid in Black's store.

The draw curved to the left up ahead; the trail was out of sight.

"They're slowin down," the kid said. "Be grazin around this bend."

"Maybe," Charley said, but he did not take his rifle out of the holster.

They rounded the bend and came suddenly in sight of a couple of old bulls. These threw up their heads and charged into the herd, stampeding them before Charley got his rifle out. He had hoped to get a standing shot, but now he'd have to run them, like a lousy Indian.

The kid was already gone, leaning over the horse's withers, holding his shiny revolver over his head as if he intended to throw it.

The trail was worse than ever now, with clumps of sagebrush and greasewood belly-deep to a horse and in and between the brush patches round smooth rocks from egg size on up. Only a pure damn fool would run a horse through this, he thought, trying to hold the bay in.

The kid reached the herd at least fifty yards in the lead. He picked out a big bull and cut in alongside. Charley lost sight of him then, watching his own way. He was still too far behind to get a shot when he heard the kid start shooting, and looked up. The kid shot five times from a range of about fifteen feet. Little puffs of dust rose off the hide where the lead hit, but the bull kept running, working farther in toward the middle.

The kid saved his last shot and cut into the herd, crowding the running animals with his horse, jumping rocks and sagebrush. Coming alongside of the bull, he leaned out of the saddle, and fired from not a foot away. The buffalo slowed, then lost his feet. The kid let out a yell and rode on, reloading.

What a mess of damn fools I got mixed up with, Charley thought. He gritted his teeth and let the bay go. He forgot about the trail after that; he was even calm. When he came in range, he picked out his bull and dropped him with the first shot. He stopped then and waved the kid back.

The bull was still kicking when they started to skin.

CHAPTER

5

SANDY WAS RIDING IN THE LEAD WHEN FROM THE top of a hill he sighted Sand River, winding and shining in the yellow light of a clear sunset. Overhead the sky was a darkening, icy blue after a sudden storm of hail and rain. Down in the shadows of the hills the thin patchy grass, wet by the quick rain and frozen as suddenly, whispered brittle under the sweep of hooves.

For an hour they had traveled through scattered herds of buffalo feeding in the little valleys between the hills. Now, ahead, on the last rise before camp a lone, huge bull paused against the brassy light of sunset, tried the wind and moved on slowly, bobbing and bowing his shaggy mop in a crippled walk, one front leg swinging loosely from the knee. Behind him, at a respectful distance, three patient wolves held his trail. The bull moved quartering across the hill, dropping slowly under the line of horizon, shadowlike.

Sandy followed the line of the bull's course down across the hill to the head of a draw and a single dry and twisted cottonwood where the bull would stop, where the long wait would begin and end. He watched, fascinated, as the bull, grey now in the thickening dark, moved in his curious bowing progress toward the dark, twisted spire of the cottonwood; the wolves, hardly visible now in the hill's shadow, following unhurried, patient for the waiting ceremony.

He turned and rode back to meet the wagon.

"We better scout the camp," he told Charley. "There's been hunters around, maybe Indians."

"Did you see em?"

"Buffalo with a broken leg."

"He could've broke it some other way," Charley said.

"Yeah, sure."

They left the wagon to follow later and separated as they came over the last hill that sloped off down to the rimrock to approach from two angles. Sandy saw the smoke then, a thin plume, grey and unstable above the trees. He decided instinctively that it was not a campfire — the smoke was somehow not right for cottonwood — there was too much blackness in it.

Buffalo were feeding close to the grove so probably there was no one there. Still, there was no use taking chances. He moved fast after he crossed the hill, traveling the same general direction the bull had come. Out on the flat he turned directly in toward the grove, riding at a run, bent low over his horse.

It was almost dark now. From a distance he could not see into the trees. Coming in close, he swung suddenly to the right, dropping low on the side of his horse, his foot hooked over the cantle. He skirted the grove, looking into the trees from under the horse's throat, and swung out along the river, in the saddle again. He turned, then, and rode back into the grove and dismounted.

Charley rode up, grinning.

"I damn near mistook you for an Indian, the way you rode in here. That's a good trick." He was being a little sarcastic, Sandy thought; but he shrugged and walked on, leading his horse. Skirting the grove he had not seen his old wagon; he expected it to be gone. Instead, parts of it were lying at the edge of a circle of ashes. Two of the wheels with burned stubs of the axle trees in them had flopped out to the side, unburned. In the center was a wad of slashed, partly burned buffalo hides that were still smoking slightly.

"Damn," Sandy said. "Now I got mules and no wagon. Don't seem like I can get organized."

"Lousy Indians," Charley said.

"Why?"

"A white man woulda took the hides and maybe the wagon too. He wouldn't of burned em."

"Maybe," Sandy said. "It was Indians all right, though. Sioux. They got no use for a hide hunter."

"It's no love lost then."

"Well, we can throw away that patched-up wheel of yours, anyway," Sandy said, "and use one of these."

"Yeah, that's right." Charley brightened. "Those lousy thievin Indians, though. Too bad."

"Didn't steal anything," Sandy said. "Unless it was a little chuck."

"Dog it, Sandy, I don't understand you. You stickin up for em?"

"No. I just thought maybe you'd remember why you figured it was Indians." He left then to bring the wagon in.

Afterwards they made camp in the dark, hobbled the mules and staked the horses in close.

"We'll keep our eyes peeled tonight," Sandy said. "It'll be moonlight, and they might make a try for the stock. Tomorrow we'll fix up a little better before we start killin — a corral for the stock in case of trouble and some kind of a shack."

They had a supper of hard bread and jerky and coffee, sitting around a small campfire.

Woodfoot sat hunched over, wrapped up in a buffalo robe with only his hands and scarred, pinched-up face sticking out, mouselike — bright-eyed, a curious contrast to the uncomfortable and mournful Charley who sat by him. Charley took the cold as a personal injury, Sandy thought, fighting it like he fought everything else.

Jimmy, of all of them, was the most at home. He was dressed lightly but he didn't seem cold. He finished eating first and disappeared into the trees toward the river. Later he came back from a different direction.

"We got a buffalo right here in the trees," he told Sandy. "A cow. You want her?"

"Naw," Sandy laughed. "Unless you want to skin in the dark. Or when it's froze up in the morning. Anyhow, it'll stink plenty around here without a carcass right by the campfire."

Woodfoot was through eating. He brought out his banjo and struck a few chords, but playing it exposed him too much to the cold so he laid it aside. He was muffled completely in his robe now except for a breathing hole. He began singing in a cracked voice the tune of Canaday-I-O, but the words were different.

*It's now we've crossed Pease River, boys, our troubles have be-
    gun —
The first damned tail I went to rip, gosh! how I cut my thumb.
While skinning the damned old stinkers our lives didn't stand
    a show,
For the Indians watched to pick us off while skinning the buffalo.
Our meat was always buffalo hump and iron wedge bread.
And all we had to sleep on was a buffalo robe for a bed;
The fleas and graybacks worked on us, oh boys it was not slow
I'll tell you there's no worse hell on earth than the range of the
    buffalo.*

As he sang he peeped through the darkness at Charley who sat appearing not to listen. When he came to the part where the skinners have the argument about wages with Crego, the hunter, and leave "his damned old bones to bleach on the range of the buffalo," he was grinning mischievously.

Sandy laughed. He had heard that version of the song in Dodge City after the last big hunt on the Cimarron. The tune he had known before he left the old settlement at Pembina on the Red River.

But there was something ludicrous and out of place — Woodfoot singing now — though it was a comment, a personal expression of independence, Sandy thought, a humorous defiance that was Woodfoot. Irrepressible, he was, and scarred up to prove it. He wasn't crazy, as Charley thought. He was just too damn brave — or reckless. The wooden leg was a badge, a decoration he carried proudly — or that carried him. A badge and a cross, both.

There was moonlight now, washing whitely down from the hills on the frosty grass into the edge of the trees, and no sound but the far yapping and hoo-hooing of coyotes and now and then the drawn-out howl of a wolf. He remembered the buffalo bull, then, seeing him in his long wait under the dark tree.

"We better keep a lookout tonight, I guess," he said. "How long since they were here, Jimmy?"

"Yesterday," Jimmy said. "There were only two. They won't likely be back."

Charley laughed, a rasping derisive cackle.

Sandy cut him off. "All right. We'll keep a watch anyway. Jimmy, you take it first, then me, and I'll wake Charley. We better let Woodfoot nurse his sore bones."

"Don't favor me," Woodfoot said. "I'll make out."

Sandy looked at the stock before turning in. On the flat the grass was plated, clear to the long shadow of the rimrock, with ice and light; out of it the scattered clumps of sagebrush and grease-wood, buffalo and mules grazing against the light thrust black as rocks out of water.

He had not yet slept when Jimmy called him, though the moon was high in the South. He rolled out and took his rifle and walked to get his blood going.

He went out of the trees and walked first to the mouth of the slough where the stampede had crossed, where he had lost his cattle. There was no sign left save the stripped carcass of the bull Charley had shot and the ones killed by the wolves, frosted like the grass and shining; and no wolves. The wind had gone down and the river was smooth except where the currents curled and wrinkled, flashing light, at the surface.

He turned and walked north along the river through the trees to look at the horses staked on the other side. Nearing the edge of the grove he saw the buffalo cow, standing with her head down, in a little open place that was laced in the moonlight with the shadows of the leafless, twisted branches of the cottonwoods. Calving, Sandy knew, seeing her bow up as a spasm took her.

A warm goatlike smell rose with the steam that flickered up through the shadows from the wet ground under her. Soon now, he thought.

The cow had not seen or smelled him. She stood quietly waiting, her ragged, bleached wool beaded with moisture, dappled like the earth in the patchy light. He was close enough to hear her breathing, the long, caught and extruded exhalation of the spasm and the steady whisper in between.

Then the feet appeared, and the head in one shining mass out of shadow into light. And then down slowly in pulses and out, unshaped to the release; the drop in the bright sheath to earth with a wet slapping sound like a lump of mud; then the kicking and, the shining case gone, the cord broken, a calf appeared, drew up its legs and raised its head, gasping.

Birth finished, the cow turned to lick the shivering wet shape, to nudge it with her nose till it rose shaking, slowly as if out of the ground, into the patchy light — an animal now, a form out of earth. It sought, nudging with upturned, wrinkling nose till the cow maneuvered into place and it found the teat.

Sandy backed quietly away and went out of the trees into the open flat. He felt tired now, and it was a long wait till he called Charley.

CHAPTER
6

Jimmy awakened to a morning of misty light and a clear sky. Charley was building a fire near the wagon, fanning and blowing and piling on sticks. He had found some small dry twigs, but the rest of the wood he had gathered was glazed with ice. The twigs burned vigorously but the other wood sizzled and hissed before catching, dripping water into the fire below and sending up white puffs of steam mixed with the smoke. The fire almost went out before the wood on top was dry enough to burn. Charley went on poking at it, piling on more wood, delaying the fire he seemed so anxious to start, scowling and walking around. The fire grew slowly to a huge blaze; then Charley stepped back, holding his hands out toward the flame, smiling triumphantly.

Jimmy rolled out and went over to the fire. He was interested in Charley, awed by his ability with a gun and curious about him otherwise.

Charley seemed pleased with the fire he had fought into an uncomfortable blaze. He turned in front of it, resisting the heat but being slowly driven back.

"A white man's fire," he observed to Jimmy.

Jimmy nodded. "We can keep warm packin wood."

"Sure, you can," Charley agreed, laughing but not amused.

Jimmy grinned, not really resenting Charley's attitude. He would do now what he had always considered women's work — he would carry wood and skin buffalo. But he would earn money too, and learn, in the meantime accepting the position without fighting it any more than he had to.

He left the fire, stopping at each tree to break off all the dead limbs he could reach from the ground, piling them for later gathering. The large ones broke with an icy shock that left his fingers tingling and showered him with frost.

The first sunlight was slanting into the trees, splintering on the iced-over twigs and branches into little showers of needled light. Above the trees a wedge of geese swept northward with a windy sound of wings and musical chattering. From the stream south came the raucous quacking of ducks, and from the flats the grunting of feeding buffalo.

Most of the trees big enough to scratch a buffalo were partly dead or dead. Those exposed on all sides were completely barked in a broad ring around the trunk and polished to a dark, oily finish. Around these, deep circular trails were cut. The only trees undamaged were the young trees growing close together in patches. All through the grove the ground was grassed with bleached brown hair and wool.

At the spot where he had seen the buffalo in the evening he read the signs of the recent birth. Working out to the edge of the trees, he saw the cow and calf down river beyond the horses and mules, standing apart from the others in the increasing sun. The cow saw him and moved a few rods down the river and stopped. The calf stayed close to her heels, walking awkwardly but strongly. When the cow stopped, the calf turned broadside to Jimmy and stood facing the sun, wiggling its little rounded ears and snubbing its nose at the bright warm light.

When he came back to the fire with an armful of wood, Sandy and Woodfoot were up. Woodfoot walked around stiffly, testing his sore muscles as if he thought they might break. There was a long blue welt across his forehead. When he saw Jimmy watching him, he mimicked his own movements, laughter stirring the scars on his wrinkled, shrunken face.

Woodfoot had assumed the job of cook. He went about it busily now, fussing with pots and pans and supplies like a woman, stopping to wash things that had only a little dust settled on them from the trip.

He served up fried hump meat and stewed dried apples, coffee and biscuits which he baked in an iron skillet propped up by the fire — the same meal as the others he had cooked.

"You eat that bread," he told Jimmy. "It'll stick to your ribs. I use buffalo hair for a binder. Yes, sir," he went on, "bread is my specialty. I can take fifty pounds of flour and make five hundred pounds of bread. It's a fact. I can cook a meal in five minutes you can't eat in a week."

After breakfast they went to work making a camp.

Sandy organized the work. "We'll fence in the grove as a corral for the stock. We'll need poles for that and for a frame for a shack. The grove's a little too big as it is, so we'll cut the trees at the edge and trim it down some. We'll use the small ones for the shack and the big ones to make the corral. The limbs we'll cut and stack for firewood."

Sandy and Charley took the job of cutting the trees. Jimmy limbed them. Woodfoot brought in one of the mules, a big grey, and harnessed him to snake the logs around.

The sun was up warm now. On the east side, where they started, the trees began dripping as the ice melted from the limbs. A warm steamy smell came out of the earth and mixed with the sweet strong smell of the cut wood and the buffalo smell that was always there but stronger with the dampness and the warm sun.

The trees fell out from the grove, icy side up. The axe bit into the frozen limbs with a brittle crack, the wood seeming to break rather than cut. Where the ice was heaviest in a clear coat on the limbs, it shattered white back from the cut of the axe and little showers scattered on the ground like snow.

By noon they had the grove trimmed down to a rough half-circle on the riverbank, maybe twenty yards deep. At the front in the middle of it they cleared off a little spot about ten by twenty feet for the shack, then quit for dinner.

In the afternoon they sorted out the smallest, straightest poles and started building the shack. They cut the poles to length and set seven posts around the plot they had laid out, four at the front, wtih two close together for a door and three at the back.

There were still some rawhide strips left from the repair of the wagon wheel. They used these to tie together a frame around the tops of the posts they had set. They now had the skeleton of a two-room shack, the front wall higher than the back. They began laying poles across the top from front to back for a sloping roof and setting more posts around the ends and sides.

Here they ran out of rawhide. Charley volunteered to bring in a hide and set off down the river afoot toward the nearest buffalo, which were now about half a mile away. Jimmy got his knives and followed.

They walked over to the riverbank, passed the mules and the picketed horses and came in sight of the cow and calf still standing in the sun near the river. The cow was facing away from them, licking the calf. Jimmy could see it wobble a little under the pressure of her tongue.

"We got the wind in our favor," Charley remarked. "We'll take the cow. Save walkin."

The buffalo beyond the cow began moving first, gathering into a closer bunch, but still not running. The cow continued to stand till they came to about four hundred yards, then started moving nervously. She started away fast, then came back for the calf.

Charley dropped to his knees, set up his prongstick, and when the cow turned broadside, fired.

She crowned up her back, walked a few steps, turned around twice nosing the ground like a dog, then keeled over slow, kicking.

The buffalo beyond ran a few hundred yards, stopped and began grazing.

"That's shootin," Jimmy said admiringly. He studied the gun with an excited interest as Charley reloaded. From seeing the guns at Sandpoint, he recognized it as a Sharps Creedmoor. But it was a fancy model. It had a long pistol grip stock of red-looking polished wood. The grip and forearm were checked, and it had a silver plate with Charley's name on it.

"That's a real gun," Charley said. "The Indians got nothing like that, have they?"

Jimmy shook his head.

"I'll get em farther than that if I have to."

The calf, a little bull, was walking around and around the cow nosing her, as they approached. When they came close he ran off a few steps, then hurried back. He stood a few feet away watching as they started to skin, shaking a little along the flank.

They skinned out the legs first and split the hide down the belly. When Charley twisted the head back under the shoulder for a block to keep the carcass from rolling, the calf came close and smelled him. After that, whenever he straightened up and backed away from the carcass he bumped into the calf. He swore a few times, but otherwise seemed not to notice.

They worked in silence, the only sound their own breathing and the skinning sounds — the slicing whisper of the knives and the tearing sound of the hide giving from the flesh under a pull. There was the warm sweet smell of meat and the steam rising from the marbled flesh into the cold air.

They skinned out one side, then rolled the carcass over on the spread-out hide and skinned the other. Jimmy cut the hump meat off both sides and took the tongue while Charley waited.

"It's a waste of time to take any more," Charley said. "There'll be meat from hell to breakfast in a day or two."

They rolled the carcass off and Jimmy folded the hide and threw it on his shoulder, leaving Charley the meat, the knives and his gun. When they started, the calf sniffed at the carcass, then attached himself to Charley. Charley did not even look back till the calf, following too close, ran up on his heels and almost tripped him. He turned then and booted the calf a couple of times, trying to shoo him back toward the carcass. But the calf was stubborn. He sucked up his belly with each kick and sidled away, but when Charley started, was on his heels again. This time he stayed farther back and Charley went on.

When Woodfoot saw Charley and the calf, he grinned widely and bawled like a calf.

Charley looked disgusted but said nothing.

Sandy did not laugh. He seemed a little startled.

"A bull hide would of been better," he said roughly.

Charley shrugged. "Hell, I took what I could get. There ain't enough difference in em for me to run foot races all over the damn prairie."

"No, I guess not," Sandy said, turning back to his work.

Sandy and Charley finished the frame for the shack, then built a rack for drying meat. They set posts with forks on the tops at the corners of a ten-foot square and laid poles across them. Across these they laid other poles for hanging the meat.

The calf stuck with Charley the rest of the day, getting in the way at every turn. Woodfoot, snaking the logs around for the corral, stopped now and then to watch and laugh.

"You'll be a good ma," he told Charley. "But how'll you feed him? You ain't built right."

"Feed, hell," Charley sputtered. "He'll be meat before the day's out."

They made a two-pole corral, using the trees for supports where they could, but otherwise setting double posts, then tying the poles in between with rawhide. They made two gates with removable poles. It was dark when they finished.

The moon moved up red over the low hills, paling slowly as it climbed. Jimmy, coming back in after rounding up the mules and moving the staked horses, was struck by the change in the grove. The cut tops of the stumps showed bright under the moonlight and around them the chips flaked white like bones on the dark ground. The corral was a crooked, bony line, the twisted misshapen logs running in and out between the posts, the stumps of their cut limbs horning out in all directions, shining where the moonlight struck the cuts. And beyond, the skeletons of the shack and the drying rack rose up formless, grotesque and out of place. It was a little thing, but it bothered him.

Woodfoot was busy rustling up another meal and laying it out in skillets to warm. Sandy was building a fire. Charley came up from the watering place with a bucket of water, still followed by the little bull calf. He climbed over a middle section of the fence and the calf tried to go between the bars but fell backward on his haunches and rolled over.

Charley was smiling when he came over to the fire and sat down on a robe. The calf got up and began trotting back and forth making little nasal grunting sounds.

"You got a lifelong friend," Woodfoot said. "You don't seem like a motherly sort to me, but a man can never tell. Under that rough — "

"Aw, lay off," Charley growled.

"All right, all right. You ain't motherly, then. In which case that calf is makin a big mistake."

"Goddamn calf," Charley said.

The calf, in the meantime making longer trips, found a place he could go under. He trotted over to the fire, stopping suddenly with his front feet spread when he felt the heat. He stood sniffing at the warmth, snubbing his reddish nose up and down, running out his little black tongue. In the firelight his coat, wavy from the mother's tongue, shone red. He backed away and trotted around the fire till he found Charley and began nosing him eagerly. Charley pushed him away, but he kept coming back, making little sucking noises with his tongue.

"The hell with it," Charley said suddenly.

He stood up and walked out of the enclosure, followed by the calf.

Woodfoot stood up. "Save your lead," he told Charley. "We'll make meat out of him." He found an axe and a knife. Walking up to the calf, with no hesitation he knocked it in the head with the back of the axe. The calf folded silently and rolled on his side. Woodfoot put his hand under the chin and drew the head back, cutting the throat with a quick slash. The blood spurted with a hissing sound, black and steamy in the dim light, and there was a gurgling sound of breathing.

Woodfoot stepped back, straightening up; and suddenly the calf came to his feet and staggered away in the direction he was facing — toward Charley. Charley stood his ground till the calf, scattering blood, came close; then turned and ran. He jumped up on a stump and stood there looking back. The calf ran into it and fell in the shadow, his kicking feet softly drumming on the wood. Jimmy could hardly see him in the black moonshade. Charley still stood there looking scared and foolish.

Sandy, who had been watching silently from the fire, laughed softly.

"Well I'll be damned," he said. And that was all.

Jimmy and Woodfoot skinned out the calf and hung it on the meat rack.

CHAPTER

7

CHARLEY AWAKENED IN COMPLETE DARKNESS, breathing hard as if from running. He turned on his back and searched above for stars or a show of moonlight; but saw nothing; the dark pressed in on him, weighted like a depth of inky water. Involuntarily he put out his hand with a pushing movement, then brought it back to his face and rubbed his eyes. There was a tightness in his chest and he could feel the blood pulsing in his throat.

There was no sound but the crazy, unreal voicings of coyotes coming from everywhere and the liquid, uneven sounds of the river. Wide awake now, he sat up and listened till he heard the snort of a horse, then lay back, knowing that he must have been dreaming, relieved.

He could not remember the dream. Lying there, unable to sleep, he felt an itching in his muscles to move; to jump up and run or yell out into the black night. He ground his shoulders down hard against the rough earth.

He remembered the calf with its head cut halfway off chasing him across the clearing. He could almost hear the gargled breath

and the muffled pounding on the wood under him as the calf fell
and kicked itself out. The hoof wasn't hardened yet, he thought.

The blood had been black in the moonlight, not red. When
Woodfoot cut the throat the blood hissed out steaming, blackening
a new wood-chip till it seemed to disappear into the earth. It was
that, he thought, had made him run. No sense getting bloodied up.
As if the blood were dirty or would not come off. The hell with it.
He shrugged his shoulders against the hard earth.

Anyway, it was scary enough, the damn calf getting up and running when it was supposed to be dead with its throat cut. There
was a fearful ghostly quality about it he couldn't quite name.

He lay looking toward the sky, sometimes, through a thin spot
in the drift of cloud, seeing a star. Lying there trying to sleep he
remembered something that had happened when he was a kid,
something he hadn't thought of in years. He had killed an old
white cat, hitting it on the head with a stick as it came out from
under the woodpile. Instead of falling the cat ran up his leg, bleeding from the eyes and mouth and ears. He dropped the stick and
caught the cat by the neck and choked it while it sank its claws
deeper and deeper into his ribs and belly. Blood trickled down
over his hands, staining the white fur, and in the open mouth he
saw the teeth, worn down almost to nothing. He stayed frozen
to the cat till he was sure it was dead, then shook its claws loose
from his clothes and left it — without taking the fur, as he had intended. He had nightmares about it for a long time after that.

Light came slowly under the heavy cloud drift. He lay watching blurred emerging shapes that seemed to move toward him out
of a mist and grow, as yet colorless — grey, unfamiliar shapes like
half-remembered things that set him thinking about the war.
Maybe, he thought, because grey was the main color of those
memories, the images all in black and white like tintypes and maybe
the unfamiliar quality of the images themselves.

He had left Chicago and enlisted in Kansas when he was nineteen.
He could remember the new blue uniform, and the blue platoons
drilling and all the color and flash. And then the marching with all
the color gone, and the dust and mud, as if the mind itself were
dirtied from the remembering.

His first battle came to him through a haze, and there was still a tightening in his stomach that was partly shame and partly remembered fear. His regiment had faced a charge of infantry, and he had frozen in position, not even conscious of his rifle till a lieutenant pushed him down behind the breastwork.

He remembered lining up the grey running figures in the sights of his rifle, surprised at the ease with which he could draw a bead, even through all the smoke and confusion. The charge wavered and petered out, and in the clearing smoke and the lull that followed, he discovered that he had not fired a shot.

He did all right, though, after that. He was good with a gun. He practiced some, but it seemed like he had been good from the first. He could beat anyone in the regiment with rifle or pistol.

He was only in a few more skirmishes after that, but he came out all right. There was nothing to shooting a man if you didn't have to look at him afterward. And he took a good deal of pride in his shooting. It always bothered him though, having other men shoot at him, wondering what they thought about him when they shot.

Sandy was up first, building the fire. He started it with a little kindling and instead of laying the sticks across the fire, burning them in the middle, he laid them all the same way with just the one end in the fire.

Charley went over and stood watching curiously.

"It's a good way," Sandy explained. "You just keep pushing them in as they burn. Saves wood."

"Hell, we got plenty wood."

Sandy shrugged. "Just a habit. You get out by yourself sometime. You'll see."

Charley was silent. He could tell he was rubbing Sandy the wrong way. And he didn't intend to. He meant to be friendly, but it always seemed to come out wrong.

He knew now he had done wrong to pass himself off as a buffalo hunter when actually about the only ones he had ever hunted had been for sport. He could shoot with anybody, he knew that, but he knew also that he had a lot to learn about the whole business. And instinctively he knew he could learn it from Sandy.

Well, it was done now, and he felt a little nervous wondering how he would make out.

"It'll be a good day," Sandy observed. "No wind to speak of and clear. I always do best on a warm, quiet day. Feller can sometimes get himself a stand. But not a windy day. Never knowed anyone to handle a herd with the wind blowing. It's always shoot and run on a windy day."

Charley nodded, searching for the word that would keep Sandy going. What he said was, "Yeah. A quiet day's best. But you can get em in the wind too if you shoot right."

"Sure. A man can. And waste a lot of powder and lead and run his damn legs off too. A buffalo is flighty in the wind. He don't scare so much from what he can see and hear, but what he smells. And it's like he don't much trust his smeller either with too much wind. So he just keeps movin. Upwind, like he was lookin for somethin to be scared of."

Jimmy came over to the fire. "I'd like to shoot some too, if I get a chance. I always shot em off a horse though. And mostly with a bow and arrow."

"Small potatoes," Charley said.

"Well now," Sandy put in. "It's a good way. For a fact, I think it's the best way, if it's just meat you're after. There's some sport to it, and it gives the critters a chance. Lancin em, now there's my idea of a man's way to kill buffalo. From a horse. A man can get hurt that way."

"It don't amount to a damn for hide-huntin, though," Charley said. "You wouldn't git enough hides to spit on that way."

"No, that's so," Sandy admitted. He went on, talking to Jimmy. "When you're just after the hide you gotta get a lot of em, and fast. So you learn how to manage em and shoot em down like hogs in a pen. It's a sorry business to be in, without you got a strong stomach." He paused. "But lancin, now. There's my idea."

The sun came up, taking the chill out of the frosty clearing, drying the near sides of the crooked frames of the shack and the meat rack. Frozen blood clots on the neck of the calf's carcass began to shine in the warming light.

He could see buffalo from where he sat. They had been close in

but now were pulling out farther, leaving a gap around the camp.
They were still within range.

"We could start shootin from right here," he remarked to Sandy.

"Wouldn't be smart," Sandy said. "It'd scare the hull damned
herd out of the country. The thing to do is work the little bunches
that's out of sight of the main herd. Git out in the hills and work
the little draws and valleys. That way we git buffalo and don't have
to move camp every day or two."

Charley caught his horse and rode out alone after breakfast,
heading for the hills as Sandy had suggested. Sandy stayed to help
unload the wagon and get it ready for hauling hides.

"I'll git the boys started," he said. "We maybe better start em
off easy like. So they don't git discouraged on us and serve us like
pore old Crego."

When Charley reached the first rise, he looked back and saw
Sandy just leaving camp, riding to strike the hills somewhere to the
north. It was a good day for hunting. The sun was up warm,
raising little skifts of mist, and the air was cold but quiet, what
movement there was from the north.

Beyond the first hill, he found buffalo, maybe forty or fifty,
mostly young ones, spike bulls and cows with calves and only eight
or ten big bulls. He left his horse standing with the reins dropped
and worked south along the ridge till he passed the herd, then went
up over and down.

He worked slantwise down the hill, hoping to get to the bottom
before the animals got restless, and so avoid a down shot. Shooting
down it was easy to overshoot, and not only that, it was hard to
make a lung or heart shot that way.

One of the bulls, an old stub horn, was feeding out away from the
rest. Something caught his attention and he threw up his head,
sniffing the air. He shifted around and stood looking straight up
the hill at Charley.

Charley stopped and stood quiet, knowing that any movement
would send the bull charging into the herd. It was still a long
shot, and he knew only a lucky one would drop the bull, facing
as he was. So he stood frozen till the bull started feeding again.

He started down again, slower, but still moving slantwise down the hill to get down and closer at the same time. But the bull caught the movement again and snorted and trotted in among the others. They all stopped feeding then, threw up their heads and milled a little, sniffing the air. Charley lowered himself slowly and set up his prong stick. It was too far for comfort, but he'd have to do it or the whole damn kaboodle would run off and leave him.

He waited till they stopped moving again and picked out a bull standing just inside the edge of the herd, broadside. A cow was standing on the near side of the bull, but back a little, her head near his middle.

Charley drew down, shooting for a spot well down and behind the shoulder just at the edge of the long hair, and squeezed the trigger, seeing in that instant that the cow had stepped into the shot. She drew her head in the air, twisting it back around to the side till it almost touched her shoulder, at the same time running a circle out away from the herd and back into it, starting a stampede.

He reloaded and dropped her with the next shot, but the herd was running then. He tried one more shot at a bull out in the lead, hoping to drop him and turn the herd back, knowing as he did it that the shot was too long and too hard and feeling foolish for even trying it.

The bull went down as the bullet struck. His hind end sloughed off to the side and dropped. His front quarters balanced for just an instant, then flopped over. But he was up, almost as soon as he hit, his right hind leg flopping and swinging as he ran. The herd had passed him now and he was trailing along at the rear, bouncing awkwardly, but still making good time.

Charley came to his feet swearing, reloaded, and took out after them, knowing as he ran that the herd would not stop for a while. Not with the wounded bull charging into them every time they slowed. Still he ran, hoping for another chance.

He was weighted down with guns and ammunition. His revolver flopped at his side dragging at his hips, forced down by the weight of the two belts of cartridges he carried. The Sharps itself weighed over fourteen pounds and was an awkward weight to run with.

He cut down to the bottom of the draw to get off the sidehill, then ran along it, following a crooked, deep-cut trail, keeping his eye on the running buffalo. He saw the herd slow down, then speed up again as the bull caught up.

He hardly looked at the cow as he passed her, noticing only that one horn had been clipped off, probably by his first shot. He ran on, out of breath, and the herd was still moving. He was breathing so hard he almost missed the sound of running hooves behind him.

Glancing back, he saw the cow not twenty feet away, head down and coming fast. He caught the black shine of the one good horn curving sharp out of the curly wool of her mop.

He dropped his rifle and cut off the trail to the left, running a tight circle around a clump of sagebrush. The cow followed, but her speed carried her out wide. He turned in toward the center of the circle and drew his revolver as he turned and stopped. The cow was coming in but still swinging wide on the circle almost broadside to him. He picked a spot behind her shoulder and fired twice and she was almost on him.

He dodged off to the side and she fell on the spot where he had stood. She belched a big mouthful of blood that spread out from her nose in the short fuzzy grass, gathering dust at the edges.

He could see the herd still moving at the end of the draw where it opened out onto the flats, at least a mile away, he judged. Too far to follow on foot.

He walked back along the trail, picked up his gun and wiped the dirt off it. He was still breathing hard and he felt shaky and slightly sick. It had been a close shave — but he had not been much afraid. It was the failure that bothered him. He felt discouraged; things were breaking wrong, he thought angrily, everything was against him in this godforsaken country, even the animals.

He walked back toward his horse, feeling strange and out of place — even under the warm sunlight the place had become hostile, inimical.

When he reached his horse he stopped and thought back, trying to figure out what he had done wrong. Looking down the way he had gone, the path he had followed approaching the herd, he remembered something Sandy had said about lateral movement catching a buffalo's eye. That was what he had done wrong, going down the hill slantwise; he should have moved straight toward them, even if he had to shoot down.

He knew what his mistake had been; but knowing it made little difference in the way he felt.

He heard shots then, coming from the direction the buffalo had gone. He mounted and rode north along the ridge till he could see the mouth of the draw, still hearing the shots steady and spaced, about one a minute.

The buffalo had stopped about a quarter of a mile out on the flats and were bunched up close now, milling and bawling — all but about ten head that were down around the edges. He could see Sandy about two hundred yards to the south of the herd, his rifle to his prong stick shooting, a little puff of smoke hanging over him in the quiet air.

While he watched, a bull detached itself from the herd and began hooking one of the downed animals. Even at that distance Charley could hear the flat, metallic bawl of buffalo that smelled blood. With the sound of a shot he saw the bull flinch and hump up, then turn to go back to the herd, and in turning fall.

It was the last bull in the herd. Sandy shot two more cows that started to lead off from the bunch, then stopped firing. He sat up and started cleaning his gun, and the animals moved off, not running. Charley counted sixteen dead ones. He saw the skinners pulling out from camp with the wagon before he turned and rode into the hills.

CHAPTER

8

Woodfoot had a team of mules up — the crazy mule and the old grey — when he heard the first shot; Charley's, he knew, because he could still see Sandy on the flats. By the time he had hitched up he heard Sandy cut loose and saw the little herd bunched at the mouth of the draw.

He drove out slowly, hearing the steady continuation of shots. He had no relish for the skinning job and was in no hurry to start. He was used to it now, but he still remembered how it had been in the beginning.

He had first skinned for a meat hunter on the Santa Fe after the war, and it was bad then, getting used to a wooden leg and learning to skin to boot. It was man-killing work at best, bent over all day, pulling and lifting till your guts hurt and grease and dust in your clothes, caked stiff, and the smell of yourself enough to knock a dog off a gut wagon.

When the Santa Fe stopped construction in the fall of '72, he hired out to a merchant in Dodge City for fifty a month and keep. There were hunters all over Kansas that year, so thick it was like the war again with all the rifle fire and the stink of rotten carcasses wherever a man went. And worse the next year, till the buffalo were that scarce you could ride all day and never lay eyes on one, save maybe an old lone bull and he more than likely packing lead.

He remembered traveling along the Arkansas before that in the fall of the year and the buffalo as thick as cattle at a roundup — for two hundred miles or more, nothing but buffalo, till it seemed like there was no end of them. Dead buffalo floating in the little eddies or quicksanded along the banks, and the live ones making a racket you could hear for miles — bulls fighting among themselves and chasing the cows, and the cows and calves bawling.

But in '74 they were gone, the live ones, and the bones and rotten carcasses left wherever you looked. And the stink. Lord God, he could still smell it, a whole country open and flat as far as the eye traveled, a whole damned world, it seemed like, stinking even with a breeze moving, till a man couldn't get the smell out of his nose awake or asleep.

It was something to remember even after he got used to it, the way it hit him then. The stinking carcasses and bones that whitened the ground like alkali, and the black spots of unskinned bull heads with dried shriveled noses. And in place of the buffalo, flies till a man was afraid to open his mouth.

It had seemed, then, that the whole country was changing, not just a little spot a man might dig up with a hoe to plant corn, but the whole damned shittaree.

Then the nesters coming in and picking bones for a start, and all the buffalo in Kansas gone, clear to the Arkansas and Indian territory . . .

In '74 he hired out to a man named Walker for eighty a month and moved into Indian country, down on the Cimmaron and the Canadian. And there was Indian trouble, then, bad, the Indians fighting for the buffalo, but the hunters still moving in. There were a good many that never came back, but others made out good, coming into Dodge City with a slew of hides.

A couple of hide buyers organized a regular expedition that year, into the territory. They forted up on the Canadian at a place called 'Dobe Walls, and there was a big fight. A few hunters were killed and a sight of Indians — no one knew how many — but there were dead ponies scattered around the fort so thick it was like some one had got a stand on them, taking them for buffalo.

And there was worse fighting farther south at Anadarko, he heard tell of, till General Sheridan moved in and put it down. General Sheridan it was who had suggested a medal for the buffalo hunters — a dead buffalo on one side and a dead Indian on the other. The army was always behind the hunters then, for all it was against the law to hunt below the Arkansas.

He had fought Indians twice down on the Red River with Walker, and the last time on the Salt Fork a band of Kiowas nearly rubbed him out. They had camped on a little flat near the stream, and in the night the Indians got all the horses and mules. At day-light they moved in and all there was for breastwork was a few buffalo hides. But two thicknesses of dry bull hide would stop anything the Indians had.

They fought off and on all day, using their rifles at long range and their Spencer carbines when the Indians came in close. They winged a few, but the others carried them away almost before they hit the ground. If they killed any Indians, they never knew it.

The last big charge in the afternoon got both Walker and the other skinner, though likely the Indians never knew — not till later anyway. They moved off down the river and he thought they were pulling out, but he didn't dare leave, not afoot, and the only trail out down the river. So he loaded the guns and waited.

It was a clear night, and moonlit, so he saw the Indian plainly as he came pounding in alone on a spotted pony. There wasn't a chance to hit him at any distance, flattened down as he was on the horse's withers. So he held his fire. He thought of dropping the horse, but waited, feeling a sudden excitement rising in him. All afternoon he had fought calmly, but now the blood was pumping through him in a flood and he was shaking like a kid — as if the craziness of the damned fool Indian was catching.

So he lay there waiting while the Indian came on, the white legs of the pinto flashing in the moonlight and the eyes shining.

The horse jumped the pile of hides and came up against the wagon, and the Indian fired first and missed.

Woodfoot shot him then with a revolver and caught the rawhide rope out of his hand as he slid off. The horse shied out to the end of the rope, his mouth open, working his tongue against the rawhide looped around his jaw. Woodfoot stuck the pistol in his belt and worked up the rope hand over hand, feeling the pony shaking.

He remembered to mount on the off side, but even then he almost fell off as the pony started, jumping and running as if he didn't know how to buck.

He could hear the other Indians coming in then. He rode straight at them, yelling, with only one revolver and it half empty, knowing sure as hell he was done for, but not scared. He felt like he was breathing again after having his wind knocked out.

He went in low on his horse in a confused rattle of rifle and musket fire and the feathered whisper of arrows. The mass of horses split and he went through, hardly believing it till he heard a united yell from the bunch and the chatter of hooves as the horses got under way behind him.

It seemed then like he was quilled with arrows, and there was a ball in his hip he'd carried ever since.

But he could still ride. He threw the revolver away and it took all his guts to stay on, with the arrows flapping in their shallow holds and the gunshot starting in after the numbness. But he stayed with it. And hearing the noise dimming behind him, he knew he had a horse that could run.

After that things got hazy. He remembered pulling the shafts of two arrows out of the horse's shoulder. The heads stayed in the flesh, like they always did with a war arrow. Running his hand over the wounds he could feel the blood coming in little spurts in time with the pony's stride.

He didn't try to pull the arrows out of himself — but he counted them. There were three, two in the muscles of his back standing up straight as they had entered as he lay on the horse's withers, and one in his thigh from behind.

He had no way of knowing how long he rode, but the horse died under him. He felt bad about that, all out of proportion, he thought, as he remembered back. He managed to crawl off the trail into a hackberry thicket and lay there cursing himself about the horse till he passed out.

Some Mexican hunters picked him up and took him into their

camp. They told him later he had put up a fuss about leaving the horse, but he didn't remember that.

He moved north then, back Kansas way, but it had crowded up so he kept on going, up the Missouri. He got a job whacking bulls on the Carrol Road over to Helena, but it was too much walking for a man with a wooden leg. He drifted into Sandpoint broke and ran into this Charley in a saloon, and now here he was again, back on the buffalo range.

Sandy was waiting by the dead buffalo.

"I got me a little bit of a stand," he said. "But it was a poor bunch, kips mostly, so I let em go. Charley run em out of the draw so maybe he's got some in there."

"It's a good start," Woodfoot said. "It ain't every day a man gets himself a stand — and it ain't every man can handle it when he does." Buffalo hunters, Woodfoot thought, were on the whole a pretty sorry lot, for all their toughness.

"Purely accident," Sandy grinned. "Though I reckon I've had my share of em. But it ain't something I'm rightly proud of. I knew a butcher once went crazy as a loon just stickin pigs. It's the blood, I guess. Times when I get a stand, it gives me a turn. It does. And skinnin is worse," he said, reining his horse to go. "I'm thinkin it's a good thing I got you boys to help."

Woodfoot unhitched the mules and tied them to the wagon. He buckled on his knife belt and went around and cut out the tongues of all the animals, taking them out through the lower jaw. That was always where the birds started — that and the eyes — and the tongues were worth saving.

Jimmy was already skinning. He had picked a bull to start on, Woodfoot noticed, and he was going at it as if he knew how. He had turned the big animal partly on its back and twisted the head back around under the shoulder to keep it from rolling. He had girdled the legs and head and was splitting the hide down the belly, working with clean, deft movements.

Woodfoot turned, knowing that the kid would do all right, and went to work on the first animal he came to. He had a new set of knives, but he didn't like the way they were sharpened — not enough taper to the edge. Time would fix that.

It was a bull he started on — a stub horn, the hunters would say. The horns were ringed with age at the base, worn flat on the outer curve from wallowing in the dirt and broken back on the ends, revealing little jet-black points like new horns growing inside the old.

When he rolled it over, he saw that the right hind leg was broken just above the hock. Charley, he thought. Maybe he ain't such a hunter for all his shooting. It wasn't Sandy, he knew, because one shot like that would ruin any stand.

The bull was big — anyway sixteen hundred, Woodfoot thought — but the hide was a sight, a patchwork of bleached brown wool and shiny brown hide. On the neck and shoulders where the new hair had grown, the old still clung in tangles. But the head looked good; the hair was new and curly, maybe three or four inches long, and a shiny black. But you couldn't skin a bull's head — not and make time, so the only part of a summer hide that looked like anything you had to leave. Even the mop on top of the head, since it was still too short to bother with.

Poor, too, the bull was, and gaunt, with ticks crawling on his belly trying to get under cover in the short hair. He girdled the legs and skinned them out and made a cut around the neck just back of the horns in the inch-thick, spongy-looking hide, and began ripping it open along the belly, not thinking about the separate movements, just letting his hands do the work while his mind wandered.

The old boy wintered hard, he thought, rooting snow and fighting blizzards and wolves, working like hell to keep his hide in one piece to last him to another breeding season. Maybe that's what a buffalo would think anyway. And even if he didn't think about it, he sure God had a set of equipment to work with when the time came. At any rate he hadn't counted on any tannery wanting his leather, but that was where the wheel had stopped.

It was a caution, he thought, the ways a man could look at it, this buffalo-hunting. It was a lot of animal to kill for a little piece of leather — a thousand pounds of meat shot to hell for a couple hundred pounds or so of green hide. And that was a lot of waste, sure, especially if you looked at it like an Indian might. And then again, for all his size a buffalo only had one life, no more than a bug, so maybe it was like stepping on a bug that was in too big a plenty.

But if you looked at it that way, a man was like a bug, too. And an Indian was a man, and sure as hell he didn't stand as much of a show to get too plentiful as the white man did, even if you left him the buffalo and he didn't starve.

You could bet your sweet life, though, that killing so many big animals would make a lot of changes you couldn't figure ahead.

He skinned the up-side back from the belly, pulling hard where the hide came clean, cutting with long light strokes along the flank and around the front legs where thin layers of meat stuck to the hide; the tearing sound of the hide giving to a pull and the knife point sliding and the sweet steamy smell and the tension of muscles all one feeling that he didn't separate in his mind.

He straightened to touch up his skinning knife on the steel hanging at his belt, and stood till the ache was gone out of the small of his back.

It was warming up now, the breeze down and the big sun washing the hills with an intense light that was unbelievable to a man from the south, as if the air were thinner or cleaner and the sunlight thinner too, with more light and less heat.

A magpie slanted down from the direction of the river with mincing flat wing strokes flashing black and white, and settled on one of the buffalo. He hopped back and forth along the ribs, chattering in a gossipy tone, then slid to the ground and started pecking at a glossy open eye. Woodfoot noticed his own eye winking and laughed.

A crow came down from high up, flapping his wings in an awkwardness that belied that way he could really fly. He sailed back and forth a few times looking things over before he lit.

Woodfoot finished skinning the one side as far down over the back and under as he could reach. Then he gathered the loose hide up next to the back and propped the hind legs over with a forked stick he carried in the wagon. Then he worked his shoulders under the front legs and rolled the carcass over, leaving the loose hide almost free. There was a knack to rolling a buffalo, but even if you knew how, you could still bust a gut on one this big.

He stopped for a breath and saw that the place was alive with crows and magpies. Jimmy had finished his first buffalo but was having a hard time getting the hide out from under. Woodfoot bunched the hide under one side and helped him roll the carcass off.

"Do that with the first side you skin," he said. "That way you only turn em once."

"I will," Jimmy said. "I'm used to saving the meat is all. I hate to see it get dirty."

"You'll get used to that," Woodfoot grinned. "But it'll take practice."

Jimmy folded the hide up and carried it to the wagon. Standing there afterwards he drew his revolver and tried a couple of shots at a magpie. He was wide with the first but the second sprayed the bird with dirt as he rose. The whole flock puffed into the air and scattered in a whirl, but settled almost as quickly. A buzzard was sailing high in the blue air.

Jimmy reloaded, picked up the empty shells and moved on to the next buffalo. Woodfoot went back to work.

A big green blowfly was buzzing around his head, alighting now and then on the warm flesh and each time rising with a higher pitch to the sound of his wings. It was early yet for flies, cold. But it always seemed like flies didn't do much growing. They just appeared with the first warm sun wherever there was something dead. Maybe they just came out of the ground full grown. He didn't know. But it was a kind of thing to puzzle a man.

And wolves. He hadn't seen any yet. But they'd be there before long, he knew. But how did they know? The smell, maybe. But they'd come from upwind too. So maybe it was the sound of the guns or maybe they just naturally spread the news around among themselves. Anyway, wherever the buffalo hunters went there was always a passel of wolves that seemed to spring up like the flies.

Woodfoot finished his first buffalo and moved on to the next. By the time he had girdled the legs and head, he saw the first coyote. Two of them with ragged worn fur trotted up within gunshot and sat down, cocking their heads from side to side. As more appeared, they moved in gradually toward the skinned carcasses. When he finished the one he was on, the coyotes were working on the first skinned carcass. But they didn't stay long. A big grey wolf loped up and scattered them without so much as a snarl. The coyotes stopped and sat down on their tails to wait. He could see little drops of saliva stringing white from their red licking tongues.

They finished the little bunch before noon, and after picking up Charley's cow, moved on north following the sound of Sandy's gun. Late in the afternoon they were skinning the last of Sandy's kill in a little flat west of the Medicine Rocks.

Woodfoot was dead tired now, and when he straightened up to rest his back, spots and circles moved dizzily before his eyes against the bright blue of the sky. East, beyond a brush-lined creek, the rocks glared brilliant white in the sun, the cracks and crevices grey and shadowy, blurring and changing shapes in the first unsteadiness of his sight. He blinked his eyes against the dizziness and shook his head, scanning the rocks curiously, wondering — as he did each time he looked at them — how they came to be there, so white and conspicuous in a land of grey mud and sandstone and rusty slate; and yet they were not white either but a dusty grey — they only looked white in sunlight, and that was curious too. There was maybe a square mile of them, a jumble of buttes, escarpments, ridges, carved by erosion to a confusion of forms — caves, archways, fluted and spiraled columns, reminding him always of a strange and ruined city.

The kink in his back straightened out gradually, but his sight was still blurred. He gave up then and walked over to the wagon for the flask of whiskey in the toolbox, and coming back, sat down on the last unskinned buffalo. Jimmy was still going strong, though he paused to grin, seeing the whiskey.

Woodfoot tipped the flask up, amused at his own weakness, and took a long pull. He shuddered at the raw taste and the fire of it in his throat, then held the bottle before his eyes against the glare of the rocks, feeling the warmth slowly wash out the tension of his muscles. Through the amber whiskey he saw the rocks blurred and golden but steadying now, moving only with the movement of the liquid, the distortion of the glass.

He put the bottle down, closing his eyes against the light, then opened them and saw a movement in the shadows among the rocks, indistinct and hazy, the way it had been through the dizziness. He stood up for a better look, feeling steady from the drink, knowing his sight was not tricking him now, and saw the movement again, a strange humped form, still in shadow, moving slowly out between two buttresses of rock. An animal, he thought; but seeing it emerge into the light, he was shocked to see it was a man. He heard Jimmy's indrawn breath and glanced over to see him standing with his hand to his mouth, his eyes wide with surprise.

Woodfoot looked back to the moving figure, an old man he saw then, bent nearly double, walking with his eyes fixed on the ground, a sack over his shoulder. His hair and beard were white, shining in the sun with the same light as the rocks. As he neared the creek, Woodfoot saw him pick something off the ground and put it in the sack.

He could not tell what it was the old man had picked up, but he felt a sudden relief, realizing with embarrassment and self-derision that he had not quite believed in the reality of the odd humped figure until that moment; it had taken that much, he thought wryly, to dispel a ghost, to clear his own head. He glanced over at Jimmy again and saw him still in the attitude of astonishment and wonder.

"Old Man?" Woodfoot grinned, "or just an old man?"

Jimmy did not answer or even seem to hear.

The old man disappeared into the creek bed and reappeared a moment later on the near side, still intent on the ground and still, Woodfoot knew, unaware of them. He moved with a curious bowing motion that reminded Woodfoot of buffalo; and the white rawhide sack he carried stood up from his back like a hump. As he approached he paused, and bending over slowly, picked up a dry buffalo chip and put it in the sack.

Woodfoot laughed quietly, not knowing quite why it struck him so funny. But there was just something ludicrous about the whole thing — the weirdness he had felt on first seeing the strange figure among the rocks, and now this: an old man gathering buffalo chips, bodewash. The ghost, he thought laughingly, was earthy enough, after all.

"Old Man," he said softly to Jimmy. "He's got enough chips to make big medicine."

Jimmy only looked at him reprovingly; but fearfully too, Woodfoot thought.

The old man came on, within thirty yards, moving obliquely toward them, still unaware that he was watched.

Woodfoot could see now that his hair was not pure white as he had thought — nor the beard — but stained grey and brown. Like the rocks and the sand around them, it only seemed white from a distance. His buckskin clothes and the rawhide bag were tinged green with the dust of the chips.

Woodfoot called then. The old man started and twisted his head to one side to look — he did not straighten up. He hesitated, then came on toward them slowly, watching the ground just ahead.

"There's better wood along the creek than what the buffalo cut," Woodfoot said slyly.

The old man did not answer immediately but came on. Stopping a few feet away, he turned and twisted his head to the side in order to look into Woodfoot's face. He did not put the sack down.

Woodfoot realized then that he could not raise his head. There was a scar on his throat partly concealed by the stringy growth of whiskers, an old knife wound, it looked like.

"It ain't for wood," the old man whispered hoarsely. "It's manure. For my garden." He gestured toward the rocks.

"A garden?" Woodfoot asked incredulously. "In pure sand? A whole damn country full of good land and you got to pick a spot that won't even grow a good crop of sand grass?" He laughed, at the same time feeling an embarrassment he could not account for.

"It's not good land," the old man admitted. "But it's quiet. Another thing, there's nothing in it — nobody's likely to want it or spoil it. If I make something out of a little piece of it, no one will miss it or object." He was still whispering, and Woodfoot looked again at the scar, thinking it was probably the reason.

"You ain't askin a hell of a lot," Woodfoot observed. "Or takin many chances. You didn't count on buffalo hunters, though, did you?"

"It was bound to come, I guess. I thought it might miss me."

"It won't change things much for you anyway, except you'll be pickin cow chips instead of buffalo. It ain't likely anyone'll be damn fool enough to try and farm this country."

It would change though, Woodfoot knew, remembering Kansas. And somebody would try to farm it, too.

"It'll change things, all right," the old man said, smiling. "It'll change things just with the buffalo gone, and the Indians."

He had his eyes on the bottle between Woodfoot's feet now, and Woodfoot saw the movement of his mouth puckering under the stained beard. He had a terrible dry, Woodfoot thought, feeling a curious satisfaction at finding this weakness. He picked the bottle up and held it to the light, then slowly and deliberately put it in his coat pocket, all the while watching the old man's face, seeing his eyes light up, then darken as the bottle disappeared.

"You don't pack a gun," Woodfoot observed. "Don't it bother you a little, the Indians and all?"

The old man shook his head. "I don't carry one. I don't need to." He paused, then continued in a whisper so faint Woodfoot could hardly hear him. "A gun is an attitude, a state of mind — it's a way a man feels about what's outside of him."

"It's a handy attitude, sometimes," Woodfoot laughed, "to keep a man alive."

"To keep a man alive," the old man nodded, "and kill men."

"It's a highfalutin idea," Woodfoot said. "It'd take a saint to believe it and live. You may be a saint — but by the looks of your neck, you've had a close call or two."

"A few," he said. "A man ain't perfect. But he can learn." The old man whispered calmly, watching the ground now, smiling. He looked strong for all the frailness of his bones.

Watching him, Woodfoot realized that he had nothing further to say; he was uncomfortable in the old man's presence and resentful because of it.

He thought of the whiskey again and took the bottle out, holding it briefly to the light, then stood passing it back and forth from one hand to the other, watching the slight, fascinated movement of the old man's eyes following. Finally, grinning at Jimmy, he held it out, watching closely and curiously as the old man's eyes lit up again and he extended a shaking hand. He uncorked the bottle and turning his head to the side, drank eagerly, the scar on his throat contorting with every swallow. A thin trickle of whiskey escaped from the lower corner of his mouth and sprinkled on the ground.

Woodfoot was holding out his hand in protest when the old man stopped. The whiskey was half gone.

"By Jesus," he exclaimed, "you drink like you had a hole in your neck, sure enough! That ain't water, old man. Fire is more like what it is."

"Many thanks," the old man whispered breathlessly, smiling

again at the ground, silently and with an air of concentration, as if he were living wholly within himself, in the fire and feeling of the whiskey. After a while he began almost imperceptibly swaying, rocking forward on his toes and back again, rhythmically as if hearing music, the movement increasing till it seemed he would fall. But he stood, miraculously — as if rooted in the earth.

As he stood there rocking silently back and forth, Woodfoot noticed that the sun was setting. He glanced backward toward the west to see the edge of the sun just striking the hills, and for a little while the air was filled with liquid, shining color — the river, the flats, the hills beyond, and east the Rocks were tinged with red. In that instant he felt an intense awareness of the country that he had never known before. He would remember it that way; the color would fix it in his mind, the way he saw it now.

The old man left then, walking slowly and unsteadily back toward the Rocks. He disappeared into the creek bed, and it seemed like a long time waiting for him to reappear.

The sun was gone now and with it the color — only in the west the clear air held the shining. East the land became one grey — the rocks, the sand, the dark-veined hills that swept upward to the divide. It looked bleak now, and suddenly changed.

The old man reappeared, hardly visible against the sand beyond the creek, looking small and insubstantial, moving slowly and painfully, as if the sack held a tremendous weight. He moved blurring and indistinct toward the grey rocks, disappearing into a wide avenue of darkness.

Woodfoot turned then, seeing that Jimmy was already hitching the mules to the wagon. But all the way to camp the memory of the old man haunted him, puzzling and insistent.

CHAPTER

9

CLOUDS CAME UP IN THE AFTERNOON, PILING UP in solid drifts over the hills west, toppling inward above the prairie and spreading out like water over a glass ball. But there was no wind.

The day had started right for killing buffalo, Sandy thought, and it was still all right, but it couldn't last; not with a storm moving in.

He felt a little relieved and checked his horse near the top of the ridge to turn back, hesitated, then rode on to the top. There would be buffalo in the draw beyond the ridge, he knew, and was amused at the little dodge of turning back before he saw them.

He felt tired, for no good reason — as if he had made a big killing, which he hadn't. His revolver and two cartridge belts and the knives he always carried pulled at his hips with an unusual weight. His horse moved in a drag-footed walk on up the hill.

He was still short of a good day's kill. As near as he could remember, he had killed twenty-four, mostly bulls. Which wasn't so bad if Charley matched it; but he was sure now that Charley would not. He had guessed in the beginning that his new partner would be either very good or no good at all. His cocksureness and skill with guns had been in his favor. But now it looked like he didn't know buffalo. It was something he would probably learn; meanwhile, Sandy reflected with sudden, overpowering irritation, he himself would have to kill more to keep the outfit going.

Skinners to pay now — a regular damn business. The thought was distasteful to him. He had always considered himself a hunter, not a businessman, and the attitude, he saw now, had made it easier for him in the hide-hunting game.

He had always gone it alone before, hide-hunting, and when a man did all his own work it seemed like there was less waste for the money he made. But this was something else again with skinners and a big outfit. He was in the business now, not the game.

As for hunting with Charley — well, he had let himself in for it, so there was no help. It was the price he had to pay for his in-decision. But still it was a hell of a time to get saddled with a partner when all his life he had shied away from it.

Charley killing the old bull that first day was what had turned the trick. He had been in a bad spot and except for Charley's fast shooting, he might have wound up with a horn in his ribs. He had felt obliged at the time, though it came to him later that it was partly Charley's fault for stirring up the bull in the first place. But it was done now and no going back on it.

He shook himself involuntarily, like a dog coming out of water, as if, he thought, he could shake off his worries the same way; and for that moment he seemed a stranger to himself. In all his life he could not remember being so distracted and puzzled.

There were buffalo beyond the ridge, a few bulls and a slew of cows and calves. He dismounted, and staying below the line of sight, he moved along the ridge till he was directly above them. He dropped to his knees and crawled over the brow of the hill in sight of the buffalo, wondering as he set up his prongstick whether it would be a stand. He shucked off a cartridge belt and laid it to his hand, moving slowly and deliberately, feeling a distaste that was new to him. A womanish streak, he thought, and fell automatically into a concentration on his gun.

He picked a big bull at the edge of the herd and fired and saw the puff of dust below the hump where the bullet hit; the bull flinched and stood bowed up in the middle, then lay quietly down. The others crowded around bawling in the strange flat voice they always used when they smelled blood; and it looked like a stand. Then they broke away up the draw following an old cow. He dropped her and the herd turned back in confusion. The little calves trailing at the rear fanned out and scattered like ants to get out of the way. He dropped two more before they passed him going down the draw, and took one last shot and saw a bull go down, then get up and run again.

He left his prongstick and cartridge belt and ran for his horse, knowing the herd was too stirred up to catch on foot, regretting the last shot. He mounted and took out after them, feeling a need to get the wounded animal.

The buffalo had a big start on him now, anyway a quarter of a mile, and were still going as fast as they could hump it. He held his pony to a run along the draw, jumping rocks and sagebrush and clumps of greasewood, risking his neck at every jump, he knew, and feeling foolish for doing it, but still he did not stop. A willful waste of horseflesh, he told himself, and nothing to gain in the end but a poor, ragged bull hide.

He shortened the distance at first, but the pony was tired, and slowed till he was only holding his own. Still Sandy kept going, seeing the wounded bull tailing the herd and falling back.

He was excited now, angry at the pony for being tired and kicking his guts with a fierceness that surprised him as he thought back on it later. He gained on the bull slowly till he could see the pink froth stringing from the bobbing muzzle. The bull saw him and speeded up. They ran that way till Sandy felt a break in the pony's stride and knew he had to stop.

He reined up suddenly and was out of the saddle before the horse stopped moving and shot quick offhand, and was amazed to see the bullet find. The bull's hind end flew up and he fell head first as if his front feet had caught in a trap.

The pony was standing spraddle-legged, head down, breathing with a snoring sound. Sandy loosened the cinch, ran his hand along the pony's neck then led him the rest of the way. He would skin the bull out since he was so far away from the others.

The excitement was gone out of him and he felt tired again, and disgusted with himself. He stood for a while looking down at the buffalo, hardly seeing it; then broke out of the mood and forced himself to start skinning. Revulsion from the whole business was in him like a sickness, and he caught himself resolving to get out of it again as soon as he got a stake together.

He laughed bitterly, remembering the times he had tried to break loose before, only to wind up falling back into it as if he were tied to the damn buffalo for good and all.

He shook himself again and concentrated on his work, hauling roughly at the tough hide, working twice as hard as necessary, he knew, as if something were after him.

He slowed gradually and was startled to find himself reliving an incident out of his boyhood, and it came to him strange but clear.

It was winter with a little snow — he remembered that, and the bare spots on the ridges where the wind swept. The hunt had been long and cold and game scarce. He remembered the long line of Red River carts slung with spare axles and the endless screeching and squeaking of the wheels on their wooden bearings.

He must have been small then — though he had certainly not considered himself so — because he was riding in a sled pulled by two dogs, Indian dogs they were, mostly wolf. During the long trip he had learned to handle the dogs till he was sure he knew them by heart. At first he had a few short, fast rides after rabbits, but the dogs soon learned they were too slow with the drag of the sled, and settled down to a slow trot that kept him even with his father's cart. The dogs learned to stop and start at a word, or turn left or right. He had always been proud of himself for his way with animals; he had been thinking that when they sighted buffalo for the first time.

That was in the afternoon, coming over the brow of a hill that sloped down into a long flat, sprinkled around the edges with a light growth of sagebrush and blacked in the middle with buffalo, just as the scouts had reported. All the men in the outfit mounted their buffalo horses to wait for the captain's orders, and in the confusion his dogs lit out for the herd with himself trying his best to stop them, but in a way glad of a chance to see the buffalo close up. A few loose dogs beat him to the herd, but he was there ahead of any of the men. Going down the hill the sled clipped the tops of the sagebrush, scattering it in his face, along with the spray of snow coming off the dogs' feet. There was a strong smell in the air from the broken sagebrush that changed to the goaty odor of buffalo as he neared the herd. He could not see much. The flying snow and the rush of cold wind in his eyes made them water to a blur in which the herd, now moving, seemed to flow rather than run. He could not let go of the sled long enough to rub his eyes; the ground in the flat was a studding of frozen buffalo chips that rocked the sled up first on one runner, then the other, till he was sure it would turn over.

He was so busy balancing the rocking sled that he was not aware at first of coming up with the buffalo, not till the dogs began jumping and snarling at the heels of the big bulls trailing in the rear of the herd. Above the snarling of the dogs and the rush of wind in his ears was a thundering, vibrating sound that he felt as much as heard.

The sled ran smoother now in the wake of the animals, but up close there was a steady hail of hard-packed lumps of ice and snow from the hooves of the buffalo that hurt like rocks when they hit him. He ducked his head down between his knees and held it there, till the dogs began moving up the flank of the herd.

The bulls looked big to him then, bigger than horses, and when one swerved off to the side chasing the loose dogs, his mouth open in short blasts of sound and his tail up, he looked mean to Sandy, and terrible in a way he had never before imagined. Before then he had thought of buffalo as simply meat. Now he felt a respect for the big animals growing in him, and more than a little fear. Still he did not roll off the sled and stop, though he knew he could do it and without much hurt to himself.

The loose dogs were on ahead, moving up the flank of the herd; the slower buffalo were falling back and stringing out. His own dogs, held back by the sled, had stopped worrying the buffalo and seemed interested only in catching the other dogs. But they were close alongside of the buffalo. Once when a big bull cut out to the side after the loose dogs, his own dogs had almost run into the big animal. They had dodged to the side and the sled had just grazed the bull's hind legs as he turned into the herd. Sandy had been close enough to see the little beads of ice whipping on the long hair of the forelegs. He caught a flash of white in the bull's eye as he passed and was sure the big animal was coming after him. He was afraid to look back.

By then he could hear shooting behind him and knew the hunters were coming up. Instead of being relieved he began to be afraid someone would shoot one of his dogs to stop them. He worried about that, forgetting his own danger for the moment, and observed with interest that he was catching up with the other dogs.

Another big bull came out of the herd after one of the loose dogs. He was too slow to get the dog he was after, but his charge brought him out just right to intercept the two sled dogs.

Sandy saw the bull vividly, the shine of his curly black hide, the way the head swept down not breaking the rhythm of his stride till the beard dragged in snow, and up in an arc, the caught dog only a blur in the air; then the jerk of the sled and the bull again running.

One of the near dogs was impaled squirming on the big horn, snapping at the air. A harness strap was caught around the base of the other horn pressing the black mop down, revealing the curved black length of horn. The other dog was half dragged, half carried till he slipped free of the harness and tumbled to the side. The sled struck his side passing and Sandy heard him yelp.

The bull was galloping sidewise now, shaking his head, nearly upsetting the sled at every jump. It skidded zigzag with each jerk of the bull's head.

The dog stopped squirming and hung limp, his head flopping off to the side. Spatters of blood from his mouth struck the snow in the path of the sled.

Sandy felt helpless then. Before, he had known the dogs would stop. But a buffalo might just keep on running. To leave the sled was impossible, it seemed then. He felt paralyzed, his hands frozen to the sides of the sled. It seemed a long time before a rider came alongside and he saw it was his father.

His father moved on by, his gun balanced across the horse's withers. Sandy saw the barrel move down; the gun gave a spit of flame. He felt rather than saw the bull drop. The sled went on by, whipped at the end of the traces, and he was suddenly rolling over and over in the snow.

In his memory that was the end of the incident, though he remembered being very proud of his experience later. It became a landmark in his boyhood. He had been seven at the time, and his other early memories grouped themselves around this incident, either before or after. It was the way he judged how old he was when something particular happened.

But there was something strange about it now, something important that he could not quite set his mind to — an unfamiliar quality, as if it had happened to someone else, but clear.

He felt the same helplessness now that he had felt when the buffalo was dragging him, the same sense of being hauled along against his will. He puzzled about it for a long time before he let it go.

That had been the last big organized buffalo hunt out of the Red River country and it was a poor one in the end.

His father went back to farming after that and it was a hard go for a while with no buffalo meat for the winter. It had been a shock to his father, he knew. But his grandfather — his father's father — had been pleased in a somber way.

"Y'r bonny kittle cattle are gone," he would say to Sandy's father, "and a good thing it is. Y're a farmer, and ye had best learn it and settle down to the land in a Christian fashion. The whole settlement has been daft these thirty years chasing after the wild beasts like savages. And yourself, ye'll suffer for it now, and a good thing it'll be."

Maybe those were not the exact words, Sandy thought, but they came to him without composition, clear in his head as if he could hear the old man speaking. And see him, a small leathery man, strong and tireless at sixty, with clear grey eyes and grey hair that shone around his head like a frost.

And a frosty old codger he was, humorless and austere, but showing a surreptitious warmth in the way he handled his animals and his tireless care of the little vegetable plots he tore painfully from the thick sod of the valley.

Sandy had feared the old man then, and hated him for his tireless drive. But looking back now he felt a respect, understanding that the grandfather had kept the family going, and in his very stubbornness and backwardness had pointed out the only road left for the settlers to follow.

But it had seemed like poor doings compared with the free and careless life of the hunter. The road of the Indian, heathen as it seemed, had drawn even the earliest crofters from Scotland. In a country where game was plenty the hoe was a poor tool compared with the rifle.

But the time had gone, and the hoggishness of the white hunters mostly to blame. They suffered like the Indians for a while, but learned again to be farmers.

His grandfather was one of those who had not turned hunter. He had looked at it as a moral degeneration that took a man away from his religion and his rightful work with the soil. He would not even sell horses and equipment to the hunters when they were making up their expeditions. He was hardheaded about it, running a big risk for himself and family. He was shot at more than once for his stubbornness, and had his horses stolen by the very hunters who had tried to buy them.

So he saw the end of the buffalo with some satisfaction, seeing in it a justification of his position. It gave him a power in the family he had not had before. And so it was Sandy remembered him, a hard master who had no doubts of his own rightness. He had been especially zealous in his treatment of Sandy, driving him religiously as if salvaging a lost soul, knowing his own son to be lost beyond redemption. And his very concern was a gall to Sandy, who had been completely, before that, a son of his father — and of the Indian woman who had taken the place of his mother.

His mother had died before he was seven and he remembered nothing of her, nor of the coming of the Indian woman, which, he learned later, had been a bitter defeat for his grandfather. It was something that never could have happened after that last big hunt. Before that, his father had been a strong man; but it seemed like his strength left him with the buffalo. The only place he showed his iron around the home after that was in defense of the Indian woman.

Her, Sandy remembered vividly. She was of the Sioux, a woman of much laughter and a steady rippling of chatter — half French, half Indian — which in memory gave him a feeling of warmth like the feel of her fingers combing his hair or walking playfully up and down his ribs under his shirt. But even she had been dampened by the presence of the old man.

So that from the time he was seven till he left home, he could remember little of pleasure that was not connected with hunting. Once a year, in the fall, his father broke away from the farm to go to the mountains. And those were the times Sandy remembered. It was as if all his life in those years had been lived in the fall, with the leaves yellow and frost on the wind and glassed along the water's edge mornings; the geese moving south and snow coming. All the rest of the year — the monotonous repetition of chores, the grind of all the hand work in the fields — all this was the price he paid for the short weeks of freedom in the fall.

Sometimes the Indian woman came with them. She kept the camp and took care of the meat and skins. And these were the pleasantest times of all.

His father was a different man on the hunting trips. Around home he was morose and irritable, getting drunk at every chance and resisting in a passive way the energetic direction of the old man. He worked on the farm, but listlessly.

On the hunting trips he was different. The farther into the woods they went, the more he smiled and capered. He was a man awakening after a long sleep, or getting well after sickness. Walking ahead along the trail he talked to the horses and sang, or argued with the Indian woman, in a playful voice, about the character of all the animals or birds they happened to see. And though he pretended disbelief in all the legends of animal life the Indian woman told — stories of peculiarly warm, half-human beings — still he liked them and only teased her to hear them over again.

Sandy had learned to watch for these signs of awakening in his father with a joyful anticipation, his own feeling brimming till he felt like running and singing. But he was quiet. In the presence of these two older people who suddenly became young at heart he felt an awkwardness, a grownupness, a feeling he began to lose at the end of each trip, but never completely.

It seemed as if he could not change from one life to the other as easily or as quickly as the others, so that his freedom at the end of each hunting trip was overlaid by the gloom of the trip home.

And the oppressiveness of home was never so bad as those months of winter after the hunt. Then his grandfather's disapproval was at its highest, the tension between the two men the tightest — and with himself the object of contention.

"Have ye no shame," the old man would say, "but that ye maun yourself act the savage and drag your ane son along with ye into the bargain, and he with no life to look ahead to but what he can fashion out of the soil wi his two hands? Och, will ye look at the lad wi his leather claes and the glowerin look of an Indian, and naething to mark him as a Christian but the color of his hair."

His father would not answer, but would listen sullenly for a while, then leave the house to come home later, most often drunk, and sit for hours watching the Indian woman and Sandy with a sad angry stare, as if they were to blame for all his troubles.

The last hunt with his father and the Indian woman and the time afterward Sandy remembered as a summing up of his life in the settlement — and a conclusion.

He had been fifteen then, a tall awkward kid with a cumbrous energy that led the Indian woman to call him Walking Bear in Sioux talk, a name his father took up and called him afterward till he left home — to the immense disgust of his grandfather.

The harvest was late and followed by a hundred little jobs, de-signed, he suspected, by his grandfather to delay the hunt till the weather might prevent it altogether. But the weather held and they made their preparations in a frenzy of energy, and set out on a cold sun-bright morning of late fall, going north into Cree territory, each with a pony and pack horse.

It was dangerous then, hunting on Indian ground. The Crees, seeing the destruction of the buffalo by the white and half-breed hunters, had decided, too late, to close their hunting grounds.

So they traveled close to the hills, avoiding the open stretches of prairie. They found buffalo in little bands grazing close to the hills. But these they avoided, preferring to hunt what deer or elk or small bands of buffalo they found in the timbered pine hills and canyons where concealment was better. Hunting buffalo in the open was a sure way to be found by the Indians. One bunch disturbed might run for miles, gathering other herds, creating a disturbance sure to be noticed by hunting parties that were always out.

But the danger did not weigh on them. They set up camp in an old war house they found far up in the hills, where game seemed plenty. The war house was a big one made of poles set up in a cone-like tepee, covered with brush and limbs. It was in bad shape, with some of the poles knocked off and most of the covering blown down. They spent some time patching it and re-covering it with pine boughs and brush, leaving an entrance hole, on which they tied an elk-hide flap, and holes around the loose poles at the top for the smoke to come out of.

Hunting was good, and most of their time was spent cutting the meat into strips for drying and hanging it on the racks. The woman spent hours in front of the house with her graining tool, working down the elk and deer hides, or stretching and drying the furs they caught with the few traps they had. As the game thinned out around camp, they hunted farther, using their pack horses to bring in the meat.

It was hard work. The first week Sandy was always tired, but he hardened to it. But it seemed as if he had only begun to feel good when it was time to leave.

As it was, they waited till they knew there was a storm moving in before they got ready to leave. They spent one day at it, intending to leave next morning. But in the night the snow started, slow at first with no wind. By morning there was almost a foot of snow. And their horses were gone.

They had left them in the shelter of some timber in a little valley below camp. Under the trees, where the snow was thin, they found the tracks of moccasins mixed with the tracks of horses and knew the story. There was no finding the trail; all they could do was go back to camp and dig in for the storm and cut wood and stack it. And for days the snow kept coming, floating down in a damp feathery silence till it rose far up the war house, ending in a blizzard that blew itself out in a day, leaving the house completely covered except for the crossed poles at the top.

They tunneled out into a world of brilliant sunshine and air so quiet the thin line of smoke rising from the ragged tangle of sticks that was the top of the house stood high above them in the air, straight as a dropped thread. And cold: the kind of cold he didn't notice at first, but for the sting as it froze the hairs of his nose and stiffened his fingers. There was a crust on the snow he could walk on and not break if he walked easy.

Standing at the top of the steep slope that led down to where the horses had been, Sandy realized suddenly that they were snowed in for the winter, or at least till the first thaw, and safe, for the present, from any raiding parties. On an impulse that surprised even himself he let out a long whoop and dived off down the slope, coasting on his belly like an otter clear to the bottom. He got up digging the snow out of the neck of his parka, feeling foolish till he heard his father yell and saw him sliding down the path he had made.

The Indian woman disappeared into the tunnel, to appear a moment later with an armful of buffalo rib bones and some rawhide thongs. She tied the bones together into a rough-looking sled and was soon coasting down the slope, laughing and squealing. They played with a reckless childish joy, as if given sudden liberty, till they were completely spent and crawled back down the tunnel to lie laughing and chattering breathlessly on their buffalo robes spread round the fire.

He relaxed then, forgetting his grandfather, and hunted and trapped, in good weather scouting the country far along the hills.

He located an Indian village in a steep-sided little valley and studied it from a distance, high on the hills, till he knew the lay of the land and the set of every tepee. Two days he watched it, marking the movement of men and animals with intense interest; then returned to camp with a curious excitement in him he did not understand.

An early chinook settled the snow in glassy plots veined with little ribbons of water that laced the hills down to the draws and streams, and it was time to go. He knew then why he had scouted the village. They had to have horses.

They came to the village in the night, himself and his father, and the wind was still in the south but cold, though melted snow lay in sheets in the low places till the prairie east was a lake of many islands in the thin moonlight. The air pushed at his back and swirled under his clothes like water. He shivered and pulled his robe tighter, then loosened it, surprised to find himself sweating. There was a rushing, impelling sound to the wind that gave him a feeling of speed, of traveling swiftly ahead into the darkness.

There was a strangeness about the country, though he had seen it before. He recognized most of the little draws and valleys that opened out of the pine hills, having seen them from above on his scouting trips. So it was not really strange to him. Maybe, he thought, seeing it in the night had something to do with it, the thin, scattering moonlight that filtered through the rush of white clouds flowing over them on into the north. There was a dream-like quality about the whole thing; he found himself searching constantly for landmarks, smiling to himself when he saw a familiar curve of hill or line of trees.

He was not afraid of losing his way — he knew exactly where he was and where he was going. But still he looked for familiar things as if for friends. They comforted him, like the calm presence of his father coming along behind him. Oddly, he kept remembering the grey, frosty face of his grandfather.

The mouth of the valley opened out before them, just as he remembered it, and they crossed the creek and started up the north side to have the favor of the wind.

The village was set back in the valley, maybe half a mile, and beyond it was the horse herd. This he knew from the vivid picture in his mind, though now all he could see was a blur against the hills. He was feeling a little scared now, and jumpy with intense excitement.

He would have liked to come down the hills at the head of the valley, but it was steep and all the climbing would have taken time. So they would have to pass the village twice, going in afoot and coming out with the horses. He remembered a wide strip on either side of the valley between the lodges and the hills; but maybe it had just looked wide from above. He was walking into a trap and knew it, and still pushed on, feeling then as if a gate were closing behind him, but not looking back.

So he moved on, forcing himself to be cautious, fighting the strange numbness of mind that gave him a feeling of recklessness; a conviction that what was going to happen would happen in spite of anything he could ever see or think.

But he was quiet, more out of habit than resolution. He could hear the wind making a soughing noise in the timber way up the ridges, wolves and coyotes, and underfoot the faint crackling of the thin crust that froze on the mud at night, even in the chinook.

He watched where he knew the village stood and saw the tepees rise up in shadows and group themselves, black but for a faint lightness on the side toward the moon. They were farther away than he expected, directly upwind now. He caught the smell of Indians then — the smell of leather and cooked meat, the smell of dogs and a faint sweetish odor he thought maybe was the smell of man.

Suddenly, out of the almost-silence, rose a tremendous racket of dogs from the direction of the village. He dropped to his knees and froze, feeling the noise, tangible as a club, beating at his ears. He thought he could see a scurrying of figures among the tepees. Then the barking and howling died downward to silence. He did not move, but he could feel the thousand little bumps on his skin smoothing out and a little relaxing movement in the hair on the back of his neck.

And again sound thrust at him, but near this time, starting low, swelling as the pitch rose, till the sound stood towering in the darkness; then sloped downward to nothing. He thought he saw the grey figure of a wolf upwind between himself and the village before the answering wave of dog-noise again struck him. But he was not sure; everywhere he looked now he seemed to see a fleeting of shadows. He heard his father blow out a lungful of air in the darkness near him and stood up, feeling the muscles of his legs jerking as he rose.

They moved on quietly. The tepees dropped again into the shadows, the noise of the dogs died down till the loudest sound once more was the wind high in the timber.

They found the horses standing in a bunch at the head of the valley in the shelter of some trees. Sandy heard and smelled rather than saw them. Stopping, he searched ahead of him till he made out the shape of the trees and placed the dark shadow of the horses. He unslung the coil of rawhide rope off his shoulder, found the end and made a loop, straining his eyes into the darkness to locate the little cut-bank gulley that he knew lay beyond the horses at the very head of the valley. But he could make out nothing except the upward slope of the high, black hills.

There would be water running in the gulley, he knew, but it was a natural trap for horses if they could get some into it. That was the only chance. They wouldn't stand a show to catch the horses in the open, once the animals got the smell of strangers in their noses. He indicated the lay of things to his father, and they separated and moved in on the horses.

It turned out just as he expected, except that they got closer than he had hoped before the horses got wind of them. There was a loud snort and a sudden vibration of hooves striking the earth. The solid shadow of the herd was suddenly moving, spreading like a thrown bucket of water, flowing away from them up the slope and coming together again as the sides of the gulley closed in; then stopping and coming out again, and himself and his father rushing in to reach the mouth of the gulley before they all got out.

He ran straight into them, swinging his rope, feeling their very breath and wind as they rushed by on either side. He reached the mouth of the gulley alone with horses still breaking past him; there was the rushing sound of water, and he knew the gulley was now a creek.

He crowded over to the edge and the line stopped, turning back on itself and flowing in shadow to the other end of the gulley and crossing the creek in a roar of water and clatter of hooves on stone; then back the other side. He could see the horses then in the moonlight that struck the north side of the gulley, not half a dozen stretched out in a dead run, head to tail; and it was too late to cross the creek and head them.

He was still swinging the loop of the rope; he threw it, watching just ahead and above the first horse, not even seeing the loop but feeling the coils slip out between the fingers of his left hand. The rope stayed slack in his hand for what seemed too long and he was sure in that instant that he had missed; then the rope pulled lightly, slipped and jerked solid, yanking him off his feet and into the creek. But he held on, even with water choking his nose and throat, blinding him till all his senses were a blur of dark violent motion. The knotted end of the rawhide was slipping in the heel of his hand and somehow he got his right hand on the rope above it. He dragged to a stop and came out of the water coughing but holding the rope tight in both hands, feeling the horse back away at the other end, tossing his head as he took up the slack. Only then Sandy felt the cold; his stomach was tight as if he had been hit, his breathing hard in the constriction of his chest.

He walked up the rope hand over hand, still holding the knotted end, feeling the horse trembling tight against the rope, breathing in long snorts from the choking of the loop. The horse was standing with front feet braced wide apart, head flung back in a strained position as if pulling against a great tension. But he stood.

Sandy made a loop in the free end of the rope, made a double half-hitch in the loop, and slipped it on the horse's lower jaw just behind the chin and pulled it tight; then he loosened the rope on the neck and slipped the loop off. The horse drew in his breath with a long sigh and straightened up, dancing, while Sandy coiled up the rope.

His father came up from across the creek.

"They ran right smack over me," he told Sandy. "Time I got myself gathered up it was too late. Then I heard you over here. By golly, I don't know how you caught anything in this dark. Damned if you ain't just a natural hoss thief."

"It was pure accident," Sandy said. "Like snaggin a fish in deep water."

He could hear the horses whinnying and snorting down the creek a ways.

"The damn things'll stir up Injuns sure as hell," his father said. "You want to clear out? We can still climb out of here."

"You mean leave this horse? Naw, I don't. You stay here and I'll bring some more back down the other side. Those Indians ain't got any horses caught up and how they gonna catch em in the dark? Or us either?"

He started to mount on the left side, but the horse went sideways out from under him and he fell. He got up still holding the coil, hearing his father's laughter warm in the night.

"This time," his father said, "try the other side."

He felt quieter then. When he mounted, the horse turned, crossed the creek of his own accord, and lit out in a tight-muscled run, letting out his breath in little snorts at every jump. Sandy hauled on the rope to slow him down, but he kept running, head stuck out to the side, going it blind. So he eased up and the horse stretched out in a long run, guiding easy under the pressure of his knees. His wet clothes stiffened with frost till he could hear them crinkle with the sound of paper in time with the pony's stride. Only his robe stayed limber, lying warm and soft across his shoulders.

He swung in a wide circle over to the north side of the valley, then back south below the horses. They threw up their heads and stampeded again as he came pounding in on them, back along the creek toward the gulley, with only a few smart ones cutting off to the left and circling back. He let these go, staying close to the main bunch, whacking the slow ones on the rump with his coil of rope. He rode with his head down close over the pony's neck to keep from getting a face full of the mud flying up off the horses' feet.

The bunch piled up in the gulley. Some had already crossed the creek to come back, but as he rode up he could see his father whipping them back.

He crowded up and dropped his loop on the nearest horse and drew him out of the herd. Loosening one of the lead ropes he had tied around his waist, he knotted it around the horse's neck and re- moved his loop, then shook it out again and caught another. Across the creek he saw his father already mounted, with two led horses. Dismounting, he tied one of his extra horses to the tail of the other, coiled up the long rawhide and remounted as his father crossed the creek.

He saw fires springing up then at the sides of the village and heard a faint sound of shouting.

"They've got wind of us now," his father told him. "We're in the soup good, and nothin but luck'll get us out. I'm sorry now I got you into this." He wheeled his horse over away from the creek and Sandy followed. The horse herd broke out of the gulley and passed them along the creek.

"They're gonna be waitin for us," his father went on. "We don't stand a show to ride through em alone, so we'll try to stampede this herd through em. Now git in among em when we go by."

His father cut in behind the herd, yelling, and there was a strange exultant note in his voice, like joy, Sandy thought.

He swung in beside his father, surprised at the way his horses were leading up, like they were trying to get up among the herd themselves. He was yelling himself hoarse now, and not so scared any more, as if he were part of the stampede and not directing it at all but completely involved in the blind speed and the noise of it.

Ahead of the horses he could see lights waving, a line of torches and fires on either side of the village. He heard his father yelling, whipping up the stragglers, and as they came close to the line he saw the leaders pitching and running sideways trying to turn back. He heard a quick volley of gunfire and thought he saw some of the horses in front go down; and the herd stopped as if it had hit a solid wall, piling up in the middle some riding others, their heads thrown up wildly against the torchlight.

He kneed his horse to the left instinctively to avoid the mixup, and found himself riding straight into the circle of lodges. He did not try to turn or slow his horse. He ducked his head and dug in his heels, whipping his horse on the flank with the coil of rope he held in his right hand, holding the led horses in close on the left to keep them from splitting off to go around a tepee the wrong way.

The pony did not break his step or change his speed, dodging in and out like a rabbit — as if he knew where he was going, Sandy thought. He could smell powder and see the flash of muskets going off around him, but none of them seemed close. He heard women screaming among the tents and saw figures scurrying to get out of his way as he came through.

He saw his way clear of the village; but at the edge a figure seemed to rise out of the ground in front of him and stand instead of dodging to the side as the others had done. The pony went sideways and he saw fire blossom just to the right of the pony's head. He did not hear the report.

Something jerked at his leg, forcing it back along the pony's side till it almost knocked him off. He tried to pull it back down into place, but he felt no movement; the leg seemed to be sticking back and away from the horse. He reached down with the hand that held the coil of rope, rubbing his wrist down along his body, and found the leg in place where it should be. Something warm and sticky came away on his wrist, cooling like water in the wind, and he knew he was hit.

He felt sick, but not excited, as if his mind were numb too, like his leg. The only thing that seemed worth thinking about was staying on, and it was touch and go whether he would or not without the use of his leg or even the feel of it, till he got the knack of riding with his butt off to the right side and using just his left leg to ride with like he did sometimes when he was sore from too much riding.

But he kept flopping back and forth in a limp, sleepy way, as if his muscles had turned watery; and he felt that way, like he was under water with everything hazy and slow-moving and airless. He had no thought of where he was going; there was a roaring sound in his ears like water, and he had the feeling of fighting against a strong current, just holding his own and the dark shores not moving.

Pain was starting up in his leg; not sharp or steady, but recurring and swelling like sound, as if the pain had a voice and was screaming in his ears. He had an urgent need to think, but the noise was too loud. The sound changed then; above the clamor of pain he heard a familiar repeated sound that he recognized suddenly as his name. He was aware dimly of his father riding beside him then in the dark.

"Damn it, boy," his father said, "you been leading me a hell of a chase. You lost?"

"I guess so," he admitted weakly, his breath coming thin out of the tightness of his chest. "I can't tell for all the noise."

His father's voice was changed then. "There ain't any noise, boy. You're hurt. Where you hit?" He was talking in a choked-up voice like he used sometimes feeling ashamed of himself.

Sandy felt his horse slow down then and knew his father had hold of the rope. He was talking steady now in a quiet voice that somehow made Sandy's own mind settle down.

"You caught a good horse, boy, with that wild throw. I had a time keepin up after we got out of there. And you did good coming through the lodges, but I didn't think you got hurt, not bein out in front like that. Time I came through they was waitin for me but they never touched me." Like he was accusing himself for not being hit, Sandy thought.

He let himself go then, sinking down into the dark water. And the next thing he knew his father was shaking him.

"We got to ride, boy. Can you do it?"

There was feeling in his leg now, as well as the pain. There was something tight around it and stiff up the sides of his thigh. He got onto his good leg and raised himself up and his father mostly carried him to his horse and legged him on.

"It's not broke, I don't think," he told Sandy. "I just braced it up in case."

They were riding then, his father in the lead with all the led horses. They crossed a stream that was bigger than the creek where it came out by the village, and Sandy knew he must have come a long way down it, almost to the river. Glancing up at the stars he saw they were traveling south.

"Maybe just as well we come out of the way," his father said. "It'll throw em off trailing us in the morning."

He was feeling better now, clear-headed, and the pain was something he could stand. He was tired and weak and kind of limp, but thinking back on the whole incident, the strong fast parts of it, put something warm and good moving in his blood, firing him up like a drink of whiskey. And the pain was part of it too, a badge pinned in the flesh; and the danger yet and the price still to pay in the long ride back. He felt a fulfillment, somehow, a pride that was strong in him and deep, that contained him and joined him to the clear swift beauty of the act — the wind, high in the timber, the dogs, the wolf; moonlight through the white, fast-moving clouds caught in frosty little lights on the earth; the feel of the caught, plunging horse and the cold blackness of the water; the blind speed of running horses, the sight of them rearing and whirling against the torchlight; the ride through the village and the final flower of the gunshot — all to stay forever in his mind and flesh.

The sky cleared. Moonlight was a beaded wash over the curving earth. The pine hills off to the left, snow-capped, were bright clouds rising out of the dark earth into the blue-black sky lanced with little knife points of stars. He found himself shivering but not cold; as if his senses had opened suddenly onto the night and the cool air blowing in.

The Indian woman was waiting for them at the foot of the slope below the war house. He got off his horse alone and stood straight and proud on his good leg while his father told the story. She came to him then, running her warm hands over his face, her laughter like crying, chattering Sioux talk. And for just a little he could not hold back the tears.

They helped him up the slope between them, and he lay in the war house while they packed, half asleep and stiff and in pain but with the good feeling warm around him with the smell of leather and smoke and pine. Then he was riding again and on his left in the east the sun came up.

They traveled steady all morning, as fast as the heavy packs would allow. All the life had gone out of him now and he barely managed to sit his horse for drowsiness. But the pain in his leg from the jogging of the horse kept rousing him when it seemed like nothing could ever keep him from sleep.

The woman had made him an Indian saddle of a bag of buffalo hair that made riding a little easier; and the horse was easy riding. He moved in a running walk that was equal to the jog trot of the others. Seeing the horse for the first time in the daylight, he had been pleased, and even now in all his discomfort he was proud and grateful for his luck. The horse was pintoed red and white, with a short swelled neck, a deep chest and a short back. He had a way of tossing his head till his little short ears almost touched Sandy's face, and a way of looking back showing a lot of white in his eye.

They stopped at noon to rest the horses and eat. Sandy stretched out on the ground to try to sleep, but the pain in his leg kept jerking him awake. The woman removed the binding and washed the wound with cold water. It had swollen against the bandage and the release of the pressure made it feel better. He dropped immediately to sleep.

In the afternoon they ran into a little band of buffalo coming down out of a draw. His father shot a young cow and gutted it. The Indian woman cut off part of the stomach and bound it with a good part of the contents on the wound in his leg. The dressing was warm and soft and seemed to ease the pain.

He did not remember much of the trip after that till they reached home. The old man was surprised when they rode in, and pleased in spite of himself. But with the sight of the strange horses and Sandy with his leg hurt, he soon got control of himself.

Sandy was almost unconscious from weariness when he rode into the yard; his leg was like a timber nailed to his hip, the nails biting into his flesh at every movement. But when he saw the old man, first with his smile, then the sternness settling into his face like ice forming, he began to awaken. But instead of the tight, sullen gloom that usually took him after a trip, he felt a strange buoyancy lifting him up out of his weariness till he could not help smiling. He even felt glad to see the old man. Dismounting, watching his grandfather the while, he could see concern for himself balanced with disapproval in the old man's face.

He could bend his hurt leg just enough to clear the ground as he hopped on the other. The Indian woman took his horse and turned it into the corral with the others, and he turned and hopped into the house, refusing the help of both his father and the old man even though the hurt leg seemed to be tearing itself loose from his body with each jolt. Inside he sat down and began painfully to remove his moccasins. In the closeness of the cabin he caught strongly the smell of old blood and buffalo gut rising from his leg. The slit in his legging that his father had made to expose the wound was tied together with a rawhide thong passed through the two holes made by the musket ball. The leather around the holes was black with dried blood, and around the slit and downward was a greenish brown plaster of manure from the buffalo stomach still strapped to his leg.

The old man was standing in the middle of the room, his face, usually leathery and immobile, working as if he were talking, but he was voiceless. It seemed like a long time before he made any sound.

"Och," he said, speaking to Sandy's father but still keeping his eyes on Sandy. "Ye needna tell me the story . . . The horses ye stole from the savages, and the lad there, a young warrior nae less, initiated with maybe a coup counted, and the pride of it in his face like a pictograph on a shield." The tone of his voice was mocking and full of anger, but there was a grudging note of respect in it, too. His eyes moved from Sandy and leveled like a rifle at his father. "And you," he said contemptuously, "to make a savage of your ane son, nae less than should ye turn him over to the tribe itself, een-structing him in the ways of thievery and bloodshed and you a Christian."

Sandy's father was sitting on a bench in front of the window, his face darkened against the light, looking at the floor, his shoulders hunched as if under a lash. "We only got our horses back," he said. "We had to have horses. Maybe I should have done it alone. I don't know. Anyhow, it wasn't stealin, exactly."

"Nae, lad, not stealin for the puir savage. It's the way he lives and he knowns nae ither way. But if ye can show me how ye came by the horses and it be not stealin, I shall be much obleegit to ye."

Sandy's father fell into a sullen silence. The old man stood watching him a while, his frosty eyes glittering with disgust. He turned finally to Sandy, and his voice softened a little. "It'll be a wonder an ye don't lose the leg, laddie, wi all that filth strapped to it like a poultice."

"The buffalo gut was good for it," Sandy said definitely.

The old man seemed about to shout at him. Instead he bent over and began undoing the thongs that held the plaster on the wound, and his hands were shaking. He washed the wound with cold water, turning up his nose at the smell of the manure. The wound was better. It was swollen and ugly-looking, but the fever had gone out of it. It had started bleeding from the recent exertion and the blood was red and fresh.

"I dinna see how it happened," the old man said, shaking his head. "Ye maun be a strong lad — a wound like that wi naught but dung fer plaister, and all the ridin to the back of it. A braw young savage." He looked up at Sandy, startled a little by what he had just said. Sandy grinned and the old man's eyes wrinkled at the corners as he looked down again. He sprinkled soda on the wound and bound it up with a cloth.

Sandy slept steadily for almost three days, then he was up and working, against the protests of his father and the old man, refusing even the crutch they gave him. He favored his leg but still he walked on it, feeling somehow that using it would make it better. And it mended fast.

He was lighthearted then, doing his work around the place with no compulsion from his grandfather as in the past. In fact, the old man seemed shy with him, as if he had suddenly become a stranger, and a man at that, no longer a boy. He milked his cows and split and hauled wood with a joyfulness, as if something pleasant and exciting were waiting at the end of each job. It was a feeling he could not explain, but it stayed with him.

The Indian woman was different with him too, more reserved and less playful, but somehow more affectionate. She made him beaded moccasins that he was very proud of later, and treated him with a respect that made him feel very grown up.

It was an early spring, coming to him like the fulfillment of a promise, with a beauty and excitement he had never known before in spring. He was no longer looking forward to fall; not looking forward at all, but dreaming and remembering vividly and working with an energy that expanded in him like an inhaled breath. The geese came north from he wondered what strange southern land, their high wavering spearheads piercing the cold air, their journeying cries dropping to him as he stopped work below to watch, bringing unreasonable tears to his eyes.

The color of green came slowly into the far grey-brown prairies west, the sun moved south as slowly, and the ducks came and all the birds that traveled south to winter and then again came north. He wondered how it must have been before when the buffalo too moved north as the grass came, blacking the earth as his father remembered, clear to the distant curve of the skyline, numberless as the new grass that now greened it. He had a bitter sense of being born too late, of having missed a beauty that perhaps no man would ever know again; thinking then that farther west it still might be.

He worked through the spring with his grandfather, plowing and working the land and then planting.

Of his father then he remembered nothing. It was as if he had dropped out of the family completely, though he was still there, Sandy knew. There were no more quarrels between the two men — himself as the object being withdrawn, there seemed to be no further reason for contention. And as if it had been the struggle that had kept him going, the old man began to lose his drive. He worked strongly through the plowing and planting, then suddenly stopped. He would walk through the little plots of planted ground as if searching for something he had lost, then stand for hours looking out across the prairie with a resignation in his eyes, and all the stiffness and pride gone out of the way he stood, and the frost out of his face.

He took suddenly ill, and within a day or two Sandy knew he was dying. He seemed to shrivel up and go dry like a withered plant. He talked some toward the last, mostly to Sandy, about Scotland and his life there in a burr so thick that Sandy could scarcely understand him.

"Ye're a guid lad," he told Sandy, "and ye hae my blessin." He stopped and his eyes receded. "The blessin of an auld man in a strange new land, and Scotland monie a mile beyant the water. It's nae a new Scotland in the new land."

During those last days, Sandy's father was continually drunk. On himself fell all the responsibility of the business of death — the night watching, the laying out, the arrangements for the funeral and finally the burial. He remembered standing in a light spring rain watching the final dirt being thrown on the grave, feeling a keen sense of loss and the sense of something ended, something other than one man's life. He puzzled about it, dry-eyed, standing there in the rain, hearing as from a distance the wailing of the Indian woman.

He came back with her to the cabin late in the afternoon and caught up his horse and saddled it. He brought his blankets and clothes and a sack of dried meat, rolled them up and tied them behind the saddle and came back in for his rifle. The Indian woman was waiting for him with a beaded medicine bag and another set of moccasins she had made for him. She gave them to him and stood with her hands on his shoulders looking at him with a pride and softness in her eyes that almost made him cry again.

He walked blindly to where the pinto was standing with dropped rein, climbed into the saddle and rode out of the yard, west. The clouds had broken over the curved horizon and in the sunset the whole earth was washed in an unbelievable liquid pink that drained off slowly with the western light till the sky was black, and the earth, and all he could see in the world before him was the western star in a widening patch of blue-black sky. He did not look back . . .

Naw, he had not gone back, Sandy thought, biting his lip as he again started skinning. And maybe it was wrong to go back even in your mind and lacerate old wounds. It was like that, like a knife probing for an old ball carried for years and almost forgotten. As if the kid on the pinto were another now, and himself watching and able to see the future and laugh at the irony, the laughter in his heart like the knife turning in the scarred flesh.

It was not like himself, going back in time; not remembering but going back, the thoughts vivid as dreams and as uncontrolled; his mind turning and sniffing in the past, an old dog hunting buried and forgotten bones.

Maybe it was age, he thought, remembering his grandfather; or maybe a man lost something at whatever age, something intangible, even unthinkable, that drained out of him like the color of that re-membered sunset and left him strengthless.

He finished skinning the buffalo and rolled him off the hide, noticing as he always noticed the way the flesh gathered the grass and dirt rolling and the dust that settled on the dead and glassy open eye. He folded the hide, tied it behind the saddle and rode back up the draw the way he had come. Looking back, he saw the carcass lying almost as it had fallen, the stubbed horns and the un-seeing eye pointed back along its trail.

He was dead tired now, leached out and his mind a blank. And all he felt above his weariness was a sense of having seen something important and missed its meaning.

CHAPTER 10

THE MOON WAS COMING UP BY THE TIME WOOD-
foot finished his camp chores. He dug his banjo out of his plunder
in the shack and sat down by the fire, his back to a stump, and
tuned her up. The first time, he thought, and here it was a month,
damn near, and this the first decent night with no wind or rain — or
snow. And not so warm either, but good enough for the mosquitoes.
Not many, but enough to bother a man; and how they hatched
out of the ice water and stood the cold nights to boot was more
than he could see. He slapped at them between chords, trying to
keep in time, amused a little at his own antics.

Sandy was squatted by the fire spooning hot lead out of a skillet
into his bullet molds. When he finished the set, he looked up with
a sly half-smile.

"You play us up a lively one," he said to Woodfoot. "Say
'Turkey in the Straw.' You'll catch more skeeters that way."

"And beat hell out of myself," Woodfoot grinned. He was
pleased at getting a rise out of Sandy. Sandy was a gloomy cuss,

what Woodfoot had seen of him since they hit camp, but it wasn't his nature, a man could see that. Something was bothering him.

"What really beats hell out of me though," Woodfoot continued, "is how come they don't bother you. Don't seem as if they like you the way they do me. You maybe got too much vinegar in your blood. I don't see you slappin at em."

Sandy laughed, taking the joke all right. He wiped his hand across the back of his neck and held it to the firelight, showing three or four stains of blood.

"They seem to like me all right, once they get their bills in. The thing is, you and Charley keep em thinned down to where they don't bother me much."

Charley was pouring powder into the shells he had lined up on the top of a stump with a brass loading tube. He pulled out the tube too quick on the last one, reaching to slap a mosquito, and knocked the shell off the stump.

"The goddamn bugs!" he said. And the anger that showed on his face was real. He looked up at Woodfoot's laughter. "I don't see anything so damn funny. That powder costs like gold."

Woodfoot said nothing, but went back to plucking his banjo, still smiling.

Charley looked at Sandy, and his eyes paused a moment.

"It's so, by God," he said to Woodfoot, "what you said. The damn bugs ain't botherin him at all, and you and me slappin ourselves blind."

Sandy broke open his mold and took out the bullets. He worked slow and sure, as if he had to think about what he did, but it seemed like nothing he ever did was wrong. His big hands looked awkward, but there was nothing awkward in the way they worked.

"There's two things you boys don't seem to savvy," he said. "It's partly in the nature of the skeeter, and partly it's just in your head. Now what you got in your heads," he went on, grinning, "maybe ain't worth mentioning. But a man can learn something about a skeeter just watching him. Now if you was to sit dead still, not even breathin, I'm thinkin you wouldn't get bit hardly at all, except what skeeters happened to light on you accidental, the way they light on a tree or a bush. But then you start movin and mister skeeter begins to take notice. And the more skeeters that take notice the more you move, till purty quick you ain't nothin but a walkin windmill."

There was probably some truth in what he said, Woodfoot thought, whether a man could apply it or not. But it wasn't as simple as that. And maybe that was what Sandy meant when he said it was partly in your head. It seemed like if it was a man's nature to slap at mosquitoes and even get sore at them the way Charley did, then nothing could keep him from slapping them. Leastways it would take a lot of will power. So maybe the main profit you could take from it was that the way a man behaved with mosquitoes was a sign of the way he was inside. If you knew how to read it, anyway.

His eyes came back to Sandy, who was pouring more bullets. The blue light of the hot lead and the red from the coals gave his face a purple cast, a sad, gloomy color, Woodfoot thought, like it was the color maybe of his thoughts.

Sandy finished with his molding, sat down by a stump and began swaging the bullets. He liked the work of reloading, Woodfoot could see by the way he rolled the finished bullets around in his hand, examining each one with care before wrapping on the linen paper patch. But he was not fast at it, not the way Charley was. He preferred to do his loads a few at a time and go through the whole operation several times. He was more careful than Charley, but even so his loads were probably not as accurate as Charley's.

Charley, on the other hand, lined out a whole slew of them, and once he got an operation started he went through it like there was something after him. He had thin, delicate hands that seemed to move of themselves with no direction from his mind, fast and accurate. When he was going good he had a detached look on his face that was as near as he ever came to showing pleasure. Any interruption threw him off his rhythm and seemed to irritate him out of all proportion. Like the mosquitoes. Woodfoot could see him trying to ignore them like Sandy had suggested. But he could only stand it a few seconds, then he would cut loose with a string of cussing, break out of his work and slap at them with a vicious accuracy. He was death on mosquitoes, that was a fact. If one ever got its beak into Charley it was a goner sure.

But, outside of the irritation of the mosquitoes, the work seemed to set Charley up too, though not in the same way it did Sandy. You could see that all Charley's pride was in the speed and accuracy of the operation, not in any tangible quality of the finished work. He never failed to remark in an offhand manner the number of shells he loaded in a certain time, always watching Sandy for his reaction, showing a kind of irritation when Sandy failed to notice. But he was good, you had to admit that, even if he wasn't much of a buffalo hunter. Not yet anyway. He was learning fast, though. Whenever Sandy talked buffalo, Charley was all ears, and humble now, asking a question now and then and not shooting off his face the way he had the first day or two.

Woodfoot switched to another tune on his banjo. He was being a little hard on Charley — Charley wasn't as bad as all that. You could even like him once you got it through your head that he was just humorless. He just couldn't back off and see anything funny in himself. He was too serious. And dead set on being the best in everything he did.

Charley finished his loading and put away his tools. He left the fire and Woodfoot could hear him cracking around in the brush by the river. When he came back he was carrying an armful of green, wet brush.

"I'll fix these damn bugs," he said.

Sandy looked up from his work. "Doggone it, Charley, you ain't never satisfied. Here it is the first nice night we've had, and here's you fixin to smoke us plumb out of camp. Naw. You just make yourself a nice seat out of that brush and fight your battle with the skeeters any way you want — just so you don't include me in with the skeeters, like with the smudgin."

Charley stood uncertainly by the fire, still holding on to the brush.

Sandy went into the shack and came back with a red claystone pipe and tobacco in a beaded buckskin sack. He offered them to Charley. When Charley hesitated, he said, "Go on, you danged fire eater, take em."

Charley, looking sheepish, dropped the brush and took the pipe and tobacco. Without a word he sat down by the stump and began to load the pipe.

"That tobacco is half brush, anyway," Sandy said. "Kinnekinnic. So you got your own private smudge and me and Woodfoot's got peace."

"Peace pipe," Woodfoot remarked.

Sandy grinned but Charley did not look up from the pipe. When he had it loaded he sat passing it nervously from one hand to the other, running his fingers up and down the stem. He was sitting back from the fire and raising more smoke than the fire itself, Woodfoot thought. His hands were like birds cutting back and forth in the moonlight.

Sandy sat down cross-legged by the fire and Woodfoot settled back against the stump, just chording slow. He let his mind drift and found he was playing a tune from back home, a tune called "Shennydore." He played it a couple of times, then sang it, watching Sandy as he sang.

Sandy was staring off across the fire into the night. The light on his red, weathered face and shining on his eyes gave him a feverish look, a look of agitation even though he sat perfectly still. A two day's growth of beard darkened his jaw, showing the color of rust and just a touch of grey. That was part of it, Woodfoot thought; the beard was unusual with Sandy. He usually shaved every morning with an old Green River knife he always kept honed and a can of cold water. He was the only one in camp who shaved so often, Woodfoot thought, running his hand through his own matted beard when he finished the tune.

Sandy nodded his appreciation of the music. Woodfoot struck up a light one and finished it, then put the banjo away. He felt like talking, but how could you talk to a gloomy cuss like Sandy? It was like pulling teeth to get him started.

Charley, now, was another case. After a good kill, he'd talk a leg off you. But not Sandy. It seemed like the better he did the less he talked — which was an odd thing when you came to think of it.

He came back with his own pipe, loaded it and lit up with an ember. "Where you from, Sandy?" he asked.

"Canada. Red River of the north, but it's a long time. Mostly I guess you'd say I'm from wherever there's been buffalo."

"That'll make you a native of Montana in a year or two, then."

"How's that?"

"I figure that's about how long these'll last. You can be from here from then on."

Sandy grinned, a little ruefully. "Maybe," he said. "I think it'll be longer than that though. Seems like there's a sight of em left. But nothin like in Kansas or the Southwest."

Charley laughed brittlely. "Hell, there's no end to em. You'll never live to see the last of em."

Woodfoot ignored him. "They're thinnin out around here right now," he said to Sandy.

"Goin north is all. They'll keep comin for a while yet."

"And after that?"

"That's about it for the season. There's some'll summer out here but not enough to keep an outfit goin. A man by himself, or two maybe, might make wages, but no more than that. They start comin back around November."

"If there's any to come back." Woodfoot was deliberately spurring Sandy to get him to talk. He himself did not expect the end of the buffalo so soon. "Indians and half-breeds'll take a share of em."

"Lousy Indians," Charley said.

"Not many," Sandy said, as if Charley had not spoken. "Most of the Indians this side of the line are cooped up on reservations. The government's trailin cattle clear from Texas to feed em and tryin to get the Indians to raise some themselves. But hell, there ain't a cow in the world can stand the winters here. I seen em freeze to death standin up, down on the Powder, and starve by golly with good grass right there under the snow, not knowing how to get it. Naw, a cow ain't in it with a buffalo when it comes to standin cold and snow.

"A buffalo now, he'll root in the snow like a hog and if there's any grass he'll find it. And he'll face a blizzard and keep movin where a cow'll turn tail and drift or just stand there and freeze.

"Now there's a thing for you to think about, why a buffalo'll most generally move upwind. Even in the summer, you scare a bunch and they'll most likely take out upwind. Or when they lay down to rest you usually find em with their noses upwind.

"But in a blizzard they'll do it every time. There was a bunch went over a bluff just out of Cheyenne Wells one time, in a blizzard. I didn't see it, but I was there two or three years later and seen the bones. It was a sight for a man to remember. The bluff was about fifty feet high, and long, maybe a mile, and the prairie slopin up to it on one side and there it was. The buffalo was movin upwind the way they will, in the night, crowdin together to keep warm and shovin ahead. The only ones that didn't go over was the drags.

"That was in the winter of 'sixty I seen it. Bones and hide and buffalo hair, ten-fifteen feet high and near a mile long. A hundred thousand buffalo in that pile, some figured. It was a good season for wolves."

"Some sight for a skinner," Woodfoot commented.

"Indians used to hunt em that way," Sandy went on, "though I never seen it, drivin em over a bluff. It wasn't so common, though, I'm thinkin. Buffalo ain't so easy to drive."

"It's something to think about, all right," Woodfoot said. "All those animals pilin up like that, in the dark and snow, kickin and bellerin at the bottom and more comin over. It ain't like it was a stampede. They was just followin a good instinct, to face the storm and maybe find shelter, and that's what it got em. It gives a man a kind of a funny feeling just to think how it must have been."

"It does now, don't it?" Sandy said eagerly, as if pleased to find someone who saw it the way he did. "It's like a bunch of men'll do sometimes, start out on something that seems good, and maybe it is at the time, then maybe it changes. But they're in the drift of it, and they can't stop even if they go over the cliff."

"Ain't nothin but stupidity," Charley said. "A bunch of dumb animals, what can you expect?"

"That's it," Woodfoot laughed.

Charley looked at him blankly. "What's it?"

"A bunch of dumb animals, the buffalo and the men too. The whole shittaree. Kill off the buffalo for their hides, then trail in cattle for meat — and them freezin to death."

"It's somethin like that," Sandy said. He was quiet for a while. "It's more than a man's mind can handle, what happened there at Cheyenne Wells. One hundred thousand buffalo. Say they'd go a thousand pounds each, which is high, but just to make it easy. That's fifty thousand tons of animals, alive and breathin like you and me, fightin a blizzard, and in the time of a few minutes — gone under." He made a sinking gesture with his usually quiet hands.

"A lot of wasted meat," Woodfoot said. "A regular nightmare for a Scotchman." He smiled, watching Sandy.

Sandy grinned, looking away across the fire. "You got it in the right words," he said. "You got a way of pickin words that mean more than they say. A nightmare is what it was. I remember after I saw it, I'd wake up sometimes thinkin about it, as if I'd seen it happen, watchin from below as they came over, and then realize it was a dream — or a nightmare, like you said. But a Scotchman's nightmare — I wonder how much you said there."

"Just talk," Woodfoot said. "I guess a Scotchman's no thriftier than the next." Sandy's comment about the right words had an inverted value — he saw more than you said.

"No, that's so. But that ain't what I mean. The waste I thought of and I hate waste as much as another man — bein a Scotchman. But there's somethin more than that, and maybe a sensible man wouldn't even try to put it into words. But what was I doin under that cliff with all those animals comin down at me and me too scared to move and not even wantin to move? I wasn't thinkin about waste then.

"Naw, there's more to it than that. Maybe it's the other side of the dollar. Maybe a Scotchman — or a Dutchman, for all that — hates the richness more than the waste. How can a man be thrifty and dig in the dirt for a livin and raise hogs when there's a few million tons of meat to be got by pullin a trigger? The way the Indians made a livin, killin meat like men and never layin hand to a hoe. But a buffalo hunter ain't killin meat when he pulls a trigger. He's killin richness, it seems like, so he can git back to bein thrifty and diggin in the dirt. And bein a Scotchman. That could be a Scotchman's nightmare. Or a Dutchman's." Sandy talked in a self-conscious way, smiling, deriding himself for the things he was saying. But he was really serious. Woodfoot sensed it from the intensity of his voice, the way his heavy brows worked in the silences as he looked out into the darkness beyond the fire. He was really studying, looking for something. He kept coming back to the Cheyenne Wells incident, as if it meant something he couldn't cipher.

"Maybe it don't mean anything," Sandy said, as if picking up out of Woodfoot's thoughts. "Maybe it's all in my head. It was an accident and it looks big because it all happened at once and in the same place. But if you stand off a ways and look at it, the animals that went over that cliff was only a drop in the bucket to the ones killed for hides. Hell, I do believe I've seen that many hides at one time in Charlie Rath's yard in Dodge City and him shippin em out as fast as he could get cars and more comin in. And Hays City and Fort Griffin, back in 'seventy-three. And the bones not even a speck to what I seen scattered out in Kansas and Texas. In 'seventy-six it was I come out of the Panhandle — the buffalo was gone — and come north across Kansas with a little freight outfit. And no buffalo — maybe an old bull now and then and him not fit for meat. Nothin but bones layin white in the sun like an alkali flat, all the old huntin grounds nothin but a bone yard. From the Brazos all the way up the Platte — the Red River, the Canadian, the Cimmarron and the Arkansas, the Republican and Smoky Hill — bones, by golly, and the wagon wheels breakin em like sticks. It was no sight for a man to be proud of.

"There was fellers in Dodge City then makin money on bones, haulin em in to the Santa Fe to ship east for fertilizer. I seen em ricked up along the tracks till hell wouldn't have you. Bones was as good as money there in those days, like hides before.

"Bonepickers and broke buffalo hunters every which way. There was hunters had made a sight of money on hides didn't have a dime. And too proud to pick bones.

"There was one though, a man I knowed by the name of Jim Cook, took up a little homestead there out of Dodge and picked bones for a start — what he made on hides had gone for whiskey like with most — and all the old hunters callin him bonepicker and laughin. But he stuck it out like a man till the bones got scarce as the buffalo.

"A good hunter he was when I knowed him. He was big and cocky and loud, but a good enough feller underneath. He killed a sight of buffalo. I knew him to get five thousand in one season out in the Smoky Hill country on some little crick. Slaughter

Crick he called it and laughed. He was free with his money, them days, and his whiskey, and he was crazy-like and mean when he was drunk. There was no man he wouldn't fight at the drop of a hat.

"He was changed some when I seen him that time in 'seventy-six. Quiet and sober and dressed like ary other nester — fool hoe-men, the old hunters called em — with a span of old grey mules and an old thimble skein wagon he used for haulin bones. He didn't say much but I had the feelin he was a better man than before. Even though it looked like he knuckled under.

"It was funny, though, about the bonepickin. He was serious about it, not ashamed, like it was some kind of a religion. And he kept at it, I heard tell, long after there was any money in it. It's a thing to study on, what happened to Jim."

Woodfoot nodded, absorbed.

Sandy stopped talking, breathing hard, as if talk were work. And yet the words seemed to come easy enough for him. Woodfoot had a curious feeling of looking inside of Sandy, of seeing him clear and yet distorted, like looking through water or bent glass. His mind came back to Jim Cook — a pilgrim with a burden of bones, he thought wryly, or a cross. A cross. Skull and crossbones. He checked his mind, feeling sheepish.

Charley stirred at the edge of the firelight. "A damn bonepicker," he said, and blew out a long breath of smoke. "I seen the Indians off the reservation down at Fort Sill pickin em. It ain't a kind of work for a white man. Nigger work."

Sandy's eyes rested a moment on Charley and came back to the fire. There was a sadness in his face.

"You'll be a buffalo hunter yet, Charley," he said.

Charley looked puzzled. He half bristled up to say something but thought better of it.

"This Jim Cook," Woodfoot said. "Was he religious, maybe?"

"Naw. No more than me. If there was aught he thought over-much about, it was the country. He was older than me and he had a memory for places — not name places but places he'd been as a young buck, where he'd trapped and maybe been the first white man to see. This is Jim's country here, this and farther north. That was odd, too, him settlin in Kansas."

"Was he ever at Cheyenne Wells?"

Sandy laughed, seeing the parallel between himself and Jim Cook.

Charley finished the pipe, knocked it out on the heel of his boot and offered it to Sandy.

"Keep it," Sandy said, "if you can stand an Indian pipe."

Charley nodded his thanks. Before throwing the tobacco he stopped to examine the pattern of the bead work on the buckskin sack, holding it up to the firelight with an exaggerated gesture. "Purty," he said. "Like what a school kid might do." He threw it to Sandy, his face lit up momentarily with a mocking half smile. "It took a man to make the one I got."

Woodfoot laughed aloud, watching Charley dig into his pocket for his tobacco pouch. He had seen the pouch before — made of a squaw's breast, it was, oak-tanned to a dark shade of brown. It was soft and pliable and unrecognizable except when you looked close enough to see the shriveled nipple.

"Did you make it, Charley?" Woodfoot asked.

Charley shook his head. "A friend of mine in the Texas Rangers." He held the pouch up for Sandy to see, but Sandy did not look.

"It ain't much for tough, though," Charley said. "It's about wore out." He put it back in his pocket.

Sandy was filling another pipe, ignoring Charley. He held a pinch of the tobacco under his nose to smell it, nodding to himself in a way he had when he liked something.

"It'd make a better smudge," Charley said, "just to throw it on the fire."

"Most men I know like it," Sandy said indifferently.

Woodfoot laughed, wondering if Sandy intended the joke; deciding by his very indifference that he did.

Charley looked curiously from Sandy to Woodfoot, then moved around in front of the stump to face the fire. His hands were free now, Woodfoot thought. He'd probably start talking.

The moon moved up now, white and lopsided, growing smaller as it climbed away from the low hills and the rolled line of light-edged clouds just above them. The moon looked bright, but there was no color under its light, just shadings of black and silver. It struck him then as odd that the clouds directly below the moon caught the light and gave it back in a fiery tone.

"The way you birds talk is enough to sour milk," Charley said. "Christ amighty, it ain't any crime to hunt buffalo. There's no law against it, is there? So if we don't get em, somebody else will, that's simple enough for me." He was sitting on the west side of the fire, facing east, and something about the way the light struck his face gave him a fierce look, not just sour, but fiery, like maybe there was something in his nature you could only see under a certain light. A horse of a different color, Woodfoot thought, and that was all. Just reflections from the surface. He was certain that if there was one man he could call the turn on it was Charley. Still it was odd the way things looked different in the moonlight.

Charley was watching Sandy, as if for vindication, leaning forward, waiting. Like a kid, in some ways, Woodfoot thought. He worked hard for Sandy's approval, but he was going about it wrong. And maybe for him there wasn't any right way, Sandy being what he was. The only way Charley could work for approval was in excelling; and his excellences Sandy was not likely to approve. It was a contradictory situation and you felt a little sorry for Charley. Charley could be either a good or bad hunter and still not shine with Sandy. The contradiction was mostly in Sandy, but how could Charley ever understand that? Right now he was thinking that Woodfoot was attacking Sandy and was putting in for him. It was curious and funny but also a little bit pathetic, that Charley's logic should lead him so far from an understanding of the situation.

"What the hell's wrong with you birds, anyhow?" Charley asked, turning to Woodfoot. "Can't you answer?"

"No argument," Woodfoot said. "You couldn't get an argument out of me with a club. Go ahead and talk, though, if you want — I've no objection."

Charley snorted and looked away. He would sulk a little, Woodfoot thought. But he would also talk.

"You birds," Charley went on, "talk like you think the buffalo's about gone. Which they ain't. But just for the argument we'll say they are. What about it? What hurt's it gonna do? None," he answered himself. "All this country's good for is raising cattle. And you can't raise cattle with a lot of damn buffalo eatin up the feed and stampedin em. It's the only way the country's gonna get settled up."

"All right," Woodfoot said.

"And the Indians," Charley went on. "There ain't any better way to tame an Indian than to spoil his huntin ground. It's the one thing that's took the fight out of them. Buffalo hunters have done more than the army for tamin the Indians."

"It works," Woodfoot said.

"Starve em. Let em dig in the dirt to make a livin, it's good enough for em. Let em pick bones." Charley paused.

While he was quiet Woodfoot heard the mules snorting down along the river. Sandy was moving before the sound died. Charley followed him. By the time Woodfoot found his gun, they were coming back into the firelight following Jimmy, who was prodding an Indian ahead of him with his pistol. Sioux, Woodfoot thought.

The Indian stopped by the fire. His eyes took in the camp briefly, moved on out into the night and stopped. He had a blanket thrown over one shoulder and under it a coil of rawhide rope. Tall, he was, Woodfoot thought, as tall as Charley, with the same sour look, but with a steadiness about him, a pride that seemed to make him bigger than he was there in the firelight.

Jimmy stepped back diffidently and holstered his pistol, showing nothing of his excitement save a liveliness of his eyes as he glanced around at the others. It was like him, Woodfoot thought, to be out looking around when everyone else was in camp.

Charley moved around the fire to face the Indian, the fingers of his right hand walking nervously on the butt of his revolver. His face was alive now and the fiery look on it like a light. He looked like a starving man at a feast, lean and eager.

Sandy was the last to come up, moving slow, showing no emotion on his face. He looked at Charley and the Indian, then at Woodfoot and pointedly back at Charley. Woodfoot nodded and sat back down by the stump. He found his pipe, knocked the ashes out of it and began reloading. Sandy also sat down and reached his pipe off the stump where he had laid it and started filling it. He seemed to concentrate on the pipe, but Woodfoot knew he was studying Charley and the Indian.

"What the hell you birds gonna do," Charley almost shouted. "Let this damned horse thief make a break for it? By God, I'm not."

"Don't get excited, Charley," Sandy said quietly. "Sit down. He won't run."

The Indian was still staring off into the night, but Woodfoot sensed he was really watching Charley.

"You're damn tootin he won't," Charley said, "not if he wants to keep his hair."

"Sit down, you dang fire-eater," Sandy said again. Indulgently, Woodfoot thought, like he was talking to a kid. "And take your hand away from that popgun before somebody gets hurt."

Still Charley hesitated.

"Sit down," Sandy said sharply, and this time there was iron in his voice that even Charley could feel.

Charley grumbled but sat down. The Indian seemed to relax then, just a little droop of his shoulders and a movement in his legs like he was settling down off his toes. Sandy spoke to him, something in Indian talk, and he turned slowly. His hand came out from under his robe and pointed at his chest. "Yanktoni, me."

Sandy questioned him then. The Indian answered him briefly, the corners of his wide thin mouth curling after each answer with a contempt that took in the whole camp. It was hard on Charley, Woodfoot could see. He sat fidgeting, hardly restraining himself, his hands moving continually above his crossed legs.

Sandy stopped talking finally and settled back. "He says he was one of a hunting party that got in a little fracas with some buffalo hunters back to the south of us. The hunters nailed two of em and shot this one's horse from under him. He hid out in the brush till dark, then come looking for a horse to get back to the reservation with. He says he would have done it too except for those damn green mules."

Jimmy nodded. "He would, too. I noticed the mules actin up and went over. I seen him makin for Charley's horse and I cut him off. He tried for one of the mules then." Jimmy paused, grinning. "But his medicine was bad. He picked that crazy mule and she threw him. That's when you heard the snortin."

Charley laughed, more heartily than Woodfoot had ever heard him laugh before. He sobered suddenly. "By God," he said, "suppose this damn thief had got my horse. I'd be in a hell of a fix now, wouldn't I? You birds ain't fixin to turn him loose, are you?"

Sandy spoke to Jimmy, ignoring Charley. "You suppose there's more of em?"

Jimmy shrugged, then shook his head. "I believe him."

"I do myself," Sandy said. "A man with the guts this one has ain't likely to be lyin."

"I don't," Charley put in. "A damn savage like that's got no more sense of truth than a wild animal, and they ain't but a little cut above one in any other way. I seen a few Indians myself, down in Texas. By golly, I'm in favor of stringin him up, like any other horse thief."

"By golly," Sandy laughed, "you been drinkin blood for breakfast, Charley? Hell, it's an Indian's nature to steal horses. They don't figure it's any sin. It's been their way in this country ever since there was horses, I guess."

The Indian sensed what was going on, Woodfoot thought. His hands came out of the blanket again, unfastened it and threw it and the coil of rope to the ground. He turned his right side to the light and raised his arm. His whole side, all the way down to his moccasin, was sodden with blood, some of it red and fresh. He had on the sleeves and shoulders of a checkered flannel shirt — the rest he had torn into strips and tied around his chest over the wound just below his armpit. He had bound what looked to be a part of the stomach of a buffalo next to the wound. Some of the manure had dribbled down his side, streaking the red with green. Woodfoot thought he could hear a whistling noise under the bandage then as the Indian breathed.

Sandy got up and came closer.

"Jesus," he said admiringly, "this bird's got more guts than I thought." He said something to the Indian, then went into the shack and came back with a roll of white cloth and a jar of salve.

Charley was craning his neck for a better look, his eyes lit in fascination. He looked a little pale around the gills, Woodfoot thought with relief. So he was right after all. Charley didn't have as much of a stomach for blood as he liked to let on.

Charley laughed then, settling back against the stump. "Just like I said, not even a cut above an animal. He don't even know he's hurt, plasterin buffalo manure on a wound like that. No white man would be walking around with a hole like that in him, let alone plasterin it with shit — washin it with bodewash."

Sandy was taking the flannel strips off the wound. He looked briefly at Charley. "You're a damn fool, Charley."

Charley rose part way to his feet, then dropped back. Sandy did not so much as glance around. He finished undressing the wound and dipped water out of the drinking can to wash it.

The wound was the deep furrow of a bullet that had entered from the front, moving upward almost with the slant of the ribs, emerging at the back in a jagged hole quilled with little splinters of bone from a rib. The length of it was clotted with dark-looking blood, but at the middle fresh blood was oozing out in little bubbles in time with the breathing.

Sandy removed one of the splinters, jerking it quick. Woodfoot watched the Indian's eyes for a sign of pain, but saw nothing — the eyes never shifted from whatever star they watched out beyond the campfire.

Sandy went back into the shack and returned with a flask of whiskey which he offered the Indian. Woodfoot saw the eyes light up with a hunger, then go blank again as the Indian shook his head and looked again out into the sky.

Sandy removed more of the splinters, smeared the wound with salve, and bandaged it, passing the strip of cloth clear around the chest, fastening it with a needle and sinew thread. Finally he found a wide gun belt of tanned elk hide, which he buckled over the bandage. He said something to the Indian then and the Indian tightened the belt more.

It was funny, Woodfoot thought, the way Sandy had perked up working with the Indian. He worked in an easy, relieved way like someone turning loose of a big load. His face looked less strained and it seemed like there were more crinkles of laughter at the corners of his eyes.

Sandy sat down cross-legged by the fire and said something to the Indian, who turned slowly, picked up his blanket, approached Sandy and sat down, lowering himself lightly, with a dancer's ease.

Jimmy sat down between Charley and Woodfoot, making a circle around the fire.

Across the fire, Charley was unusually quiet — even his hands — and his eyes were set on the fire in a glassy, concentrated stare.

Again Woodfoot had the uneasy feeling of having missed something about Charley. For an instant he felt a complete stranger to the set bony face bronzed by the firelight.

Sandy loaded his pipe, lit it with the burning end of a stick and pointed the stem in the four directions and up and down in a serious and very deliberate manner before passing it to the Indian. The Indian accepted the pipe, puffed deeply at it and held it out to Charley.

Charley came out of his trance, surprised, and his hand came out instinctively, but he drew it back and turned his eyes away, curling his lip in scorn.

Jimmy reached over and took the pipe and smoked it and passed it on to Woodfoot.

It was a vote, Woodfoot thought, tasting the pleasant bitterness of the kinnekinnic, a vote on what happened to the Indian. He wondered if that were all of Sandy's purpose in smoking or if maybe Sandy simply liked the ceremony itself. He seemed to be enjoying himself now, in spite of Charley, as if he felt some kind of brotherhood with this hard-looking redskin. And maybe that was partly what was galling Charley, that Sandy should suddenly take a shine to this Indian horse thief, while still holding Charley himself at a distance.

Sandy puffed quietly at the pipe, then laying it aside, he again offered the whiskey. This time the Indian accepted, tipping the bottle and drinking in big swallows like it was water and then holding it up to the light before passing it on. Charley refused as before and the bottle came back to Sandy, who finished it and laid it aside.

There was silence then, a tense, waiting silence. There would be no more talk, Woodfoot knew, till whatever was coming had happened.

The Indian moved first. He did not speak or even so much as ask with his eyes. He just stood up slowly, found his rope and moved away from the fire past Sandy. Not fast, but slow and slouchy for an Indian, the easy swing of his shoulders coming like a dare to the eye.

Charley was up first, his eyes set on the Indian's back, his gun coming up fast, when Sandy stepped in front of him. Sandy had no gun on him but his hand rested lightly on the big skinning knife he had in his belt. When he spoke, in a low light voice, Woodfoot was surprised by a trace of Scotch in his accent.

"Put your damn popgun awa, Charley," he said, "if it happens ye're of a mind to stay in one piece."

Charley lowered his gun, but it was still pointed at Sandy. "You damned old fool," he laughed humorlessly, "I could shoot out both your eyes before you moved out of your tracks."

"No doubt," Sandy said placatingly. "I believe it. But should ye shoot out my brains, I should yet gut you belly to brisket."

It was over then. Woodfoot saw the doubt come into Charley's face and saw him cover it with a halfhearted laugh.

"Hell," he said, "I need a little practice. And if there's one thing I like to practice on better than a wolf, it's an Indian."

Sandy's voice was back to natural when he spoke. "You're a great one for wastin lead, Charley."

CHAPTER

11

CHARLEY WAS COLD WHEN HE BROUGHT HIS
horse into the corral — he felt shivery and empty for all the hot
coffee he'd had for breakfast. The morning was grey with a low,
cold fog so thick it ran like water against the skin, but shallow,
showing the brightness of the sun.

He saddled roughly, throwing the blanket on with his left hand
and following it so closely with the saddle that the blanket hardly
had time to settle; he was not sure there were no wrinkles in it. He
caught the cinch as it flopped under the belly on the first swing,
strung it with the latigo and hauled up strongly against the bay's
expanding barrel, hearing with satisfaction the horse's breath caught
at the sudden pressure. The horse danced out against the reins,
snorting the cold air in his nose and humping a little under the
saddle. Charley led him out of the corral and mounted without his
rifle, knowing the bay would buck and fiercely glad of a fight, sure
beforehand he would come out on top.

The bay got his head the first jump and Charley knew he meant
business. For just an instant he was sorry he had not smoothed the

blanket — if he took a fall the other men would see it. Then the doubt was gone. If there was one thing he could do, it was ride.

There was nothing fancy about the way the horse bucked, and thinking of the men watching, Charley almost regretted it. The bay was big and rawboned and when he came down stiff-legged there was no spring in him. It wasn't much to look at, but it was the hardest kind of ride to make.

But the fear was gone out of Charley; he was taking up some of the jar with his legs, sure now that nothing the bay could do would surprise him. He could hear the horse's gut slapping around inside of him and the involuntary expulsion of his own breath at the end of every jump. There were lights flashing in his eyes but he could see well enough, and the hot feel of winning was flaring in his blood.

The horse eased up and Charley pulled him up and rode back to the shack, aware of the back still humped and the switching tail.

He was warm now and feeling good, even though his neck hurt and his gut felt jarred and sore; and seeing the look in the eyes of the other men, he was proud. Woodfoot was grinning as usual, but it was a friendly grin. He would have some wisecrack to make, Charley thought, shifting his eyes as he dismounted. There was open admiration on Jimmy's face and Charley could not help smiling.

"You can straddle a horse and no mistake," Sandy said.

Charley knew he meant it and the pride rose in him strong. He knew, in that instant, that he liked Sandy as well as he would ever like any man, and he felt warm inside and good; then the memory of the set-to about the Indian closed on his insides like a clenching fist. Woodfoot was speaking but Charley only heard the last of what he said.

". . . like he had a burr under the saddle blanket."

All the good feeling was gone.

"Naw," Charley said, knowing himself to be partly wrong. "It's just his damn-fool nature to buck on a cold morning."

He strapped on his revolver, picked up his rifle and mounted holding the bay's head up, trying not to show the hurt of his feelings in his face. He rode out of camp knowing that something under the saddle was hurting the horse and, oddly, glad of it. He kicked the bay to a lope and held him there for a long time before he was calm enough to begin thinking again.

The fog cleared as he left the river, opening and closing on little patches of sunshine that looked rather than felt warm as he rode through them, thinning as he climbed into the hills to little puffs that twisted and curled along the ground like blown tobacco smoke. There was a yellow color in the light, warm as fire, that almost visibly melted the fog.

He stopped finally and unsaddled, finding a small stick of rose brier under the blanket next to the horse's hide. Already it had peeled a place the size of a dollar close to the backbone. Another saddle mark, he thought, noticing the sprinkling of white marks along the horse's back.

He shook out the blanket and refolded it, smoothing it down good before he saddled up again. After that the bay settled down to a long-stepping jog and Charley relaxed. He felt better, though he could not help thinking about Sandy and the Indian.

He was above the fog now, on the east side of a hill, with the sun slanting in warm and yellow out of a clear blue sky, and below, the fog shining and white as snow, but moving, gapping here and there on patches of brown earth. Looking back now, he had a feeling of release and relief; of coming out of darkness into light. The grey fog and little patches of light as he came through had been like his mood; now he felt stable again, clear. He wondered how much the weather had to do with it.

It would be a perfect day for hunting, the kind of day a man was likely to get a stand, he thought, yet holding it back from his mind as more than he could hope for — but still thinking he might. He had the feeling that it was today or never, though. He had been on the verge of quitting for a long time now but had put it off, always thinking that another day might change his luck and bring him out on top. It was impossible for him to go on being the under-dog in camp; it was too hard on his self-respect. It had been the same in the war, starting in at the bottom and working himself up by his skill with a gun; and again, down in Texas, where he had drifted after his discharge. He had felt the same way then, but he had finally come out all right.

He had hired out as a cow hand to a rancher in the Big Loss Valley, having ridden in on a high-stepping cavalry mare he had bought with his mustering-out pay. He looked good on a horse and thought he was good till he made his first ride with a couple of old brush poppers to bring in some wild cattle.

It was at night, because that was the only time the wild ones came out of the brush, but moonlight, so you could see a little, out in the open at least. They left a hungry decoy herd grazing in a little park and withdrew to watch from a little brush patch down wind. The wild ones came out like deer into the park, noses high, testing the wind, mixing finally with the decoys.

Waiting, he had noticed the little Indian ponies of the other two men trembling with excitement, and his own mare seemed to catch it from them, till he could hardly hold her in; and the two men grinning together about some private joke.

They seemed comical to him then, the two ragged-looking little men on their pot-bellied ponies. One, Billy Sanchez, was a Mexican, small, seeming hardly more than a boy till you looked at his face; sort of roly-poly, he was, and always clowning. The other was a thin-jawed northerner named Sanders, small too, but with a raw-hide look and hard blue eyes that did not laugh with the rest of his face. He looked fierce, all right, but with his banty size, a little funny too.

Charley saw only a few of the longhorn cattle come out of the brush, but the herd swelled under his eyes so he knew he was not seeing them all. He had not thought it possible for cattle to be so stealthy.

Sanders gave the signal to ride, taking out through the brush at a dead run with Billy right behind him. The idea, Charley supposed, was to get behind the herd and haze them toward open country, keeping the wild ones together with the tame ones. The only instructions Sanders had given him were to stay in sight and watch how it was done.

The two men were out of sight before his mare got out of her tracks — it was dark and in the brush besides — so all he could do was give her rein and let her follow. She ran crazy though, with her head way up, like she was afraid of scratching her nose on the underbrush. He could tell from the unevenness of her stride, the way her front legs jarred in the rough places, that she was not watching the ground. He was blind, himself, riding with his eyes almost shut against the brush popping him in the face; even where the brush was low he could not see the ground for shadows. It was wild and confusing, all the speed and darkness, with no control over where you went nor how, and the horse blind too and crazy.

He tried to stop, but the mare kept going, crooking her neck around and higher when he pulled on the reins. She fell then, in a tangle of hackberry bushes, throwing him clear but stunning him. She got up and tried to run, but by some chance he still held a rein. She dragged him out of the bushes and stopped, hanging back at the end of the rein, trembling like she was scared of him.

When his head cleared he mounted again, but he was lost. Something crashed by him through the brush, a cow he supposed, and the mare grabbed the bit and followed. He was afraid to try stopping her again so he gritted his teeth and let her go. He seemed to explode into the open, hard on the tail of a spotted longhorn cow.

He tried to stop, but it was too late and he plunged into the middle of the decoy herd and came up solid against a big steer that was slow getting out of the way. The mare almost went down but caught herself and staggered dizzily in a circle to the left. The cattle stampeded with a crackling vibration of hooves, fanning out like sparks from a fire, striking the brush now on all sides of the park and crashing on, leaving the park suddenly cleared and quiet, the sound of their flight dimming in the distance.

The mare came out of her staggers and was running again as something burst out of the brush into the park behind him. He caught just a glimpse of a horse and rider as the mare hit the brush again, and he knew it was Sanders.

He did not look back again, but he could hear the pound of hooves gaining on him; the mare was jumping through the brush rather than running, but she was not wild now. She was zigzagging around the big clumps so fast it kept him guessing just to stay in the saddle.

Sanders was yelling like he was hazing a steer along. As he came close he yelled, "By God, if you can't ride her, I'll drive her."

Charley heard the sing of a rope in the air and felt the mare flinch as it struck her a welt across the haunches. She missed her footing for a few jumps, almost falling again, and Sanders kept laying the rope across her hind end fast and heavy. She put her head down then and settled down to run.

"Now git the hell on home, you damn tenderfoot," he heard Sanders yell, feeling in the same instant the cut of the rope across his shoulders.

He swung the mare off to the left, almost throwing her, drawing his gun as he turned; but Sanders had turned back and was lost to sight in the brush.

The mare kept going, fast, flashing in and out of the little open spaces where the moonlight struck, following a buffalo trail. He was yanking at the bit with his left hand, his gun still out, cursing and weeping with the humiliation, the welt of the rope lying across his shoulders like a snake.

It was daylight when he rode up to the ranch. The boss met him at the bunkhouse, no more than laughing and looking at him a little critically when he told about his part in the stampede. After breakfast he put Charley to herding a little bunch of wild ones in the flats around the ranch buildings. These had been corralled and starved for several days, and the wildest ones hobbled or toggled so they were glad to graze, making no attempt to get away.

The next day Sanders and Billy showed up with the decoy herd and about as many wild ones. Neither of the men said anything to Charley about the stampede or about his horse, but he could see the contempt and amusement in their eyes. Oddly, he found himself resenting Billy more than he did Sanders. He was outraged at the laughter in the face of the little roly-poly Mexican — it was like being made fun of by a kid — or an animal. He tried to raise a fight with Billy later, but the little Mexican only pretended not to understand, and walked away neither scared nor angry, smiling.

He helped corral the herd the two men had brought in, taking orders from Sanders as if nothing had happened, suppressing his resentment.

The corral was a heavy log enclosure with wings running out in a V shape for maybe a hundred yards on each side, to guide the cattle into the gate. They brought the herd in fast so that the decoys, used to the work, would carry the wild ones in with them through the gate before they sensed the danger.

It worked fine except that a big blue steer among the drags turned back just before he reached the gate. He came straight for Charley. The mare, scared from the work of the night before, cut off to the side and let him by. Sanders rode on to the corral and slammed the gate shut while Billy took out after the steer.

The steer headed for open country as tight as he could run, tail in the air, but Billy caught him before he had gone a hundred yards. Riding close alongside, he leaned over, caught the end of the steer's tail and took a dally on his saddle horn. In the same instant the pony cut off to the side and the steer slammed over on his side and rolled. He lay there in a puff of dust, stunned, and Billy rode back fast and started to dismount, a short length of rope between his teeth. But the steer came out of it, then. He stood up quick and turned, shaking his head. Seeing the horse and rider, he dropped his head and charged. The pony shied, dodging the steer, and Billy, hanging by the horn and one stirrup, made it back into the saddle as the pony settled into a run.

The steer followed Billy toward the gate, the sweep of his horns just missing the pony's tail for the first few jumps. Sanders opened the gate and Billy rode through into the herd and circled, losing the steer among the others.

The boss came out then on a big rawboned bay colt he was breaking. He talked for a while with Sanders, apart, shaking his head now and then and looking at Charley.

Charley turned and busied himself with his saddle, determined not to watch any more. He was sure now he would lose his job — before he had a chance even to start.

When he looked again Billy had opened the gate and the boss and Sanders were riding into the corral. The boss beckoned with his head. "You can help with the cutting if you want, Charley," he said diffidently, "that is, if you can get your horse into the corral."

Charley rode in as Billy closed the gate.

"The idea," the boss said, "is to cut out the tame ones and let em out to graze. We'll starve the others a while to quiet em down some. So you just more or less stay out of the way, helping wherever you see a chance, and me and Sanders here will do the most of it."

They bunched the cattle in the far end of the corral, letting the tame ones break back whenever they could. The wild ones, afraid of the riders, crowded to the back, making it easier to get out the tame ones. When they got a little bunch cut out, Billy would open the gate and let them go, shutting it like a dodge gate on any wild one that happened to get by. It was simple till they got down to the last few. Then they had a lively time, with cattle dodging every which way, and Charley's mare too scared to work in close. The boss, on the big colt, was too slow to be much help, so most of the work fell on Sanders. He did all the cutting while Charley and the boss held the bunch. He would pick out a cow and the pony would do the rest, snaking around through the herd at a run, following the cow till she broke for the other end of the corral.

Charley could see the big blue steer in the bunch at the far end. Every time Sanders cut into the bunch the steer would try to climb the fence, each time falling back on his haunches. He would come to his feet then and whirl, facing the rider with his head lowered as if to charge. It happened that way several times with Sanders appearing not to notice, before the steer finally charged. Then it seemed like he had been waiting for the chance.

Sanders was crowded between two big cows in the corner of the corral when he saw the steer coming. He reared his pony around, drawing his pistol at the same time, and fired. The bullet grazed one of the steer's horns and sang out into the air, and the big animal veered and came out of the herd straight for the boss. Sanders' next shot took him in the hind end and only seemed to speed him up.

The big colt just stood there watching, his ears tilted forward in curiosity — too dumb to be scared, Charley thought — and the boss hauling away at the reins and kicking his ribs to move him.

Charley drew then and fired quick, taking the steer in the middle of the forehead, dropping him right under the colt's nose. He holstered his gun, knowing from the look in the boss's eyes that he was still good for a job.

He felt relieved, not so much because of the job, he realized later, but because of the kind of shooting he had just seen from Sanders.

Afterwards the boss offered to trade horses, and Charley ac-

cepted, thinking himself cheated, but willing to take the loss in order
to keep his job. In the long run it turned out that he got the best of
the deal.

His shooting and the horse, Charley realized later, were the
things that had kept him on the payroll. He had never really learned
about cattle; at a roundup he was always in the wrong place, cutting
out the wrong cattle, misreading brands. It seemed like he didn't
have the knack of working with a crew of men.

But he got to be good with the wild ones, working with Sanders
and Billy. For the most part they used decoys, but sometimes even
the decoys stampeded. Then all a man could do was save what he
could by roping them or tailing them down and tying them — it
was impossible to use a lasso in the brush. It was dangerous work,
not so much from the hell-bent riding as from the cattle themselves.
Tailed down, they were usually stunned long enough to tie, but it
made them mad too, and if they came out of it too soon, it was
either shoot them or get a horn in the ribs — and shoot quick.

He did all right there. And with the buffalo.

The ranch was located in a little steep-sided valley that opened
out onto the prairie. The boss usually had a rider out to keep the
buffalo from coming in with the cattle, but occasionally a big herd
would sweep in. It was easy enough to drive them out, but getting
all the cattle combed out of the herd afterwards was another story.
It took some hard riding that not every horse could stand up under.
As it turned out, he had the best horse in the outfit for that job. The
big bay was fast and it seemed like he could run all day and never
give out. He was the kind of horse the Indians used for hunting
buffalo. And indirectly he had been the cause of Charley's first
run-in with Indians.

A herd of buffalo had come into the valley, taking with them as
they left a hundred or so head of cattle. The next morning he and
Billy set out to bring the cattle back, finding the main bunch already separated from the buffalo and grazing by themselves at the
mouth of a draw that led off into the hills. Riding into the draw,
Charley found the trail of a small mixed herd of cattle and buffalo
leading back into the hills — the splayed pointed hoof mark of a
cow was easy to spot among the round clean prints of the buffalo.
Leaving Billy to take the main bunch back to the ranch, Charley

rode on into the draw.

He rode into the bunch fast, and the buffalo stampeded first, leaving most of the cattle running in the rear. He came up alongside, getting most of the cattle with the first cut, though he had to shoot a couple of old steers that refused to turn.

He combed out the remaining few, shooting a few buffalo as he rode, partly for practice and partly to get them out of the way. Coming back with the last of the cattle, he stopped to take some of the buffalo tongues, and that was when he first spotted the Indians. There were two of them, riding up the draw, cutting off his back trail, so there was nothing to do but unsheath his rifle and wait.

They came on slowly, making no show of hostility, finally dismounting and leading their horses the last few yards. Mounted, they had looked strong and sure and somehow fearful. But on the ground they were just two Indians, the one short and bowlegged and old, the other young and dirty with a mean sullen look in his eye. They were upwind from him, and the smell of them had reached him before they dismounted, a kind of wet-dog smell that, close now, gave him a queasy feeling in the stomach.

He stopped them at a distance with a gesture of his rifle, saying nothing but watching them closely. The younger was armed with a short bow held in the same hand as his lead rope; the other carried an old Hudson's Bay fusee. This one extended his hand, grinning, but Charley shook his head, and again moved the rifle.

"Whatever you got to say," he said, "I can hear from where you're standing."

The Indian swung his arm around in front of the young one, as if to restrain him. When he spoke, Charley was surprised, then amused at the depth and power of his voice. There was something ludicrous about that kind of a voice coming from an old flea-bitten savage; the solemnity was out of place, like a preacher in a barroom. And with all that, the childish accent of the English words was especially laughable. Charley found himself smiling, listening to the old man talk.

"Buffalo," the Indian said, pausing and pointing to the dead animal beside Charley, "Indian cattle. Spotted buffalo," he swung his arm toward the bunched-up cattle down the draw, "white man's cattle. Indian shoot spotted buffalo to eat, white man makes war.

White man, not hungry, shoot buffalo just the same, what road shall Indian take?" He stopped and folded his arms, looking unbelievably serious and dignified. Charley laughed outright.

"Hell," he said, "buffalo don't belong to anybody. They're there for anybody to shoot, me just the same as you."

The Indian shook his head, pointing again to the dead buffalo, then to himself.

Charley shook his head. "No, by God, if you want meat, go shoot it. This is mine." He indicated with his rifle the way the buffalo had gone.

The young Indian turned suddenly then, mounted and rode off at a run; the old one followed with surprising swiftness, whacking his horse with the old fusee trying to catch up. At about thirty yards the young one swung off to the right, with the old one trying to head him off, and circled back toward Charley. As he came close, he dropped off the far side of his pony, his heel hooked over the cantle of the saddle. In the same instant that Charley saw his head and arms appear under the horse's neck, he heard the zip and thud of an arrow and saw it sticking in the dead buffalo beside him. He dropped then to take a rest on the carcass and the Indian moved out in a wider circle, having missed his chance. The old one came by then and fired and Charley ducked, seeing the flash and smoke of the old rifle. The ball went overhead and he heard the sound of the other horse pounding in behind him. He climbed over the carcass to the other side and turning, saw the young Indian in the saddle now sweeping down on the bay colt. The horse threw up his head and ran and the Indian came alongside and grabbed the reins and moved off at an angle down the draw. Charley got a bead on him then, giving him just a shade of lead, and fired. The Indian came out of the saddle, the bay cut off to the side to avoid stepping on him and the two horses separated, leaving him kicking in a circle on the ground.

The old one had ridden on out and reloaded. Now, seeing the wounded Indian, he came back in, lying low over his horse. Charley got a bead on him and fired and thought he saw the Indian jerk in the saddle. But he kept coming.

Charley dropped the breach of his rifle to reload, and the shell was stuck. He dug at it, breaking his thumbnail, but it was solid.

And the Indian was still coming, low over the pony, cutting to the side now. Charley dropped the rifle and drew his revolver, but he did not fire. The Indian swung off then without shooting, maybe, Charley thought, because he was wounded, and rode back to where the young Indian was still squirming on the ground, out of pistol range.

The young Indian was trying to get up, but it seemed like only one side of him was working, so that when he tried to raise himself up with his arms he only turned himself over. But he kept trying.

Charley was poking at the stuck shell then with his wiping rod, watching the two Indians, the old one trying to boost the young one onto his horse and he still kicking and squirming. The old one finally hoisted the other to his shoulder and backed up against the horse and loaded him.

It was a perfect chance to get two Indians with one shot, Charley thought, poking furiously at the stuck shell. He wondered why the old one did not at least keep on the other side of the horse.

The wounded Indian was on his belly across the saddle, one leg jerking out to the side, and the old one up behind, riding off toward the two horses that were grazing down the draw. Charley almost ran after them, but thought better of it and sat down on the buffalo, thinking of the long walk back to the ranch.

The old one caught the lead rope of the Indian pony and, turning, waved with his rifle and rode on, leaving the bay grazing. Charley got up then, feeling shaky in the knees and puzzled and somehow regretful. He stood watching the brown back of the Indian and the two buckskin ponies fade into the heat-shimmered brown distance as if they were riding straight into the hill that curved far below, sloping, into the prairie. And they were gone, with only the drift of little wisps of dust to show where the horses had passed; disappeared into the sagebrush and the tall spined cactus like a coyote or a wolf.

He shivered, standing there in the heat, feeling a sudden strangeness, as if the passing of the Indians had somehow revealed to him the country; looking around him, he had the sudden sharp feeling of a stranger in an alien land — the far sweep and quiet of the hills, the dry lifeless distance and the intense blue of the sky that cupped it under a burning sun were ominous and unfriendly. Only the spotted, longhorn cattle, scattered out in the scant shade of the cactus and tall clumps of sagebrush, were familiar.

He picked up the tongue he had taken from the buffalo, but dropped it and walked quickly to his horse, feeling a desire to move, to put distance between himself and that spot; noticing as he passed, the smeared circle of blood the Indian had left. Rounding up the cattle, he had a jumpy, half-scared feeling that stuck with him long after he passed the mouth of the valley into the familiar range, a feeling he could not understand or ever forget.

It was a long time before he hunted buffalo again. But he fought Indians often enough, horse thieves that raided the valley every time there was good moonlight, and killed a sight of them — then and later with the rangers. And the feeling passed as he came to know the country, till killing an Indian was no different from killing a wolf except it was more dangerous. But hunting buffalo he always remembered the incident. It puzzled him with its insistence, and angered him.

The memory stayed with him now as he rode into the hills looking for buffalo; and the feeling was the same except there was no fear in it, but anger. Maybe, he thought, it was a similarity of the country — not the cactus, or the heat, but the same feeling of distance and quiet, of endless space yet cupped by the intense blue of the sky, and himself small and at the center. And for all the calmness, a vague feeling of hostility.

He moved steadily northeast, roughly paralleling the river, working the little draws and valleys. By noon he had running shots on half a dozen small bands and his count stood at ten, scattered out over a distance of four or five miles. He crossed Rock Creek, east of Medicine Rocks, then turned west and moved down toward the river. There was a good watering place at the mouth of the creek and a little swampy flat full of buffalo wallows. It would be a good place to try.

There were no buffalo in the flat, but to the north of it, just coming down out of the hills, was a band of maybe a hundred and fifty. They were strung out along the trail, moving lazily down to water.

It was warm, the sun high in the south, with just a whiff of breeze from the north. And quiet, so that even from a distance he could hear the buffalo.

He had ridden up to the edge of the bluff that overlooked the flat. Now he rode back, out of sight, and turned south to the creek. He left his horse tied to a clump of willows and followed the creek bed down around the end of the bluff, then climbed the cut bank and picked a spot behind a sandstone boulder that gave him a good view of the flat. He set up his prong stick and settled himself to wait, a fierce excitement boiling up in his chest.

The flat was splashed with puddles of water from the springs at the foot of the bluff and patched with swamp grass. At the far end were deep pools with gravel bottoms where the buffalo watered. Near the bluff on his right was a scattering of big boulders of grey sandstone, worn smooth and oiled by the scratching of buffalo, standing up from the circular ditches cut by hooves. Around them the ground was furred thick with the shed wool. Below him at the mouth of the creek was a little grove of cottonwoods.

After watering, the buffalo spread out slowly into the flat, some lying down or wallowing in the puddles, grunting and tearing up the sod with their horns, others drifting on out to scratch on the rocks. The nearest ones were not over a hundred yards away, the far ones not a hundred more, and all of them full of water and lazy. A stand, if he handled it right, Charley knew. He forced himself to lie quiet and wait till all of them had watered and settled down in the flat, meanwhile trying to remember all that Sandy had told him. He was tense now, and shaky, fighting the desire to start shooting. The nearness of the big animals tormented him, filling him with a crazy, inexplicable anger.

The stragglers moved up from the watering places and spread out, moving in a hazy light that was maybe the heat, Charley thought, and maybe a trick of his eyesight. The grip of his rifle was slick now with the sweat from his hand and there was a halo around the front sight that blurred against the mass of buffalo. There was a buzzing in his ears that disturbed him — as if the noise might scare the buffalo.

He kept sighting experimentally and adjusting his sights, trying to calm himself, picking half a dozen animals before he decided on one to start with. Then he picked a cow standing alone at the edge of the herd, and suddenly his hand was steady, the blur of light gone, and he fired. The cow did not even flinch, the report came back off the bluff like thunder, and he half rose, cursing himself for the miss, expecting the stampede; then dropped back unbelieving as the herd stood, the only movement a few buffalo getting up slowly, front end first, like horses, and staring curiously toward the bluff.

The cow moved then, bowing up in the middle and belching, and he saw the stream of bright blood from her mouth spatter on the ground in front of her; and she turned and lay down, easy, and rolled onto her side.

The nearest buffalo, catching the scent of blood, gathered around the cow, their mouths open, tongues extended, bellowing in short brassy blasts. An old cow moved out of the herd, away from the group, with a half dozen others following her. He dropped her, and the followers turned back and split up.

He was calm now and sure, in spite of the crazy talk of the buffalo circling the downed animals like rings of dancers, hooking them in a senseless frustrated rage — as if only part of his mind were aware of them, feeling the weirdness, hearing the eerie sounds they never made except at the smell of blood. There was an odd metallic taste in his mouth, hot in the flow of spit that kept him swallowing between shots, in his nose like the smell of blood; and his mind questioned the reality of the smell — it was too far to smell, not enough wind, and the acrid haze of powder smoke around him, thick as a fog.

His hand was sure and steady on the gun, but eager, so that he had to force himself to count between shots so as not to overheat the barrel — and still it grew hot, hot enough to burn the finger at the touch, and even though all his shots found, he had a feeling they were becoming erratic, and cursed himself for not remembering to bring his canteen to cool the barrel — advice Sandy had offered and he had not considered. He wiped the barrel and tried to wait for it to cool, but he could not; his eagerness was burning him like a fire, fear of breaking the spell tormenting him.

His shoulder was numb from the constant kick of the rifle, his hand hot and sweaty on the grip. There was a deafness in his ears from the battering noise of the rifle so that the sound of the buffalo now seemed to come from far off; a haze that he knew was mostly the gun smoke around him, seemed to hang over the flat, giving it an odd peaceful look, like heat might but more tangible and oppressive. Some of the buffalo still lay in their mud holes, the dead ones scattered around them, stretched out as if in sleep.

He heard a new sound then from the cottonwoods along the river, faint but clamorous between shots — the idiotic gibbering of magpies commenting senselessly, endlessly. The sound disturbed him, rasped on his nerves, and he searched between shots for the white flash of bird wings.

The gun barrel became so hot he could feel the heat on his face when he sighted; he forced himself to stop and clean it. Then, glancing back of him with the feeling someone might be watching, but moving slowly and cautiously, he reversed the gun and, holding the hot steel with the end of a gun belt, made water down the barrel. He heard the hiss of steam, and the sweet, sickening odor of burnt urine rose to his face in a cloud; he held his breath with a quick feeling of suffocation. But he stayed with it till he was dry, breathing finally in shallow gasps through his mouth to avoid the smell; but still thinking he could taste it and almost vomiting.

The buffalo that were left were moving in two small groups by the time he got his rifle back to the prong stick. But he broke up the groups by shooting the leaders and they split up again and began milling aimlessly. There were only a few cows left now, and some young ones, spike bulls and heifers and a whole raft of spring calves scattered out among the carcasses. He shot the remaining cows carefully, slowly, cursing himself for the shakiness he could not control that seemed to be coming up out of his chest into his arms. His nerves were edgy, raw from all the noise, and he heard with a sudden anger the continued chattering of the magpies along the river. On impulse he threw a shot into the trees. He heard the bullet ricochet out into the sky with an unexpected racket; the young bulls bunched up and started moving and he knew the stand was over. He shot the leaders with quick amazing accuracy, but the bunch was running now and there was no stopping it. He rose to run after them for another shot but his knee buckled and he fell and rose again, almost weeping in a suffocating rage. He forced himself to stop then, reasoning that he had lost nothing but a few kip hides, not worth the skinning; but still he watched the retreating animals — not over two dozen — with a terrible sense of loss.

He turned then to count his kill, stopping at fifty with a sudden sickening distaste, then finished the count feeling only a dull surprise and no elation to learn he had killed almost a hundred — the biggest stand he had yet heard of.

Exhaustion took him till he could hardly stand. He walked unevenly back to his belts and prong stick. He felt drunk and empty; picking up the shell cases, his hands fumbled with an unnatural awkwardness. Afterward he stretched out face downward on the ground, feeling the earth rolling under him with a thunderous noise.

CHAPTER
12

Jimmy was lying in the back of the wagon on a pile of fresh hides as they moved north toward the sound of Charley's gun. The sun, high and polished in the south, cast an unusual warmth around him, as if drawn to the buffalo hides layered in the bottom of the wagon. He was tired, and the softness of the hides pressed warm and tight against the sore muscles of his back. But he felt curiously uneasy. The hides, for all their weight and bulk, jiggled liquidly with the jarring of the wagon; they had the stretchy slide of flesh with none of the stability of bone.

He had been sleepy when he climbed into the wagon, but now he was wide awake, unable as always to sleep in a moving wagon with its unpredictable motion and jarring. It seemed like he always had to watch where he was going to be comfortable. It wasn't that he didn't trust Woodfoot; it was just that he had to have some solid connection with the earth — his own feet or the living bone and muscle of a horse, which always became an extension of himself, so that he knew as if with his own touch the quality of the ground he traveled, and the shape of it, knowing before the horse stepped exactly where he would put his foot.

Lying now, trying to rest, he had the feeling that his medicine was working, trying to warn him of impending danger; he sat up, searching the country around him for any sign, but seeing nothing. He lay back determinedly, knowing he had read the feeling wrong. It was mostly riding in the wagon watching the sky and the only friendly presence to reassure him, the sun.

Yet even sitting up, with the familiar hills and the river line clear and steady in his eyes, the feeling lay faint but insistent in the depths of his mind. There was a strangeness about the country he could not account for, not in any change he could detect. It was the same as it had always been as far back as he could remember, with only the sprinkling of buffalo carcasses to change the looks — and the smell. Often now he caught a whiff of putrid flesh and knew without looking they were passing by some naked carcass. Sometimes on a warm day he would hear them explode with a great pop and sigh.

The death of animals had never bothered him before — it was how a man lived, killing his meat. But all the rotting flesh and the hides, worthless for robes, staked out drying around camp like some strange growth and the new grass curling yellow underneath, weighed on him, invading even his dreams. Sometimes in the dark of early morning he would awaken with a vivid sense of strange presences that he could not shake even in the daylight. It made him uneasy and vaguely dissatisfied. He did not like the work he was doing. But he could not stop; he could not go back.

It was a trap, the reservation, a cage to hold a man till he rotted or went crazy, the old life dead and all the men who had known it dead or dried up, living backward, the decay in the air as heavy as the smell of swollen buffalo, the rot-wind of death. He could not live on the reservation.

He remembered his father, a big Irishman, a squaw man who had fought beside Crazy Horse on the Rosebud and again on the Little Bighorn, and then afterwards had quit the tribe and his woman, saying he could not stand the smell of sickness, the smell of the reservation. He had been killed later, hunting buffalo down on the Canadian, by a band of Comanches.

It wasn't the smell, Jimmy knew. That was only a way of speaking. But how could you put into words the thing that was in the air — the old men, distant-eyed now and hopeless, who had been the hunters and the fighters of the tribe, who now refused to work with the ill-smelling cattle and the awkward plows, sitting in their ragged canvas tents reliving old action; and the young men, excluded even from that reflected glory with no coups counted, no symbol of manhood to clothe them against the silent, unsaid and even unthought scorn of the old ones; going sullenly about their farm work days, at night drinking and fighting, or risking their lives or losing them to steal horses which the agent only took from them and returned.

Jimmy had taken part in some horse-stealing raids; and with Spotted Hand, his friend, had spent time in jail for it and had his hair cut off. There had been a thrill in the danger of it and in the silent approval of the old people of the tribe. And for Spotted Hand, this had seemed worth the price they paid. But not for Jimmy. After the first time, he went only because of Spotted Hand, against his own better judgment and against the advice of Grey Elk.

"It is no good to look backward," Grey Elk would tell them. "The old ways were good, but they are not the ways of the white man. What hope now to fight the long knives? They are numberless as the leaves. For the Indian the battle is done. There is no hope nor honor to fight longer."

Spotted Hand would not listen. He would walk away scornfully and Grey Elk would watch him go without anger but with a sadness in his eyes and something like admiration. At these times Jimmy would sense a bond between the two, a brotherhood in spite of all the enmity. It made him feel apart, a stranger to these his two best friends — Grey Elk his uncle, a medicine man and a leader of his people, who had been his teacher and friend and in all things closer to him than his father had ever been; and Spotted Hand, his companion since childhood, with whom he had shared the deepest experiences of his life. Yet he had gone a different road and where his trail split off he could not tell at the time. But now, looking back, he could see and understand. Grey Elk had pointed him the way, encouraged him to leave. Yet he could never have left except for what had happened to himself and Spotted Hand.

They had come of age at the same time, and through tradition — there were no more wars to fight — had gone out to find their medicine, their protector in battle. It came easy for himself, the vision. He went alone into the hills, fasting and going without water, remembering the many stories he had heard of protective animal spirits, intent only on seeing one. And on the fourth day in a kind of waking dream he saw what he wanted to see. He could see it now with a breathless clarity, the cool blue water of the lake, then far above the eagle, flying upward into the sun, till he was gone; and again the blue water. It was the lake he could see now, and feel. But the eagle he had chosen for his medicine — he had shot one and skinned it and he carried the feathers in his medicine bag until the final break. But he was not sure. It had come too easy, and with an unsettled separation — the broad calm water and the shadow of the bird, disappearing. It made him uneasy remembering it.

But to Spotted Hand the vision came hard and after a long vigil; and then he had refused to accept it. It was as if his body had refused the vision before it came, so that he almost killed himself with fasting before his mind opened and saw and then closed again. And he would not accept and tried again.

He had been gone too long when Jimmy, unable to wait longer, had found him. He watched from a distance for days while his friend tortured himself on the hot hill, bare-bodied in the sun and at night in the cold wind, his strength against him like an enemy. And Jimmy watching, sick and desperate, with all his will fighting the impulse to interfere. And he waited almost too long.

Coming to watch one morning, he found Spotted Hand stretched out motionless and bloody at the foot of a ledge and at first believed him dead. He made a travois and hauled his friend to camp and used up the last of his own strength waiting while Grey Elk made medicine.

Spotted Hand was delirious for a day and night, talking incoherently and with unmistakable terror of a burning tree. The fear shook him like a wind, distorting the usually calm round face almost beyond recognition, communicating itself to Jimmy and even, Jimmy thought, to old Grey Elk.

It was hard now, remembering, to separate in his mind his own image of the tree from what Spotted Hand had said then and later. But there was a vividness about it, a reality beyond anything he had experienced since, that even now quickened his blood — as if the terror were a glass that cleared and magnified the image. He had seen a tree struck by lightning once, enveloped suddenly in a yellow tower of flame, then almost as suddenly black and smoking against a muddy sky. That had become part of the image. And maybe the only part that had come from Spotted Hand was the spiraling of the frantic birds ascending the flames, disappearing finally in the tall smoke, leaving their cries floating downward then like ashes. Not any birds he could name, but strange, bright-plumed beings birthed maybe in the mind of his friend, but clear and somehow terrible. And the sound of flames even now a rushing in his ears.

Spotted Hand lapsed finally into quiet, and Jimmy rolled up in a robe and slept in Grey Elk's lodge. He awakened a day later to the quiet sound of voices and heard his two friends talking in an un-usual intimacy. Lying there listening, feeling weak and shaky, he was flooded with a wave of relief, a sense of release that seemed to wash over him clean and cool, leaving him finally with a sense of drifting.

He lay puzzling over the feeling for a long time, becoming aware finally of a changed quality in the voices. Listening, he heard Grey Elk explaining the vision and Spotted Hand in an angry voice denying it, leaving the lodge finally on unsteady legs.

Grey Elk sat looking at the fire, sadness and resignation heavy on his face. Seeing Jimmy, he said roughly, "Let him go. You cannot follow him where he is going now."

Jimmy shrugged, not understanding. "He is my friend," he said simply, and left.

He found Spotted Hand in his lodge — he lived alone, refusing to enter the log house adopted by his parents — and found him preparing to leave. He looked up at Jimmy with a reluctant wel-come in his eyes, but he said nothing.

They traveled westward toward the old hunting grounds on the Yellowstone, keeping away from the wagon roads and white men's houses, hiding out in the daytime in the brush patches, riding only at night. They lived on what small game they could get with arrows, neither having a gun, saving their dried meat for future need.

It was then, under the constant shadow of danger, that Spotted Hand came alive. He shed his sullenness with the white man's clothing he had worn, leaving the reservation. He bundled up the black coat and trousers to tie behind the saddle, then on impulse threw them aside into the brush with no comment but with finality, as if he had reached a decision. After that he was in unusually good spirits.

Sitting by a campfire one afternoon under a big cottonwood, the only one for miles along the river, where the smoke would disperse upward through the tree, Spotted Hand scratched a handful of small stones out of the dirt and heated them in the fire. Picking two of them out with a pair of flat sticks, he placed one on the back of his left hand and gave the other to Jimmy, his small black eyes glittering in his round friendly face.

Jimmy placed the stone on the back of his hand, gritting his teeth, gripping the wrist with the free hand as if the arm were a being apart from himself, and held it struggling, smelling the singed flesh. But his body would not stand it; the wrist turned in his grip dropping the stone, the hand came to his mouth, and he tasted the burn.

Glancing at Spotted Hand, he saw the pebble still lying on the flesh, looking cool now and the hand not moving, the mischievous smile still in his friend's eyes. He declined the next pebble, and watched the boy burn another spot on his hand, and start a third; then jumped him, knocking the pebble off, and pinned him to the ground with a headlock, throwing all his weight and strength into his shoulder.

Spotted Hand did not even struggle at first; with a methodical calm, he began flipping his legs and body up and back. Jimmy had the head solid in his arm, the chin hooked, but his power was going. And the head began to slip, the neck seeming to shorten, and with a final flip, Spotted Hand broke the hold, landing on his hands and knees. Reaching through under his belly and behind his arm, Jimmy caught him by the neck and far shoulder and with a sudden pull downward and a shove, flipped him onto his back and pinned him again, knowing if he lost the hold again it was the last time.

It seemed like a long time he held on, all his weight on his friend's chest, holding the one arm with his hands and the other in a grip between his legs, and Spotted Hand did not move, but held himself in a constant tension, wearing away at Jimmy's strength till his muscles seemed to melt. He let go and threw himself clear to try for another hold, but came up too slow and went down under his friend's weight, kicking and struggling wildly now, knowing he was through. Spotted Hand got a wrist lock on him, throwing his endless strength on it till Jimmy thought the bone would break; but he would not yell. He had dropped the hot stone, but nothing could make him yell, as if his mind had control of his voice and not his wrist.

He was wet with sweat and feeling dizzy when Spotted Hand turned him loose; the hand would not work for a long time. But he was pleased, knowing it was worth the pain, seeing the approval in his friend's eyes.

He felt faint and a little sick. He wondered then if Spotted Hand ever had that feeling to fight; it was as if his friend did not have that separation of mind and body that Jimmy found in himself.

But he was restless, Jimmy thought, sitting under the big cottonwood waiting for evening. Not that the restlessness showed in any movements he made — he sat quietly under the tree, leaving Jimmy to do the watching. But about him Jimmy sensed a concentration, a turning inward, a blankness which he could not analyze but which left him with an uneasy, lonesome feeling.

Unable to sit longer, Jimmy left the fire and skirted the brush that surrounded the big tree, scanning the puddled flat and the little draw that led down out of the hills. They had been following the river, moving south and west. Now a long steep ridge slanting down to the river blocked their way. They would have to turn back and find a place to ford or take to the hills along the trail that followed the draw. He came back and climbed the tree for a look up and down the river but saw nothing.

It was a cold day near evening, but with an unusual greyness in the air, an oppressive, leaden quality, even with the movement of the rising wind. A gust seemed to catch in the tree, rocking it out over the river till he was sure it was going down, but it righted itself and came back slowly, as if with effort. Looking down through the leafless branches, he could see the movement of the uncovered roots that trailed down the steep-cut bank into the choppy water, rising and falling with the motion of the tree, drifting a little in the slow current. Little gusts of wind struck here and there in the low brush along the bank with a rattling, irregular sound like live things. West, high in the hills, he thought he could hear the sound of the big wind coming down. He imagined he could see the blue-black cedars straining against the wind as against a current of water and farther down the sagebrush bending. He waited fearfully for the impact of the wind on the tree, but it did not come.

Finally he climbed down and found Spotted Hand preparing to leave. He had both horses in and was saddling his own, moving fast. Jimmy saddled his pony, surprised that Spotted Hand should be leaving camp before dusk, but not questioning. He was glad of a chance to get moving, to meet the storm before it struck.

They rode out of the brush up onto the flat, striking a deep-cut buffalo trail that curved away from the river toward the draw that led up into the hills. Spotted Hand took the lead, riding steady but with no caution. Jimmy found himself hanging back, searching the hills ahead for any unusual movement — bird flight or running rabbit, any sign of what lay beyond the curving mouth of the draw — but saw nothing, only the straining motion of the wind that struck them now, and held steady, slowing them, needling their faces with blown sand. Looking back, Jimmy saw the big tree, leaning in tension with the wind, but still standing high over the river.

They rode into the shadow of the hills into an unnatural early darkness. There was less wind. Above the eddying currents of air he could hear the main stream of it striking the hill tops and pouring on over toward the river.

There were two trails cutting in and out of the sagebrush and running almost parallel, the one shallow and hoof-marked, the other cut too deep for use, filled in here and there with rocks and caved-in dirt or clogged with weeds and brush gathered by the spring freshets.

Spotted Hand was on ahead riding at a jog trot that Jimmy could not match with his own horse — a trot was too fast, a walk too slow. He raised his horse to a trot now, to catch up before the next bend in the trail, feeling the tall brush catch at his feet with brittle fingers. He was almost up when he heard the first sound of horses and looking up saw the wave of riders envelope Spotted Hand as his horse reared to turn; saw him strike with his club and then go down under a rifle butt swung from behind; this while his own horse spun in terror and headed back down the trail. A rider plunged by him on the left bucking the sagebrush, to head him off, but went down in the old buffalo trail. From the corner of his eye he saw the rider jump clear, then fall, and rode on hearing the pound of other hooves close behind. He dropped low on his horse hearing the sing of a rope past his ear, and brushed it aside with his arm as the loop touched his shoulder. Looking back, he saw the rider trying frantically to shake the loop free of the sagebrush, saw him stop and turn full in the path and heard the cursing as the two other cowboys cut into the sagebrush on either side to get by. By the time they got back into the trail he had a good lead and held it and gained a little on the twisty narrow trail coming down the draw. His horse was little and wiry but not fast, he knew, so he rode hard in the dangerous ground, knowing he would lose what he gained on the open flat.

It was almost dark in the draw, but coming out onto the flat the light still seemed full. He had a sinking feeling then — as if darkness were his only chance. Glancing back, he saw one of the riders take off to the left to cut him off from the trail down river and he knew then there was no use trying to outrun them. So he rode straight for the river, whipping his horse across the flank with his bow, hearing the steady pound of hooves behind him, knowing he was losing ground with every jump. He struck the brush a little below the big cottonwood, the low willows striking his legs with the sting of whips, and the pony snorted and tried to turn down river in spite of the guiding pressure of his knees. He struck the turned head with his bow and dug in his heels and the horse went over and dropped toward the black water.

He left the saddle under water, taking a shove off the horse's side, and stayed under, swimming upstream. It was dark under the muddy water, and the only thing to guide him the feel of the current and the last split-second memory of direction before he went under. He stayed in the deep water, hugging the bottom till he could feel the pressure on his ears, and knew almost in panic that he was moving too far out from the bank.

He headed back in, forcing himself to keep the slow hard stroke and the long glide afterward. He brushed the upturn of the bank with his left hand and straightened out to swim farther, his chest heaving to suck in the denied air but his arms and legs sure and controlled and his mind still clear.

He strained his eyes into the muddy black water for a sign of the tree roots but saw nothing and thought maybe he had passed the tree, then knew he had not. The current was faster under the surface; he had not thought of that. He had misjudged it. And his wind was running out. The blackness before his eyes was more than the darkness of the water; there was a spinning, a turning in front of his eyes that was not real.

He increased his stroke in a last surge, knowing he had to surface, and felt roots brush his neck like friendly fingers, turned toward the bank and stroked again and came up slow, reaching upward with his hands for a hold on the roots.

He put just his face out of the water and sucked in the air slowly for all the frantic need and hurry in his chest, seeing not much but a wavering, whirling of dim light that gradually steadied, and hearing a thunderous crash of shots overhead. He pulled himself slowly back against the caved-out bank in the darkness among the tangle of the big tree's uncovered roots.

He lay against the bank with just his head out. Overhead he could see the bare roots of the tree arching out, drooping finally, and tapering, haired thick with fine little feeder roots that fluttered in the wind or below trailed out waving like moss in the current.

Through the open spaces he could see his horse swimming, far out now and downstream, little spouts of water rising where the bullets struck. He saw the dark otter skin of his medicine bag floating downstream away from the saddle, looking like the head of a swimmer rising and falling with the choppy waves. As he watched, flinching a little at the sound of the guns, he saw the horse's head drop, thrusting forward suddenly into the water. He saw the water splash white as the body rolled and the feet for an instant thrashed the surface. Then movement stopped and the horse settled, looking in the dim evening light, like a drift of wood. Beyond, floating loose now from the saddle, the medicine bag still bobbed on the surface.

The shooting stopped. He heard movements in the brush on the river bank above and, over the sound of the wind, voices though he could not make out the words. Then the noises stopped and the only sound was the wind and the little lapping, sucking sounds of the river. With each lull in the wind he could feel the tree roots rise, then settle again with the next gust.

He lay there for what seemed a long time in the cold water waiting for full darkness before moving. Then he ducked out from under the roots and started to climb up; but a peculiar, far-off wail sent him back under. With his head out of water he could still hear the sound, coming closer, something between a cry and a bellow, an animal of some kind, maybe, but a sound in it of human pain, something that raised the hair on the back of his neck and tightened his muscles. There was an unearthly quality about it, an unreality that sent his hands feeling among the roots in the darkness, that made him want to shout to hear the sound of his own voice.

He heard the sound of horses then, snorting and cracking in the brush, and men's voices, and the bellowing was loud now and clear, rising and falling in a rhythm that did not change. It came closer till it seemed to come from the very tree above him, then stopped moving and stayed steady.

A voice that he recognized from hearing it on the riverbank a while before came to him loud, the words clear. "Here's your tree, boss, if you still feel like goin through with the sorry mess."

A deeper voice answered, "You're damn right we are. We agreed on this before we started and there ain't any reason to change now. We'll string this one up, and ary other we can catch off the reservation. It's the only way I can figure to stop em from killin our cattle like they was buffalo. And stealin horses."

"Huh," the other snorted. "You can't scare an Indian like that. Won't any more'n make em mad."

Another voice, then, soft and with a strange musical drawl came to him. He could not make out the first of it, but the last words came clear, ". . . like with the niggahs."

"It's a damn shame you let the other get away," the deep voice said. "Two of em in the tree'd look better than just one. Why didn't you shoot the horse from under him?"

The other was slow answering, "That ain't my style, boss. Old dead-eye here did shoot the horse — after he was halfway across the river."

The soft voice came again, "I wasn't shootin at the hawse, but whatevah was floatin down below. It looked like a cap to me."

"That was jist a bag. The kid's drowned. Don't know as I'd have shot him if I'd seen him, the way he rode his horse over that bank."

"He was white," the soft voice said. "A redhead."

"All right, let's get it over with. Git your damn ropes out, this bellerin is gettin on my nerves."

"Keep your shirt on, Teddy," the deep voice said. "Let im come around a little so he'll appreciate it."

"You can't teach the niggah anything when he's out of his head."

"All you can teach him, he won't remember long anyhow," the one called Teddy answered. "Come on now."

A new voice came in then, "Maybe he's a Heyoka."

"What's that?"

"It's just a crazy Indian, one that acts crazy, anyhow. Claim the bad spirits has put a hex on em or some such. Maybe this is one of em."

"Naw," the deep voice said. "That rifle butt hurt his brain some way. You hit him too hard, Tex. I seen a dog act that way once though and come out of it. This one may too. He's got a strong look to him."

It was full dark now under the tree and nothing to see but streaks of lesser darkness through the openings in the roots, a veiled shining on the choppy surface of the river. The wind seemed stronger in the night, a long low breathing, rising and falling, bearing up the crazy bellowing that he knew now was Spotted Hand like little ripples on the swell of waves. There was a sound coming from the tree too, a shuddering of strained wood that he felt, not heard, through his hands on the roots, coming with each change of the wind.

And there was a shuddering in his own cold soaked body, a

trembling beyond his power to control and inside him a watery feeling, as if the river had soaked through him and softened his bones.

"It's too damn dark," he heard the deep voice. "Some of you birds rustle up some wood. Hell's fires, you can't hang an Injun in the dark."

He heard low, grumbled answers but not the words, then here and there the crackle of breaking willows.

He lay in a curious mental suspension, not thinking but feeling, as if all the nerves in his body had suddenly come alive after a long numbness. Cold swept him with waves of shivering, the sound of the wind came to him with a screaming pitch, and the bellowing beat painfully at his ears. In between, the separate sounds of the firebuilding came to him vividly, and the smell of muddy water and wood and on the wind the smell of sage; the smoke smell of burning willows and on the water the flicker of firelight; fragments of talk dropped him by the wind, unconnected in his mind and meaningless, but clear.

Then the bellowing stopped with a choking sound, and all he could hear was wind and water.

And suddenly the shaking tension of his mind and body was more than he could bear; a screaming, unreasoning necessity to move seized him. His legs doubled under him and shot him into the open and he was climbing the tree roots with a strength and swiftness beyond all his experience.

He was almost to the level of the bank when he missed a handhold and hung there with the other, feeling the weakness of the lame wrist, clawing with broken nails at the rough bark at the base of the tree; then fell backward, seeing in that instant of fall the tree above, lit with the red light of the fire and the darkness hung above like smoke; then the crash and blackness of water. He remembered to stroke back under the screen of roots before coming up.

"Bank cave-in," he heard the deep voice say as he came up.

And directly above him the voice of Teddy, "Cave-in, all right. Christ amighty, I don't see what's holdin this old tree up. It's undermined. Hell, boss, you're wastin your time. If the wind gets any stronger the damn tree'll go over and all your advertisin with it."

There was no answer.

Jimmy lay weak and unnerved in the water, considering himself, amazed at what he had almost done; knowing he could not have helped doing it, but knowing also that he would not do it again. It was something Spotted Hand would have done and not failed at. And something he himself might have done that one time except for a lost handhold, ironically a weakened wrist. And he was alive now and Spotted Hand was dead and something was finished.

His feeling was bitterness, almost a taste in his mouth, a sadness and a vague, objectless anger. He was amazed at the lack of revengefulness in him. Even, he thought, if he put his knife to the source of the deep voice and the soft voice nothing would be changed, as if the men on the riverbank above had nothing to do with the death of his friend, as if he had been dead before they ever hurt his brain with a rifle butt.

He could hear the voices again now, and understand them.

"It's not a professional job we-all did," the soft voice said. "The rope didn't break his neck, it only choked him."

"He had a tough neck," the deep voice said, "for such a young one."

"Maybe we-all could make it look a little bettah."

"Let's get out of here," a new voice said. "I ain't cravin to camp here."

"Me neither," Teddy said. "I'm headin for camp. You comin, Tex?"

"Me?" the soft voice asked. "Not in this storm. Here's a fire and plenty of wood and here's where I stay till morning. And come fall I'm headin south again to where it's warm. How about you, boss?"

"No. I'll be goin."

He heard the sound of horses getting under way and a little later the sound of a man walking back through the brush dragging something, a saddle, he guessed, and heard the leathery squeak of it dropping to the ground. With his head out from under the roots he saw the light of the fire brighten and heard the little stirring sounds of the man settling himself to sleep.

He lay considering then, deciding, he told himself, knowing inside that the decision was already made and what he had to do he would do in spite of the bitter distaste he felt for it. He could swim the river and be without a horse, he thought — he had no way of knowing how far he would have to swim downstream to climb out on the side he was on. The only other way he knew was to climb the tree roots. He could do that later when the man was asleep and take the horse and leave — knowing he would not do that either, carefully keeping from his mind the anticipation of what he would have to do, not even considering the way he would do it, knowing it would come to him at the time. And there was no fear in him nor anger, but a kind of sickness, a sense of loss; not defeat, but a drive to do and be finished with it.

He lay there freezing in the icy water, but not shivering now and not impatient, only glancing upward now and then to notice the fire's brightness. As the light dimmed, he swam silently against the current to get his blood going again and take the stiffness out of his muscles.

Finally, when the fire was almost out, he began climbing, feeling carefully for his handholds, testing each. At the level of the bank he paused and located the sleeping figure in the thin shining of the coals, and came on out hugging the tree. He moved slowly, knife in hand, diving the last few feet as the man stirred, and plunged the knife, feeling the warm splash on his hand. The arms and legs came up and the body rolled powerfully under him, jerking the knife out of his hand; then convulsed in spasms, all purpose gone. He found the knife then and wiped it and sheathed it in his belt, turning to the tree to search the darkness for the body of his friend. He saw it swinging in the wind, turning and re-turning against the twist of the rope in a curious weightless dance.

He found the rope tied off around the base of a willow bush, untied the knot and lowered the body, letting the rope slide through his hands. He straightened the body on its back, cut the rope from the neck, pulled it on over the limb and coiled it and laid the coil by the fire.

He built up the fire then and took off his coat and shirt and propped them on sticks by the fire to dry and stripped the coat from the dead cowboy and put it on, feeling with a shock the warmth in the shoulders and the wet cold spot of blood down the front and side.

The wind was higher now, rising and falling with a keening

sound high in the old tree, whipping the flames of the little fire back and forth in the shelter of the brush. There was the smell of rain in the wind.

He left the fire and from memory located a clump of the largest willows and cut four of the best ones with his knife and trimmed them to lengths a little taller than himself. These he brought back to the fire and tied in a bundle at one end of the rope and climbed the tree with the other end between his teeth. He searched the tree high up till he found a spot where four limbs came up at points almost in a square, and hauled the bundle up hand over hand. Hanging the bundle on a limb, he cut four short lengths from the end of the rope and, working mostly by feel, tied the willows in a square between the four limbs, forming a rough platform. On the ground again he collected another stack of willows which he hauled up and laid across the platform for a floor and tested it, feeling the twist and slide of the sticks with the varying movements of the tree limbs.

He hauled the body of his friend up then, fighting the heavy swinging weight on the rope for a long time before he succeeded, and laid it out straight on the platform. He sat there for a while exhausted, feeling the strain and twist and shudder of the big tree, hearing the whistle of the limbs tearing the streaming air, and seeing far off now the crazy, slashing knives of the lightning cut the dark; feeling himself the center of the storm, within himself at once the tortured straining of the tree and the drive and thrust of the big wind.

With an effort of will he forced himself to move again, coming back to the ground to the body of the dead cowboy. Taking a hold in the thin silky hair on top of the head, he made a careful, circular cut in the scalp. Placing his knee on the head to keep it from rolling, he pulled sideways on the hair, felt it give, heard the tearing sound of the scalp coming loose from the skull, like the hide from fresh-killed buffalo, and on a current of air caught the warm-sweet unmistakable odor of human flesh.

He climbed back up then and placed the scalp beside the body of Spotted Hand and piled brush and sticks on top. He sat for a long time living the violence of the storm, releasing himself to the danger of that swinging perch, not fearfully, as if awaiting the final reso-

lution of the storm, the balance point that would settle the turbu-
lence in his own feeling.

Lightning flashed with an instant, violent crash of thunder,
spreading a sheet of bluish light over the river, and the rain broke,
slow at first, coming from the side on a long slant with the wind,
then increasing till the gusts of wind came like waves out of the
darkness.

He climbed down then, before the peak of the storm, as if released by the icy waves of rain.

He found the horse picketed at the edge of the brush, standing
humped up with his hind end to the storm, and brought him in and
saddled. He found his clothes in the brief flashes of lightning and
bundled them behind the saddle. Buckling on the dead man's gun
belt, he mounted and rode out of the brush, back up the river.

The unwilling horse paced sideways across the wet current of the
wind. There was no shelter now and in the blackness and drive of
the increasing storm it was like riding under water. But he felt
strong, a power rising in him to meet the force of the wind, the
cold cut of the rain against his face.

He told the story to Grey Elk, not having said yet in his mind
that he would leave, but feeling it and waiting only for Grey Elk
to give it words.

"You go," Grey Elk had said. "Your medicine is strong, the
dream clear."

"It wasn't a dream."

"Not a dream," Grey Elk corrected himself. "No difference."

But he was not satisfied, feeling an uncertainty, maybe even a
sense of shame, needing to be reassured but not having words to
ask for it.

"You go," Grey Elk went on. "Maybe find a people among the
long knives. Maybe understand their medicine."

"Did I do wrong?"

"Not wrong. Just not Indian. Maybe not white either. Better
to go. Young animals learn fast. Better to learn among the living."

"If I stay?"

"What is here for a young man with strength? To live in square
houses and do the work of women — no medicine in that. For you

the road is open, for Indian — " He made a chopping motion with his hand. "The circle broken, buffalo gone — no medicine now to help."

He left then with a feeling of tearing loose, the pain but the freedom too, and no fear, but the feeling of a world of time and distance before him . . .

He was standing up in the wagon watching the ground ahead to keep his balance when they crossed the creek and came in sight of the flat.

The shooting had stopped but there was no sign of Charley yet. There was a kind of haze in the air under the bright sunlight, a moveless, brittle quality of light, that glazed the ground like a picture under glass. Flat and dead, it looked, lethargic and sleepy.

He had to look twice to see Charley lying face down near the creek bank below the bluff. As Woodfoot swung the wagon over, Charley seemed to awaken and got to his feet looking sheepish and pale, staggering slightly as he walked, as if he were drunk.

It was only then that Jimmy realized that all the buffalo were dead. He had felt that all the quiet animals would rouse out of their lethargy and run. But his mind now grasped the fact that they were dead with a jolting sensation like coming out of a dream. It had been a trick of the haze in the flat, of the unshattered silence.

The color was coming back into Charley's face under the smoke and sweat and with it a self-conscious look of pride.

"That kind of killin is work," he said. "I like to burnt up my gun."

"God amighty," Woodfoot exploded. "Did you leave any at all? It'll be all night skinnin and then some."

"Dog it all, that's what you're here for, ain't it?"

His tone was jocular, Jimmy thought, but not enough to cover the intent of his words. He could not handle Woodfoot's style of humor.

Woodfoot shook out the lines and drove on out among the carcasses. He sat for a while looking, as if amazed by the sight, then climbed down and began unhitching.

"We'll never hear the last of this," he said. "He's gonna be hard to live with now and no mistake."

Charley came out and sat on one of the carcasses by the wagon
to clean his rifle. He was nervous, Jimmy could see, but not tense.
There was a flushed look in his face, a curious looseness as if he
had just had a woman. The slim hand on the wiping rod was not
shaky, but slower than usual, and blunt in movement.

Woodfoot still had a look of amazement on his face. "I golly,
Charley," he said, "I never saw shootin like that before. Did you
make ary bad shot at all?"

Charley shook his head. "Maybe two or three I shot twice."

"I never saw the beat," Woodfoot said, and there was an unusual,
grudging tone of admiration in his voice. "The hell of it is, there's
a lot of kip hides there. It's a waste. And we'll have to pull some
out of the mud before we can skin em."

"Let em go," Charley said with an offhand tone of generosity,
"if they're too much trouble."

Woodfoot shrugged and went to work, stopping now and then to
shake his head in a gesture of wonderment.

Charley still sat on the ragged carcass of the buffalo, wiping his
gun mechanically, a dreamy look on his face.

"It ain't that I haven't seen stands before," Woodfoot went on,
"and almost this big too, but it always strikes me the same, kindy
strange, how a bunch of animals will stand like that and be slaugh-
tered — like maybe they was hypnotized. But hell, Charley ain't
got that kind of an eye. It beats me, it does now. What kind of
medicine you got on em, Charley?"

Jimmy was startled to hear his own thoughts put into words,
even though the tone was joking. He turned and went to work
before Charley answered, feeling a reticence about looking at him.
He felt strangely involved with Charley.

"It's jist a matter of judgment," Charley said, "that's all. You
gotta get em at the right time, then hold em. Like with me. When
I first sighted em, I seen they wasn't ready for a stand, just comin
down to water like they was, so I waited. I let em fill up on water
and get settled before I went to work."

Glancing up then as he whetted his knife, Jimmy saw that Woodfoot had stopped work and was watching Charley out of the
corner of his eye, speculatively and with a veiled anticipation.

Jimmy looked down again, making the first cut in the hide, feeling a sudden aversion to the thing that was going on between these two men. There was something inhuman in Woodfoot's curiosity, the way he prodded Charley with his eye and mind, that called up a sudden memory of a snake nosing a stricken gopher with a cold desire.

He still did not look at Charley, but he had the odd notion that he could feel him, as if the very air between were a connecting tissue of spirit that made him a reluctant partner in another man's vision — as he had been that once with Spotted Hand.

He looked around to shake the feeling and saw Charley, standing now, putting a new shell in his gun with a slow unnatural movement of his smooth hand, still with his face dreamy and far-focused eyes.

"How did you come on em, Charley?" Woodfoot asked. His voice was hardly above a whisper, soft and wheedling, "Where did you shoot from?"

Charley did not seem to hear. He was walking back up the hill toward the spot where they had first seen him. He started talking then as he walked, slowly and not as loud as usual. There was no other sound but the mules switching mosquitoes and along the river the tentative, musical chatter of a single magpie that had just alighted. But even in the silence he could hardly make out what Charley was saying.

"I first seen em from the bluff," Charley pointed, "strung out on the trail in from the hills, and I knew they was after water. So I backed off and worked down around to a better spot, figuring they'd spread out on the flat after drinking, which they did." He stopped and turned and stood looking down past them, his rifle resting loose across his left arm, his right hand fingering the checked grip.

"They drunk and commenced to scatter out, some of em wallowin in the mud like hogs and gruntin, and some rollin like horses to scratch theirselves, or just layin in the sun, and some rubbin on the rocks. It was hard to wait, but I done it till they got settled, then laid my gun to the prong stick and started." He stopped and just stood there rocking back and forth, slow and easy on the balls of his feet, sweeping the flat with his eyes and the gun barrel.

"After that it was just shootin, pickin the outside ones and the ones that tried to leave. And by God it was hard work."

There were more magpies in the trees now, loud and confident in their chattering.

"I was about here," Charley said, his voice even lower, but tense-sounding now, and hoarse. "I kept on shootin, spacin the shots, and the smoke hangin like a fog — like in the war again — and the barrel hot . . ." He stopped to look at one of his hands and looked back up with a blank, puzzled expression. His gun was still resting across his arm, pointing off to the left toward the trees and swinging back and forth with the motion of his body.

There was a sudden commotion among the magpies, a squawking and flutter of wings. Turning, Jimmy saw a hawk slanting in from upriver. In the same instant a shot exploded. He ducked instinctively, hearing the ball sing out across the river.

He looked up to see Charley still standing with the gun across his arm staring in a real confusion as if suddenly awakened.

A plume of smoke was curling upward from the gun barrel.

Woodfoot was laughing, harshly and with little humor.

Charley ejected the empty shell and came back down to the wagon, slapping at mosquitoes, a childlike look of hurt and chagrin on his face.

"That's too far to kill a bird, even for Charley," Woodfoot said. "But a shot like that could break up a stand," he added irrelevantly.

Charley stopped walking, stiffening for just an instant, then turned to put his gun in the wagon, and leaned against it, holding himself up with his hands. He looked dead tired, shot out, Jimmy thought, and shaky like an old man.

Jimmy walked to the front of the wagon, found Woodfoot's flask of whiskey in the box and brought it back to Charley, handing it to him without speaking. He did not meet Charley's eyes.

Woodfoot watched in amusement but said nothing.

Charley drank, handing the bottle back with a shudder. He said, "Thanks," with an openness of feeling that made Jimmy feel at once sorry for him and repelled.

Woodfoot laughed aloud. "They ain't nothin like the good old fire-water to drive away the bad spirits," he said to Jimmy. "You better have a little yourself, boy."

"Go to hell," Jimmy said. He was annoyed with Woodfoot, his

shrewdness and lack of feeling.

Charley was himself again. He had found knives and a steel in the wagon, and was working now with something like anger in his movements. Every now and then he stopped to slap at the mosquitoes and swear.

Woodfoot was still grinning. "Bad spirits must be swarmin around this place like the skeeters. Buffalo spirits anyway. Charley got a mess of em hangin over him."

"You're talkin a lot of foolishness," Charley said. "Now cut it out. You bother a man like a damn gadfly."

"Or a magpie," Woodfoot laughed.

Jimmy was not amused. He was not inclined to joke about the spirits, even though he could not honestly say he believed in them. But he sensed a deeper truth than he could put into words, that these white men would not understand or admit if he did say it — a kinship, it was, a spiritual connection with these animals he skinned that would never allow him to look at them as strictly leather on the hoof. And yet he had a hunch these men were as much affected by it as himself or any Indian, even though they chose to fight it.

He had to hump it to keep up with Charley skinning. Charley did not know the tricks but he was fast of hand and he attacked the work with a savage hostility. And the longer he worked, the faster he went. He was really picking up his stride now, Jimmy thought, fighting everything — and winning. Yet he knew he had just seen Charley as clearly as it was possible to see another man; had sensed the fear and turmoil within him, and pitied him. It was hard to reconcile the two pictures. He was a man alone, Charley was, out of touch with the spirits and without a people, in an alien land. Jimmy wondered if that was what it meant to be white, and thought he would never be that way himself. And yet, for all that, he felt a touching-point with Charley, a bond of common feeling he could not quite explain.

At dark they stopped to wait for moonrise. They boiled a pot of coffee and made a meal of jerky and cold biscuits.

Charley was talkative, then, expansive and superior.

"You oughtta learn to shoot," he told Jimmy. "It's a good thing to know . . . I'm gonna let you take my gun and practice, once you learn how to take care of it. Shoot a few buffalo and maybe make yourself a stand. It'll make a man out of you."

He was being as genuinely friendly and generous as it was possible for him to be, Jimmy knew. And yet he could not help resenting the condescension. "That'll take some doin," he said.

Woodfoot winked at him from across the fire. "Hell," he said to Charley, "he's got too much Indian in him to be any hand with a gun."

"That ain't so," Charley said. "I seen Indians that was plenty good. Maybe not so accurate, but fast. And they got meat. Anyways," he said to Jimmy, "you ain't really an Indian. Whoever heard of a redheaded Indian?"

Jimmy grinned but said nothing.

"I can show you a thing or two about that pistol too," Charley went on. "By God if you're gonna wear a pistol, you want to know how to use it. I seen you draw a few times and you don't do it right. You never got time to reach down and pull it out. You knock it out." He stood up to demonstrate, and the slap of his hand on the pistol and the leathery sound as it came out all seemed part of the same sound. It was too fast, Jimmy thought, to be real. It was part of Charley's medicine. He wondered if he could ever be that good. He would try: among these men it seemed to be important.

"A real gun-slick from the Wild West," Woodfoot mocked. But there was admiration in his voice too, and a certain respect.

When the moon pushed up big and yellow over the hills, Woodfoot hitched up a pair of mules and began dragging out the carcasses that were in the mud holes. Charley did not repeat his offer to leave them. "Might as well," he said. "Every dollar counts."

The carcasses came out of the mud with reluctant sucking sounds, looking in the moonlight as slick as new-born calves.

They worked without talking then, the mosquitoes a steady, insistent hum, broken now and then by Charley's angry grunts and the whispering of the knives, hide tearing from flesh, and the sing of knife on steel.

They did not finish. Woodfoot gave out first and climbed into the wagon to sleep. Jimmy finished the one he was on and straightened up slowly to get the kink out of his back. The moon was high overhead, touching the wet grass and pools of water with a frosty light. The naked carcasses rose up shining out of dense shadow that was rocklike, thrusting upward. At the edges of the flat he saw the grey shadows of wolves, some already tearing at the more distant carcasses, others just sitting, watching.

He spread out the hide he had just taken and rolled up in it, hearing Charley still at work, cursing the mosquitoes and grunting . . .

He came out of sleep in a suffocation of fear, struggling wildly with the green hide that bound him till he stood completely free of it. The beating of his heart quieted as he looked around the flat, seeing it almost as it had been when he went to sleep. But it was alive now with wolves — he had never seen so many in one place. It had been the noise of their feeding that awakened him; but his fear he could not understand.

Charley had rolled up in a hide nearby with just his nose out, and Jimmy could hear him breathing in long, gurgling snores.

He spread out the hide again and lay down reluctantly, just doubling it over him this time. He was just dropping into sleep when a sound like far-off screaming brought him up again in the same jolting terror. A mountain lion, he thought, till the sound came again, near and shocking; and though he knew now it was Charley, his heart leapt and the hair rose on the back of his neck. It was not the sound of a man in fear — it was a startling, catlike sound. He moved to awaken Charley; but the sound came again, thrusting him back.

Charley rolled suddenly free of the hide. He stood up, his eyes shining coldly in the silver light, his gun already drawn, and fired with incredible speed into a knot of wolves at the edge of the flat.

Jimmy saw two wolves drop. A third ran a few jumps and fell, giving a series of piercing yelps that died down to a gurgling moan.

"What the good goddamn is goin on out there?" Woodfoot yelled.

"That'll keep em quiet for a while," Charley said. He reloaded his pistol and rolled himself up again in the hide.

Jimmy lay down and doubled the hide over him; but he could not sleep for all his weariness. The sound Charley had made seemed to hang bodiless in the air, becoming audible each time he came near sleep.

CHAPTER

13

LOOKING WEST DOWN OFF THE DIVIDE TOWARD
Sand River into the far-red color of afternoon was, Sandy thought,
like looking into another land, a land of color that divided itself
from the grey jagged foreground with an almost visible line. Here,
the gashed, eroded sandstone, gullied on the down-slope like the
marks of claws, all plastered with a wrinkled layer of clay and
sand. And beyond, the color — not in a haze — it was too early yet
for summer haze — but an emanation of the land, brown of the old
grass, the new green, and over all the pink, as if the air had leached
the color of the rocks like water and lay now a thinly dyed pool
over the country.

And on out past the river the prairie seemed to rise, stretching
out and up toward the far, purple mountains, the low hills, curved
and waved or rising soft and oval as a woman's breast. Specks of
animals appeared and disappeared, moving among the hills — yellow
spots of antelope flashing white as they turned and the brown,
earthen lumps of buffalo, humped like the land and natural to the
hills as grass, as if truly, he thought, they came out of the earth as

the Indians believed. Off to the right and far out he could see the white jumble of Medicine Rocks.

Riding up the divide with no purpose in mind, he had felt an urgency, a need to move upward, as if, climbing, he could leave below the torment of mind — as if the height could cleanse him.

It was a long ride up — a fool thing, he told himself, the day near gone and not a dozen hides made yet. But still he rode, picking a trail through the veinwork of dry creek beds and washes with a vivid concentration. Grass thinned to nothing on the ridges till all that lived was a scattering of stunted sagebrush and low, vine-like cedar, and in the bottoms of the washes thorny spots of greasewood took the place of chokecherry and buffalo berry.

In the badlands of the divide there was nothing — cut banks of clay and sandstone marked here and there with dirty streaks of alkali; sudden mounds in the bottoms, shapes of ball or breadloaf or standing pillar, striped horizontally with black or grey — the exact grey of wood ashes — capped maybe with tilted planes of burnt red rock eroded here and there with grillworks of vertical furrows. But nothing lived.

It was like working out a maze to find a trail up, but he stuck with it, feeling an anticipation as he worked upward into the dead grey land of the divide, as if there were a place here for him, a meaning which as yet he could not grasp. No work here, maybe, he thought, smiling at himself with bitterness, no buffalo; yet knowing there was more than that, a deeper meaning. A drive of instinct maybe, like the instinct of a dying animal to find cover, a quiet place to die. He had once followed a trail of a sick wolf that had dragged himself almost a mile to die by a tiny clump of sagebrush no more than a foot high. It was a drive like that in a man, maybe, that turned him toward the mountains in his trouble.

He came out at the top then, on the long sloping hogback of the main divide. He stopped, and turning, looked backward down toward Sand River, and it was like looking homeward from another country. The feeling in him was sharp and painful as the cut of steel.

He had not expected this, that the color, the sweep and distance of the country, could hurt him like a knife drawn through flesh. Silence ballooned out and upward like the sky, and there was nothing — only distance and light, the land rising to the colored west beyond all power of seeing; and himself alone.

It was like looking backward in time, seeing the country as he had first known it with no litter of swollen, stinking carcasses and whitened bones, expecting beyond any hill to see the clean cones of leather tepees shining under the sun; herds of horses grazing on the sidehills and all the bushes red with drying meat.

The time was gone now; no going back. But it was not the memory that pained him, he thought. It was the sight itself.

He reined his horse around and rode on along the divide, sweating, breathing hard in a feeling of suffocation. He was sick of himself, he thought, and sick of his job. But he had to make more hides. There was no other way out now — till he got a stake, he had to hunt buffalo.

Maybe in the fall — maybe get enough together for a little freight outfit and run a line off the railroad. A man might do all right and get shut of the damned rifle. He was sick of it, had been for a long time. But it seemed like he couldn't break loose.

There had been a time when it was different — a long time ago. He had been proud then to make a living with his gun. When he was making meat it was all right — even meat for the railroad. There had been some style to it then, running buffalo the way he had learned it from the Indians. But it had been mostly wasteful even then, the cooks using only the best parts and hollering for more. And the sport hunters, buying tickets to the little dead-end terminal towns for nothing but the chance to shoot buffalo from the moving trains, leaving the dead ones to rot and the wounded to die the long slow death. The parties out for trophies.

He quit the job after a year and came back north and tried freighting; and did all right till the war between the states cut off his supplies and he went broke. Then the hide hunting in Kansas and down in Texas, quitting and always going back — as if, like the Indians, he had no other way to live but on the buffalo.

He picked a ridge that led off toward the Medicine Rocks and started down, thinking of nothing now but picking a trail, shutting his mind off from the laceration of his thinking. He could see buffalo above the Rocks, moving in a snaky line toward the shine of water in the stream bed. They would drink and laze around for a while, if nothing disturbed them. It would be a good bunch to try.

Sundown was no more than an hour away when he came again in sight of them. Clouds banked in the west had changed from white to a smoky orange, an ember color that glowed as from heat.

It was a poor time to be starting a hunt, but he had to chance it now. He followed the cut of Rock Creek down out of the hills till he knew he was close. Leaving his horse, he climbed up out of the stream bed with his rifle and canteen and saw them to the north at maybe a thousand yards. Most of them were lying down with their noses pointed upwind, directly away from him. He could smell them strong, with a wet earthy smell from the water and the powder of dust in the air. A few of the bulls were rolling, plowing up the sand with big sweeps of their horns, arching and straightening their bodies, then flopping over to the other side, like horses. Some were grazing back in the shadows of the rocks, reminding him of cattle in the streets of a ruined city.

There was an eerie feeling about the rocks, a startling quality. A jumble of sandstone buttes thrust up sharp out of the soft flowing mounds of prairie: square buttes with flat tops, fluted and carved by wind and rain; tall cones; columns with spiral markings, a maze of corridors darkened now by shadows; black spots of caves.

He moved in slowly toward the animals, avoiding any lateral movement that would draw their eyes, watching them carefully for any signs of uneasiness. At about half the distance he stopped, lowered himself carefully to his knees and began crawling. There was still no uneasiness in the herd. He watched a tremendous bull approach a wallow where three others were rolling and drive them out and lie down. The three turned and stood watching, their necks bowed as if they had a notion to fight.

At maybe two hundred yards he stopped and set up his prong stick, feeling a quickening of his blood in spite of his weariness. He took the canteen and cartridge belt off his shoulder and laid them on the ground and jointed together his wiping rod, forcing himself to move slowly.

The big bull he had noticed was standing now, broadside to him but looking directly toward him; the other three still stood at the edge of the wallow, still tensed.

He drew down on the big one then, his eyes finding the spot for the lungs. The sights came into line and steadied, the rifle bucked against his shoulder. He saw the puff of dust where the bullet struck; then the rattle of echoes like a score of rifles came crashing back at him from the rocks. He had not thought of that.

The herd came up and he half rose as he worked the lever expecting to have to run for the next shot; but in that instant the three bulls charged the big one. He went down under their weight and they swarmed around him bawling and hooking, the power of the great curved necks lifting and jerking the big carcass. When their heads came free he could see the horns wet and shiny. Instead of running, the herd moved in to watch the fracas and he knew he had a stand.

Some more bulls plowed into the mixup till there was a regular knot of crazy, fighting animals. He picked the ones at the edges, waiting each time till he got a good shot. And the buffalo kept clustering around, crowding in among the dead ones. Then suddenly a bull detached himself from the group and shot outward, stopping after a few jumps to look back. He looked scared, Sandy thought, bringing him into the sights, scared and suspicious. When the bullet found, the bull looked directly at him, walked a few steps, nosing the ground like a dog looking for a soft place, circled a few times and lay down.

He did not know how long he kept shooting. It seemed like buffalo kept appearing, coming in among the dead ones, up from the stream bed and from in among the rocks — from places he could not even see. Every five or six shots he stopped to run the wiping rod down the gun barrel and pour a little water through it to keep it cool. He was sweating, even with the cold breeze blowing on his face; his mind seemed numb and sluggish.

He was working in the shadows now. The western sky streamed upward brilliantly, but the rocks were dark, only the sides to the west reflecting a little light. The front sight blurred against them, looming big as his finger. But he could not miss. It seemed as if the rifle worked itself, as if the mind and the will had gone out of himself into the hot steel. He felt weak and shaky, but the gun was steady, moving slow and sure, and the buffalo kept coming into the half-light and standing quietly and going down easy. And no ani-

mal sound now, nothing but the crash of gunfire, echoes multiplied
and clattering among the rocks. There was no end to it, he thought
— he could not stop, nor the gun, nor the buffalo appearing endlessly as if out of the earth.

To the west the sky shone purpled red, changing to flame color
beyond the last hill. The sun was down.

It was then, with no shock, no surprise, he saw the white one.
At first he thought it was a rock caught in some freak of light. But
it moved, like a light moving in the shadows, an animal of the sun.

It was a trick of sight, he thought, a vision of white buffalo like he
had heard told among the Indians, that he might yet tell himself; it
would go with the light. A memory of something familiar stirred
then in his mind, but would not come.

He went on firing at the dark ones — the real ones — till there
was nothing standing in all the flat but the one figure of white. It
stood broadside to him, outlined clear, as if with inner light, against
the black shadows of the rocks.

A cow, he saw, from the lines. A white cow.

The memory came then, as the sights lined up, words of an old
medicine man in his high-chanting voice . . . Spirit of the Buffalo —
the sight was clear and black against the white — be there with Thy
White Cow. . . . The trigger gave and the shot crashed and echoed
among the rocks. The figure still stood against the shadows. He
fired again and heard the bullet whine off the rocks and knew he
had missed. The cow dropped slowly then, and the light was gone.

There was a stampede of shadows, out of his sight, the sound of
running.

He dropped the gun as if it had burned him. It fell forward with
the prong stick, and he lay face downward on the sand.

Darkness came as he lay unseeing.

Then light came again and he knew the moon was up. He stood
up and saw the rocks emerge from darkness as from water streaming silver and shining, the shadowed spaces black and velvet; above
in the blue night, the clean flakes of stars.

A single coyote howled, the drawn, rising wail breaking at the
end in a shower of yelps that multiplied crazily among the rocks.
A wolf howled from along the stream bed and he saw a shadow
moving among the carcasses. He moved and the shadow disap-

peared. He walked forward toward the blot of dead buffalo, stopping at the first one, aware then of another sound under the noise of wolves and coyotes, a sound like breathing — a low grunt, followed by a long bubbling wheeze.

He walked first to the white one and thought he saw a slight movement of the distended belly. He drew his revolver and fired into the head. The only movement was the jar of the lead striking. When the echoes died he could still hear the breathing, coming from nowhere and everywhere.

For what seemed a long while he searched for the wounded animal. Then he began firing a shot into the head of each one he came to. After a while the sound stopped.

He was reloading his pistol when he saw the old man. He was standing by the carcass of the white buffalo with a sack over his shoulder that gave him a peculiar humped look. His head was dropped far forward and the grizzled white hair and beard — the same silver as the rocks — hung grotesquely around his face, stirring slightly in the breeze. Sandy had not seen him come; he had just appeared as if arisen out of the earth. He stood looking down at the white buffalo so completely motionless that for an instant Sandy thought again that his eyesight was tricking him, that he was seeing what was not there. Then the old man's head turned sidewise and, walking toward him, Sandy saw that his lips were moving; but he could hear nothing — only the ringing in his ears from the rifle fire. As he came near the lips moved again and this time he heard the whisper.

"Did you run out of live ones," the old man asked, smiling strangely, "that you have to be shootin the dead?"

"There was still one alive," Sandy said, confused.

"But you couldn't tell it from the dead?"

Sandy did not answer. He felt intensely ashamed, as if he had been discovered in some terrible crime. He had an impulse to run, to hide in the darkness; but he could not.

"You must have good eyesight to shoot the way you do — and a hog-blindness too. What'll you do with all the meat? Or is it the hides only you want?"

Again Sandy could not answer. He stood, still holding the revolver, feeling helpless, unarmed before the old man's contempt.

The old man was not looking at him now. His eyes were turned downward to the white buffalo. A little gust of wind stirred the hair on the carcass, a movement like that of grass. He bent over and touched it lightly, then stood up and turned away. He spoke again without looking at Sandy, the whisper so soft that Sandy had to lean forward and down to catch the words.

"I thought it was at least a battle. And find nothin but a hide hunter makin a stand on dead buffalo." He started away without looking at Sandy.

"You campin around here?" Sandy asked, not wanting him to leave yet. He was uncomfortable with the old man; but he was suddenly afraid of being alone — a way he had not felt since childhood.

"I live here — I've got me a little garden among the Rocks — and expected a little peace in my last days. Quiet and the clean smell of prairie to my nose. Now this." He turned back suddenly toward Sandy. "Man," he whispered piercingly, "were you born without love of the earth or fear? Are you proud of such doins?"

Sandy holstered his gun, suddenly and unreasonably angry. There was no answering the old man; yet he had a need to humble him, to find his weakness. "Who are you anyway, old man? No doubt a man who never set a trap for beaver or sold meat or a robe. A saint maybe, a farmer in this desert?"

The old man left then, moving slowly and carefully, bent forward against the weight of his sack. He looked small and frail under the burden.

Sandy felt shame then and regret. He felt like running after the retreating figure, but it seemed like he could not move. Instead he called, "Have some meat, old man."

The figure did not pause, but moved on into the rock shadows and was gone.

There was the sound of hooves running, then, and he saw his horse coming in from up the creek, snorting in fear. Wolves, maybe, he thought, or a panther. He ran out and caught the horse and quieted him, feeling as if he had just awakened from a dream. He heard with relief the rattle of the wagon coming in, rode out across the creek to meet it, and guided it in on a buffalo trail. The banks were steep but graded down some by the buffalo. Even so it was a rough crossing.

"We'll never make it out of here in the dark," Woodfoot commented. "Not with any hides, anyway."

"We won't need to," Sandy told him. "We got a night's work here and then some."

He helped unhitch the mules, feeling a reassurance and pleasure in the work — the familiar clinking of the harness chains, the lather smell of sweating mules, the squeak of leather. He coiled up a line and slipped the coil through the ring and up over the copper knob of the hame, the oily flatness of the strap sliding pleasantly in his hands. He unharnessed the mule and hobbled him, lingering, aware that Jimmy and Woodfoot had already finished the other five.

"You better have a bite to eat," Woodfoot told him. "We had ours."

"Thanks," Sandy told him, "but I ain't got much of a stomach for it right now. We'll get started first."

Jimmy had been walking around among the carcasses. Sandy saw him stop as he came to the white one and step back, bringing his hand to his mouth in an involuntary gesture of surprise.

"White buffalo!" he exclaimed in Sioux. He glanced around self-consciously then and repeated in English.

Woodfoot hopped over, using his peg for every other step but moving with surprising speed.

"Hell's afire," he said. "He shoots a white one and don't even say boo. Damned if it ain't the first I ever see."

Jimmy had drawn back, visibly agitated.

"You ever see one, Jimmy?" Woodfoot asked.

Jimmy nodded, fumbling for a knife and whetting it on the steel that hung at his belt. "It's big medicine. With Indians, that is," he added.

"But it ain't with you." Woodfoot grinned.

Jimmy turned away without answering, picking a bull to start on.

"Here," Woodfoot said, "why don't you start on this one? Be nice and easy to see, a white one like that."

"You do it," Jimmy answered. "I got good eyes." Sandy thought his voice was shaking a little.

"Leave him alone," Sandy said roughly, regretting immediately the anger in his voice, seeing Woodfoot stiffen. "I'm sorry," he said quickly. "I didn't mean it to sound that way." He seldom spoke that way, he thought with shame, or found it so hard to apologize.

"Forget it," Woodfoot said, looking at him curiously. "The damn thing must be big medicine. Too bad it ain't prime, though. It'd make a dandy robe. It'll be worth plenty, though, just as a curiosity."

Sandy nodded and turned to go to work, driving himself with all his will against the weariness that gripped him.

They worked till the moon went down and were up again at daylight. Sandy and Jimmy skinned while Woodfoot got breakfast. They were just sitting down to eat when Charley rode in.

"I timed it just right," he observed.

"Except we ain't through skinnin," Woodfoot said.

Charley ignored him. "Looks like you finally made a fair killin," he said grudgingly to Sandy. "How many?"

"A hundred and ten," Woodfoot put in. "And a white one. Gives you a new mark to shoot at, boy." He watched Charley maliciously out of the corner of his eye.

But Charley did not seem to notice. His face lit up. "Where is it?" he asked, already running among the stretched out hides. He found it and turned it over, looking a little disappointed, Sandy thought. The hide did not look so white in the daylight. There was a yellow stain at the base of the hair and tag ends of shed fur sticking out of it. Charley spread it out again, fur side down.

"Anyhow," he said, coming back to the fire, "it's probably worth as much as all the rest put together. I heard of one sellin for two thousand once. This oughtta be worth half that, at least, and that ain't bad." He was really pleased, Sandy thought.

They were starting to work again when Sandy saw the two Indians coming in from the south, each leading a pinto horse. They stopped out a way and one of them held up a pipe. Sandy waved them in. The reservation hats they wore and the black coats made it hard to tell at a distance what tribe they belonged to.

They came in slowly, their old cap and ball rifles balanced across their horses' withers. The one with the pipe was an old man, he saw as they came in closer, the other not much more than a kid. Sioux. They dismounted at a distance and the old man walked forward, leaving the other to hold the horses. He was short for an Indian, Sandy thought, but broad of shoulder. An old scar creased the dry wrinkles of his face.

He shook hands all around except with Charley, who stepped back and began whetting his knife, ignoring the outstretched hand. Indicating all the skinned carcasses and the tongues strung up on a rack on the wagon, the Indian said simply, "Much meat." It sounded like "moosh mitt" and Sandy knew he could not speak English.

Jimmy spoke then in Sioux. "You want meat?" he asked. "Help yourselves." He turned to Sandy. "It's all right if they take meat, ain't it?"

Sandy nodded.

"Oughtta charge 'em a little," Charley grumbled, "or they'll be followin us around like stray dogs. Ain't nothin like easy meat to draw Indians. Or flies," he added, grinning.

The young Indian moved up closer now. He was tall, rather thin, with a way of holding his head up and back, his nostrils flaring as he breathed. His hair was braided in the old way in spite of the hat and he had on bearded leggings and cowboy boots. The coat hung loosely on him, but somehow did not detract from his dignity. It was unbuttoned and, blowing back now and then, exposed a battered-looking Colt revolver.

He was watching Charley, as if he knew what was going on. Charley met his gaze for an instant and Sandy thought he flushed.

The old one turned and taking the lead ropes of his two horses, tied them to the horns of the nearest buffalo. He leaned his rifle against the carcass and began looking around for the best meat. The young one tied his horses in the same manner, but he hung on to his rifle while he looked around.

The old one had already started cutting meat when the other found the white buffalo. He saw the hair on the unskinned muzzle and feet, and the light horns first, then saw the hide stretched out beside. His hand went to his mouth in the same gesture of surprise Jimmy had used and he called the old man.

The old one came over and knelt down, folding the hide back on itself and brushing the dirt off carefully. He knelt there looking at the dirty-white hide, his hands pressed flat against the earth, his lips moving in words that Sandy could hear faintly but could not understand.

He got up then and walked over to Jimmy. "We would like the white one," he said. "Does the white man care to trade?"

"You want to trade the white one?" Jimmy asked Sandy.

Sandy did not answer immediately. Before he could speak Charley laughed.

"What the hell have they got to trade?" he asked. "These damned old crow-baits?"

"What will you give?" Jimmy asked.

The old one walked silently to his two horses, untied them and led them over to Sandy and dropped the lead ropes in front of him, then stepped back and folded his arms across his chest, watching Sandy.

Both of the horses were poor, the ribs showing plain under their ragged hides. The one the old man had been riding was old; but the other was a good horse in spite of his ragged looks. He was a pinto, deep in the chest with a short curved neck, wide-set eyes and large, flared nostrils. Sandy found himself remembering the horse he had stolen from the Crees the time he had been wounded. He became aware then that all the other men were watching him. The old Indian was still waiting with no change in his expression.

Sandy shook his head, resenting deeply the fix he was in.

"I can't trade," he told the old Indian, speaking in Sioux for the first time. "It belongs to him too," he said, indicating Charley. "He'll never trade."

The old man brought the other two horses, as if he had not heard, and again stood back with his arms folded. When Sandy did not answer he brought his rifle and laid it on the ground, motioning to the young Indian to put his gun down too. The young one hesitated a moment before he complied. It was almost more than his pride could stand, Sandy thought.

Charley was watching Sandy closely.

"That ain't even half what it's worth," he said. "But just for curiosity see if they'd part with these silly damned hats too."

Charley had assumed that he would not trade, Sandy realized; that he was just playing a game. The thought galled him more than he could bear. He had to hold himself in as he spoke.

"Don't crowd me, Charley," he said. "Or I might just make that little trade. Come right down to it, it's just a ragged piece of leather for four horses."

"What the hell do we want with the damn crow-baits?" Charley was not backing down this time. "Anyway," he went on, "that hide is half mine and I say no go. It's me you got to deal with now."

Sandy saw the skinning knife drop from Charley's hand and stick in the ground beside his boot. He was pale, a little bit scared, Sandy thought, and dangerous.

For just an instant, anger flamed in him; then he caught himself, knowing Charley to be right. His own indecision had put him in the fix. The anger went out in the returning flood of his weariness.

"You're right," he said. He forced himself to turn away from the old Indian and his offer and walk over to face Charley. There was no anger in him now — or fear. But he had to set Charley right.

"Do me a favor, Charley," he said, "and don't make any more of your cheap threats."

It was a damn fool thing to do, he knew, putting Charley on the spot like that. In his new-found strength, he would never back down. It was as if he drew his strength from the buffalo he killed; he had changed that much lately.

For that moment he was joined with Charley as surely as with a bond of flesh and blood, knowing his feeling and his very thinking. It was odd, he thought, to be so intimate with your own death and feel nothing but fatigue; there was not even a thrill to it.

Then the moment passed. He followed the shift of Charley's eyes and saw the young Indian picking up his rifle. There was something impetuous and angry in the way he moved, though he said nothing.

"That one'll do to watch," Woodfoot said. "He's got half a notion to fight."

The old one was talking in a low voice to the other, trying to cool him off, Sandy thought, though he could not hear the words.

"Jimmy," Charley said suddenly, "if that damned Injun wants to fight, tell him I'll fight him for the hide."

"You mean with your hands?"

Charley laughed harshly. "Hell, he carries a pistol too, don't he?"

With despair Sandy realized then what he had brought about. It seemed like the more he struggled the worse things got. It was no use now. The hell with it. He could not have predicted that Charley would move in that direction. But he had put Charley where he had to move; and Charley had taken what he thought was the least dangerous way.

Jimmy had already put it to the young Indian.

The Indian puzzled a moment before he spoke. "I don't understand. If I shoot him I get the robe — if the other white man gives it to me. But if he shoots me he gets nothing. It's plain he doesn't need any more meat," he said with just the trace of a smile as he looked at all the carcasses. "What good would it do him?"

"He wants to know what you stand to gain by it," Jimmy told Charley. "He don't savvy."

Charley grinned. "Just pleasure. Just pure pleasure."

"That don't explain much," Jimmy said, hesitating.

"That is," Woodfoot laughed, "it don't explain much to anybody that don't know Charley."

"All right," Charley said, "on second thought, tell him it's the hide against the four horses — and the two hats."

The old Indian had withdrawn a little. He did not even look at Sandy when he spoke.

"Take your young man and go," Sandy told him in Sioux, "before he gets himself rubbed out. This man is dangerous."

The Indian shrugged, but he looked sad and defeated. "I am an old man," he said. "My nephew is strong-willed and too brave."

Jimmy had explained Charley's proposition again.

The young Indian shook his head. "Only two," he said, indicating his own horses.

"Good enough," Charley agreed. "I'll have to get along some way without the hats." He turned to Woodfoot, grinning. "Step off fifty paces," he said. "Or rather twenty-five paces and twenty-five limps, and mark it."

Woodfoot picked an open spot and stepped it off, looking a bit ludicrous trying to take measured steps and limp too. The peg left little cone-shaped tracks in the sandy earth.

The Indian stripped off his clothes, piled them on a hide, and stood naked except for his breechclout and gun belt. He took an eagle feather out of the medicine bundle hanging on his saddle and braided it into his hair, singing in a low, earnest voice. He rubbed red paint on his face and made a few symmetrical marks on his body, not hurrying, Sandy noticed, but now and then he glanced at Charley.

Charley seemed unperturbed by the little ceremony. It was the sort of thing that would bother most men under the same circumstances, Sandy knew. But Charley seemed merely amused and scornful.

The old Indian spoke once more to the young one, but he only shook his head and went on singing.

The fracas would be little better than murder, Sandy knew, and himself to blame. And yet he did not feel sorry for the young Indian. There was nothing pitiful about him; he had made his own decision. He had a dignity that was beyond condescension.

And yet there was something fantastic about the whole situation, something ludicrous even and nightmarish in its headlong, uncontrolled development. He had a feeling of helplessness that was not just weariness but an emotional and moral paralysis.

The young Indian finished painting himself and stopped singing. "It's a good day to die," he said to the old one. He checked his pistol, and unbuckling the gun belt, let it fall.

Charley had already checked his gun and replaced it in the holster. His eyes were steady on the Indian.

"I better explain to him he's gotta draw," Jimmy said.

"Let it go," Charley told him. "I'll give him that much of an edge." He backed off to the mark Woodfoot had made, still watching the Indian.

The Indian walked to the other mark and stood watching Charley, uncertain but alert.

"Tell him to let er buck," Charley said. He was standing stooped just a little, his hand out, poised over the shiny grip of his pistol. His eyes were bright and feverish, but steady and unblinking.

The Indian stood just a second studying Charley, his gun pointing straight down; then he dropped forward, the gun coming up as he fell, and fired almost as he hit. The bullet kicked up the dirt between Charley's feet.

With the first movement Charley's hand dropped and the gun was out and leveled; but he waited till the movement stopped and fired.

The Indian was dead, Sandy thought, before the echoes died off the rocks. The back of his head exploding had knocked off the eagle feather. It skittered along the ground in a sudden gust of wind, flashing a spot of red.

Charley blew the smoke out of his gun and reloaded. His eyes went to the two horses.

The old Indian loaded the body onto his pinto and rode off, drooped forward in his saddle, looking shrunken and sorrowful.

"What I want to know," Charley said hoarsely, "is why did he want that hide so damn bad. What would he do with it?"

"Religion," Woodfoot said. "An offering to the sun. He'd stretch it out on a platform and leave it to rot."

"I'll be damned," Charley said, wonderingly.

CHAPTER
14

WOODFOOT FINISHED SKINNING THE LAST BUF-
falo and raised up, squinting at the lowering sun, letting the aching
muscles of his back straighten out slowly. Jimmy had loaded the
hides, all but this last, and was hitching the mules, eager to head
for camp.

Charley had shot only once since leaving this bunch — way off to
the east in the badlands toward the head of Greasewood Creek, it
sounded like. It was too late now to drive up there, at least for one
buffalo; and anyhow Charley had said he was through for the day.
Charley hated to skin, and no mistake.

Woodfoot threw the hide on and climbed stiffly into the seat.
He was about fagged and camp chores to do yet, a meal to rustle
up.

Sandy was already in camp and had built a fire, Woodfoot noticed gratefully; Charley arrived a little later, coming in at a lope,
looking excited. He did not get off his horse.

"Looks like we got neighbors," he told Sandy. "An outfit with a couple of wagons just pulled in to the river about a mile up. Buffalo hunters, probably."

Sandy nodded, with little show of interest.

"I figure we better move em on," Charley went on. "Hell, buffalo's gettin scarce around here the way it is."

Sandy shrugged. "We don't own the country. No use stirrin up trouble."

"We was here first," Charley said, "so it's our territory, and what buffalo are left in it by rights belong to us. So let's go move em. Buffalo's scattered out bad enough without any more hunters chasin em."

Sandy shook his head.

"You mean I got it to do alone?"

"Yes, if you're bound to start a fight."

Charley reined his horse around. "It's a hell of a note," he said as he rode off. "One man havin to do all the killin and all the fightin too."

That was Charley, Woodfoot thought. He had killed more buffalo in the last few days, but on the whole he was still a long way behind Sandy.

Sandy stood looking after Charley till he was out of sight around the bend of the creek, then turned shaking his head, and sat down by the fire.

"I wouldn't worry about him," Woodfoot said. "If I know Charley, he's not likely to start anything he can't handle."

Sandy looked up, surprised. "I ain't worryin about Charley," he said. "He'll get along all right, Charley will."

Charley was back in time for supper. He came in looking flushed — the way he always looked after a drink or two — and in rare high spirits.

"A bunch of tenderfeet," he said. "The outfit belongs to a zoologist or some such — out to study the 'monarch of the plains in his native habitat.' Old Black from Sand Point is along and a whole crew of greenhorns. I jollied em a little about Indians so they're moving over next to us for safety. We'll have some fun out of this yet. We got any meat, Woodfoot? I promised em some."

Woodfoot nodded, amused and interested in this new aspect of Charley. He was really relishing the thought of the tenderfeet.

Charley sat down to eat, grinning to himself.

"They want to have a go at shootin some buffalo — the Doc wants some heads and such — and the crew's all excited about it. All they got is a bunch of undersized pea shooters — Spencers and the like. The merchant's got the only decent gun and it's only a Remington. So it ought to be a real show! Not only that, the Doc don't know it, but the cook's got a whole keg of good rye whiskey. Things are lookin real good."

"For a guy who was just complainin about the buffalo gettin scattered out," Woodfoot commented, "it seems to me like you've changed your tune considerable."

"I got that figured out too," Charley said. "This afternoon I ran onto a bunch in that little strip of badlands up toward the head of Greasewood Creek, and they was ripe for a stand. But I figured it was too late to start so I wounded one — shot a big bull in the loins and left him settin there. The rest'll stick around till he dies or someone runs em off. Now what give me the idea was all the life and meanness that old boy had, even without the use of his hind legs. So in the morning I'll just lope up there and fix up the rest like that and this bunch of tenderfeet can have a real buffalo hunt and nobody'll be out anything. And the rest of us'll get a real show."

Sandy was watching Charley with something like amazement in his face. Woodfoot remembered now that Sandy had mentioned once the trick of wounding a buffalo to keep the rest around — but he had made it plain at the time that he didn't think much of it.

Woodfoot grinned at him. "You got a good pupil, Sandy."

Sandy shook his head. "I won't take any credit for it."

Charley looked puzzled. But he was in too good a mood to let anything bother him.

"You two birds don't make sense," he said.

The outfit pulled in after dark and set up a camp with all the comforts, even a stove for the cook. They worked fast with little confusion — even though their style was not western. It probably showed something about the boss of the outfit, Woodfoot thought — the Doc, as Charley called him.

The Doc came over when the work was under way, bringing Black and a younger man with a kind of aristocratic air. They were all dressed in hunting togs that were remarkably clean — except for a coat of dust which Woodfoot did not consider dirt.

The Doc's name turned out to be Stevens. He introduced the younger man as Ladlaw or something like it, one of his students.

"Myself and Ladlaw are making a study of the fauna of this area," Stevens explained, "in connection with an army reconnaissance. We would appreciate what help you could give us on buffalo."

Charley grinned at Woodfoot. "Sure," he said, "we'll help you. Since you're working for the Army I guess we've already helped you considerable." He indicated the hides ricked up on the stake grounds along the river.

"I don't quite understand," Stevens said.

"Well, there's upwards of a thousand hides there," Charley told him. "If every dead buffalo represents a dead Indian, like old General Sheridan said, then we're doin our share. Killin two varmints with one stone, you might say."

"That isn't my position," Stevens said angrily. "Nor is it that of the Army. In any case I've no sympathy with the hoggish destruction of the buffalo — even as a military expedient."

He was a little guy, this Stevens. But when he was mad he seemed bigger — maybe because he stood straighter, Woodfoot thought.

Charley was still grinning. Woodfoot had the feeling then that this argument had been going on between these two before. Charley was just prodding him a little.

"Maybe it ain't the Army's position," Charley said. "But maybe you can explain to me how come the Army gives away ammunition like this" — he held up a shell case — "to any man who can show he's a buffalo hunter."

"I don't believe it," Stevens said.

Charley shrugged, still smiling.

"He's right," Sandy put in, "as far as the Army goes."

Stevens seemed a little mollified talking to Sandy. "Well," he said, "the Indian had to go all right, but it seems a shame the price should be the extinction of the noblest mammal on the continent."

"Ain't an Indian a mammal?" Woodfoot asked innocently. "It looks like he's gonna be extinct, too."

"Well, they had to be tamed," Black said. "And in that sense it shows you how a businessman can be patriotic just in the line of his work. These boys killing buffalo, for instance, making a nice little sum every season and at the same time opening up the country for white men and cattle. I've got some hunters out myself, working on shares. The way I look at it, all this talk about military expedience is nonsense. It's just good business. Buffalo is a crop to be harvested and the land used for something else."

"We harvested a white one," Charley said to Stevens, "but some lousy, thievin Indian stole it."

"We don't know it was an Indian," Sandy put in.

But Stevens was not listening. He was flabbergasted. At last he was able to ask, "Pure white? A true albino?"

"It was white all right," Charley told him. "A cow. It was a damn smart Indian that stole it too. He didn't leave a trace."

"We ain't sure it was an Indian," Sandy said quietly. "It's just a guess."

"A good enough guess," Charley exploded. "Good enough to where I'll shoot every damned Indian I see around here from now on out. The hide was worth at least a thousand dollars."

"You got one consolation anyhow, Charley," Woodfoot said. "If an Indian got it, he won't sell it. For that matter, it's probably stretched out on a platform right now as an offering to the sun."

"It's a shame," Stevens snapped. "The damned heathens! I would have bought it from you. We might have got the skeleton too, but it would be no good now without the hide. It's a terrible loss. It was probably an Indian all right," he added indignantly. "They're inveterate thieves."

"What would you do with it?" Woodfoot asked.

"Why, mount it, of course, and preserve it for posterity."

"Just as a curiosity?"

"No," Stevens bristled, "as a contribution to science."

"Mounted in a glass case? A remembrance of the way the country was once? Maybe the Indian's got more right to it, at that. It's his country that's gone. And maybe a prayer makes more sense than a memento, a curiosity." He grinned into Stevens' glare.

"Hah!" Charley exploded scornfully. "It's dollars gone, that's all. Good cash money. And we shot the damn thing, not the Indian."

Woodfoot laughed aloud. He would not make any comment on the irony of Charley's speech. He glanced at Sandy and saw that he too had seen the point, but he was not amused.

The cook came over then to borrow some meat and Woodfoot left the fire to help. He always had some strips of hump meat hung up on the meat rack and a few tongues. He gave some of these to the new man. In the darkness away from the fire the cook slipped him a jar.

"Pickling brine," he said. "See if it suits your taste."

It was rye, Woodfoot could tell at a whiff, and good rye like Charley had said. After drinking he handed the bottle back.

"Keep it," the cook said. "We got a barrel of it and this looks like a good time to use it."

"Your boss a drinkin man?" Woodfoot asked.

"Naw. He's too damn serious. He's been drivin us like mules the whole damn spring, and we're gettin sick of it. He's used to havin a bunch of sojers to boss around, but with me it don't set so good. This Charley of yours has got him in a mean mood for some reason or other."

Woodfoot grinned. "I see Charley's on him. What did he say?"

"Aw, he just naturally hates buffalo hunters and he don't bother to hide it. The young guy is too good for the earth and he can't hide that."

When Woodfoot came back to the fire, Stevens had sat down by Sandy and was questioning him about buffalo, but Sandy was not saying much.

Charley and Ladlaw were talking about hunting.

"I want to try hunting them from a horse," Ladlaw was saying, "like the Indians. It's my idea that anything an Indian can do a white man can do better."

"No doubt of it," Charley said. "Can you ride?"

The young man smiled. "I'm not considered a bad horseman where I come from."

"Bareback?"

"Any way. Indians don't use saddles, do they?"

"Some. I'll tell you what. I got hold of an Indian pony here a while back. You can try him out tomorrow if you like — an old buffalo horse. But you can't use a saddle or bridle. He won't stand it."

"No bridle?"

"Naw. He's a horse you got to handle Indian style — loop a raw-hide rope around his jaw and guide him with your knees. The rope is to stop him with. You loop the free end around your wrist in case you fall off, that way he don't get away. Course if you're used to a bridle, maybe you better not."

"I'll do it," Ladlaw said.

Ladlaw left first and Charley went with him.

Stevens left a little later when the cook jangled a cow bell, and Woodfoot could hear him ordering the crew around in the other camp.

Charley did not come back. After the meal was over there was some singing and laughter that drowned out Stevens' rather brassy voice. After that it seemed like Stevens must have given up and gone to bed. And the singing and laughing went on. Woodfoot turned in then, dead tired.

When Charley finally came back it must have been along toward dawn. It took him a lot of staggering and fumbling in the dark to get his bed rolled out.

Morning came cold and grey with a wind rising. Charley was already up rousting out Jimmy to bring in the horses. After break-fast he paid a short visit to the other camp and rode out, leaving the pinto pony for young Ladlaw.

There was a lot of confused activity after that in the other camp. It looked like everybody was drunk, except Stevens and Black. And Ladlaw, who was just lit up good. Stevens was not say-ing anything this morning but he was looking plenty sore. He and Black got their own horses in and saddled up and rode off. Ladlaw, after a long struggle and with the help of the crew, finally got aboard the Indian pony and followed. He looked good though, once he got on. The rawhide rope Charley had given him was a long one — forty or fifty feet — and he had the slack coiled up in his left hand with the free end looped around his wrist. He was carrying a short Spencer carbine.

The rest of the crew loaded up in one of the wagons and with the cook driving, left camp singing and shouting. They were armed with an assortment of old muzzle loaders and needle guns — the cook had an old Hudson's Bay fusee.

When their noise faded a little, Woodfoot could hear the steady far away thud of Charley's big Sharps.

Sandy had already saddled up and gone, looking disgusted with the whole thing, Woodfoot thought. Jimmy had the mules harnessed.

It was a peculiarly grey day, cloudy but not with storm clouds. It was more like an immense depth of a thin mist, so tenuous you could not even see it moving with the wind, but grey, obscuring the sun and hanging just above the level of the hills. And a little chilly. Woodfoot brought the bottle of rye out of the shack and took a short one to warm him up before putting it in the toolbox. Jimmy did not drink, but he looked alive and interested.

"A damn funny way to hunt buffalo," he commented.

They caught up with the other wagon beyond the first fork of the creek. The cook had tried to quarter down too steep a slope. The wagon had slewed around downhill and the box had slid off and gone clear to the bottom. The team was tangled up in the harness with one horse down and the other standing in a strained attitude holding the running gears. The crew was still trying to climb back up. They were all in a bunch when Woodfoot saw them, with the cook in the lead, crawling up on all fours. When he heard the wagon he stood up to wave and lost his balance. He fell backward into the others and the whole bunch started sliding, slowly at first, then breaking up and rolling helter-skelter as they picked up speed. They came up in a shower of rocks against the wagon box, yowling and cussing.

Woodfoot straightened out the team and got them up to the top of the ridge while Jimmy tied a couple of ropes together and dropped the end down to the crew. It took them a long time to make it up the rope since they insisted on bringing their guns and a few bottles of rye.

"We got to pull the box out," Woodfoot told them. "We can get the guns then."

"Naw," the cook said. "We ain't gonna mess around with the damn box. We'll miss all the fun. We'll ride with you."

They left the team tied to the running gears and the whole bunch piled into the wagon. They were all skinned up, their clothes torn and dusty, but none was hurt bad. In fact, they didn't seem to notice their wounds, complaining mostly about the bottles broken in the mixup.

They still had plenty left though, Woodfoot thought. And nothing would do but that he take a big drink out of each bottle. By the time they reached the stretch of badlands he was a little tipsy himself.

Here the land was cut by gullies and dry creek beds, coming down to a basin, itself marked by odd-shaped hills and washes. And grey, the same as the clouds, and nowhere any color, just shadings of black and white. There was wind here with dust and sand in the air you could feel and hear but could not see. It was as if the whiskey haze had leaked out of his head and spread over the whole country in a kind of invisible fog.

There was no shooting now, but coming down into the basin, he had caught a glimpse of buffalo toward the far side. He came on them now, around a hill, scattered out in a little grassy, sunken flat below.

He stopped the wagon, amazed at what he saw, his mind struggling up out of tipsiness to stand for an instant clear with wonder.

He still did not see the other men, but the buffalo were there, scattered over the whole surface of the flat, maybe thirty or forty of them, some lying down but most of them drawn up on their forelegs in a sitting position — as if they were about to get up.

There was grass in the flat, the only color of green in the whole country of jagged, muddy-looking hills you could hardly separate from the color of the clouds. Even in the flat there were little sandy-looking mounds and spires of clay that the rains and wind had not yet flattened out — odd, intricately carved shapes of no meaning. And among them the buffalo.

He sat there looking, half expecting to see the herd get up and run, knowing at the same time they would not; that this was what he had known he would see, but had not expected the surprise of it. Even the crew of tenderfeet had stopped their racket and were looking, amazement on their faces.

Then Charley stepped into sight and waved them on down. Before Woodfoot could start the mules, the crew swarmed over the sides of the wagon, yelling and sprawling on their faces on the slope; then getting up and running downhill till their feet could no longer keep up, then falling and getting up again. At about two hundred yards they started shooting, but Woodfoot could see no effect on the buffalo. They sat quietly as stone, not even shaking their heads yet.

He drove on down toward the herd and found Charley and Black standing on a little pedestal of sandstone watching. Stevens was on down and off to the side near a big bull. He had a notebook and pencil and was drawing a picture, it looked like. Ladlaw was not in sight.

Charley was shouting with laughter watching the charging crew of hunters. Black seemed only faintly amused. In fact he looked a little green around the gills.

Woodfoot drove up close beside the rock and stopped. He was cold now, the false warmth of the whiskey dying down. He took another drink and pulled a robe around him and sat watching in a bemused numbness.

The hunters were scattered out among the buffalo, now, running back and forth and yelling and shooting. Sometimes a buffalo would shake its head and snort and maybe even drag itself forward a ways. There would be a general retreat then, giving a little intelligence to the scene. But mostly it was just crazy if you watched the whole thing.

It was maybe a little funny too if you picked out a single hunter and followed him. He would shoot and a buffalo would shake its head and he would turn and run, trying to pour powder into the muzzle of his gun as he ran; and after the powder a little wadding, maybe forgetting the ball altogether and running back to fire again. And all in a fog, a greyness coloring the very air, and the wind blowing away the sound of the shots and the crazy noise of their yelling, till it was like watching a faraway scene through glasses — foggy, unfocused ones at that. And the only reality the rage of the big bulls. Their shaggy heads showed up black and solid against the grey; as they tried to charge, dragging their useless hindquarters, their short, brassy blasts of sound came clear against the wind.

There was not a buffalo down yet, nor, even stranger, Woodfoot thought, a hunter either. They were shooting wild. Every now and then a bullet would sing overhead and Charley and Black would duck.

Stevens had finished sketching the big bull. He came over to Black, borrowed his gun and aiming carefully, shot the animal he had sketched. The bull dropped, the first of the bunch, and stretched out with hardly a quiver. Stevens went over and began taking measurements of the head.

Then for the first time Woodfoot saw young Ladlaw. He was coming up a coulee that led out of the flat, riding hell for leather after a young cow. Coming into the flat, the cow slowed down and Ladlaw came alongside for a shot; the cow veered off to the left suddenly, dodging around a big bull. The pony turned as quickly, going sidewise away from a sweep of the bull's horns, leaving his rider hung in the air. Ladlaw came down not ten feet in front of the bull and started crawling almost before he hit. He was just going good when he turned a surprising somersault and went sliding on his back toward the bull. Woodfoot saw the pony come to a sudden stop and knew then that Ladlaw had fastened himself to the end of the rope, as Charley had suggested. The bull let out a roar, and Ladlaw, almost under his nose now, began crawling again, scratching up the dirt with the one free hand, dragging the unwilling pony back up close to the buffalo.

Woodfoot heard Charley then, and turning, saw him almost falling off the rock in fits of laughter. Black's face was set in a pale, moveless mask. Jimmy was watching in amazement, just a hint of laughter in his eyes.

The bull swung around then toward the pony, stepping his front feet over the rope; the pony reared back and Ladlaw came sliding head first toward the bull again. The pony stopped just in time, and the seesaw started all over again.

The drunks had stopped their own ruckus for the moment and were cheering and whooping.

Woodfoot glanced over at Stevens then and saw him step up on the carcass of the bull he had shot to get a better look at what was going on. He stood up, tiptoe on the shoulder, straining his neck up. And suddenly he shot up into the air as if he had jumped and the bull came up under him.

The rest was a blur of movement with Stevens falling toward the curving upswing of horns; and Woodfoot had his rifle up, the sight coming down on the bull.

The barrel bucked upward then; he saw Charley's hand drop away and glanced over and saw the flare of anger as Charley met his eyes. He looked down again to see Stevens, unhurt, crawling away from the bull. Somehow his trousers had slipped or been torn and were wadded up around his knees like hobbles. His bare stern waved like a white flag as he struggled to crawl — and the bull not a yard behind, dragging himself with his front feet and fanning the bobbing rear end with short sweeps of his head — all with a dreamlike slow motion.

Charley was laughing again, choking and coughing between spasms. Woodfoot felt himself smiling again, his tension relaxed, as Stevens gained on the bull.

Ladlaw and the pony were stalemated now; he had worked around to the side to try to free the rope from the bull's front legs, but he could not. When he jerked on the rope the bull would shake his head and the pony would start rearing back. Ladlaw was hollering for help now and trying to get the rope untied from his wrist. But every time he eased forward to loosen it the pony would back off and take up the slack.

The crew went back to their own sport then, forgetting Ladlaw.

Stevens was out of danger. He had pulled his trousers up and was trying to fasten them with shaking hands.

Charley stopped laughing. Tears were streaming down his flushed face and he looked like he was choking. He picked up his rifle, climbed down off the rock and walked slowly over toward Ladlaw. Woodfoot could see his chest heaving, his face still contorted and red. About fifty yards from Ladlaw he raised his gun to shoot; then lowered it and stood looking down, his shoulders shaking. Woodfoot could not tell whether he was laughing or coughing.

Ladlaw was looking at Charley then, staring like a man seeing a ghost, still straining at the rope.

Charley raised his gun again and aimed. Looking over his shoulder Woodfoot could see he was not shooting at the bull but toward Ladlaw. The big Sharps roared, and Ladlaw fell backward. And for that instant Woodfoot thought he had been hit; then saw the pony break away and run and knew that Charley had only cut the rope with his shot.

Instinctively Woodfoot glanced down and saw Stevens with Black's rifle to his shoulder again, aiming at Charley. Woodfoot threw his own gun, knocking the barrel of the leveled rifle down just as it fired. He saw the bullet kick up sand a little way out.

Then it was over. Ladlaw was up and walking over to Charley. Stevens had dropped the rifle and was standing pale and shaken against the wagon. Black had climbed down off the rock and was puking against the side of it, his face green and distorted.

Carefully avoiding the spatter, Charley climbed back up on the rock and began picking off the wounded buffalo. He was shooting offhand, and with every shot a buffalo went down.

Between the shots Woodfoot could hear Black gagging and coughing by the rock.

CHAPTER
15

SANDY TIED HIS HORSE TO THE HITCHING RACK
in front of Black's store and followed the load of hides along the
alley to the hide yard in back. Dust was deep in the roadway,
ground to a fine powder that splashed like water from under the
wagon wheels, rising slowly and fine as steam in the windless air.
The yard was hazy with dust under the hot sky of noon, blurring
and clearing with the movement of the air in the wake of the
wagon. It was like walking under water without the buoyancy but
the same suffocating need to move upward to the clear blue air.

Woodfoot stopped the wagon at the end of the line that was
waiting to unload, and Sandy climbed up onto the seat to sit with
him above the dust. The sun was hot. And even above the worst
of the dust the air was heavy with smells: the putrid and woolly
smell of hides; insect powder; sweaty mule teams, and the barnyard
smell of oxen; and now and then the whiff of whiskey.

And sounds, like the smells, coming in puffs and swirls — drivers
swearing at their teams as they maneuvered their heavy wagons, the
explosive crack of whiplash; the rising and falling talk of a group of

drivers who had climbed from their wagons to the long rick of baled hides that lined the yard on three sides; the squeak of rope and pulley, of wood under strain and wood on wood from the back of the yard where a crew of men was operating a hide press, stacking the bales with a little derrick; the jangle of harness chains, mules stamping and shaking their heads as they fought the flies and mosquitoes that moved over them in little clouds filling the air with the furry, constant sound of their wings.

Black was watching the sorting of the hides on the unloading platform, looking out of place in all the dirt and confusion, his hair and shirt powdered with dust. When he saw Sandy he left the platform and came over, climbing up on a wheel hub to talk.

"Where's Charley?" he asked.

"He didn't come," Sandy said. "He stayed to look after the rest of the hides — afraid somebody'd walk off with em. After losin the white one, he's pretty suspicious."

"I pity the guy that tries it," Black laughed. "How's hunting?"

"Scarce. We got to let our skinners go for the summer — buffalo's scattered out from hell to yonder now. Charley figures to keep at it alone. He says if you still can use meat to send out salt and stuff to cure it."

"What about you, Sandy?"

"I don't know. Maybe I'll go back now, maybe later. I thought you might send an outfit for the rest of the hides though, and maybe give Woodfoot and Jimmy here the job. They're good men."

"All right. Come on into the store and we'll fix up the supplies. The boys can unload."

Sandy followed him, glad to be free of the dust and confusion of the hide yard and in the cool darkness of the store. He helped Black make up the list of supplies and while they were being gathered up by a clerk, walked around the store looking at the merchandise, yet not really seeing it. He was wondering what he would do now; yet not thinking. In his mind recurred the feeling he had had in the hide yard — of swimming upward through muddy water to the clear blue air. His mind kept skirting and drawing back from the decision he had to make in a weariness, a suffocation.

When Woodfoot and Jimmy came in bringing the credit slip for the hides, Sandy paid them their wages. He paid for the supplies, dividing what was left and leaving half of it with Black as a credit for Charley. He made the arrangements mechanically, and it did not occur to him till later that he had paid for half the supplies he was sending Charley.

Outside he shook hands with Woodfoot and Jimmy.

Woodfoot looked at him questioningly. "You still want us back in the fall, Sandy?"

"Sure. Charley can use you even if I ain't around. When you see Charley, by the way, tell him I'll be back before long either to stay or to settle up, one. And good luck if I don't see you again, you two."

He turned then and walked along the alley toward his horse, aware that the two of them were watching him leave curiously, as if they expected something more of him. They had been good to work with, those two, he thought; and suddenly he wondered why he had not told them so. It was a thing he would do ordinarily, but it had slipped him now, and suddenly it seemed important. Still he did not go back.

Leaving his horse at a livery stable, he found a barber and had a shave — and for the first time, on the spur of the moment, a short haircut. He went out into the street again feeling conspicuous in his dirty leather clothes, the sun hot on his exposed neck.

The town was busy even in the heat of the day with a continual movement of freight wagons, buggies and riders kicking up the dust along the narrow main street. Along both sides in the middle of town the log storefronts and buildings formed almost continuous walls, making a channel filled and flowing with dust. It silted down on the walk showing smooth along the sides except for the ragged, caved edges where it fell through the cracks between the boards.

He turned in at the first store he came to and after some hesitation bought a suit of clothes, a hat and shoes. He went to the hotel then and had a bath and changed clothes, feeling a stranger to himself as he came out onto the street again. He felt uncomfortable and constrained in the stiff new-smelling cloth; the shoes were stiff, giving an awkward feel to his walk. He found himself glancing around apprehensively for fear of running into Woodfoot and Jimmy. He smiled at himself then; but still, he thought, he would hate to face them in this new getup. The tie was choking him and he imagined he could feel the dust gathering in the sweat that was coming out on his face.

But he had to go ahead then. It was his plan to scout around and see what the prospects were for freighting and maybe get acquainted with someone he could do business with. But he did not consider further how to go about it. He went on down the street thinking vaguely that he might run into someone.

Halfway down the block he came opposite the jail where a little knot of men had formed. It was a two-story building with two windows above and two below. The two upper ones were barred and the one on the right hand side below; the other, which had been enlarged, was the show window for a taxidermy shop. He remembered the taxidermist — a clever easterner by the name of Bill Brady, who made most of his living mounting trophies for hunters, sometimes even shooting the game himself — and wondered what kind of caper he was cutting now to advertise his business. Sandy could not tell what was in the window for the crowd in front; above, all he could see was a welter of mounted heads.

He walked on toward the end of the block, then turned and crossed the street and came back along the other side. Ahead of him a young woman stepped out of a store entrance and walked toward the group of men blocking the side walk. She had on a close-fitting black silk dress that showed at once the strength and softness of her body and marked her as a dance-hall girl. Coming behind her he caught the damp flowery smell of her perfume clear in the dust, and noticed the shine of her hair under the small hat.

When she came close to the crowd she stepped off the walk to go around, placing her foot carefully in the rough street. But the group opened near the window; all the men stepped back, watching her, grinning. She stepped up lightly onto the walk again and passed close to the window, pausing to look.

Her hand came to her mouth as she stopped, quickly; then dropped away, and he saw her face clearly from the side — the lower lip caught between her teeth, her face drained, white. She looked around then, her eyes grazing his, glazed suddenly with fear like those of a cornered animal. Then she went on along the sidewalk almost running, her hand pressed to her mouth.

There was laughter among the men as they closed in to the window again.

He paused a moment before pushing in to look, remembering the girl's face — clear of skin and well featured, but drawn between the eyes with a frown that was both questioning and fearful.

At first he thought the taxidermist had stuffed an Indian — it was something he might have done — till he saw the eyes, dark and opaque, focused far beyond the crowd in front of the window, glassed with death; and pride and hate set on the face like a mask. A Cheyenne he was, sitting cross-legged on a spread-out buffalo robe, his hands pressed flat at his sides in the long wool of the robe, his arms bare and full-muscled holding him up like props.

The wound in his head was open but it was not bleeding now; the hair on that side was matted with dried blood, and around the wound was a spatter of blood-encrusted white. He could see the very brain pulsating inside the skull.

He turned questioningly to the crowd and saw they were not even aware of him; there was no humor or interest in any of the faces, only a trancelike emptiness.

"What's the story?" he asked.

No one answered at first. Finally a well-dressed merchant of some sort spoke, but quietly.

"He was resisting arrest so the marshal had to shoot him. He was supposed to be dead when they brought him in."

"What did he do?"

"I don't know for sure. Stuck a knife in someone, I think."

He pushed through the crowd and went on along the street. From a saloon a few doors beyond the jail he could hear accordion music thin and wheezy. He turned in and standing at the bar ordered a drink. The bartender set out a glass and bottle and he paid for the bottle, poured himself a drink, swallowed it and poured another; then, taking the glass and bottle walked to a table and sat down near the wall.

There were maybe eight or ten men lined up along the bar, at the far end a couple of drunk buffalo hunters he knew slightly. They had not recognized him in his new clothes. The rest were

freighters, miners or cow hands. The cow hands were mostly
youngsters wearing clean, tight-fitting clothes and wide hats, keeping for the most part to themselves.

One came in now, swinging the doors wide as he passed through,
stopping at the bar with the others and calling for a drink. He was
hardly more than a kid, dressed in California pants and a fancy
shirt.

"How come the Indian to be in that window?" he asked the bartender.

The bartender grinned. "Oh, that's jist one of old Bill's crazy
tricks. A sort of advertisin stunt, you might say."

"The son-of-a-bitch," the kid said. "I hope he goes broke." The
men along the bar turned to look at him and he met their eyes
defiantly.

"Well," the bartender said, placatingly, "it ain't really turned
out the way Bill figured. The damned Injun was dead, or so ol
Bill thought when he put him in the window. Bill borried the
carcass from the marshal thinkin it'd be a good lesson for the rest of
the damned redskins and at the same time attract a little attention
to his business. It ain't such a bad idea, if you think about it, seein
as how his business is mostly in native wild animals, you might say."
The bartender was wiping glasses, grinning at his little joke.

"Have you seen him?" the kid asked.

"Naw. I ain't curious. Besides, it keeps me busy servin drinks
to the ones that has."

"By God, you ought to have a look," one of the other cowhands
said. "You're makin money on it, ain't you?"

"It's a secret of my success. I never look a gift horse in the
mouth."

The bartender considered himself quite a humorist, Sandy could
see; but the fact that he had not looked at the Indian angered Sandy
unreasonably.

An old freighter standing farther down the bar said, "It's a good
lesson for any man that's got to die, barkeep, not only the redskins."

The bartender looked puzzled. "Anyhow," he said, "it kind of
backfired on old Bill. He ain't had a customer in the place all day.
He'd take the damned Injun out only I think he's a little scared of
him. Or he can't git anybody to help him. I sure as hell won't."

"No, it wouldn't be good business for you to help him," the kid said.

The bartender riled a little at that. "Maybe you'd like to go help, sonny," he said.

The kid shrugged but was silent.

Every now and then the two hunters at the back would burst out in roars of laughter and one or the other of them would buy drinks. They had some kind of game going that Sandy could not make out. He preferred not to look at them too closely for fear of being recognized. They were paying no attention to what was going on. But they looked up when the two women came down the stairs at the back.

The one in the lead was a large heavy-set woman, overdressed and overpainted, with a look of calculating good humor on her face. The other was a tired-looking woman of maybe thirty-five, poorly dressed and with stooped shoulders and a long pointed nose. One of the buffalo hunters pulled her over as she started to go by and she stayed with them talking.

The other one came on along the bar, greeting several of the men with a big toothy smile.

"Brandy neat, Ed," she told the bartender. "Medicinal, you know."

"Sure, Peg," the bartender grinned. "For your rheumatiz, you might say."

She tossed off the drink and he poured her another.

"We've had a hell of a run on today," she said. She glanced around at the men, grinning. "Must be the heat."

"Yeah," the bartender said, looking at the kid. "There's been several around here hot under the collar, one way or another."

Some of the men laughed and the kid flushed a little. The woman picked up her drink and turned away from the bar. When she saw Sandy she smiled and came over, taking a dance step or two in time with the music.

"You're new here, ain't you, dearie?" she asked.

"I been here before," Sandy told her. "When you was in didies, most like."

"Well now," she said, bridling a little, "that ain't so long. Who are you?" She sat down at the table.

"A man," Sandy smiled. "With two hands. The usual article."

"I mean what's your name?"

"Sandy. Yours?"

"Peggy. Just Peggy. What's your game? I mean what do you do?"

"This and that. Nothing much."

"All right, we understand each other. But I can see you're a cut above most of the men around here. A businessman, maybe."

Sandy grinned. "What's your game, Peggy?"

"As if you didn't know. You're alone. A man alone needs a woman."

"Thanks," he said dryly.

"Don't misunderstand. I don't mean me."

Sandy's eyes went to the two hunters who were pulling the woman back and forth between them, arguing and laughing.

"And not her," Peggy said, following his eyes. "There's a girl for every class of man — even for a refined gent like yourself."

"Thanks," Sandy said again.

Peggy was watching the hunters now with a hearty disgust on her face.

"You know what they're doing? They're catching lice on their shirts to see who takes her upstairs. Buffalo hunters! Well, I never."

Sandy laughed. "I wondered what the game was. Well, it's their nature. They got to be huntin."

"They won't have to hunt for anything with her." She faced him again. "I know a nice clean girl you might like to meet. Good to look at, too." She finished her drink and he filled the glass out of his bottle. She drank it and stood up. "I've got a nice place upstairs," she said. "A nice place to set and listen to the music, if nothing else."

He nodded, not looking at her. She left then and went back up the stairs.

One of the hunters had gone up with the woman; the other was looking at Sandy with recognition in his glassy eyes. He came over, staggering among the tables, carrying his empty glass.

"Damn my hide and taller, if it ain't ol Sandy, togged up like ary damn pilgrim." He was a big bullish man, red face shining through a heavy, dirty beard. He swayed above the table, waiting for Sandy to speak.

"Reg'lar damn swell," he said. "Shamed to speak to ol buff'lo hunter."

Sandy stood up then, feeling the whiskey for the first time burning his stomach. He reached over and took the man's glass and filled it with what was left of the whiskey. He handed it back, avoiding the man's eyes.

The hunter raised the glass to drink, hesitated, then poured the liquor on the floor.

"Don't want whiskey of damn swell," he said. "Too good to talk with ol buff'lo hunter. Reg'lar damn swell."

"You got the wrong man," Sandy told him, shame and anger rising hot in his blood like the whiskey.

"Naw," the man said. "Ol Sandy McSwell. Too good for damned ol buff'lo hunter." He threw the glass on the table. It shattered and scattered musically across the floor. "Go on," he said, "leave man 'lone." He reached over with his left hand to push Sandy in the chest.

Anger flashed white in Sandy's head as the hand touched him; he caught it in his own left hand, jerking the hunter forward across the table. He chopped short across with his right, striking the whiskered face hard, high on the jaw.

The man's arm relaxed and he collapsed on the table. The legs creaked as the table swayed under the weight.

All the men in the place were watching him, grinning. He started awkwardly to lift the man off onto a chair but the bartender stopped him.

"Forget it," he said. He raised one end of the table and dumped the man off onto the floor, then taking both feet dragged him along the wall till he was out of the way.

Sandy watched the hunter till he saw his breathing, then turned and walked out onto the dusty, sunlit street. He found the other entrance to the building and walked unsteadily up the cool, dark stairs.

Peggy met him at the top of the stairs and led the way into the parlor. A girl was sitting at a piano playing with stiff, mechanical fingers — the wheezy accordion was in the hands of a big wide-shouldered man with a finely trimmed, waxed mustache and slicked-back hair. He was in a vest and a white shirt with sleeves rolled up showing pale but muscular arms. As he played he leered impartially at the girls scattered around the room on chairs and sofas, his big knotted hands moving awkwardly on the keys.

The piano was decorated with paper flowers and an assortment of painted dolls — females in various stages of undress — and in the center a group figure in plaster of two modestly diapered cupids supporting a tablet with a flowery inscription to love. Half a dozen painted, tensely smiling girls were watching him. He looked at each of them without meeting their eyes, with no embarrassment but a feeling of grotesque unreality and a compulsion to act — as if he were part of a badly presented play and had forgotten his lines.

Peggy was talking to a girl who had been sitting with her back to him. She rose now and faced him, and with a shock he realized that he knew her — yet he could not think of her name. It was the eyes, he thought, a certain frightened look and in the face a sudden, painful reality of beauty. As she walked toward him he recognized her as the girl he had seen in front of the jail.

"This is Rosie," Peggy said. "Sandy."

He nodded and Peggy said something he did not quite hear and left.

He stood there studying the girl, almost impersonally, trying to resolve his own feelings, to understand the hurt and resentment and the blind anger not far beneath.

"Well, honey," she said in a shaky nasal voice, "the cat got your tongue?"

Still he did not speak, watching the eyes and seeing a growth of something like panic in them. He shook his head then, as if to clear it, and stepped toward her. She stepped backward, the terror as real in her eyes as it had been when he saw her looking at the Indian.

He forced himself to smile, knowing she was afraid of him, yet finding that hard to comprehend.

"Let's go," he said.

She went ahead of him out the door and down the dark, un-carpeted hallway, the hard heels of her shoes clicking hollowly on on the thin flooring.

She was wearing a small round hat, decorated on one side with a bunch of wax cherries and white flowers that so much resembled wild hawthorn that he imagined he caught the odor mixed with her perfume. In the darkness of the corridor he remembered the shine of her hair in sunlight.

She opened the door of a room, held it for him, closed and locked it, leaning against it for a moment before she turned to face him. Her eyes dropped before his and she stood looking at the floor.

"Honey," she said again, in the false uncertain voice, "you still haven't said anything. You haven't even said you love me."

"Quit it," he said harshly. "I don't."

She looked at him briefly and moved away till she stood with her back against the door, breathing hard, her eyes wide and the white skin of her forehead set in a questioning frown.

She stepped past him then into the room and began to undress. He could hear the thin music from the parlor moving endlessly in a repetitive melody with no change of expression and with a clocklike rhythm. It annoyed him but he could not stop listening.

The girl was weaving around the cramped little room keeping time with natural grace, undressing in a practiced routine of suggestive movements. He remembered Peggy coming toward him in the saloon with the little dance steps — her trade mark, he thought.

The girl would not meet his eyes, and in her face was still the numbness of expression; but the expression of her body was real and womanly beyond the cheapness of the dance and the false music.

He turned then to undress, his feelings torn in confusion between the falseness and the reality; and when he looked at her again she stood before him naked.

He remembered the day on the divide looking down on the Sand River country, the beauty of it striking him like a knife; and it was like that now but with a baffled anger rising under the pain.

He moved quickly then, tearing himself out of the confusion of his feelings, jerking her forward, hearing her breath escape her lips in a cry as his arms closed on her, his hard hands discovering the slenderness of her waist, the velvet of her skin, and her nakedness against him, flamelike.

He carried her to the bed, losing himself and her in the blinding drive of his maleness . . .

He lay face downward, a sense of physical weakness drowning him; and suddenly he was weeping, clenching his fists to control the jerking of his breathing.

He felt her arm moving under his forehead then, raising his face to the softness of her shoulder; her hand was moving in the hollow of his neck in a sureness of compassion. After a long time he looked at her face and there was no fear, but a fullness and softness and the wetness of tears.

When she dressed the last thing she put on was the little round hat, pinning it to her hair as she stood before the wavy, distorting mirror above the washstand. Standing close to her he thought he smelled again the sweetgrass odor of wild hawthorn. Reaching up he caught one of the small roselike flowers of the hat between his thumb and finger and it came free. He found himself crushing it under his thumbnail, amazed to find it real; the odor was strong now and unmistakable. He raised his eyes to find her looking at him accusingly and he saw again the tenseness, the fear of him, coming into her eyes over the traces of tears.

The music had stopped and from the parlor he could hear the sound of laughter and talking. He paid her and she went ahead of him down the hallway and into the parlor. She did not look back.

He stopped in the doorway for a last look at her as she walked across to Peggy.

A young cowboy came toward her — the one in California pants he had seen in the saloon — and something he saw in her face caused him to look over at Sandy with sudden, darkening anger. He started over toward the door, but the big accordion player, as if knowing this would happen, blocked his way.

Sandy went on down the other stairs to the saloon, a need for whiskey growing against the rising self-revulsion.

He passed the two buffalo hunters as he walked along the bar, and from the way they looked at him, he knew he would have to fight. He bought another bottle of whiskey and took a long drink out of it. Turning he saw the two hunters coming toward him. He set the bottle on the bar and with a fierce exultation stepped out to meet them.

The one on the right swung first and he brushed the blow aside with his right hand, holding himself solid and waiting. The other swung then, a right caught partially on his shoulder but glancing across onto his face. There was a kind of satisfaction in the pain and shock that seemed to give strength to his shoulder as he struck at the exposed face. He connected solid and saw the man start down; and the other one hit him on the side of the head. His knees gave and he went down in an instant of blackness, recovering as he hit the floor. He saw a booted foot coming at his face and rolling, managed to take it on his elbow. He kicked with a wide sweep of his leg and knocked the man's feet from under him, getting up, still dizzy and a little blind, but with his strength coming back to him in waves.

He fought wildly after that, realizing only dimly that there were more men in the fracas. He was fighting all of them, not thinking or caring whether they were for him or against him. There seemed to be no end to the strength and power in his arms — till something struck him on the head. Light blinded him for an instant before the darkness closed in . . .

There was darkness still when his mind stirred again. It seemed like his eyes were open on complete blackness and he wondered dimly if he were blind; then a greyness formed slowly in front of him and brightened till it became a silver patch, rectangular in shape and striped with black lines.

There was a pain recurring in his head that kept dropping him back into a watery darkness; but each time he surfaced, the patch was brighter till he recognized it finally as a patch of moonlight on the floor and the dark lines, bars. He was on a cot in the jail and there was no sound or any light save the silver patch. Between himself and this he could see the bars. And after a while he could make out the shape of the cell.

The room beyond, where the moonlight was, emerged slowly — there was a desk and chair, and by the window what looked like a coat rack. Directly across from him beyond the patch of light was something dark that looked like a man asleep, though he could not hear breathing.

He lay listening for some sound for a long time, feeling drowsy and drugged from the effects of whiskey and the pain in his head. When he looked at the light again he knew he had dozed. The square of light had moved.

Suddenly he found himself sitting up, breathing hard, scared like a man coming out of a nightmare, and even yet not awake. The light, shifting, had picked up the figure on the floor and as his mind came awake he knew it was the body of the Indian, dead now for sure. The head was away from the window and in the cold light the face showed clear and hard as chiseled stone. There was not light enough to see the wound in the head, but he remembered it vividly.

His hand went to his own head and came away sticky with blood. For a moment he was stricken with panic such as he had never before known. He stood up and staggered to the door of the cell and shook it with all his strength; and almost started yelling before he got control of himself.

He went back to the cot and sat down and the panic died. In its place came a terrible craving for whiskey. He forced himself to look again at the light, and by the slant of it he knew it would be a long time till morning.

CHAPTER
16

COMING UP ON THE BENCH LAND ABOVE THE river, Charley first saw the antelope — a buck standing alone way out on the flat, looking fat and golden in the afternoon sun. He stood there broadside, a beautiful target, even after the string of pack mules came up into sight.

Charley stopped his horse, a pleasant excitement welling in his blood, and the mules crowded up around him. The antelope turned then, as the mules stopped, and ran lightly off, his white rump flashing and bobbing But he would stop, Charley knew, and out of curiosity maybe even come back.

Charley eased out of the saddle, desire and determination strong in him with the excitement. He could not see the horns or the legs — the body seemed to float in a little fog of color tawny above white.

It struck him as odd that he should want the antelope so much. The mules were loaded with meat — deer and elk he had shot in the brakes below. But the thought did not spoil the good feeling. It was something he did not understand, but he knew it was good.

There was a little shakiness in his hands that he knew would leave him when the time came to shoot.

He walked out a little way and set up his prong stick and sat waiting for the buck to come back, enjoying the excitement, but not thinking about it any more. The antelope had stopped now, far out, looking yellower and more perfect with the distance.

Looking down off to the left he could see the river glittering and curving in the riffles, the gravel white and bright along the bars. The water was clear this far up so that even from the distance he could see the colored rocks in the shallow places. The cotton-woods were in full leaf now, the leaves shiny and jeweled as the washed rocks. There was hawthorn in the brushy spots, and chokecherry and serviceberry, and underneath the pink of the wild roses. It was good country here, Charley thought, smaller and friendlier than the open plains, the river bottoms closed in by hills and broken up by rock ledges and old stream beds into places a man could recognize if he saw them again. The brakes leading up out of the bottom were filled with jack pine and scrub cedar that made good cover for elk and deer. There were buffalo scattered out in the bottoms — no big bunches but enough to where a man could nearly always get what he could skin out. He regretted now that he had not kept Woodfoot to help him. But it was good being alone like this sometimes.

Sitting there waiting for the buck in the warm afternoon sun with the green river valley stretched out shining below and the haze over the hills shutting off the distance, he felt a depth of peace and richness he had never known before. The country, maybe, he thought, or the hunting; but it was more than these. The little game he was playing with the antelope was part of it too. He needed to shoot the buck for some reason he could not even explain to himself, knowing that if he did it and did it well, it would be in some way good, an experience he would remember for a long time. It was not the animal itself, the meat. He would take part of the meat, but that had nothing to do with the feeling he had. The little airily moving animal he saw along the sights did not mean meat to him. It was no good trying to explain it. He shook his thoughts away, looking more closely at the antelope, feeling a little shiver of pleasure as the animal came on, its golden hide shining, the wildness surrounding it like the glow of color.

The buck came in on a spiral path, coming toward him and walking broadside, then going away to turn and come closer on the next loop. He could see the horns now, curved at the tips, pronged just above the eyes, and the stripes of white and black under the throat.

It was hard to keep from shooting each time the buck crossed on the near side of the circle; but it was still a long shot — and Charley found himself enjoying the tension, the alternation of feeling as the animal came and crossed and again turned away. Waiting he ran his hand back and forth on his gun, enjoying the cool smoothness of the polished barrel, then the warmth and grain of the forearm, and finally the familiar roughness of the checked grip. He did this almost unconsciously, aware only of the warmth and coolness, the textures under his fingers, feeling the gun as almost a part of himself.

On the next loop the antelope stopped, standing broadside, its head turned toward him, bristling the long hair on its rump.

He guessed the range at three hundred yards and raised the rear sight, thinking it would be a long shot — a scratch shot if he made it — feeling at the same time that he had to make it; knowing he would. The front sight wavered into line, then steadied, big and solid against the misty smallness of the buck; and he squeezed slowly on the trigger. And in that instant before he felt the give in the trigger tension, he saw the prongbuck with a sudden clarity — experienced it rather, he thought later — the mystery of it, the odd-shaped head like no other animal, the forward set of the horns just above the enormous eyes; the strangeness he would always feel if he killed a thousand of them. The gun bucked at his shoulder and the antelope sprang once and fell.

Charley folded his prong stick, reloaded and laid his rifle carefully on the grass. Then he got out the red claystone pipe Sandy had given him and filled it and lit up, consciously preserving the good feeling he had — the excitement that was still warm in his blood, the richness.

The pipe had a good feel to his hand — like the rifle — smooth and solid and heavy; and he had come to like the taste of the kinnekinnic tobacco. He sat there till he finished the pipe, then rose, knowing he would have to hurry or be late to camp.

He led the horse and mules to the carcass, feeling the little disappointment he always felt, seeing an antelope he had shot. The hide was never much good; and this time of year it looked shabby up close, the long hair shedding and the short dun-colored stuff coming in underneath. He did not care much for the meat either, though he would eat some of this, he knew. Hurriedly he skinned out the hams and the loin and, tying them to the back of his saddle, headed down river for camp. He was tired and hungry now, but with a sense of wholeness, of completion. It had been a good day.

The sun was nearly down when he reached camp. Coming down off the bench land to the river bottom again, he saw smoke from a fire off to the right of that from the smokehouse and knew that Sandy was there ahead of him. There would be a fire going and maybe supper cooked and nothing left to do but unpack the mules and take care of the meat.

He liked this new camp. He had found a cave in the sandstone bluffs that lined the river bottom here, an overhang of rimrock with a level floor below. On his suggestion Sandy had built a rock wall up from the floor to the overhang, leaving just an opening for a door. It made a fine big room, with a solid homey feel to it. At the back was a crevice that made a natural flue for the fireplace, and there were little cubbyholes and shelves to store things. Not fifty paces down from the cave was a spring of cool sweet water. And the bottoms along the river were thick with blue-stem grass and slough sedge, little natural pastures for the stock.

The cave had been Charley's idea — Sandy would have preferred a tent or some kind of temporary shack. But Charley had insisted on the cave, and he was glad now.

Down by the spring Sandy had made curing vats by digging holes and lining them with buffalo hides sewn together. He had made a smokehouse also of buffalo hides strung over a willow frame with a fire pit below and an adjustable vent at the top to control circulation. They brine-cured some of the meat; the rest they cut into strips, salted, and hung in the smokehouse to make jerky. So with the meat they cured and what hides they picked up they were doing all right.

When he came into camp Sandy was down by the spring putting

away the last of his meat. He helped Charley unpack the mules without saying a word or even seeming to notice that he was there. The hides Charley had brought they stretched out on the ground flesh side up by the spring and piled the meat on them.

Charley took the mules down to a meadow by the river and hobbled them, bringing his horse back to picket with Sandy's in a little brush-enclosed park close to camp. When he came back Sandy was washing the meat in the spring and putting it in the vats.

Charley did not offer to help. Sandy was fussy about the way meat was handled, a little like a woman, Charley thought. And he was cranky these days and hard to get along with. He tended the meat and took care of camp, leaving Charley to do most of the hunting. It was a good arrangement, Charley thought. He had felt, lately, that he was the boss of the outfit, and it gave him a good feeling of strength and responsibility. But he was lonesome sometimes. Like now. He felt good, and he wanted to talk to someone. But he knew Sandy would not talk or even listen. He had been that way ever since he came back from town, quiet and morose.

Charley remembered the day Sandy had come back — before they moved the camp. At first Charley did not recognize him. His hair was cut short and he was hatless and had on different clothes — a business suit that had recently been new but was torn now and wrinkled, spotted with dirt and dried blood. There was a long cut on his head, scabbed over but still looking mean and red and the hair around it matted with old blood and dirt. He had a week's growth of beard, also dirty, and his eyes were bloodshot and swollen almost shut. He would not speak or answer at first, acting as if he were completely unaware of Charley's presence.

He turned his horse loose and got a bucket of water and soap to wash with, then squatted by the bucket looking off into space. He finally poured the water out without even touching it.

He had stayed dirty ever since, washing his hands only when he took care of the meat. The suit was full of holes and rips now, and as he moved Charley could see spots of peeling sunburn on the big muscular legs.

And yet Charley was glad to have him back. He had felt panic-stricken when Woodfoot, coming back from town with the supplies, had said that Sandy might not be back. He had thought then of going into town himself, but he had waited, making a few hides but no meat. He had all the supplies for curing, but he realized then that he had depended on Sandy to show him how to do it. So it was a big relief when Sandy showed up again, even with the way he was changed.

Sandy finished with the meat and led the way back up to the cave. He had a pot of meat boiling over a fire out in front — he would never cook inside.

They ate in silence and afterwards Sandy walked off to look at the stock. It was dark when Charley went inside, dropping the bull-hide flap in the doorway to keep out the mosquitoes. He built a small fire in the fireplace — to melt lead with, he told himself. Yet he knew he would have built it anyway. A fire inside like that was a comfort to a man. It was like home again, sort of cheerful, the crackle of the flames a friendly presence.

He loaded a few shells, taking pains to get the charge right — he was shooting better these days than he had ever done before, and he was getting more particular all the time about his reloading. He knew his ammunition was better than the factory product and he took a lot of pride in it.

He spent a long time cleaning and polishing his gun, but it was still early when he rolled out his bed by the fire. He was not sleepy — but he liked to lie and watch the play of firelight on the solid sandstone ceiling and the rough, mud-chinked wall opposite the fire.

There were pack rats that played in the chinks and crevices of the ledge, little bright-eyed animals that carried off anything left loose — shell cases, primers, anything they could carry. He had killed a few of them at first, but now he had come to like them. They were not dirty like ordinary rats, and it amused him the way they liked to collect things. Now and then he brought them little pieces of flint and bright-colored rocks, leaving these on little juttings of the sandstone so he could watch them being stolen, feeling amused and indulgent.

Sandy came back after a while and took his bedroll out — he had never yet slept in the cave.

A pack rat came out then, flickering back and forth along the ledge, shadowlike, his little beads of eyes sparking in the firelight. Charley followed lazily with his eyes till he dropped off to sleep.

It was dark when he awakened, with just a luminous pink of embers showing from the fireplace, and he knew he had been asleep for a long time. He had the feeling that something had startled him, but listening he could hear nothing. He dozed off again and when he awakened it was dawn . . . He could hear Sandy stirring around outside.

When he came out Sandy looked at him rather curiously and looked away.

Charley noticed the two horses standing in close to the fire, saddled.

"We lost our stock last night," Sandy announced bluntly.

"What? How do you know?"

"Well, I know they're gone. Is that good enough for you?" Sandy asked testily.

"Maybe they're hid out in the brush."

"Naw. I heard something last night and went down to find out about it. The mules and your two ponies were gone then. It clouded up about that time and got too dark to find out anything so I come back and brought in the two saddle horses. Leastways they missed those."

"Why the hell didn't you call me? I woke up in the night and had a hunch there was something wrong. I wish to hell you would of called me."

"What for? Can you see in the dark?"

"No," Charley said, flaring up a little. "But by God when something like that's going on I wantta know about it."

Sandy smiled. "It's the price you pay, Charley, for hibernatin in a cave like a durn bear."

There was no answer for foolishness like that, Charley thought. But he was still sore. "What we gonna do?" he asked. "Set here suckin our thumbs while a bunch of thievin Injuns make off with our stock?"

"What makes you so sure it's Indians?"

"Who else?"

Sandy shrugged. "Might as well eat. I got er ready. Anyhow, it's just now gettin light enough to track."

Charley finished first, burning his mouth on the coffee and boiled dried apples they always had with their meat. He gathered up some jerky and hard biscuits and stuffed them into his saddlebags and sat his horse waiting impatiently for Sandy. Sandy was exasperatingly slow, but Charley knew it was no use trying to hurry him. He had a notion to ride off alone but thought better of it, partly because he had a hunch Sandy would just as soon he did and partly because he knew Sandy would be a better tracker than himself.

In the meadows the tracking was easy, the lightness of dew knocked off the grass leaving a dark green path going down river. Charley rode ahead, following at a lope till the tracks turned abruptly and left the river on a buffalo trail up toward the hills. Coming out of the bottoms the trail threaded a jumble of water-smoothed sandstone boulders and passed up through an opening in the bluff. Right at the top where the rocks gave way to graveled hills, one last boulder, tall and pointed, stood beside the trail. Circling the top of it was a coil of rawhide rope and on the very point a pair of worn-out moccasins. Charley stopped to puzzle out what it meant and Sandy came up. When he saw the moccasins he laughed — the first time since he came back to camp.

It galled Charley. "I don't see a damn thing funny," he complained.

"Naw," Sandy said, "I don't suppose. But all the same it's funny. Don't those poor old wore-out moccasins say anything to you, Charley? What do you suppose that Indian put them up there for, where he knew we'd see em?"

"Damned if I know. But it ain't my idea of a joke, whatever it means."

"I'll tell you what it says to me," Sandy grinned. "It says, 'These are the moccasins I wore out and the rope I used to get me a horse to ride. Now you can do the same with em, and welcome.'"

He was enjoying himself, Sandy was, and stalling — as if he wanted the damn thieves to get away; as if he didn't give a damn about the lost stock.

Charley was outraged. Here he had just been going good, getting ahead a little and something like this had to happen. All the good feeling of the day before was slipping away from him now. He had felt desperate at first, but now he felt crazy mad. And with Sandy sitting his horse so easy and still grinning, Charley could hardly keep from cursing him.

"Blackfeet," Sandy went on, "a long ways from home. It's a good thing those two Indian ponies of yours was in with the mules or they would've looked for these and probably got em. As it is they think we're afoot — somethin else those moccasins tell you, if you stop to think. Mules'll slow em up. So we got a good chance. No use to get all het up about it. There's only two of em."

Charley swung off up the trail, knowing that what Sandy said made sense. But he was still mad, and he had to move or blow up.

The trail led up onto the long roll of prairie, and in the short brown buffalo grass the tracking was harder. They had to go slow. At one point they lost the trail altogether where a small herd of buffalo had followed it along a draw and across a flat. They had to ride a circle around the flat to pick it up again.

Before noon they were coming back to the river, the trail having swung in a big half-circle into the hills then back across the bench land where he had killed the antelope the day before. In spite of his hurry and anger he showed Sandy the spot where he had made the shot. But the rest of the carcass was gone. He rode over and saw that the Indians had taken it, probably right after he shot it.

"That was some shootin all right," Sandy said as they went on. "I never knew anyone that could handle a gun like you, Charley, or anywheres near." He was looking at Charley now, deeply and earnestly.

Charley dropped his eyes. When he looked again Sandy was watching the trail ahead, grinning.

"It's the truth," he went on, "and I've knowed a lot of men that wore guns. But it's the first time I ever knew a gun to wear a man."

Charley said nothing, but he was puzzled by Sandy's little joke. He could see nothing in it that a man should take offense at, and yet he was angry. It seemed like the anger grew in him with everything that happened, no matter what it was. It wasn't the loss of the mules so much that made him mad, it was just that he had been doing so good, it was the interruption of his plans — and by a lousy bunch of Indians, to boot.

They dropped down through the brakes on the same trail he had come out on the day before. And after that it was just riding. There was a well-cut buffalo trail along the river — the only trail, with the river cutting through a range of hills. The trail crossed and recrossed the stream, traveling the gravel bars and mud flats laid down by the water, avoiding the steep sides of the canyon.

At one point where the canyon opened out into a little flat, the tracks turned off into a grove of cottonwoods. They found the remains of a fire and in the soft earth near the river, the prints of moccasined feet. Charley saw the head and hide of the antelope.

Sandy got off and looked around briefly.

"They picked up their women here," he told Charley. "Two."

Sandy continued to search the campground slowly and deliberately. Charley waited, keeping his horse on edge by kneeing him back and forth in a little clearing and holding his head up. Sweat was showing in little patches on the bay's thick neck and little streamers of foam streaked downward from the bit as he moved his head. Coming close to Sandy's buckskin, the bay took a nip, his teeth snapping together as they slipped on the hide. The buckskin squealed and sidled away.

Sandy looked up. "Damned if you and that horse ain't a pair," he said. "Get down and cool off a minute."

Charley shook his head.

Sandy finished his inspection and came back to his horse. Instead of mounting he picked up the buckskin's front foot and pried a little rock out of the frog with his knife. "Bruised a little," he told Charley. He took some jerky out of his saddlebag and sat down by a tree to eat, beckoning Charley with the meat he held in his hand.

"Come and set," he said. "And stop frettin. We'll get our mules back all right. It's just a question of time and the right idea."

Charley did not get down or speak. He was choked up now with anger, as if the blood itself were expanding in him.

"No hurry," Sandy said. "We'll catch em tonight easy — women and mules are gonna slow em up. The trail's rough and brushy up ahead and the women'll wantta camp. What we want to do is let em get settled, then we can drift in and haze our stock back along the trail — and pay em back their compliment." He nodded toward his horse and for the first time Charley noticed the rope and moccasins hanging on the saddle. Sandy was smiling. Trying to smooth things over, Charley thought. And the thought made him furious. But he managed to keep his voice cold.

"You mean just let the damn thieves go?"

Sandy shrugged. "It ain't gonna help you to hurt em," he said. "Anyway, stealin horses ain't a sin to an Indian like to you. It's a way of livin they're raised to. Like as not those two will give the whole bunch away, if we don't get em back. An Indian don't think the same as you do, Charley. Mostly the only reason he collects things for is to give away, not just to have."

Sandy was talking earnestly now, and appealing to him, Charley thought with a certain satisfaction, not telling him as he used to.

"Hell, Charley," Sandy went on, "these are just reservation Indians. They ain't a danger to anyone."

"Look," Charley said. "I ain't arguin with you about Injuns — to me they ain't scarcely human, just one more kind of varmint. Goddammit, there's plenty of places they got a bounty on em — so much a head — any Injuns, not just horse thieves. I aim to get my mules back and if any Injun gets in the way, I'll just naturally shoot him. And I ain't gonna go sneakin around through the brush either. Now let's get the hell out of here."

"The hell of it is, Charley," Sandy said, a little weakly now, Charley noticed, "they got their women along. If it wasn't for that I wouldn't mind a little run-in."

"Hell," Charley snorted, "a squaw horse thief ain't any better than a buck."

Sandy was still sitting by the tree, making no move to leave. And suddenly Charley could stand it no longer. He reared the bay around and pounded out of the grove, ducking branches, catching just a glimpse of Sandy, half risen, an imploring look on his face.

Charley rode at a run for a long time, leaning low over the saddle horn in the brushy places, taking the whip of branches on his shoulders, only slowing at the fords to keep from getting his guns wet. The bay was sweating freely now and running easy with a long powerful stride. And he could run that way all day, Charley thought, a little feeling of pride rising above his anger. Sandy could never catch up with him on the little buckskin. He realized then that he was listening for hoofbeats behind him and looking back continually as if he himself were being chased. He was surprised that it should seem so important to leave Sandy behind. A moment before he had wanted Sandy along; now he was glad Sandy had hung back and he found himself hoping that the rock bruise in the buckskin's foot would slow him down. It was an odd thing, he thought, to be hunting Indians and have all your mind on the trail behind you.

He stopped and listened, dismounting and climbing up the side of the canyon to get away from the sound of the horse's breathing and the saddle squeak. In the quiet of afternoon there was not a sound except the murmur of the river — and he knew a running horse could be heard for miles along the trail.

He slowed down after that, holding the bay to a steady, mile-eating lope, looking ahead. At almost every bend of the river he passed an ideal spot for an ambush. But he was not worried. From what Sandy had said he was sure the Indians would not wait for him. And even if they did, he had the sure feeling he would make out all right. An Indian would never be able to hit him on the move like that.

He kept his pace steady all afternoon, stopping only occasionally to observe the freshness of horse or mule droppings. Toward evening he stopped where the animals had crossed a sandbar and studied their tracks carefully to gauge their freshness. Sandy had told him once that for a long time after an animal made a track in dry sand, there would be some movement in it — little trickles and slides moving into the bottom of the hole. He found no movement in any of the tracks he looked at and knew the Indians were still a long way ahead. He picked up his speed after that till dark, when he had to slow down and let the bay pick his own trail till the moon came up.

The canyon widened out again and he held the bay to a jog trot, searching the little flats carefully as he passed them. It would be easy to blunder right into a camp with no more than moonlight — or miss it altogether.

He was tired and hungry but he would not stop — his anger had calmed to a hard core of determination. He would get the mules. But he did not think how he would do it — when the time came he would decide. In the meantime he would not think ahead.

It was not the first time he had ridden after Indians. He had had his share of it in his year with the Rangers out of Fort Sill. Most of their job had been rounding up strays from the reservation — Kiowas mostly and Comanches — and either taking them in or taking care of them on the spot, which was much easier. It was damn few Indians they bothered to ride in with if there was much distance to go — and they had caught quite a sizable number of them.

They had been a tough outfit, the Rangers. The pay was only forty a month, but there was plenty of plunder once you got on to it. The Indians usually had something that would bring money — guns, beaded jackets, knives. Some of the Rangers skinned them and tanned the hides to a good grade of leather, making quirts and tobacco pouches and such. He had never done it himself, nor even skinned an Indian, though he had that little tobacco pouch of a squaw's breast as a souvenir. But he had seen it done plenty of times so that it did not shock him any more. Not after the first time anyway. But strangely enough, the first time was the only one he remembered. Not that it bothered him any but it came back to him often and with peculiar clarity and vividness.

He had just taken up with the Rangers and was out with a scouting party of about half a company. They had been issued new Colt .45's and new carbine needle guns, which were a big improvement over the old cap and ball navies they had had before, and they were anxious to give them a try.

It was a hot day, he remembered, and they had ridden all morning, stopping about noon up on the timbered side of a little valley to eat their lunch. They saw the Indians coming down out of the hills directly across from them, maybe two miles away. The lieutenant ordered them back into the timber and they waited there while the Indians came on. They were riding slow, raising a dust that hung motionless in the dead air marking the path they traveled, pointing a line toward where the rangers waited. They stopped at a little creek about a mile away and watered their horses and came on, seven of them, heading now for the timber a little way below. All but two were stripped to the waist and he could see the sun on their brown hide like the shine of new saddle leather. One was dressed like a white man with a wide hat and chaps.

The lieutenant scouted the timber below and when he came back he was grinning. He drew a little map on the ground showing a trail leading into the fork of a washout. "It's an old trail," he told them, "and the wash is too deep to cross — hell, it's straight up and down, fifteen, twenty feet . . . We'll have them like cattle in a corral."

They split up, leaving their horses, and hid out in the trees on both sides of the trail. By then Charley could hear the Indians laughing and talking, and he saw they were whittling out arrows as they rode. It was then that Charley saw the squaw. Mac, a big ranger who was with him, laughed at his concern. "Hell," he said. "A squaw horse thief is no better than a buck."

It was a perfect trap. And the Indians rode in without even pausing. They came right up into the fork before they looked back and saw the rangers cutting them off.

They got three bucks with the first fire, before the Indians even got their guns out. Two that were on the coolest horses came back toward them, riding hard, and someone shot the horse from under one of them and he fell right in front of the lieutenant.

The other one somehow got by, but his horse was hit. He made it out of the timber and maybe two hundred yards beyond when the horse went down.

The squaw emptied a revolver at them without hitting anyone, then jumped off her horse and ran toward them, her hands pressed to her breasts, crying, "Me squaw, me squaw." Someone shot her in the stomach and she stumbled backward with a surprised look on her face and sat down by a tree. When he looked at her a moment later she was puking blood.

The one dressed like a cowpuncher was riding what must have been a green bronc, because when the shooting began the horse, a big wall-eyed roan, started pitching, going up high and swapping ends as he came down, squealing like a pig with every jump. Maybe it was because the Indian made a poor target or because of the good ride he was making, but no one was shooting at him. He had big Mexican spurs and a quirt, but he was not using them. And he looked cool and easy, as if he had nothing else on his mind but staying in the saddle.

The roan had been working over close to the edge of the wash, still whirling; finally he came down facing the drop-off and so close his head was out over it. And it was then that the Indian put the spurs to him and stood on them, at the same time laying on the quirt. The roan bellowed and dived out over the cut bank and went out of sight without even touching.

The Indian that had been thrown in front of the lieutenant had got up and the lieutenant, who had somehow lost his gun, was clinching with him. It looked like an even match so they let it go a minute, with three Rangers keeping them covered in case the Indian got the best of it.

Charley walked over to the edge of the wash. The roan had piled up at the bottom and rolled on the rider and was just now getting up, staggering awkwardly but with no legs broken. The Indian moved then and tried to get up but his legs would not work. He pulled himself over under the horse with his arms, talking as he moved. Catching hold of a stirrup, he pulled himself up and hooked his arm through. Then, for the first time, he drew his pistol, and fired it under the horse's belly. The roan jumped once and lit out down the gully, running sidewise against the drag of the stirrup. He was disappearing around a curve in the gully before anyone started shooting.

The lieutenant was starting to weaken now and the three Rangers stepped up and put their .45's to the Indian's head.

"You gonna surrender?" one of them asked.

"No, you Texas son-of-a-bitches."

The .45's went off almost at the same time and the Indian's head disappeared, all but a little piece and that was sticking to the back of his neck.

The Indian that had made it out of the timber had crawled behind his horse; and looking down through the trees along the trail, Charley could see him bobbing up and down, just his head coming into sight. He was not trying to shoot, he was just moving up and down. Two of the Rangers were taking turns shooting at him with their new carbines. It made a difficult target because you had to shoot damned straight and time it right too. Charley drew down then, and with the first shot the Indian stopped bobbing and dropped down out of sight.

They ran for their horses to follow the Indian that had got away. But by the time they were mounted they saw him halfway across the valley, in the saddle now, and the roan running like a jack rabbit.

They rode back into the trees and Mac, who was in the lead, shot the squaw. He began ripping off her clothes with his knife before she even stopped moving. Charley watched him make the first cut to start skinning her, and turned away, afraid it might make him sick. The other Rangers gathered up what plunder they could find and started skinning the bucks, taking great pains not to make holes in the hide.

For that moment Charley was completely bewildered. His eyesight went hazy and a numbness came into his body. He felt a stricture of his heart as if from fear, and suddenly he was streaming sweat.

He came out of it, and saw the lieutenant grinning at him. "You look a little peaked, Charley," he said. "Like you was fixin to lose your lunch."

Charley shook his head. He was all right now, just feeling dizzy and suffocated. The trees around the little clearing closed him in, shutting off the air.

To get into the open he rode down to look at the Indian he had shot, and forced himself to get down and take the gun and a knife. He could not take any more.

His shot had hit the Indian over one eye, and both eyeballs were rolled upward showing white, as if he had tried to see the bullet. There were two other holes in the body.

And that was all Charley remembered.

Looking back now he could laugh at his greenness, knowing he had come a long way since then. It was just a matter of realizing that killing was, after all, just killing. And when you came right down to it, there was not much difference between killing an Indian and killing a buffalo, or in the skinning either.

He was beyond the hills now and the valley was bordered by a rough vertical wall of sandstone that curved in and out the way the river had cut. Patches of brush and trees and rocky points alternated with open meadows. The moon was high and bright, and by dismounting in the open places he could see the tracks of horses and mules, still moving ahead. He kept his jog trot, stopping now and then to check the tracks till light began to show in the east.

He knew then that Sandy had been wrong — the Indians had not stopped for the night. He had counted on catching them in camp but now it began to look like he'd have to tackle them on the move — and in the daylight. If he did that he would be sure to lose the animals the Indians were riding.

He was cursing his luck when he smelled the smoke, just a whiff and then no more. There was no wind that he could feel so he knew the fire had to be close.

The trail was near the river here, and ahead his view was blocked by a point of cottonwoods that grew almost to the rimrock. He hesitated, then tied his horse in the trees a little way off the trail, and taking his rifle, climbed up onto the rimrock and walked carefully forward.

In the meadow beyond the trees he saw the Indians. They had a fire going and were sitting around it, all four of them. The two saddle horses and two of the mules were grazing close to the fire on pickets, and the rest were scattered out over the meadow.

He worked his way forward along the rim, keeping back out of sight till he was directly across from them, then crawled out to the edge and lay down behind an upthrust of rock.

It was a good spot, close, not over a hundred and fifty yards, and the rock would make a good rest for his gun. But there was not light enough yet to shoot by. If the Indians pulled out very soon he would be left high and dry. But he could think of no other plan. He would never be able to get ahead of them on his horse without being seen. And there was no way of getting any closer.

The Indians were roasting meat over the fire on sticks they held in their hands. He could see the firelight red on the faces of the two across from him and steam coming off the meat. The smell of it came to him now and then, making his mouth water. He was starved, but he had not thought to bring anything when he left his horse. He might as well be chewing a piece of jerky while he waited. In the meantime it galled him to lie there starving while

the Indians ate — probably meat from his own antelope. The fact
that he would not have used the meat himself did not lessen the
injury.

Well, he consoled himself, a pile of good it would do them if
they just waited till he got some light on his sights. But the light
came slowly. There was dew on the meadow and in the dimness it
had a pearled grey luster, except for the black trails the grazing
animals had left. As the light increased, the grass turned silvery,
then light blue green. Beyond the meadow he could see white little
feathers of mist floating above the river among the black trees. The
shells he had arranged on the rock showed yellow, glowing faintly
against the grey.

The light was deceiving. He could see everything in the meadow
clearly and easily — even the color — till he looked along the sights.
Then things seemed to blur and lose their outlines.

The waiting was intolerable — he needed to move; but he forced
himself to lie quiet. The only movement he allowed himself was
the adjustment of his sights. As the light came the range seemed
to shorten; and since he would be shooting down he would have to
be careful not to overshoot. So he kept lowering the rear sight,
working the vernier with nervous fingers.

The hollowness in his stomach was more than hunger. He was
excited as he had not been since his big stand. And he felt the same
now, but with more confidence. It might even be a stand, he
thought, smiling.

The Indians were finishing their meal. One of the squaws got up
and began clearing up. When one of the bucks stood up, he knew
he had to start. And suddenly the sights cleared; the nervousness
went out of his hands and they strengthened and steadied. The
three shells he held ready in his hand felt clean and solid.

The one buck was stretching, his arms held out and up, facing
away from Charley toward the east. He came up on his toes just
as the sight steadied and the Sharps roared.

Charley worked the lever, not waiting to see the Indian fall,
knowing he had hit, and stuck in another shell. The squaw that had
been up and the other buck were already running toward the horses.
He followed the buck with the sights till he paused to cut the
picket rope of the pinto and nailed him as he straightened up.

The squaw had cut the other rope by the time he reloaded, but she had scared the horse. He was backing away from her, rearing against the rope. She was sliding her feet, crouching low to the ground. Charley waited till the horse stopped rearing, and fired. The rope must have been wrapped on her hand because the horse dragged her a few jumps before he broke loose.

The two mules had already pulled their picket pins and were running toward the river. The last squaw was following them, running slow, as if she were carrying something. He took a quick shot at her and was amazed to see her fall forward and lie still.

He reloaded, laid his rifle aside and gathered up the unused shells, keeping his eye peeled for any movement of the Indians. Then he sat down on the rock and lit up his pipe.

He was numb now with the excitement — he could not even taste the tobacco, though he could feel it warm and tingly on his tongue. His hands were steady but slow-moving and unwieldy. He sat there smoking, waiting for his strength and energy to come back, watching the dead Indians. He thought once of shooting them again in case any were playing possum — but it seemed like too much of an effort. He was pretty sure they were dead, except maybe the last one. It was the first time he had used the Sharps on Indians and he was a little curious to see what it had done to them. It would probably be messy.

He stayed there till the sun came up, blinding him with its brightness even before it cleared the hills. It shone warm and yellow on the grazing mules and horses and the crumpled bodies of the dead Indians.

He found a way down the rock and walked through the damp grass to the camp. The fire was down to white ashes, showing a pinkness of coals underneath. There was a piece of partly eaten meat still skewered on a stick lying in the grass. He picked it up to smell it and almost took a bite, then threw it on the ashes where it began smoking and sizzling. It was antelope meat.

He looked around quickly then, half expecting to see someone; but the meadow was quiet and peaceful in the warming sun. A meadow lark rose from the grass, soaring in a burst of tinkling song; there were red-wing blackbirds singing, magpies chattering in the willows, and ducks somewhere downstream.

There was something strange and unexpected about the weather. He realized that he had expected clouds and maybe some wind. But there was not a sign of a cloud though he searched the sky, nor a breath of breeze. He was taken aback by the light and freshness of the morning.

His shot had taken the first buck low between the shoulder blades and he had fallen forward, kicking around some, and the blood was smeared red and shining on the trampled grass. There was an amazing amount of it. He looked at the other buck and the squaw nearest, finding them both shot in almost the same place as the first one. He did not bother to walk over to the squaw that had run.

He looked once more around the meadow and came back to the first buck, hurrying now. He rolled the body over, stripped off the coat and the blood-soaked shirt and split the hide down the middle in front and around the waist. He would not take all of it, but just enough to make something with. He made incisions around the upper arms and neck like a vest, connecting them along the shoulders, then began peeling it off, starting at the ragged edges of the hole where the bullet had come out.

It was hard getting a start, but once he got a little edge between his thumb and finger, the rest was easy. He was surprised to find the skin so thick and tough. Somehow he had expected it to tear easily and stick hard to the flesh.

It was tedious work, though, compared to a buffalo. Sweat came out on his face as he worked and dripped off the end of his nose onto the dark-muscled flesh. There was a warm smell of meat mixed with the Indian smell that he could hardly stand. He found himself holding his breath for long intervals, then sucking in air through his mouth so as not to smell it.

He had finished half the front, dropping the skin back onto the grass, and started the other side, when he heard the sound — something far off and soft, too faint to recognize. But it startled him so that he cut a hole in the hide. He straightened up to look around, aware that he was breathing hard and his heart was pounding audibly in his chest.

He listened for a long time without hearing it again, turning around and around, searching. There was nothing, only the bright calm day and the sound of birds. But he could not go back to skinning. There was nothing to be afraid of — and yet he was scared. He glanced continually back along the trail, though he could see nothing beyond the point of cottonwoods. Suddenly he started toward the trees and was almost running by the time he reached them. He found his horse and rode back, feeling calmer now.

It was hard to start skinning again. He was still jumpy, though he had decided that the sound was imaginary. He skinned the other side and rolled the body over, peeling across the shoulders and back. When the hide came free he held it up to look at. It was smeared with dried blood and stuck with dry grass and dirt along the edges. On the inside there were thin strips of flesh clinging, like with the hide of any animal. But the strange thing about it was the bareness and a kind of transparency in the light. His hands were slick and oily.

He was rolling it up to pack in a saddlebag when he heard the sound again — a smothered cry, like no animal he had ever heard. His heart paused, then beat wildly and he felt the chill bumps rise on his body. He was gasping for breath; the rush of air in his throat was deafening. But he could not hold his breath, not even to listen.

And yet nothing was changed. The sun was up warm now, the air clear of mist, so that the distance seemed to unroll under his eyes forever, in every direction as he turned. Back to the south, the lightly timbered hills rose away from the river and high up he saw a herd of elk. They looked no bigger than flies and were yet clear to his sight.

And still, for all the clarity and freshness of the day, there was something ominous, an eeriness of space and distance. He thought then what a tiny speck was the little river valley in all the sweep of prairie around.

His horse, cropping grass a little way beyond the other buck, raised his head and tilted his ears forward, looking toward the river; and the sound started up again, no more than a breath at first, then rising to a squall, for all the world like the cry of a baby. Then it choked off short. He thought he saw a movement of the farther squaw and noticed that she lay in a peculiar humped-up position. He caught up his rifle, hesitated, then laid it down again.

His hands were shaking and he was weak with a confused agitation.

He went over to the squaw, approaching her gingerly; and the sound began again, choked off quick and he saw a movement of her shoulder.

She was lying on her right side with her left leg drawn up, her left elbow propped on the ground holding her shoulder up. The white buckskin dress was bloody where the bullet had creased her side, just below the armpit.

He prodded her with his toe and stepped back with his hand on his gun as she sat up lifting something with her left arm. The squalling started again and he saw the baby, just the side of its head with its face pressed to her shoulder. It was strapped on a cradleboard.

The squaw came to her knees, and laid the baby on the ground in front of her, face up. It was yelling loud now, eyes shut tight. Its face was covered with blood and he thought it had been hit, but he could see no wound. There was the print of a hand across the mouth and cheeks showing clear in the partly dried blood. He realized then that the blood was the woman's — though her bleeding seemed to have stopped.

The squaw bent forward, arching her body over the baby, touching her forehead to the ground at Charley's feet.

He stood there frozen, his hand still on the butt of his pistol, his mind blank. He could think of nothing to do.

The squaw made no more movement, but stayed there, her face to the ground as if she still expected to be killed — and she had made no sound yet.

He could not see the baby, except part of its bloody, distorted face, but its crying filled the meadow, bursting in waves against his ears. He wanted the squaw to stop it, but he could not bring himself to speak to her.

He looked down the valley, expecting Sandy to appear at any moment out of the trees. He had to finish this, one way or another, before Sandy came, and he had to do it by himself. Yet there was nothing to do. He could not think at all in the thunderous confusion of the baby's crying.

His eyes searched the meadow again and came back to the woman; and he seemed to see her for the first time — the delicate stitching of the buckskin dress, the flare of her hips from the narrow waist, the surprisingly white and slender neck with the coarse black braids of hair fallen forward in the blue-green grass. Her hair was parted in the middle, the part colored vermilion. But he could not remember her face. In his intentness on the baby, he had not noticed her face.

The baby went on crying. There were little white streaks down the side of its face where the tears had washed away the blood. Charley turned away then. It was more than he could stand.

He walked to his horse and mounted and loped out and caught the pinto horse and brought him back to the woman. She was on her knees again, cradling the baby against her breasts. The baby was quiet.

He noticed her face then, the dark wide-set eyes and the full, perfectly shaped mouth. She was young, rather tall, but strong-looking, even in her fear. She started to put the baby down again, but he motioned her toward the horse.

"Get on," he said, amazed at the roughness of his voice.

She stood up and sidled toward the horse, her eyes rounded, fear of him vivid on her face.

He watched her curiously as she tried to mount holding the baby in her arms. She seemed frantic and distracted. Finally he rode over to her, holding out his hand to take the baby. She shrank away from him, whimpering; then in a sudden calmness she strapped the cradleboard to her back and mounted expertly.

He tossed her the rope, and turned and rode back to the dead Indians to pick up the hide he had dropped, she riding close behind him. He did not look at her, but he heard her gasp when she saw the peeled Indian. He dismounted and picked up the hide. He shook off what dirt he could, then stuffed it into the saddlebag and rode off, not looking back.

He put his horse to a lope, rounding up the mules, and she stayed close to him — out to the side and a little way back. He caught the other horse and the two mules, took their ropes off and herded the whole bunch back down the trail.

At the first crossing of the river he stopped and faced the woman. He pointed to the baby and then to the water, making washing motions with the other hand on his own face. She understood and getting down, unslung the cradleboard, and propping it against her knee, dipped up the cold water with her hand and rubbed vigorously till the blood was gone. The baby protested through her fingers but stopped as soon as she finished, face pink and shiny, eyelashes gummed and dripping with water.

When the woman looked up Charley indicated her own wound. She looked at it, moved her shoulders with a belittling gesture and mounted again.

Charley rode on then, wondering what he would say when he met Sandy. He could hear her riding close behind.

CHAPTER
17

SANDY COULD HEAR THE BUFFALO GRUNTING and splashing in the low flat by the river before he came in sight of them. It was almost noon, hot under the August sun, and in the dampness of the brush close to the river the air was steamy and thick with the smell of vegetation — willows and mint and swamp grass and over it all the smell of buffalo.

He had known he would find buffalo in the flat. There was a heavy stand of slough grass sedge — the kind the Indians used when they made medicine for buffalo — and wallows filled with mud and seepage where the buffalo mudded themselves up like hogs for the coolness and protection against flies and mosquitoes.

He came slowly to the edge of the clearing and sat down in the shade of a chokecherry bush, setting up his prong stick, and adjusting his sights. There were maybe twenty animals, cows with calves mostly and half a dozen full-grown bulls. All the grown animals were either in the mud or had just come out of it and were standing in the sun lumped and shiny with black mud that lightened to grey as it dried. The new-furred heads and shiny eyes and horns looked startling and out of place on the rough, earthen bodies.

A few three- or four-month-old calves were playing along the dry edge of the flat, racing back and forth, their tails curving up over their backs like scorpions. They bucked and jumped sideways and ran twisty, zigzag courses, stopping now and then to stand spraddle-legged and alert, snorting through their wide-flared nostrils. Except for their short necks and the long hair on their shoulders, they looked like Jersey calves.

Some of the older calves were beginning to shed, and under the buff color of the old hair, the darker brown was beginning to show, giving them a comical, tattered look.

As he watched, a cow rose out of the mud and walked a little way toward the calves, stopping as one of them broke out of the group and ran toward her. It dived under her eagerly with up-turned nose, paused to spit out a wad of mud, then went on to suck, tail waggling vigorously.

He sat waiting for the calf to finish, with a vague, impersonal detachment, as if he were watching through field glasses from a distance, feeling a need to be nearer but having no energy to move.

He had felt that way for a long time — ever since he had come back from town — useless and worn out, spending most of his time just sitting or wandering slowly; not hunting but just looking at the country as if he were a stranger to it. And not thinking either or dreaming but numb of mind and body, living through his eyes, as if he had no other connection with the things around him.

He spent little time in camp, leaving early and coming back late, usually with meat but seldom with hides. He tried to avoid Charley, feeling guilty in his presence, knowing he was not doing his share of the work. The young Indian woman had assumed all the camp work, the care of meat and hides as well as the cooking, leaving both men free to hunt. But it seemed like he could not get into the swing of it — or quit either.

And Charley riding him more all the time till he knew a show-down had to come. But he did not think about it much. It was something he had neither the will nor the energy to face. So he ' let it ride, trying to avoid any open clash with Charley till he could get his own feelings straight.

It was odd how he felt about Charley — there was something inhuman about him, a machinelike quality of precision and untiring drive that Sandy could not understand. And yet he could not condemn him; he felt somehow akin to Charley, despising him and at the same time feeling responsible for him. And yet, ironically he thought, he could not even be responsible for himself. It seemed like there was nothing worth making an effort for.

The calf finished and went back to the others, and still he did not begin shooting. Two of the bulls started fighting over a cow that was in season, shoving each other back and forth through the mud. While they fought, the cow went on into the brush followed by another bull. The buffalo were leaving the mud holes now and moving slowly away from him, grazing on the sedge grass, their bodies grey now with the drying mud. He remembered the story he had heard from Indians about the buffalo coming every year out of the earth from under a lake and thought this might be the way the story had started; yet he felt a deeper truth that the story put in such simple terms — the fitness of the buffalo for the country that gave them the quality of immortality that the Indians sensed.

He raised himself up to start shooting, but dropped back, thinking of the labor of skinning — of working knee-deep in mud, and cleaning mud off the hides afterward. He did not have the energy to face it.

The buffalo moved off down the river, disappearing in the brush beyond the clearing. Sandy shook himself as if awakening and stood up, stripping a handful of chokecherries from the bush. He turned and went back through the willows to his horse, with the cherries still uneaten in his hand when he mounted. He put one in his mouth, and let the rest roll through his fingers to the ground as he rode.

He went slowly back along the river, his pack mules strung out behind, browsing on willows as they walked. In a little clearing he left the animals to graze and walked down to the river to eat his lunch.

The river was slow and deep where he sat, curving to the right upstream around a sandbar, then turning left again. The sandbar was maybe fifty yards away, the light sand clean and shining in the sun. At the point was a white log of driftwood lying partly in the water, and beside it a big blue crane, standing on one leg, staring into the shallow water.

He watched the crane for a long time, waiting for it to make a catch, pausing in his eating as he waited. But the bird remained still as the log, the only movement a feather stirring in the occasional puffs of wind.

Then suddenly the long beak came up, the head turned, and the big bird launched outward with a startled squawk, the tips of its wings striking the water the first few beats, making little pairs of concentric waves that spread and merged on the smooth surface. It turned and flew down river past him, its long legs thrust out behind, its neck in a deep curve straining ahead.

Looking back at the bar to see what had startled it, he saw the Indian woman, carrying her baby and a rawhide sack, coming out on the sand. Halfway to the water she stopped, undressed the baby and dropped him naked in the sand, leaving him to crawl after her as she walked to the point.

She dropped the sack and the baby's clothes across the log and stood looking out across the river. The buckskin of her dress, he noticed, was the exact shade of the sun-bleached driftwood.

A hawk dipped down over the bar, then curved upward again, sailing cleanly against the pure blue, circling, cutting like a knife across the white, puffed clouds, moving in spirals out across the hills and out of sight.

The hills were yellow with ripe grass, rounded soft and warm and female under the sun, coming toward him in swells out of the distance, sloping finally down to the river. The slope was patched with outcroppings of grey rock and the silvery bushes of buffalo berries — even from the distance he could see the jeweled red of the fruit. And close to the river, interspersed with willow and cottonwood, the tangles of rosebushes heavy with red-tinged berries; and around him the chokecherries red with clustered fruit; farther back were hawthorn and squawberry.

His eyes came back to the woman, who was still standing at the point of the bar, her child playing in the sand close to her feet. The curving river in front of her and the willows behind enclosed her in a rough circle with the point of the bar where she stood its center.

She undressed then, laying her clothes on the log, and stood up tall and clean-limbed in the sun, full breasted, curved and golden as the hills, the braids of her hair blue-black against her shoulders. Standing there calm by the water she seemed as much a part of the summer's richness as the ripening fruit; like the buffalo a creature of the land, a member of a life earth-born and rich.

His eyes filled with unexpected tears; he was swept by a loneliness beyond any he had ever known, detached and helpless, like that of a sick man watching from a distance the well and vital.

She waded out then and plunged into the water, swimming out a few strokes and stopping. He saw the flash of her smile as she turned, treading water, to look back.

The baby paused in his play, then without hesitation crawled down the slope at the end of the bar and into the water. His hands, reaching the drop-off, slipped and his head went clear under. The woman moved to come in, but before she got started the baby had recovered and was crawling full speed back up the bar. At a safe distance he sat up, chattering at the water in a shrill, angry little voice, subsiding finally to play again in the sand.

The woman swam downstream a little way, and he thought she would see him; but she turned and went back. He felt guilty and ashamed, not because he had seen her naked, but because his watching was furtive. It was the way he always felt in her presence, and he could not understand it.

He remembered the shock he had felt when he met Charley bringing her into camp. He had thought then that it would have been easier for him if Charley had killed her along with the others. And shame had taken him then till he could not even look at her. In all the time she had been in camp he had not yet spoken to her or heard her speak. And she in turn seemed repelled by him — not afraid as she was with Charley, but standoffish and, he felt, a little contemptuous. And as if he accepted her estimate of him, he felt humble and uncomfortable with her.

He began watching her unobserved whenever he could — except when she was with Charley — and doing it he felt small and culpable, but he could not help it. He was fascinated by her and drawn toward her but unable to approach.

And it was worse with Charley around. He felt somehow responsible to her for Charley, as if the man's very existence were his fault; as if all that had happened to her had been his own doing.

And seeing her moving in fear in Charley's presence, he felt a terrible weakness and self-loathing.

So he had stopped sleeping near the cave and moved into a little grove of cottonwoods at the foot of the slope. Evenings after supper from the shadow of the trees he watched her working outside — she seemed always to be outside, except at night — on her knees fleshing hides or scraping them or massaging the hair with brains and liver to loosen it; or standing to supple a hide, pulling it back and forth across a rawhide rope, the ends of which she had tied to the top and bottom of a juniper tree. She dried meat, cutting it in long thin strips and laying it on the racks she had made of willows. Days, she gathered berries which she also dried to use in cooking, and dug roots along the river — turnips and white apple and wild onions and others he could not name. He watched her, detached and withdrawn, but with a kind of wonder. He could not understand the vigor and energy of her movements. She worked tirelessly, moving from one job to another without hesitation, asking no questions nor accepting any directions. Her movements had a quiet rhythm, as if she listened to some inner music, and there was the serenity of music in her face.

The camp itself took on a quality of the woman. There was a neatness and cleanliness, an inhabited feeling that came with the furnishings she made — parfleche bags and containers, bleached and decorated with her own paints, back rests of peeled willows, racks for drying meat, tanned hides; and the cave was stacked with food she had dried. And mixed now with the smell of hides and drying meat was the smell of fruit, of onion and sweet sage and the subtle sweet odor of vanilla grass. It was a kind of perfume, the vanilla grass. She carried it in her clothes or boiled it into a tea that she used for hair tonic. Watching her swim now, he thought he could smell the grass, though there was none growing near him.

She finished swimming and waded out to stand in the sun. The baby climbed up by one of her legs and stood raising himself up and down on teetery limbs, chattering at her till she picked him up. He squirmed in her arms against the coldness of her wet body, but she held him and waded back out to scrub him off. He squealed breathlessly but did not cry.

She nursed the baby then, sitting on the log, her head bent forward to shield his eyes from the sun, her body rounded and protective, clothed richly with the sheen of light and water. When he finished she put him down, still naked, and dressed herself. Leaving him to play in the sand, she took her sack and walked back up the bar to pick chokecherries.

Sandy lost sight of her as she moved into the brush.

For a long time he watched the child paddling about in the sand. Then, hardly thinking what he was doing, he stood up, leaving his food uneaten, and made his way quietly along the bank to the sandbar.

The baby was facing away from him as he approached, absorbed in covering a piece of driftwood with sand. The woman was out of sight, though he could see the movement of the bushes where she worked.

He stood there silently a moment, then lowered himself carefully to the ground beside the child. He sat watching while the child continued to play, dropping tiny handfuls of sand on the driftwood, his little dark head with its whorl of hair at the back bent almost to the ground. Sandy waited, smiling a little, so close he could smell the child's damp hair and just a faint odor of vanilla grass. He felt warm and affectionate toward the baby; alive and friendly as he had not felt in a long time.

He was still smiling when the baby looked at him. The dark eyes traveled upward from the ground, resting finally on his face, then dilating slowly with fear. The little brown face screwed up; the mouth opened in a scream.

The terror in the cry was so real, so palpable that Sandy found himself looking around to see what there was to be afraid of.

The baby was crawling away now, looking back over his shoulder still screaming. And suddenly the woman was there, sweeping him up into her arms, her own face vivid with fear that changed slowly to anger as she looked at Sandy.

He stood up, smiling foolishly, the blood hot in his face. Using sign talk he tried to explain his approach to the baby. But his hands were awkward and he could not think of the characters that would convey his feelings.

As the child quieted, the anger smoothed out of her face till she was looking at him with something like amusement. In his confusion, he dropped his hands to his sides and blurted hoarsely, "He hadn't ought to be afraid of me."

She laughed, looking at him so directly that he lowered his eyes. "How could he help it? You look so fierce with all the hair on your face. And your clothes — you ought to be ashamed."

She was shaking her head at him, and in his embarrassment he was not surprised that she had spoken to him in English. The baby was peeking at him from the shelter of his mother's arms; and there was still fear in his eyes.

Sandy turned away, baffled and defeated, and walked back into the willows, the woman's warm laughter following him, the memory of the child's terror tormenting him. He rode a long time before he was calm enough to think again.

He stopped by the river and had a swim. Sitting in the sun afterward to dry off, he whetted his knife on a smooth stone and began hacking painfully at his whiskers . . .

It was late when he made it back to camp. He left the shelter of the trees and walked up to the camp feeling sheepish and denuded. When Charley saw him, his face split into a grin that became a guffaw as Sandy came closer.

"I golly," he said, "so you finally came out from behind the bushes. You look like you'd been just lightly skinned." He sat down on a rock near the fire, chuckling in his throat.

"I feel like it," Sandy admitted, running his hand over his burning face. The woman was working around the fire fixing supper, but he did not meet her eyes. She dug a dutch oven full of stew out from under the coals and ladled out two platefuls, passing one to Charley first, the other to Sandy. She gave them each a tin cup of coffee and set out a pan of boiled buffalo berries.

Charley had not yet started to eat. He sat there, following the woman's movements through half-closed eyes, looking pleased and sleek. He looked good these days, Charley did. It seemed like his face had filled out, though he was certainly no fatter, and there was a complacency in it that set off strangely the hard blue of his eyes. He talked more too — even when he knew Sandy was not listening.

"Yeah, Sandy," he went on, "I thought maybe you'd killed some-one in town and was hidin out. In disguise, so to speak."

Sandy shook his head. He did not feel like talking, but he had to listen.

"Well, it's a good sign, anyhow. For a fact, though, I thought maybe you was sick the way you was mopin around. I'll be honest with you. If it wasn't just the off season anyhow, I would of looked for another partner. But hell, we're gettin all the meat we can sell as it is; and if you'd just bring in a few hides now and then, we'd be doin good."

He was right, Sandy thought. He could not defend himself, and there was no use trying to explain. There were no words to reach Charley, no way to bridge the distance that stretched between them.

Sandy nodded, saying nothing. He was sitting cross-legged on a robe by the fire facing the entrance to the cave; the baby was peeking out from behind the flap, following his mother's move-ments. Sandy caught his eye and smiled, and the head withdrew.

"Hell," Charley said. "You can't make friends with that little papoose. He's timid as a mouse — nothin in the world but a wild animal. You'd think he'd get used to me, much as I'm around, but he don't. I can't even get close to his ma but what he hollers. Watch."

Charley caught the woman's arm as she walked by and drew her over beside him. Instantly there was a squall from the doorway, and the baby put his head around the flap, crying as lustily as if he'd been hurt.

The woman stood there quietly, looking at the ground till Charley released her, then went inside and the crying stopped. She emerged with the baby in her arms and walking a little apart she sat down with her back to the ledge and opened her dress to nurse him.

The sun was just setting and bands of light coming in almost level above the shadows islanded the hilltops bright yellow against the hazy red of the distance. It struck the ledge, catching the woman and child in a brilliant light, glowing on their brown faces and the whiteness of her breast.

"It's a fact," Charley continued. "I got to wait till he's asleep at night before I get in any licks at all. And he don't sleep very sound, either."

It occurred to Sandy then that Charley did not know the woman could understand him. Not that it would have made any difference in what he said. But it gave the whole relationship a different aspect — he felt drawn in, saddled with a responsibility he would rather have avoided.

He looked over at the woman and she raised her eyes, meeting his glance. But he could not tell what she was thinking. Her face was suffused with light and a warmth he knew was for the nursing child. He looked away quickly, aware that Charley was watching him.

Charley laughed. "Hell," he said. "She don't know what I'm sayin. And what if she did? You're blushin like there was a lady present."

Sandy could not think of anything to say to Charley. Because of the woman, he could not be jocose — though there was humor in the situation; and there was no other way of talking to Charley without getting embroiled with him. It was either be on top or on the bottom with Charley. And Sandy did not have the energy or the will for the struggle. So he hurried to get through with his meal and get away.

"Dog it Sandy, can't you talk? You act like a durn buttermilk kid. Ain't you ever been around a woman? It ain't any good to be bashful around a woman. She ain't bashful, is she?" He jerked his thumb at the woman. "Like a cow with a calf — stops any-place." He laughed and went on. "She's an Indian all right. But she's easy to get along with. Treat em rough and tell em nothin, I always say — and with her it's easy. I couldn't tell her anything if I wanted to. She understands well enough what I want, though — when I want it."

Charley started eating, smiling at his food as he ate.

Sandy finished his meal. He was just fixing to leave when the woman brought the child over and put him down on the other end of the robe he was sitting on. She said a few words softly in the Blackfoot tongue and went on about her work.

Sandy stayed, watching the child, knowing what she had meant by the gesture. He felt like getting up and running, but he could not.

The child sat facing away from him, bending forward and peeking back under his arm at Sandy. But he did not look scared now. He sat there quietly till Charley finished eating and stood up, then crawled off the robe toward his mother.

Sandy left and walked down the slope toward the trees. The sun was down now, and among the trees it was nearly dark. But west beyond them the sky still flared with color. High up, a single cloud turned slowly, glowing like an ember till it seemed like he could stretch his hands out toward it and feel the warmth.

He stayed watching till the light was gone, then went on into the trees.

PART II
FALL 1882

CHAPTER
18

SHE WAS GONE WHEN CHARLEY AWAKENED AND
reached over to touch her. The robe was still warm where she had
lain, and on over toward the side was a warm, damp spot where
the baby had been. The sweet, grassy smell of her hung pervasively
over the bed.

It was still dark inside, with only a filtering of light around the
edges of the doorway — too damned early to get up. And nothing
to stay in bed for now, either. It was no good to call her back —
the kid squawking would spoil everything.

He had awakened with a warm feeling of desire, and not much
to separate the waking from the dream until he reached out to
touch her. But he was wide awake now, the warmth drained out
of him and in its place a vague irritation and disappointment.

He turned over to try to sleep again, but it was no use. A pack
rat was moving along one of the ledges dragging something that
was too big to carry. He could only see a shadowy movement but
he could hear a papery sliding sound. Whatever the rat was
dragging must have caught in a crack then because the sliding

stopped and there was a rattling sound as if the rat were jerking on it.

There was another sound too, the soft chucking of her fleshing tool on a hide. He turned onto his back, knowing he could not sleep. Listening intently he could hear her talking to the baby as she worked, only it was not talking exactly but sort of half singing. If he had not heard it before, he thought, he would take it for some animal sound.

It was the way Indian talk always sounded to him, as if there could not possibly be any meaning back of it. And yet he had learned to say a few words of it and to understand quite a few more. But he hated to say the words. It made him feel ridiculous, as if he were trying to imitate the chatter of a bird. He had to say them, though, just to get what he wanted from her. She was either dumb or pretended it, because she would understand only the word itself and no sign talk — unless he got mad, and then it seemed like she could understand anything. But hell, a man couldn't stay mad all the time. So he would say the words — except when Sandy was around — and she would look triumphant and pleased. It made him feel uncomfortable and irritated.

She was like that with a lot of things — playing dumb — but in such a way that he could never be quite sure of it. There was a perversity about her that was almost but not quite rebellion.

What he had said to Sandy about treating her rough had been right; but he found it harder and harder to do. He felt soft toward her sometimes; and yet the more he felt that way, the more she pulled away from him. It was like with a smart horse — the more you let him get away with the worse he got. And even when she seemed tractable enough the kid was always in the way.

She had been easiest to handle when he first brought her to camp — scared then, and anxious to please. And she had not been so dumb either.

Whenever he thought about it now his mind came back to the Indian hide, as if maybe all the trouble had started there. But the more he thought about it the less able he was to say how he had felt or what he should have done.

He had really intended to flesh the thing himself and just borrow her tools to do it with. But on a kind of humorous impulse he had spread it out on the ground in front of the cave and motioned to her to bring her fleshing tool. She brought him the tool calmly enough and handed it to him, keeping her eyes averted from the hide. Maybe it was her calmness that irked him. Anyhow he had given the tool back to her and pointed to the hide, making chopping motions with his hand. She backed away from him, her eyes widening, her face losing some of its calm. She dropped the fleshing tool and fumbled around in her bag till she found a scraper and brought it to him . . . He shook his head and pointed to the fleshing tool again, but she would not pick it up. He finally picked it up himself and put it in her hand, at the same time pulling her over toward the hide. She was trembling, her whole body jerking like a scared animal. A blankness came into her eyes and she kept turning her head from side to side. But she did not try to pull away.

The papoose started hollering then and he let her go. He could not stand the crying. Taking the hide and the tools he went down the slope into the trees, walking till he could no longer hear the crying.

He stopped in a grove between two giant cottonwoods and spread the hide out on the thin grass and pegged it. The limbs of the trees arched high over him and there was no sound except the stirring of the leaves like whispers and little tapping sounds from dropping twigs. The feel of the air and the little noises gave him the curious feeling that the trees were alive like animals.

He slipped his hand through the wrist loop of the fleshing tool and began stripping off all the dried flesh and the peculiar, rancid-smelling fat. The hide was dry and the thicker pieces of flesh peeled off like paper tearing. He tried to keep from breathing through his nose because of the smell and his mouth became dry. He felt a strange excitement, a fearfulness, and all the little live noises of the trees disturbed him.

As he worked, the oil from the skin spread slick on the bone handle of the tool and onto his hands, giving them a shine that would not wipe off. It spread in so thin a film he could not even feel it — but he could see and smell it.

When he finished the fleshing, he climbed high into one of the trees and hung the hide from a branch with a piece of rawhide, out of reach of animals and out of sight. He went down to the river then and washed the tool and scrubbed his hands with sand till they were raw before he got the oil off.

He had intended to finish tanning the hide then, but he kept putting it off. So it was still hanging in the tree. He had looked at it just the day before and the magpies had pecked a hole in it and there were bugs in the creases. It was streaked and spotted with the white of bird droppings. So he had to finish it now or give it up. Maybe today. It troubled him even to think about it.

But he had a feeling that the incident was a key to his relationship with the woman. Thinking back, he was amazed that he had tried to make her work on the hide. It had been a mistake. But maybe it had been a bigger one to back down. It was hard to say. Anyhow, she was never so easy to handle after that, as if, having once seen him back down, she would never be so much afraid of him again. He was ashamed of himself for having started something he could not finish. And yet the shock she had shown seemed real. He went in circles whenever he thought about it.

He sat up in bed, too tense and nervous to lie still, and began dressing. The pack rat was still making the rattling sound on the ledge. Standing up he could see its head sticking out of a crevice. It was trying to pull a narrow piece of stiff rawhide into the crack, but the piece was crosswise and it was too stiff to bend. So the rat kept tugging at it, refusing to give up. There was plenty of room for the rawhide, Charley thought with irritation, if the damn fool would just get hold of the end.

The woman was working around the fire in front of the doorway now. She lifted the flap suddenly and came in — not even looking at him, as if he didn't exist — and took a parfleche container off the ledge and dug into it, looking for something. She brought with her the smell of smoke and a warmth as if from the fire.

He stood looking at her, feeling hurt and angry, trying to think of something to say but unable to. The kid had started crying when she came in and kept it up even after she went back out.

Charley stayed there, staring at the ledge, buckling on his gun belt. The rat had retired when she came in, but it reappeared now and picking up the rawhide in the same place, resumed its tugging. But he could not hear the noise of it for the baby's crying. His hand dropped to his gun then, and without any forethought or even aiming, he shot the rat's head off.

The report was thunderous in the little space, striking his face like the blow of a hand, leaving his ears ringing. Through the spreading acrid smoke he could see a fluttery movement in the crevice.

When she looked in he was standing in the middle of the room, the gun still smoking in his hand. She looked at him silently, just a trace of amusement in her eyes, then went on about her work, leaving him confused and embarrassed.

After breakfast, as he was leaving to hunt, she brought out a pair of fringed, beaded leggings and offered them to him. He almost took them, but a sudden picture of himself dressed like an Indian struck him; and he turned and rode off. He did not trust himself to speak to her for the weakness he felt.

He stopped by the trees and climbed up after the hide. A breeze moved in the trees, stirring the leaves, and the hide turned and swung, brushing a twig with a papery sound. He cut the thong that held it and it bounded downward through the limbs, striking the ground flat with an explosive sound that scared the mules.

He climbed down and spread it out, pressing out the creases with his feet. It crackled like heavy paper, breaking in the sharpest creases; a few bugs scurried off into the grass. He stepped off, shuffling his feet on the ground as if to clean them.

It would have to be cured with bark for a long time and suppled and dried. He would never have the patience for it, he knew. And suddenly it struck him as strange, unbelievable, that he should be involved in this — as if he dreamed all of it up to now and was just awakening; or as if someone else had started it and he were being forced to finish.

And yet it was just a piece of hide, stained with bird droppings, cracked and bleached by the sun and worm-eaten. But his eyes would not see it that way. He felt that if he touched it again he would be infected, diseased. He had a creepy feeling like he felt with mice or snakes.

But he could not leave it there. He picked it up with a stick, intending to lay it across a pack saddle — but the mule shied away from him, snorting, rearing back on the lead rope. The others

spooked too, rearing and plunging, tangling their lead ropes. Only
the steadiness of the big bay kept them from stampeding. He had
to drop the hide and untangle the mules. He rolled it up in one of
his meat canvases, and carrying it under his arm rode off up the
river. He found a dense thicket of buffalo berries and threw the
bundle out into the middle of it.

He had a good day of hunting. In the evening he came back to
camp with all the hides the mules could pack. It was quiet, the sky
close with warm colors of sunset and the air cool and sharp. Coming
down into the little valley toward camp was like coming home.
It would be hard to leave this little spot, but with fall coming on,
the time was not far off when he would have to. The old camp
down river would be the best when winter came, not for the camp
itself, but because the country with its well-grassed, windswept
plains, was better range for buffalo in winter. The wind cleared the
snow off the slopes and there were brushy coulees for shelter from
blizzards.

He wondered how it would be with Woodfoot and Jimmy back
and the woman in camp. But there was no use worrying about it
until the time came.

She met him on the hide-grounds and helped him peg out the
hides, leaving the baby to play on a robe near where they worked.
And for a change the baby was quiet. When they finished Charley
led the way up to the cave, and she fed him supper, serving herself
after he was through. Sandy, as often happened these days, did
not show up for the meal.

Charley felt relaxed and peaceful with just himself and the woman
in camp, the baby playing quietly in the warmth of the fire. Night
hawks were curving and darting silently overhead and down the
slope. They flew almost as well as bats with their gull-like wings.
Sometimes when one came close he could see it open its wide
mouth on an insect. Coyotes were beginning to tune up and now
and then a wolf.

He stayed for a while listening and watching the woman. He
liked the quick sureness of the way she worked, the dexterity, the
decisiveness. It was almost dark when he went inside to load some

shells. He made a fire of vine-cedar roots that he had stacked in the corner. On down the ledge was a cave full of these roots that the rats had gathered and stored. They burned with a yellow smokeless light with no crackling or sparking, making a perfect fire to load by. He spread out his tools and was just beginning when the woman came in. She sat on the bed and nursed the baby, putting him down when he dropped off to sleep and coming over to sit by the fire.

He wished then that he knew enough of her language to talk to her. But it was nice, just the same, having her there. He liked to have her watch him work, knowing she admired and appreciated his skill, being herself so skillful with her hands. He loaded twice as many shells as he had intended, just enjoying the work, the close firelit room and the warm feeling of her eyes on him.

Afterward he lit up his pipe and motioned her to sit closer but she seemed reluctant so he did not insist — he was feeling too good to argue. He would catch up with her in bed . . .

Overnight the weather changed. He heard the wind first when he awakened, not hard but steady, making a whining sound in the crevices of the rocks, sifting a thin haze of ashes out of the fireplace. Under the flap in the doorway, where the light was srongest, he could see little skifts of powdery sand sliding along the floor.

He dressed shivering and stepped outside, surprised and depressed by the sudden change of weather. And yet it was bound to change sometime, he thought. It was the timing of it——just when he was feeling good again — that gave him a sense of personal injury.

Clouds were moving overhead in a solid flow, steel grey and heavy, barely skimming the hilltops. Over the little valley the sky looked flat as a lid. He stood looking up till it seemed like the ground itself were drifting, the whole valley sliding.

She had a fire going and was fixing breakfast, a blanket of the same grey as the clouds around her shoulders. The baby was wrapped up tightly in a deerskin with just his hands free, sitting with his back to the ledge, shaking a rattle of deer hooves. He was partly sheltered by a slab of sandstone that was slanted up against the ledge. Playing, he slapped the rattle experimentally against the slab, oblivious to the cold.

Charley crowded up close to the fire, annoyed by the chill in him. The backs of his hands were blue, his nose dripping; and here were the woman and child looking comfortable and unconcerned. It made him feel out of place and helpless in his own camp. He had been thinking of days like this when he dreamed up the fireplace in the back of the cave. And now he was not even using it — because the woman would not. He almost went back in to build a fire himself but thought better of it.

Sandy came up the slope, clean-shaven and looking more natural than he had looked all summer. It was some time before Charley realized he was wearing a new pair of leggings over his torn and dirty trousers. The new getup suited him somehow. But as he approached he seemed apologetic, embarrassed about something. It made Charley uncomfortable himself with Sandy acting that way. He felt like slapping him to bring him out of it, like with a kid.

The woman glanced at Sandy with a pleased smile, and it was then that Charley realized that the leggings were the ones she had made for him, or at least offered him, the day before. He had refused them — and yet seeing them on Sandy he felt hurt and injured in a way he could not understand.

They were a perfect fit for Sandy. His face was clean and browned now, his hair grown out. With a breechclout and a leather shirt, Charley thought, he would look like any Indian. And the woman would make them for him, Charley knew.

Sandy dropped down cross-legged near the baby and held out a willow whistle he had made. The small hands dropped the rattle and accepted the stick, shaking it vigorously to see what kind of noise it would make. Sandy took it back, blew on it and handed it again to the baby. The child took it, looked it over carefully, then put the wrong end in his mouth.

Charley laughed and the baby's eyes came quickly to him, then back to Sandy; the face puckered.

Sandy took the whistle again and blew it repeatedly, exaggerating the effort with his expression, and the child's face relaxed. Sandy gave him the whistle again, holding it right end to, and he blew on it, making an audible sound, looking at Sandy afterward with a delighted smile.

It was something that puzzled Charley, and annoyed him too, the pains Sandy had taken to make friends with the baby. Whenever he was around he worked quietly and patiently, exactly the way a man worked with a wild animal, and gradually he had succeeded. It seemed like the kid looked forward to seeing him now; and the woman too, because of it. And Charley himself felt increasingly left out.

He might have done the same himself, he thought, if Sandy had not beat him to it. But his pride would not let him start now. And he had little desire to, knowing it would be worse to fail than not to try at all.

She gave them breakfast. Sandy came back to the fire, sitting down with his back to the ledge, across the fire from Charley. The baby had mastered the whistle now. He was alternately blowing it and pounding on the slab with it. He worked himself gradually out of the deerskin and stood up beside the rock, balancing himself with one hand and wielding the whistle with the other.

Charley settled down to eat then and stopped watching the baby. She gave him some coffee and stewed berries to start on.

When he looked again, the kid had crawled to the top of the slab, and with the whistle still in one hand, was trying to stand up. He was facing the ledge, intending to balance himself against it with his free hand. In his mind Charley could see what would happen — the kid would stand up and the slanting rock would throw him off balance. There was nothing to catch hold of on the smooth face of the ledge — so he would fall backward.

Charley saw this, an instant before it happened. But it seemed like he could not move — he froze there with a spoonful of berries halfway to his mouth.

Both Sandy and the woman had their backs to the baby. But something in Charley's own expression must have warned them. They moved simultaneously and their reaching hands almost caught the child as he flopped backward down the slab.

It seemed to Charley that he heard the head strike on the solid rock. The whistle flew from the outflung hand and the small figure wilted and rolled down the slope.

She caught him before he stopped moving, sweeping him up into her arms, supporting his limp neck against her shoulder. Only then Charley remembered himself and ate the spoonful of berries. Sandy, standing close to her, ran his fingers lightly over the back of the small, dark head. There was a little blood on them when he brought them away.

She had been rocking the baby back and forth in her arms till she saw the blood; then she walked quickly to a robe. She looked at Sandy as she laid the baby down and said one word that sounded like "Water." But Sandy was already bringing a canteen.

She poured water on to wash away the blood and examined the wound. The baby stirred and she looked up, relief bright in her eyes, with just a sign of tears. She stood up and disappeared into the cave, leaving the baby with Sandy, and reappeared with some kind of roots which she ground up on a rock and mixed with water. It made a fibrous-looking paste which she bound on the baby's head with a strip of cloth.

The baby had come to now and was hollering as good as new. She was sitting on the ground holding him to her breast, rocking back and forth. Sandy was on one knee in front of her watching the baby with a foolish, half-smiling look.

Charley went back to his meal, feeling helpless and excluded. And oddly, in his mind above the crying of the baby, he kept hearing the sound of her voice saying "Water." But maybe he had been wrong because Sandy had already been bringing the water. He would probably never know. And anyhow, what difference did it make?

He noticed that the pot of meat on the fire was burning. Impetuously he stood up and kicked it off, dumping the contents on the ground and sending the pot rolling down the slope. Before it stopped rolling he regretted what he had done. But he could only stand there, defiant.

She looked at him just a moment before moving, her face expressionless — but he had the curious feeling she was sorry for him. She stood up and, carrying the baby, recovered the pot, cleaned it and put on more meat to cook. The baby clung to her, still crying but not making so much noise. He looked pale, but otherwise all right.

Sandy was still standing, hesitant, and Charley could see that he had a notion to help her. And the idea made him furious. But he could think of nothing to say. So he tried to drink his coffee, but it was too hot and burned his mouth.

When he raised his eyes Sandy was sitting across from him looking at him with an impersonal stare, not laughing or accusing but sort of curious.

"Go on, say it," Charley exploded.

"Say what?"

"Whatever's on your mind. Or take your eyes off me."

Sandy looked genuinely surprised — and hurt — and the knowledge made Charley feel better.

"What's got into you, Charley? You're touchy as a skinned snake in the sand, lately."

"Ain't anything wrong with me. But by God we're out here to hunt — not to monkey around camp wastin time. Neither one of us," he added significantly, watching Sandy.

"You mean me especially?" Sandy asked. "Hell, Charley, you know I spend less time here than you do."

"You spend less time huntin. Nobody could tame a wild kid like that without spending time on it. And by God you can't say you've brought in your share of hides."

"No," Sandy admitted. "You're right about that. But you're barking up the wrong tree about the other. Hell, I ain't tryin to interfere with you, Charley."

"That's a lie!" Charley was on his feet now, ready to fight. But Sandy still sat, flushing now.

Charley was only half convinced himself of what he was saying, but Sandy's calmness, the tone he used, for all the world like he was quieting a kid, riled Charley and he could not stop himself. He felt naked, exposed under Sandy's eyes.

Sandy shook his head again. "Naw, Charley, I ain't." He looked away, avoiding Charley's eyes.

"Stay away from her then." He had not intended to say that; he had not even thought it before he said it. But now it was out and

Sandy was looking at him in surprise. He grinned; and it was too much for Charley.

"By God, don't laugh at me," he shouted. "Get up and fight."

Sandy did not move. "Naw," he said quietly, "you couldn't raise a fight out of me with a derrick. Now sit down, Charley — or shoot, one."

"You think I won't?"

"It ain't that," Sandy said. He was not looking at Charley, and he spoke softly as if talking to himself. There was wonder in his voice. "It ain't that," he said again. "It's just that I don't give a good goddam. Now make up your mind, Charley." He paused, then went on, grinning. "If you're gonna shoot there's no use of me eatin the rest of these berries. It'd be a waste."

Charley knew then that he could never shoot. And he could never take back the things he had said. He sat down and finished his coffee, taking a bitter pleasure in the feel of it burning his throat.

He left, not waiting for the other pot of meat to cook — he had to be moving. He worked hard lining out his horse and mules. But he could not warm up; he could not stop shivering even after he was in the saddle. It was the raw, miserable weather, he thought, the wind increasing and rain or snow coming on. It was the kind of weather he hated.

He was passing the thicket of buffalo berries where he had thrown the Indian hide the day before, when one of the mules snorted and shied, throwing the whole string into confusion. They crowded off to the side and almost pulled him out of the saddle before he got the bay reined around.

He looked back along the trail to see what had spooked them and saw the hide. It was lying close to the trail where some animal had dragged it, and even from where he was he could see it was partly eaten, laced and ragged at the edges.

He started to ride on, shrugging his shoulders. But he turned and came back. It was impossible to leave it there by the trail, in plain sight.

Leaving his horse, he picked the hide up with a stick and carried it back through the brush to a little clearing in a grove of cottonwoods near the river. He walked across to the far side, hung it on a bush, and began digging a hole, using one of his knives to loosen the dirt and scraping it out with his hands.

He felt foolish there on his hands and knees digging like a badger after a mouse — but he could not stop. He broke the point of his knife on a rock and swore at it — but kept on digging.

In spite of the cold he started to sweat, The wind, dipping into the hole, filled his eyes with dust. Tears and sweat ran down his nose, dropping off into the hole, and even after he finished, his eyes kept watering as if he were crying.

The hole was twice as big as need be, he realized. Almost big enough to bury a man. His fingers were raw from digging, the nails broken, and his lungs felt clogged from breathing the dust.

It seemed dark there in the grove — the clouds were low, barely higher than the treetops, and black and wet-looking. The wind was stronger. It whipped the trees back and forth with a screaming sound, stripping them of the last of their thin yellow leaves.

He had to hurry. He had to finish before the rain started. His thoughts came with an effort, as if his mind were straining against the wind.

He brought the hide and, taking it in his hands — he could not wait to find the stick — dropped it in the hole; and before it stopped moving he was kicking the dirt in on it, hearing a papery, raining sound till it was covered.

He mounded the extra dirt up and over and packed it with his feet; then, without pausing, began carrying rocks up from the river to cover the mound with. It was the only way to keep the animals from digging it up again. On the last trip he brought only one rock, a flat squarish one which he dropped among the others without bothering to place.

He left, walking quickly across the clearing in the beginning rain, stopping at the edge to look back. He saw it only dimly at first, through a slanting sheet of rain. But the air cleared, and for just an instant fear struck him; the back of his neck seemed to crawl. Then he realized what had happened. The last rock had stuck up edgewise at the end of the mound; and there it stood, bright in the rain, straight and square as a headstone and all the other rocks lying flat to the shape of the mound.

It took all his courage to go back and kick the rock over.

CHAPTER
19

It was still dark when Sandy heard Wood-foot roll out and walk off toward the draw where the animals were. He could hear Charley snoring under the wagon and the faint whisper of a breeze but that was all. There was no sound from inside the wagon and he concluded that the woman was still asleep. She was usually up before anyone else, but this morning Woodfoot had beat her to it — probably because of what had happened the day before. He smiled to himself now, remembering.

He had been awakened by shouts and laughter. Rising up on his elbow, he saw the woman kneeling in front of a fire she had just started and Woodfoot in his underwear hopping frantically toward her. He snatched something off the fire and hopped back to his bed, grumbling in feigned indignation, and Sandy saw that he was carrying his peg-leg. The woman was laughing with such infectious glee that he found himself laughing too, at the same time feeling sad enough to cry.

He felt that way now, reliving it, and sat up quickly and began dressing.

It was still half dark with the light of morning brighter on the frosty grass than in the sky. Clouds were piled overhead dark and solid-looking as an inversion of the hills themselves and as still. But it was cold.

They were camped at the head of a little treeless valley that curved off south and east into the yellow roll of prairie. Ahead, north, the valley narrowed to a draw that seemed to end between Twin Buttes about a mile distant and there were little side draws this side that branched off into the hills. They were three days out of the upper camp now; another day of travel would bring them to the old camp, and before the snow flew, he thought.

As he sat pulling on his shoes, he saw Woodfoot come out of one of the side draws riding Charley's pinto, leading the crazy mule. He rode up to the wagon, dismounted and pulled a harness off the wheel with a loud rattling of chains. Charley, who was sleeping under the wagon, reared up, bumping his head as usual, looking wild and ready to fight. He growled something at Woodfoot now, and lay back down. Woodfoot did not answer, but he was grinning when Sandy came over. "Got to rustle some wood," he told Sandy. "Maybe take a little ice off the camp."

Sandy looked around. "Hell," he said, "buffalo already rustled it. Cut it up too."

"Yeah," Woodfoot grinned. "Cow cuts are all right if you're up against it. But they don't cut it clean enough for me. Anyhow Charley and me like a real fire — and the cook, too."

"You ain't worrying so much about Charley," Sandy observed. "You just learned your lesson, that's all."

Woodfoot smiled good-naturedly and left, leading the mule toward one of the little side draws where the rest of the animals were. He must have located wood there because there was none anywhere else.

It was good to have him back, Sandy thought. He was solid and changeless, Woodfoot was, with his irrepressible good humor and his childlike quality of spirit. He and Jimmy had come into camp with Stevens' freight outfit just a week before. Jimmy had taken the outfit back with the last of the meat and what hides he could haul, taking Charley's other pony to ride back. Woodfoot had stayed.

At first he tried to take over his old job of cook, but the woman stood him off. After that he teased her about her cooking, sometimes sneaking in extra ingredients. She responded gleefully, showing a surprising ability for little wordless jokes — like with the wooden leg.

The exchange pleased Sandy, and saddened him too. Hearing her he felt proud, involved somehow in her laughter. But he resisted the feeling, trying to shrug it off. She was not his woman, he told himself, nor his responsibility.

She was up now, climbing quietly down out of the wagon so as not to wake the baby, bringing with her matches and a handful of kindling. She scraped the ashes out of the little trench where the fire had been, placed the kindling and began gathering buffalo chips.

Charley was up, standing by the wagon watching her, looking mournful and at the same time distracted for all his quiet. It was the way his eyes kept shifting, Sandy thought; a feverish look, flushed and bright-eyed. He had been that way quite a while now, nervous and hungry for action.

He had been reluctant to leave the upper camp; but once he pried himself loose he was in a regular lather, a constant hurry to get to buffalo. But they had seen none since they started, not even a lone bull. Not that they had scouted much. Sandy was busy with the extra mules, and Charley, in spite of all his anxiety, had stayed close to the wagon. In a way it was comical, the way he would ride ahead to the top of a rise and take just a short look and then sit waiting nervously till the wagon caught up so he could keep his eye on the woman.

And Woodfoot did not miss the humor of it, though he was more cautious than usual with his jokes. The woman and baby rode with him in the wagon, and though as far as Sandy knew she never spoke to Woodfoot in English, yet they managed with sign talk to keep some kind of interchange going. It was hard on Charley, though he had not yet said anything to Woodfoot.

She had the fire going now, the chips burning slowly and with a lot of smoke, but warm for all that. Charley came over and sat down close to it, stretching his hands out to the blaze; and even then his eyes kept traveling. When he glanced back and saw Woodfoot coming out of the draw with the mule hitched to a dry cottonwood, he grumbled, "He ought to be gettin hitched up and ready to go instead of fartin around haulin wood. Chips are all right when you're movin. He's a crazy bastard. A man can't tell what he'll do next."

In a way Charley was right, Sandy thought, as he watched Woodfoot coming in with the tree. Of all the mules in the bunch he had picked the crazy scar-faced jenny. She was snorting and plunging, staring back wild-eyed at the white-limbed tree. He was keeping her snubbed in close, grinning from ear to ear watching her. The pinto was acting up too, being a little scared of the mule and also leary of the dragging tree. It kept Woodfoot busy with the rope trying to keep them together without throwing one or the other. But he was enjoying himself.

Sometimes he seemed as crazy as the mule. And maybe, Sandy mused, it was why he liked her so well. It was a fact that he used her more than any other mule in the bunch. And he never got mad at her or used a whip the way he did with the others. Sometimes it would seem like he was getting her gentled down, then he would do something like this.

Woodfoot came in as close as he could, riding, then dismounted and led the mule the rest of the way, holding the lead rope up short. She would come a few feet and rear, almost lifting him off the ground. He was bringing the tree in close as a way of joshing the woman, Sandy knew. And she was standing by the fire with a pan of water in her hand, smiling mischievously as a kid.

Charley watched her, tight-lipped, not even glancing around when Woodfoot came up behind him with the mule. And for an instant it looked like a big curled stub of a limb would hit him; but Woodfoot stopped in time. He quieted the mule, then moved carefully back to unhook her, still hanging onto the lead rope. He was just bending over to unhook the first tug when something exploded on the fire.

Out of the corner of his eye Sandy saw a white puff of steam and smoke rise over the fire and knew she had thrown the water; the mule snorted once and lit out, dragging Woodfoot like a rag doll at the end of the rope. A limb took Charley alongside the head, keeling him over, and the big stub hooked his coat and pulled him along on his butt; and he squirming like a fish and swearing.

Woodfoot was hollering Whoa, still hanging to the lead rope, pulling the mule in a circle with his weight but hardly slowing her down. And the woman all the while standing by the fire with her head thrown back, shaking and bubbling with laughter.

They had made half the circle when Charley broke loose from the stub and rolled over and over as the rest of the limbs hit him. The mule brought up at the wagon and Woodfoot scrambled to his feet and snubbed her down to a wheel. She got one foot over a tug and every time it touched the inside of her leg she kicked with both feet. Woodfoot had a turn around a spoke and was holding the rope with one hand, trying to rub her neck with the other. He was having a lively time.

Charley was still sitting on the ground, looking dazed and ruffled. The woman ran over to him, extending her hands to help him; but he stood up by himself. Without a word he reached his left hand behind her neck and, holding her, slapped her face, hard. He let her go and she stepped back, her hand held to her cheek, her eyes fixed hypnotically on Charley's face.

Sandy felt his leg muscles jerking under him and realized that he had half risen and was crouched with his feet still crossed. He forced himself to sit back down, feeling his breath coming hard in his chest, snoring in his throat as if his windpipe were too small to carry all he needed.

The mule was still struggling and snorting, taking all Woodfoot's attention. The fracas had awakened the baby and he was crying at the top of his lungs from inside the wagon.

Charley turned away then, glancing wildly around as if he were looking for a place to hide. The whites of his eyes showed plain as his glance traveled. He moved toward the wagon, drawing his pistol as he walked.

The mule stopped snorting and held her head up against the rope, her long ears and misshapen muzzle pointed north past Charley toward the buttes; the baby stopped crying and the woman, following Charley toward the wagon, stopped and turned. The camp was suddenly silent and unmoving.

It was then Sandy heard the sound, like rain at first, but growing till it seemed like he could feel the ground shaking under his feet.

He kept his eyes on the trail between the buttes and saw the first of the buffalo appear suddenly against the grey solid sky, springing, like the sound, out of the earth. They poured out of the gap and down the narrow draw, taking the shape of the curves, flowing black and alive.

And there was no break in the line — it stretched toward them, the shapes of the leaders clearing slowly till he could see the shine of eyes and horns; the sound increased, vibrating thunderous and palpable. They came into the head of the valley eight or ten abreast, moving at a steady lope.

Maybe it was the smell reaching her, Sandy thought, or just the nearness of the buffalo; but suddenly the mule went crazy again. She got some slack in the rope and for an instant it looked like she would climb into the wagon. But she fell back tangled in the harness and threw herself. She lay there kicking her feet as if she were running.

Her sudden flurry brought Charley out of his trance; he dived into the wagon, emerging in a moment with his rifle and cartridge belts. His face was shining and he was talking in an excited monotone, low and harsh. "Look at the bastards, goddam, goddam. Look at the bastards . . . " He kept talking like that, setting up his prong stick, loading his gun.

The leaders swept past and the smell of buffalo, green and musty, drifted over thick as steam. Above the steady rumble of hooves he could hear the rattle of dew claws and anklebones, the windy sound of their breathing.

Charley started firing, but the line did not falter; it only crowded over a little farther against the side of the hill. Beyond the camp the leaders swung back to the middle of the valley, leaving the curve of their path defined by a dark rippling flood of animals. They reached the end of the little valley, bent southeast between two hills, and the flow was complete, unbroken as the momentary surfacing of an underground stream.

Charley was firing steadily, moving with an easy mechanical rhythm. He had a rapt, concentrated look now; drawn up, he was, and aimed like the gun. And he was hitting. With nearly every shot a buffalo came down, usually peeling off to the side to fall.

The mule was up again, half out of her harness, pressed tight against the wagon, trembling. Woodfoot was rubbing her neck and talking as he watched the buffalo stream by.

Sandy found his own gun then. He moved deliberately, loading and setting up his rest, trying to still the shaking in him. He gripped the rifle for the solid feel of metal; but his hands were numb. The gun seemed weightless but cumbrous and unwieldy.

Looking toward the buttes he saw the line break. For a moment the flow stopped, and he breathed relief; but as suddenly it began again.

He looked along his rifle, seeing only a muddy flow, no single animal, and fired. There was no disturbance in the line, nothing to show he had hit, and he knew he had made a gut shot. He reloaded with slow, strangely numb fingers, guiding them by sight more than feel, slapping the lever with the palm of his hand to close the breach, not hearing the click of the action for the ringing in his ears. He fired again, and lowering the rifle, saw an animal hesitate and stumble, then go on swinging a broken leg.

He reloaded and tried to shoot again but his vision blurred till he could hardly see the sights. He knelt there, staring at the movement till it seemed like the column of buffalo was the only stable thing and everything else moving, streaming under the solid unmoving sky.

He sat down then, weakness flooding over him in waves, his mind unclear and paralyzed. And yet a part of him seemed solid, looking at himself as if from an immense height. It was like having the fever again but he did not feel sick, only lightheaded and lethargic.

Mechanically he ejected the live shell from the gun, leaving it in the grass where it fell. He folded his prong stick and sat for a while not thinking, aware only of the buffalo, the jar and shake of their passing, the sound and smell of them. His strength came back slowly, expanding in him like a breath; a break occurred in the line, the sound dropped off sharply and he stood up, released.

He glanced at the live shell on the ground, then turned toward the wagon. And as he walked it came to him what he had to do. The knowledge settled on him with a weight that was almost more than he could bear. But he had it to bear, he knew now, and he would find the strength and courage for it.

The woman was sitting in the wagon under the canvas top nursing the baby. In that instant before she saw him she was looking down, her lips full and parted, her eyes shining and moist. One of her braids had fallen forward and a small hand was tugging it lightly.

In the thin light seeping through the canvas he could see the print of Charley's hand on her face.

She looked up as he put his head in, and smiled at him without speaking and looked down again at the child.

He climbed in and sat down, hearing the sound of Charley's gun crashing steadily above the rumble of hooves; and then he forgot even that. He felt absorbed by the warmth and nearness of her as if the air closed in under the oval canvas were a part of her, and himself and the child enclosed in it. She looked up at him again calmly and he met her eyes; and there was no longer embarrassment in him or shame.

He did not know how long it was before he spoke, but when he did his voice was harsh and rough as if he had not used it in a long time.

He said simply, "You've got to leave."

She nodded, her face showing neither surprise nor pleasure. She only waited for him to go on, her eyes on his, unwavering.

"You get out as soon as Charley's asleep and meet me in the draw where the animals are. I'll be there with an outfit."

He reached over and touched the baby's hair and went out.

The buffalo were still coming, with now and then a break in the line, still moving at a steady lope. Charley was blazing away steadily, cleaning his gun during the breaks, and dead buffalo were scattered out like boulders along the trail almost to the end of the little valley.

It was noon before they stopped coming. The line shortened, the end passed and disappeared between the two hills like a string drawn into a hole, and the noise died.

Charley got up and came over to the wagon, staggering as if he were drunk. His face was black with smoke, striped with the light traces of sweat. The cheek where the limb had struck him was puffed up, giving his face a leer. His teeth and the corners of his eyes were white and startling in his blackened face.

"I brought down a sight of the bastards," he exulted. "Lord God, I thought there never would be an end to em. Jesus Christ what a bunch of animals; a regular damned river of hides."

He walked around as he talked, loosely and aimlessly, not tense as he had been before. His eyes were glazed and he looked as if he would keel over if he stopped. He noticed the mule still tied to the wagon and burst out laughing.

"By God, Woodfoot," he said, "you finally got her quieted. But it's only temporary. If the buffalo hadn't came along just when they did, I'd of quieted her for you — and permanent."

The woman had been chopping wood with an easy over-the-shoulder motion. She came by now with an armful and as she passed, Charley slapped her resoundingly behind. She twisted lithely to the side and, tossing her head, went on about her work.

"She's got good control of it, ain't she?" He laughed, following her movements with a hungry, wistful look in his eyes.

He was all good humor now, Sandy thought, as if all the meanness and bitterness had gone out of him with the killing of the buffalo. His talk and laughter were loud and full; and yet Sandy sensed a shakiness in the voice, a touch of hysteria in the laughter.

Sandy had been standing quietly studying Charley, feeling cold toward him and impersonal as he would toward a rather complex machine that he could not understand. But now, knowing what he himself had to do, he felt a burst of compassion, a brief vivid sense of Charley's loneliness.

He turned away, looking down the valley the way the buffalo had gone, feeling a nameless, overpowering regret. He shrugged and smiled ruefully. Here he was about to hurt Charley and feeling sorry for him; knowing at the same time that Charley would likely kill him for his pains.

He could not comprehend the complexities of his feelings. He knew only that he had to get the woman and her child out of camp, no matter what. There were good reasons for it, he knew, but he distrusted his ability to reason about something which he felt so deeply. He had to be right.

About the woman and child he had no doubts — what he would do for them he had to do, though maybe his motives were not so clear — nor honest — as he thought.

But it was Charley who caused him the uneasiness. There was an air of violence about him, of riding wild in the night. That he was dangerous to everyone around him Sandy had always known; but that Charley himself was as much a victim as any man he ever killed had never occurred to Sandy so clearly before. There would be no fulfillment for Charley, no release except in the final violence of his own death. His feeling for this woman, under all the armor of his prejudice, was the nearest he would ever come. And he, Sandy, was about to take even that away. There was nothing else he could do.

It was dark before they finished skinning the buffalo Charley had shot. After supper Woodfoot got out his banjo and began plucking it softly. The baby, playing by the fire, crawled over to him and sat watching, making little bubbling sounds with his mouth.

Charley was still in good humor, but he looked tired and pale. He lay on a robe by the fire, staring at the coals, only raising his eyes when the woman came near.

It was then Sandy thought of the whiskey.

"I got a mighty dry," he said suddenly to Woodfoot. "You ain't by any chance got a bottle?" Seeing the way Charley brightened, Sandy felt ashamed of what he was doing.

Woodfoot smiled. "It just happens I do. Snakebite remedy it is."

"Well, I'm bit bad."

"I golly," Charley said, "I wouldn't refuse a drink myself."

"Rustle your own whiskey," Sandy told him, winking. "I nailed him first."

"It's all right," Woodfoot said. "Once I open a bottle I can't keep it long. Lose too much by evaporation."

He brought a quart and handed it to Sandy. "It's real old snake juice," he said. "A cure or a cause, either one, accordin to how much you drink."

Sandy drank and passed the bottle to Charley.

"Ol Sandy just wants the cure," Charley grinned. "But me, I ain't been bit." He tilted the bottle and drank in long thirsty swallows, his big Adam's apple bobbing vigorously in his throat. He shivered from his toes up when he stopped.

"It's real firewater," he said breathily. "By God, but it's warm."

"It's hot, sure enough," Woodfoot said. "A man got to take his pants down to fart. Or burn holes in his britches, one."

After two or three drinks Charley's pallor was gone. He laughed raucously at everything, following the woman all the while with humble eyes. In spite of his laughter his face became torpid and stiff; only his hands stayed alive, and they moved constantly, restlessly.

Woodfoot was not drinking much. He played and sang a few songs — love songs mostly — watching Charley with alert, curious eyes. He had seemed puzzled at first by Sandy's temperate drinking. But he must have caught on, because now he kept pressing Charley to drink more. And Charley did not have to be coaxed.

Sandy found himself resenting Woodfoot's help, resenting the amusement he found in Charley. There was a coldness about Woodfoot for all his humor, an insensitiveness. He was an experimenter in human nature, a shrewd but callous observer. Oddly, Sandy felt sorry for Charley under Woodfoot's dissecting gaze.

Charley was aware of it too — but for once he was not irritated. He sang one of the songs with Woodfoot in a hoarse, quavering voice. The woman came by while he was singing and he reached up to touch her. She brushed on by, leaving him with his delicate hands extended upward, his face frozen in a sorrowful, distorted look. He stayed that way a moment, forgetting to sing. Seeing him like that, Sandy was suddenly ashamed; he did not like to see any man so intimately.

Woodfoot ended the song and burst into a lively tune on his banjo to cover his laughter.

Charley dropped his hands and took a drink without changing the expression on his face.

The baby was between Charley and Woodfoot now, still watching the banjo, fascinated. Charley leaned toward him to pass the bottle to Woodfoot and dropped his other hand lightly to the baby's head as he did so, his face still frozen but his hand eloquent. Instantly the baby dropped onto his hands and knees and skedaddled around to the other side of the fire. He did not cry but his eyes were big, looking back.

"Didn' hurt im," Charley said thickly. "Wil' lil coyote. Ain't scarcely human. Ain't anyways near as human as his ma. Wil' lil coyote."

The woman picked up the baby and disappeared into the wagon.

They had another round of drinks to finish the bottle and Charley stood up to follow the woman. He leaned forward and made two steps, then started backing up. He would have backed into the fire if Sandy had not caught him. Sandy gave him a little shove and he made it the few steps to the wagon, grabbing the front wheel just as he started backing up again. He steadied himself by the wheel a minute, then, setting his sights on the rear wheel, leaned forward and caught it. He sidled around to the back and made a grab for the endgate. But he missed. Grasping frantically at it with his hands, he backed away, going faster and faster till he fell. His arms were still extended, pointing skyward now. Sandy saw the fingers relax first; then the arms crumpled and dropped to the ground beside him. He was snoring when Sandy dragged him under the wagon and covered him up.

She met him in the draw. The clouds were gone, the sky was glittering and blue with just a piece of a moon among the stars. She was carrying the baby wrapped up in a tight bundle against her shoulder. He stirred sleepily when she stopped walking.

Sandy had all three of the horses in, a pack outfit on the pinto and his own buckskin saddled for her to ride. Charley's bay he had tied to the pack saddle.

"Take the bay as far as the Medicine Rocks and leave him," he told her. "He means quite a bit to Charley."

She nodded, then said questioningly, "Medicine Rocks?"

"He'll expect you to go back the way you came. So you better go the other way. You can cross over to the Musselshell about there and follow it up."

"For Indians the Musselshell is bad medicine," she said.

"So much the better. No one'll bother you."

He gave her a carbine and shells. "Can you use it?"

She nodded.

Watching her, he knew she was paying only half a mind to what he was saying. She watched him with large, steady eyes as if she expected something more of him.

But he could not sort out his feelings toward her. That what he was doing was right, he knew — as if this act were beyond and clear of his own personal feelings and hers — and he could not let anything spoil it or interfere. Beyond this, he was uncertain.

In his mind he followed the way she would have to travel and saw it lonesome and long. But he could not go with her. He had accepted this responsibility and he had to stay. But he was sure that she would be all right. She was a strong and capable woman, and she was not afraid.

He felt himself drawn strongly toward her and toward the child, enveloped with them in the wholeness, the unity, that he had felt there in the wagon. But he could not touch her yet. He could not take her away from Charley for himself.

The picture of Charley with his arms upraised was a shadow between them.

As if sensing his thoughts, she said, "Charley will try to kill you."

He nodded. "It's what I got to face. I owe him that much."

"And after that?"

"I don't know," he said simply.

She turned away from him for just an instant and he thought she would cry. Instead she turned back quickly and gave him the baby to hold while she mounted. She caught the pinto's lead rope and tied it to the saddle horn, then put the buckskin over close and leaned down to take the baby.

He was awake now and had worked one hand free of his wrapping. He reached up and Sandy caught the small hand in the same instant that she reached down. Her hand paused on his briefly and when he met her eyes she was smiling.

She took the child then, saying only "Goodbye," and rode off.

He followed to the mouth of the draw and watched her ride into the darkness toward the buttes.

CHAPTER
2 0

IT WAS PAST MIDNIGHT WHEN WOODFOOT HEARD the buffalo start passing again. Sandy was back, already asleep, and the moon was down. There was hardly a sound at first — only the wind sweeping down from between the buttes and Charley snoring close to him under the wagon. So he heard the buffalo before they reached the camp, moving at a quiet walk — a faint vibration of the ground at first, then the sound of hooves and the rattle of dew-claws. The leaders passed following the trail of the others; but when they reached the first of the skinned carcasses they began bawling.

The noise was sudden and startling, wild-sounding in the night. It was enough to raise the hair on your neck if you hadn't heard it before, especially coming in the night and so close. The sound was many-throated, flat and brassy like horns, blasting at first but attenuating as if blown away by the wind. And it kept growing as more buffalo moved down and smelled the blood.

He saw Charley move under the wagon and thought for a moment he was awake; but he did not sit up. He rolled back and forth struggling as if he were wrestling with someone and whimpered like a whipped dog.

Sandy was sitting up now, but he was watching Charley instead of the buffalo.

"Poor devil," he said to Woodfoot. "Maybe we better wake him up."

"Naw. Let im sleep. It wouldn't do im any good. Ain't anybody gonna separate im from his conscience. Or you from yours." He grinned.

The line was starting to back up now, filling the space around camp as more animals came down. It was beginning to look dangerous when finally the pressure forced the leaders on down the valley. But the bawling and bellowing kept up even after the line straightened out again.

Charley had kicked around till he was uncovered, but he was quiet now. He was lying on his back with his eyes open wide, his face twisted and frowning, but he was not awake. He did not even blink his eyes when Sandy came over and threw the robe back over him; he just lay there breathing hard and staring straight up. Sandy watched him till his eyes closed and he started snoring again, then went back to bed.

Woodfoot lay back down, listening to the buffalo till he got used to the noise. But he could not sleep. He kept trying to imagine what Charley would do when he found his woman gone. It was an explosive situation for sure, and someone was likely to get hurt.

Sandy had amazed him by turning the woman loose. It was just beginning to look like Charley had Sandy completely buffaloed when all of a sudden he had done the one thing that would make Charley the maddest. Of course, if he played it smart he could make Charley think she had gone by herself. But it was not like Sandy to do it. He would probably delay Charley all he could and then wind up telling him the truth. And Christ himself couldn't tell what Charley would do then. Start shooting probably, unless Sandy bluffed him. But it looked like it was too late for that now. And if Charley started shooting it was curtains for Sandy and no mistake. The hell of it was, there was nothing a man could do to stop it, short of bushwhacking Charley. The only thing that might help would be to delay him as much as possible and give him time to cool off. A man could do that at least.

He lay there thinking till he was sure Sandy was asleep, then dressed and headed for the draw where the mules were. It was dark now with the moon gone and he had to make his way mostly by memory. The buffalo were still coming through between the buttes in a solid line so he had to keep on the hillside till he reached the draw. He unhobbled all the mules, keeping the old grey to ride, and, waiting till there was a break in the line, he hazed them out of the draw and down the valley. When he reached camp, he turned the grey loose with the others and made sure the buffalo took them on down. They would be scattered from hell to breakfast by morning.

Charley awakened him about daylight. He was sitting up under the wagon, pointing down the valley. Woodfoot raised up and saw one of the mules grazing toward the lower end.

"By God, something's happened to the stock," Charley said. He looked bad, Woodfoot thought, pale and shaky and bleary-eyed.

"One of the mules," Woodfoot said. "I'll get a horse after breakfast and haze him back in."

"Naw," Charley said. "One mule wouldn't take out all by itself. By God, we'll be lucky if there's ary one left."

Sandy sat up looking puzzled. "Buffalo must have pushed em out," he said. He was too puzzled to look guilty, Woodfoot thought. He was glad Sandy did not know the truth.

"I'll go take a look," Woodfoot said.

He dressed and started out, surprised to find Charley following.

When they reached the draw, Charley was in the lead. He took one look, then got down on his hands and knees to study the tracks coming out.

"They're gone all right," he said. "Just as I thought. And no buffalo pushed em out either. They was drove out of here — unhobbled to boot."

"Looks that way, don't it?" Woodfoot agreed. "Indians, maybe."

Charley shrugged. "Maybe."

Woodfoot was surprised that he was not more enthusiastic about the suggestion.

Charley went back up the draw a way, studying the tracks, but the grass was too thick there, Woodfoot knew, to reveal much. Finally he came back out and headed for camp, walking fast. The first thing he did when he reached camp was to look in the wagon. He lifted the canvas and looked in, then just stood there gripping the endgate, stunned.

"What's the matter, Charley?" Woodfoot asked. "Ain't a ghost in there, is there?"

"She's gone," Charley whispered. He was not accusing anyone, nor even speaking to anyone. His hands on the endgate began to shake, his face paled, and for a little it looked like he would faint. Instead he leaned over and puked. And he kept on puking even after his stomach was empty.

Sandy had been building a fire. He came over now. "You got any more whiskey, Woodfoot? Give him a nip. It'll settle his stomach."

Woodfoot hesitated. "It'd be better just to put him back to bed."

"Bed, hell," Charley protested between spasms. "We got to light out after that stock."

Woodfoot brought another bottle, his last. "Here it is, Charley, the hair of the dog. Snake, that is. Take a big one or it'll just bounce."

Charley only smelled it and went into another spasm.

"Lay down and take it easy, Charley," Sandy said. "When the heaves stop, take a drink. Me and Woodfoot'll fix up a bite to eat."

"No, by God," Charley said. "We got to start movin or we never will catch her. By God, she was smart, wasn't she?" He started off toward the mule, heaving as he walked. Sandy caught him and pulled him back.

"Take it easy, Charley, you'll just keel over if you try to move now. Woodfoot here can bring in that mule quicker than you can walk out there. And while he's gone I'll fix breakfast."

Charley allowed himself to be led back to his bed and lay down, still racked with dry heaves.

The mule turned out to be the crazy jenny. Woodfoot caught her easy enough, but it took him a while to get on her. And when he did, she stood there shaking, looking back at him over her shoulder. After a lot of talking and babying he got her around the bend out of sight, then he got off and led her. He found the rest of the mules a little farther on, grazing up on a sidehill. The damn things would have been miles away, any other time, Woodfoot mused.

He caught the old grey, hazed the others on along the trail, and rode back into camp leading the jenny.

"The first ones I come to," he apologized. "The rest was way the hellagone down the trail."

Charley didn't even look up. He was sitting by the fire holding the bottle. He must have had a drink and was concentrating on holding it down.

Sandy smiled, seeing the mules. "You can give me the old grey," he said. "He's just about my style."

Charley stood up, as if to go, but he sat down again quick, holding his head.

"Get some coffee in you now," Sandy told him, "and maybe a little meat. You'll be good as new."

He looked so miserable, Charley did, that Woodfoot felt a little sorry for him. He almost regretted bringing in the crazy mule. But it was done now, and the delay might do some good.

Charley looked better after breakfast. He had managed to drink some coffee and eat a little, but he still looked pretty peaked.

Sandy took the grey and Woodfoot brought the jenny over to Charley.

"She ain't broke so good for ridin," he told Charley. "You got to treat her kindy easy."

"Hell," Charley said. "Didn't I see you on her a little bit ago?"

Woodfoot nodded.

"Well," Charley growled. He put a loop on her nose and climbed on, giving her a good boot with his heels when he got his seat.

The mule squatted and stayed that way for just a second. Then she shot up, arching her back like a cat.

Charley sailed gracefully over her head, turning over in the air and coming down on his shoulder. He rolled over a couple of times and sat up, drawing his gun all in the same motion.

Woodfoot felt a stricture of his breathing and tensed for the shot, resisting an urge to duck.

But it was the mule Charley was watching. She was already running, holding her head out to the side, dragging her rope. Charley's shot took her to the side of the head just over the eye, and she did a somersault, landing on her back and rolling onto her side. Her feet kept galloping for a while after she dropped.

It had all happened so suddenly it was hard to believe it was over. But it had been close, Woodfoot knew. He had almost stopped a bullet for his pains.

Charley still sat on the ground looking numb and sick. His breakfast almost came up, but he put his hand over his mouth and swallowed hard to keep it down. When he stood up he was sweating.

"I'll take this mule," he said, shakily. "I'll get me another as I go by and start the rest back this way. I'll look for tracks where we came down out of the hills, and if I don't find anything I'm comin back. I got a hunch she went the other way." He rode off then and they stood watching.

"Things are lookin good," Woodfoot observed.

"Yeah," Sandy said, not very heartily. "The poor son-of-a-bitch."

"The time to feel sorry for Charley," Woodfoot said, "is when he's pullin his gun. Me, I ain't got it in me."

"You had a close call," Sandy told him soberly. "Damned if you ain't got a genius for rilin him. You're gonna set your spurs too deep though, if you ain't careful."

"Just tryin to help."

"I know," Sandy said quickly. "I appreciate it. I ain't been givin you much support either."

"Actin ain't your long suit, I got to admit," Woodfoot grinned.

"It ain't that. If I could hate him I'd do all right. I ain't sayin I like him. I just don't hate him."

"Well, anyhow, all you got to do now is sit tight and keep your mouth shut. She's got enough start to where he'll never in God's world catch her. Not on a mule, anyway."

"Maybe," Sandy said. "I'm gonna stay with him, though, in case anything turns up."

"Like what?"

"Suppose he gets hold of a horse, or something."

"Fat chance. If I was you I'd stay as far away from him as possible."

"Naw. I'll bring the mules in and catch him when he comes back this way. It's the thing I got to do."

He found a rope and went on down the trail, walking softly and awkwardly as a bear, with the same look of drowsy, latent strength.

Woodfoot stood looking after him feeling puzzled and regretful. And yet he had done all he could. All he could do now was wait.

CHAPTER
21

Sandy was waiting in camp with an extra mule when Charley came back through. It was still early in the forenoon, but the clouds had broken and were moving now, slowly and ponderously, overhead.

Charley came all the way up the valley at a gallop, pounding the mule at every jump with a thick piece of green willow. When he stopped the mule spraddled its legs and stood head down, breathing through its mouth in long noisy gasps.

"By God," Charley said sarcastically, "I see you been waitin faithfully. You might, by God, have done a little ridin yourself, seeing that you lose a horse too. What in hell are you hangin around here for?"

"You said you'd be back through," Sandy said.

"I said 'maybe.' How did you know she went the other way?"

"Take it easy, Charley," Sandy said quietly. "It just seemed like the logical thing to do, that's all. It's what I'd have done myself."

"Well, why in hell didn't you take out after her, if that's what you thought?"

"To tell you the truth," Sandy said openly, "it'd suit me just as well if you didn't catch her."

"I can see that. But for Christ sake, even if she ain't your woman, you lost a horse and saddle."

"It ain't what I'd kill myself to get back. Or her either, for that matter."

"Well, it's a hell of a note that I can't get just a little help in this goddamn camp."

He switched his bridle to the other mule and mounted. "At least," he admitted, calming down a little, "you got a mule in for me. That's somethin."

Woodfoot had been watching Sandy from where he stood by the wagon, a look of consternation on his face. He put his hand over his mouth whenever he caught Sandy's eye.

Sandy suddenly felt grateful to him for his concern. As he mounted he winked and pointed his finger at Woodfoot, like a pistol, crooking it and clucking his tongue. He rode off smiling. For once Woodfoot missed the humor of the situation. He stood there looking as if he'd lost his best friend.

At the buttes they met another herd of buffalo coming through and had to ride off the trail and wait while it passed. Charley sat his mule nervously, cursing the delay.

"If I had my rifle," he complained, "I could at least make some hides and give Woodfoot somethin to do. But by God everything's gone wrong — the lousy cold weather, the damn buffalo so thick you can't get through. Millions of em," he said, looking out into the distance, "millions of em and no gun."

He rode over and tried shooting with his .45, but mostly he wasted his shells. He dropped some but most of them went on down with the herd. He kept at it till he was almost out of shells, then rode back over to Sandy.

"At least I speeded em up," he said. "It'll save some time." He got down to wait. "By God, I hate a mule. They ain't no more fit to ride than a cow."

The buttes were high. Beyond them the land sloped off into

gentle hills that stretched off to the north brown and oval under the broken sky. Spots of sunshine moved across them with yellow, brilliant color, and herds of buffalo marked them in black living patches. Here and there the lines of dry creek beds wandered off toward Sand River showing little stretches of trees or brush. Sandy could see pieces of the river, crooked segments of narrow grey ribbon far down to the west.

On to the north, past the old camp, a patch of sunlight touched the Medicine Rocks, and for a moment he saw them clean and white as snow. But when the light passed they disappeared into the grey distance.

East the land sloped upward to the high butte country and north, to the divide between Sand River and Antelope Creek. He remembered the day he had ridden up there and looked down on the same country he was seeing now, the beauty of it striking him like the cut of a knife. There had been a nostalgia in his feeling then, a sense of loss, of the land changed and violated; a sense of looking for the last time at a place he had loved.

But it was different now, the way he felt, as different as the land itself looked. It was cold and there was no color in all the grey world save the yellow of the rare spots of sunlight and the blue patches of sky where they broke through.

Yet for all that, there was a warmth and beauty that stirred him deeply — it was like coming home. It was strange, he thought, how a man changed, not knowing it from within himself but only seeing it in the way things looked, things that did not change so much themselves. His life, he realized suddenly, had become important to him again; and in that moment he thought with regret of the chances he was taking with it.

He smiled at his fearfulness. Ironically, he thought, what he was doing now was probably the source of his strength. That it would be dangerous he had known when he started out, so there was no room for regret. Action was a requisite of manhood and it was almost always dangerous.

The herd passed and they rode on down, Charley taking the lead, hurrying his mule so that Sandy could hardly keep up. Waiting, Charley had been distracted, explosive, as if all the forces in him could not be contained in one place. Now, moving, he was again drawn together and purposeful. He was after something now, hunting.

Riding a little way back watching him, Sandy was suddenly struck with the impossibility of ever knowing him. Thinking of Charley without seeing him, Sandy remembered only his face, the mournful hungry expression, the distracted eyes. But in motion he was different; there was a gracefulness in the way he moved, a concentration; a kind of beauty. He looked good riding, even on a mule. He had square shoulders and a long straight back that bent easily at the waist with the motion of the animal. The way his arms moved, the set of his neck, all were in perfect accord. It was strange, he thought, that the memory should be so far from the man he was seeing.

They rode steadily after that. There were no tracks for Charley to follow with all the buffalo moving, but neither were there any forks in the trail. So he was guessing right. The test would come, though, where the old trail forked off for the Musselshell — if he guessed right there he would have to be delayed. It was a long stretch across there, and only one trail, maybe two days' ride — with the baby she could not ride much at night. She had maybe ten hours lead now; give her that much more she would be safe. There would be too many trails behind her for him to work out. Well, Sandy thought, he would arrange the delay when the need came — there was no use worrying ahead. Very likely it would work itself out anyhow.

They were traveling through country now that they had hunted in the spring, and it was all familiar. There was no change except the season's change. The grass was bleached to a yellow-grey, cropped close and trampled far out on each side of the trail and dotted with buffalo droppings. Along the draws and coulees the brush and trees were leafless, the only green the faraway cedar on the divide and, along the trail the light dusty color of prickly pear under the white whiskering of their spines.

Carcasses of buffalo they had killed showed white now against the hills, the flesh torn off by animals or what was left shrunken and bleached, clinging to the white bones in shreds. Only the unskinned legs and the heads of the bulls showed dark now; the shriveled black nostrils, the shining jet of the horns. Another year and only the skeletons would show. They were durable, the bones.

And yet for all the country's familiarity, he had remembered it only vaguely. He was seeing it vividly, the way he would remember it from now.

It was after dark when they reached the old camp. The clouds had closed in solid and the wind died. The darkness was so complete they could never have found the camp except that the mules pulled off the trail by instinct and went down to it. They found the shack by feel and built a fire to warm up some meat. While they were eating, some snow fell and Charley almost cried for anger and frustration. "Of all the damn luck," he kept saying. But the snow stopped and was gone by morning.

Charley awakened him at the first show of light, and they went on, coming in sight of the Rocks sometime before noon. Seeing the Rocks he thought of Charley's saddle horse. She would have left him tied somewhere among the Rocks and it would be up to Sandy to find him. He would arrange it, somehow, on the way back.

"If we don't find any tracks at the forks," Charley said, "we'll take the trail over to the Musselshell. I doubt if she'd try to cross the Missouri this far down."

Sandy said nothing. There was no use, he knew, in trying to change Charley's mind. Well, they would have to swim the river — that would maybe be a good chance to cause some kind of delay. If worst came to worst, he could always put a gun in Charley's back and make him stop. He thought of it, and yet he knew he would never do it. He was certain that Charley would try to fight and he would have to shoot him. It would be impossible.

They were almost to the forks of the trail when they saw the horse. He was grazing off to the right of the trail, his lead rope tied up around his neck.

"By God," Charley said, "my luck's changin. He must have got away from her."

"He was turned loose, with his rope done up like that. Somebody turned him loose."

"What do you mean, somebody?"

"It don't look like she would, does it?" Sandy countered.

He was amazed and chagrined. Surely the woman would not

have done it. And suddenly it struck him — the old man. The old man he had seen there when he killed the white buffalo. It was the only answer — and his own fault, since he had forgotten. But he had not really forgotten; it was just that he had not quite believed in the old man. There had been too much unreality and strangeness connected with him; he seemed like part of a dream.

He should have told her to leave the horse some other place — or not at all. But it was too late now. Charley was already riding off the trail toward the horse. Once he got aboard, Sandy knew, he was almost sure to catch her.

He swore at himself briefly for getting into such a fix. He could not shoot Charley down from behind; and in a gun fight he would not stand a chance, not even to cause a delay. It had to be something else.

He had been following Charley automatically. Now he stopped by a little clump of prickly pear and dismounted, pretending to make water. When Charley went on he cut three or four of the flat pear-shaped joints, and barehanded, put them in the pocket of his coat. Then he rode on after Charley, only half aware of the stinging where the spines had pierced his hand.

They had a hard time catching the horse. He was shy of the mules, and every time they came close, he would tear off at a high run, moving northeast toward the Medicine Rocks — back, Sandy guessed, toward where she had left him.

The delay annoyed Charley, but he kept at it patiently, knowing that if the bay made a break past them and got on the trail back to camp, they would never catch him.

The horse kept moving on toward the Rocks, entering the creek bed near the place where Sandy had shot the white buffalo, then going downstream. They could hear him racking through the little pools of the almost dry creek, though he was out of sight.

Charley cut off downstream and headed him, and they bottled him up in a steep-sided wash that led off toward the Rocks. They stopped at the mouth of the wash, and Charley dismounted, taking the bridle off the mule and tossing the lead rope to Sandy.

As soon as Charley entered the wash, Sandy got off and led the mules upstream out of sight. He tied up the lead rope of Charley's mule and the bridle reins of his own, and, one after the other, he slipped a joint of the prickly pear under their tails.

The mules took out upstream, their tails tucked down hard on the stinging cactus, grunting and bucking, but at the same time not forgetting to run. They fogged through a big pool of water and climbed the bank, heading south toward camp as they disappeared.

He hurried on into the wash after Charley and helped him corner the bay at the end of it. Charley caught the horse and slipped on the bridle.

"You can take those damn mules back to camp," he told Sandy "I'll do some ridin now."

Sandy said nothing but moved closer to the horse, smiling inside himself at the irony of Charley's last remark.

Charley gathered up the reins and jumped onto his belly across the horse's withers. He was just throwing his leg over when Sandy lifted the bay's tail and slipped the joint of cactus under it like a crupper.

The bay clamped down with his tail, pulled his rump under him and scooted down close to the ground for a few short jumps; then he gave a squeal and started throwing high ones. In the first few jumps before the bay got his head, Charley latched onto a handful of mane. He hung on tight, and for a few seconds he made a beautiful ride. It was beginning to look like he would last till the horse started running when, at the top of a jump, the mane came loose. Charley sailed up and out still holding the handful of mane. He came down on his feet on the sloping side of a cave-off and fell, rolling to the bottom. He sat up facing the mouth of the wash just as the bay made the turn and headed up the creek bed, running now, his tail clamped tight to his rump.

It had been a mean thing to do, Sandy thought, but comical too. And seeing Charley get up unhurt, he could hardly keep from laughing.

Charley turned toward him, his face pinched with anger, his eyes white and wild.

"By God," he shouted, "you done that!" He stayed in the same spot, his feet spread out, his body easy and loose, except for the hand that hung hawk-like over his gun.

Sandy stood there, saying nothing.

"I'll kill you for that," Charley told him, his voice hardly more than a whisper, but tense and squeaky. "By God, I can see now you been at the bottom of it all along."

Sandy still did not speak or move. He felt hypnotized under Charley's stare, fascinated. It struck him as odd, then, that he should not be afraid — mostly he just felt drowsy.

"You damn coward," Charley hissed. "Will you stand there and be shot like a lousy buffalo? You got a gun, now use it!"

Sandy knew he would have to move; he did not feel like shooting at Charley, even in the face of the threat — but he would have to try. His hand felt cold and stiff above his gun.

Still he hesitated, watching Charley, conscious suddenly of the grey carved sides of the wash, steep and smooth as the walls of a grave. Above and behind him were the Rocks. He remembered them now, even as he moved, as he had seen them in the night, washed and gleaming in the moonlight.

His hand moved with dreamlike slowness; his gun came up, not even clearing the holster before the first shot struck him, throwing him backward with terrible force. His gun kept coming up and the next shot struck him in the side. He pulled the trigger in darkness, feeling the leap of the gun, but hearing no sound . . .

CHAPTER

22

CHARLEY SAW THE SECOND SHOT STRIKE SANDY and turn him halfway around just as his gun cleared the holster. The gun came up slowly, pointed off at the side of the wash and fired, caving a slab of dirt off where the bullet hit. The echoes of the shot died far off among the rocks and he could hear then the raining sound of dirt where the slab had fallen. Sandy went to his knees slowly and stretched out face down like a man going to sleep.

Charley stood there, holding his breath, listening, with the feeling that he would hear something, that something sudden would happen. But there was nothing; not a breath of wind or the sound of any living thing; nothing but a pulsing ringing in his ears.

The powder smoke from his two shots hung in front of him, blurring his vision, choking him. Over the square-sided wash the clouds were low and flat as a lid, dirty-looking and oppressive.

He holstered his gun and walked over to Sandy, stumbling, a tingling sensation in his legs as if they had been asleep. He saw Sandy through a haze, even when he bent down close, and he saw no sign of life. He could not bring himself to touch the still form.

He turned then and ran, coming out into the creek bed with a momentary sense of relief — as if he had expected the mouth of the wash to be closed off and himself walled in. But he kept running, climbing the steep bank of the creek on all fours and heading south toward the old camp.

He ran wildly, not looking ahead or back, nor even thinking, but concentrating wholly on moving. He had no sense of time passing nor distance, so that when he fell in complete exhaustion, it seemed like he had only just left the wash. He lay face down, his eyes shut and pressed tight against his arms till the urgency of his breathing subsided. Gradually he became aware of a damp coldness on the back of his neck, and raising his head, he saw that it was snowing. The air was damp and warm and the big flakes fluttered down like small white birds, to disappear in the grass.

He stood up, still weak and breathless, but his sight cleared. He walked to the top of a ridge and searched the country for the horse and mules, seeing them finally through the dimness of the falling snow, three scattered dots off to the south moving away from him along the trail.

He stood a moment, searching for any other sign of life, but there was no movement nor any sound save the hiss of falling snow. There was not even a bird or a rabbit. He felt suddenly small and exposed there on the hill, and hurried on toward the animals, feeling a need of them that was more than just the need for a mount.

He gained on them slowly, coming up with the horse about half way to the old camp. The mules were on ahead, traveling steadily, but the horse was stopping now and then to graze. When Charley came close, he raised his head and trotted off, switching his tail vigorously. He had broken off both bridle reins stepping on them, so there was nothing now to slow him down.

It went on that way clear to the old camp — he would get close, sometimes almost close enough to touch the bay, only to have him break away and stop again a hundred yards or so farther on. He tried circling to cut him off in front, but the horse kept warily just ahead of him. Anger grew in him till he could hardly contain it. Repeatedly he stifled the urge to shoot the horse, directing his anger at Sandy and Woodfoot for the trouble they had caused him.

Near the old camp the horse came down to the river where the
mules were grazing and Charley drove him into the corral by the
shack. Leading him by the cheek strap, he caught Sandy's mule
and switched bridles. Then he mounted and lit out north again at
a run, pounding the bay with his heels.

It was snowing harder now. The ground was white, but wet and
slippery from the snow that had melted. He could hear mud and
snow from the bay's hooves raining on the ground behind. Coming
up out of the flat he saw the river off to the left, black as ink beyond the swirl of snow; ahead and to the right he could see nothing but the falling snow. The grey light was shadowless, giving
the ground an illusory flatness. Under the mask of whiteness, the
familiar country had turned suddenly strange. He rode with his
head down to shield his eyes from the snowflakes, knowing the
contour of the ground only through the feel of his horse.

The bay dropped gradually to an easy lope, and Charley held
him there, leaving him to pick his own way through the increasing
snowfall. He settled into a drowsiness after that. In the open
country he could not tell where he was, nor guess the time by light
or shadow. He seemed to travel continuously in an enclosure of
space no bigger than a room.

Toward evening the snow slacked off and the range of his vision
increased. The clouds thinned in the west till a misty shadowy light
came through, giving the snow a brilliant whiteness. Against it the
Rocks looked grey and bleak.

Farther on the bay turned off the trail of his own accord and
headed toward the Rocks. Charley reined him roughly back onto
the trail, turned left at the forks and came down to the river. He
stopped at the edge of the ford to let his horse drink; but afterwards he could not go on. He had an intense perception of darkness gathering, of winter and the loneliness of the trail ahead. He
sat there numb and suspended with no power of will to move.

A wolf howled from the dusk across the river, a lonesome fearful sound that rose through the silence, sending a chill through him.
He let the reins go slack in his hands and the bay turned and went
back along the trail. Beyond the forks Charley turned off, steeling
himself for what was ahead. He was losing precious time, he
knew, but he could not go on without taking one more look.

He could not leave Sandy for the wolves to tear.

He struck the creek above the wash and turned downstream, pausing a moment before going into the wash. Then he kneed the bay resolutely and rode on in.

It was half dark now; the bottom of the wash lay clean and unbroken between the raw grey walls. Along the sides where dirt had caved off, there were smooth white mounds. But the middle, where he had last seen Sandy, was flat and even as a floor.

At first he was only startled, but as he searched the wash clear to the head still finding no sign, terror struck him sharply as a thrown knife.

He reined his horse around, drawing his gun, and looked upward and back along the wash, half expecting the crash of a rifle. But he saw nothing. With his gun still drawn, he rode back along the wash and out, his heart thundering in his chest. He forced himself to search up and down the creek bed, and came at last back to the wash unable to believe his senses, and rode up and down it till there was hardly a foot of it unmarked by the muddy prints of his horse's hooves. He thought of getting off to search more carefully, but he did not. He could not bring himself to step down onto the muddy floor of the wash.

He gave it up then in the falling darkness and rode out of the creek bed at a run and back toward the river. The bay slowed at the ford, but Charley forced him on out till he was belly deep in the dark water.

But he did not go on. He stopped and stared at the black, faintly shining expanse swirling and coiling ahead of him, and beyond it the white hills sweeping upward untracked and stainless.

He was struck by a sudden overpowering aversion to the water, a strange, premonitory feeling that its deep blackness would stain him or destroy him if he entered. He could not go on.

He turned once more and rode back along the trail, shutting his ears against the far lonesome cry of the wolf across the river.

CHAPTER

23

THE SUN WAS NOT YET UP WHEN THEY PASSED the summit of the Antelope Creek divide and started down. But eastward the far white edge of prairie turned upward in sudden coppery light, fading above to a brassy yellow against the sky. There was no wind and no clouds that Jimmy could see, only a pale, luminous sky that darkened behind him toward the west where a few stars were still showing.

He paused at the top to rest his horse and Woodfoot and Charley went on, dropping out of sight as the trail entered a coulee. In the cold quiet of the air he could hear their horses' hooves grinding the frozen snow. Then the sound was gone and he was completely alone on the summit and there was nothing. The frozen white earth stretched off east to the bright limits of the sunrise and in all that space he could see no sign of life. The sun pushed up a curving edge of fire, touching himself before it touched the land below; the almost imperceptible warmth on his face spread through him like the feel of whiskey. He felt strong and clean, but suddenly lonely, as if there were no other like him in all the glittering white world.

He reined his horse onto the trail and started down. But he was in no hurry to catch the others; he needed the time to himself, and it was the first he had had in almost three months, the first day with no buffalo to skin.

It was Christmas day — not that it mattered much to him — but Charley and Woodfoot had got wind of some kind of celebration at a hide station that Black had set up across the divide. They had lit out bright and early, all decked out in their best clothes, leaving him to come or stay as he chose. He was following out of curiosity mostly, not anticipating much pleasure. A lot of buffalo hunters it would be, probably, and a lot of whiskey. Well, he would have a try at the whiskey; and as long as there were no women around, he might make out.

It was Letty, he thought, who had caused him all the trouble. She was the first white woman he had ever known, and even now he could not understand her. He could not reconcile the way he felt about her with the way she acted. She was like two people, and only one of them a natural woman; the other he could not understand at all except that in a vague way she reminded him of Charley. Maybe the ambiguity was a quality of white people, something he would have to learn to accept.

He remembered how he had felt about her the first time he met her, seeing her as desirable and desiring him — he knew she felt that way as much as he — and he was sure of her then, even after he woke up in the alley with a knot on his head and no money. He was not so sure now.

He could not quite trust his feelings any more. And yet it was the only way he could ever know anyone — he did not have the mind for analyzing people the way Woodfoot did, nor the detachment. And he would never trust it if he did. There was a necessity within him for being close to people with his total self; this itself requiring a total judgment which was too finely shaded and complex for his mind to handle. He had to depend on his instinct. And maybe it was right.

He could not believe that Letty's dishonesty was real, that it was true to the way she was deep down. It was something put on like the fancy clothes she wore. That was the way he felt. But right or wrong, it did not help him much in knowing how to act.

That first time he met her and wound up in the alley, he had come to think of as none of her doing. He found out later who it was that hit him — a faro dealer by the name of Thimmes who was known chiefly for the fast and reckless way he handled a gun. He was a sallow, skinny little man with a face like a bird and a way of regarding you with the corner of his eye as if you were some kind of bug he might take a notion to eat. He moved quickly and in spurts, jerking his head with each step, and he had thin, womanish white hands. What his connection with Letty was Jimmy did not know, but he was always around when there was trouble over her — which was quite often. And it seemed like every one in Sandpoint was afraid of him.

He had been around the next time Jimmy saw her, after he had taken the freighting job with Black. It was his first trip with the outfit — a freight wagon with two trail wagons and a twelve mule team, loaded with hides to go down the river. Woodfoot helped him get lined out and started down the road. He was riding the near wheeler, controlling the leaders with a jerk line, and he was doing all right until he reached the middle of town.

The street was clear ahead when suddenly a woman left the sidewalk to cross in front of him. She paused at the side of the street and he thought she was waiting for him to go by, so instead of stopping, he swung over to the left a little to give her more room. But she started moving again, directly into his path; and as she looked toward him he saw that it was Letty. In the shock of recognition he forgot to yell Whoa; instead he tried to swing back to the right. But he forgot how many times to jerk on the line, and the leaders kept swinging left, directly toward her. She got scared then and started to run, but she tripped in a rut and fell in a ruffled heap of petticoats and skirts. He heard shouts of laughter from some men on the sidewalk — and heard it cut off short as Thimmes stepped out into the street to help her up.

The mules, still swinging to the left, turned short of her and made a half-circle in the wide street. And Jimmy was tangled in the slack of the jerk line, looking right into the eyes of his leaders.

A man yelled, "Look out for Injuns, boys, he's fortin up!" and peals of laughter rolled along the street. He slid off then and caught the leaders and led them back around to get them straightened out, hearing the laughter and banter from the sidewalk, aware dimly that she was no longer in the street.

He heard Thimmes say, "He thought it was himself comin back, but it was another jackass all the time."

He ran back along the still-moving line and climbed the near wheeler again, seeing as he passed that Letty was back on the same side of the street she had started from, looking red-faced and ruffled. But she was laughing at him too. Hearing her laughter, he did not mind the others, not even Thimmes.

He was back a few days later in the evening, and he searched for her through the town, meeting her finally on the street, alone. She walked deliberately into his arms and relaxed against him, her eyes warm.

He was too surprised to act, or even speak; and she pulled away as quickly as she had come and went on along the sidewalk without having spoken. He waited a moment, recovering, then out of the exuberance of his feeling, he cut loose with a yell that echoed raucously along the quiet street. She stiffened as if she had been hit and turned her head to look, tripping on an uneven board in the walk and almost falling again. He caught her eye, grinning, and yelled once more. Her mouth formed an O of indignation and she threw up her head and hurried on. He did not follow her, but he knew he would see her again.

He turned to go on and saw Thimmes coming toward him along the walk. His eyes were set straight ahead, looking beyond Jimmy as if he did not exist. Jimmy watched him curiously, wondering if he would change his course at the last instant. Thimmes came on, no change of expression on his face, his head jerking with each step and at the last possible moment Jimmy stepped aside and let him pass, noticing that in passing Thimmes regarded him speculatively out of the corner of his eye.

Jimmy stood looking after him, puzzled. He did not understand why he had stepped aside — he was not afraid — nor why the little beady-eyed man possessed so much assurance.

He met her again that evening in the gambling hall. He had
bought a drink and was idly watching the faro game when she
came out on the stage and sang. She finished, making a little bow
to the applause, and came down among the tables and along the
bar. She paused to drink with someone at the bar, a man in a black
suit with a tall, hard-boiled hat. He began trying in a drunk,
fumbling way to get his hand on her breasts, following her along
the bar. Smiling and unperturbed, she kept just out of his reach.
He stopped a moment to drink and fished a gold piece out of his
pocket and held it up to the light, moving it enticingly in front of
her. She snatched it dexterously from his awkward fingers; then
moving slowly for anyone to see, she dropped it in her dress between her white full breasts, moving her body in a mockery of the
way he had moved the gold piece. He reached toward her to touch
where the coin had touched, but she stepped back laughing and
slid a chair between them. He fell forward over it, spilling his
drink, and she left him, walking away among the tables, acknowl-
edging the laughter with the little bow she had made after the
song.

She came over toward the faro table then, smiling and talking on
the way, showing just a trace of surprise at seeing Jimmy, then
giving him a smile that was in no way different from the one she
gave to everyone.

"Are you playing?" she asked him.

He shook his head. "I don't savvy it."

"I'll show you." She stood watching him expectantly till he
realized she was waiting for money. He gave her five dollars and
she stepped to the table just as the deal was starting and laid the
five on one of the face cards painted on the table — a queen.

"You play against the house," she told him. "The first card wins
for them, the second for you."

The fourth card out of the box was a queen and Thimmes, who
was dealing, slid out a five which she tucked into her dress, leaving
the other on the table.

"You try it," she said smiling. "It's easy."

He tried it, winning once, then losing steadily till he ran out of
money and realized he had lost almost a month's wages. Letty was

still standing by him, having won almost as often as he had lost.

He held out his hand. "Give me a five," he said. "I'll pay it back."

She shook her head and her lips formed words, but they were drowned in the laughter of the other players. He looked around at them, seeing no friendly faces, puzzled and hurt by their derision.

"This buttermilk thinks he's hell with women, don't he?" Thimmes laughed.

When he turned to face Letty again she was gone and he saw her moving quickly among the tables toward the stage. A moment later she was singing again, smiling impartially at everyone, moving her body suggestively, beautiful as a ripe fruit. Under the stage lights her hair was alive as fire.

A big hairy-faced waiter bumped into him as he stood watching. "Excuse me, sonny," he said. "You want another drink?"

Jimmy shook his head. "I'm out of money."

"Well get the hell out of here then," the waiter told him. "This here ain't a hotel."

He hesitated, then went out and back to the room he shared with Woodfoot in the hotel.

Woodfoot was playing cards with himself. "You get her all tore up?" he asked.

"To hell with her," Jimmy said. He threw his hat on the floor and kicked it and began walking up and down.

The next time he saw her he was on his way to Miles City to pick up some mules for Black. Three or four miles out of Sandpoint he stopped to water his horse where the road came down close to the river. Seeing the water so clear and cool-looking, he rode down along the river and put his horse to graze in a grove of cottonwoods, then peeled down for a swim. Sitting on the bank afterwards, thinking about her, he heard horses. He walked back up the bank and saw a man and woman coming along the road.

The man was riding a big, slim bay that paced along sideways, fighting for his head. The woman rode sidesaddle on a little droop-headed buckskin. They came down to the river to water their horses and Jimmy stepped back into the trees. When he looked again he saw that it was Thimmes and Letty. She was red-faced from the heat and she looked uncomfortable and pouty as a little girl.

Thimmes dismounted and helped her down. He held the horses while they drank, then tied them to a willow bush up the bank. The two of them walked upstream to a log of driftwood and sat down.

Jimmy started to leave, then turned abruptly back through the trees till he was above the horses and moved down to them quietly and slowly. Keeping his eye on Thimmes, he drew the bay around behind the willow bush and cut the reins where they buckled to the bit, leaving little more than the natural hook of the leather holding. Then he went back to his horse, mounted and sat waiting.

After a while the couple came up onto the road again and started back toward town. He gave them time for a start, then put his horse onto the road at a run, and cutting loose with a string of warwhoops, bore down on them.

The big bay reared, looking back along the road, and started plunging. Thimmes was holding the reins with one hand, trying to dig his gun out from under his coat with the other — and the reins came loose. He lost his gun and almost lost his seat; but as he fell sideways he caught the horn and got back aboard. The bay took out down the road with his nose stuck out in front like an elk in timber, with Thimmes waving the reins helplessly and hanging on.

The buckskin was running now and Letty, scared white, was hanging on with both hands to the horns of the saddle, bouncing awkwardly with every jump. She was making no effort to control the horse.

For a while it looked like the buckskin would outrun him, and, seeing Letty's terror, he regretted what he had done. But gradually he came alongside and, catching hold of the bridle, pulled the buckskin to a stop.

Thimmes had gone out of sight over a hill, but Jimmy could still hear the pounding of the bay's hooves.

When the buckskin stopped, Letty almost fainted. She went limp in the saddle and he caught her arm to keep her from falling. She looked at him then, and suddenly the color came back into her face. Her eyes blazed and she started to speak. But the trembling of her lips kept her from saying anything and she started crying, covering her eyes with her hand.

He could think of nothing to say to her so he turned and led the buckskin back along the road to where Thimmes had dropped his gun. He picked it up without getting off and led the buckskin off the road, down into the trees.

She was still crying. When he dismounted, she slid off limply into his arms and burrowed her face against his shoulder, sobbing. He held her tight against him, brushing his face against her hair, till she stopped crying. Then, still holding her, he forced her head back with his chin and kissed her lips, tasting the salt of tears on them. She tried to hide her face again, but with one hand he caught her hair and held her head back, smiling at her till she smiled too.

He released her hair and she put her face back to his shoulder and her arms came up around his neck. She was soft in his arms now, and the smell and color of her hair was against his face like a flame.

He drew her over to a spot of grass under a tree and made her sit down. But as soon as she touched the ground she sat up straight and stiff, and the warmth of her went out like a match.

He touched her face, knowing the moment had passed. She shivered slightly and moved away, pulling the skirt of her dress up off the grass and brushing it.

"If you're worried about your dress," he grinned, "take it off and I'll hang it in the tree."

She shook her head, blushing. "Tim'll be back in a minute. He'd see us."

"Not right away. He was travelin too fast and in the wrong direction. Anyway we'll hear him."

She shook her head decisively. "I can't. Not here. For a minute I thought I was going to, but not now."

He looked at her hungrily, knowing that if he touched her again she would leave. Her skin, flushed from sunburn on her cheeks, was unbelievably white and transparent, shining with tiny beads of sweat on her forehead and along her lips. Her mouth was full and wide naturally but it was compressed now. There was a scattering of freckles on her nose, and her eyes were green. Her beauty was delicate and fragile as snow flowers and here, he thought, as out of place.

He looked away, clenching his hands, the need of her swelling and tingling through all his body. When he looked at her again an ant was crawling on her dress and she was brushing at it in panic.

She stood up then, looking around her through the trees. She looked scared, Jimmy thought, as if she had just awakened in a strange place — a fearful one at that.

He was puzzled. It was a friendly spot — the blue grass thick under the trees in the cool shade; cotton drifting down gently here and there and white as blossoms among the leaves. Near the river were thickets of chokecherry, shining with clusters of fruit and red and yellow wild currants. There was the soft sound of the river and a little breeze in the tree tops like breathing.

"Have a swim with me anyway," he offered. "The water's nice. I just got out."

"I know," she said, bending down and running her hand through his wet hair. "I'd like to go with you, but I can't. There isn't time. Tim'll be back and if he finds you with me he's likely to shoot you."

"Naw. I got his gun."

"You're a crazy kid. You haven't got sense enough to be afraid, have you?"

"I don't see much to be afraid of. Are you his woman?"

"In a way, but not exactly. We're kind of business partners. But he's jealous, anyway."

"Anyhow," Jimmy said. "You don't need to worry about him for a while. I cut his bridle reins, and that old bay was headin for town. He'll be lucky if he don't overshoot."

"I wondered what you did," she said, and there was a grudging note of admiration in her voice. "He'll be furious."

She went to her horse then and tried to get on, but every time she got her skirts hitched up far enough to put her foot in the stirrup, the horse moved sideways and lost her. After a few trys she turned to Jimmy, her eyes flashing with anger, her lower lip pushed out and starting to tremble again.

"You get that silly grin off your face and help me, you —

you—" She stamped her foot and turned to try again.

He came over and held the buckskin quiet, holding the stirrup for her with the other hand. She pulled her skirts up till he could almost see her knees; then seeing his face, she dropped them again.

"You're supposed to look the other way. You're not much of a gentleman."

"I don't know what that is, but it can't be much fun. Go on now, if you want me to help."

"Oh," she gasped, "if I had a club, I'd—I'd fix you."

He laughed delightedly. "I got one here that'd fix both of us if you'd just use it."

She blushed and almost smiled; and the light danced in her eyes. She pulled her skirts up with a flirt and, catching the handhold, swung herself up—awkwardly but showing as little of herself as possible.

"I hope you got an eyeful," she sniffed, putting her knee between the two horns.

"Not enough to blind me." He blinked his eyes, then told her seriously, "You ought to ride a regular saddle instead of this contraption, at least till you learn to ride. I don't see how it can hurt you to spread your legs a little as long as you stay on the horse." He paused and grinned at her, holding her eyes. "With all these horns, this one might do it even if you stay on."

"Do what?"

"Hurt you. The way I'd like to."

She kept her face straight, but he knew she was laughing inside.

"Give me his gun," she said. "And stay away from both of us for a while. I can control him up to a certain point, but after that— And you better not tell anyone what you did to him, either."

He shrugged. "I'll be gone for a while, so I can't do much different. But I'll be back."

"All right. Go on now, start riding, in case he tries to follow you."

"I ain't in any hurry."

Her eyes snapped and she started to say something, but she caught herself and rode up out of the trees. He watched her till she was out of sight, then turned reluctantly to his horse. It was a long ride ahead of him—and a long way back.

When he came back she was gone. He searched for her every time he was in town, but he did not see her again till late in the fall. He had brought a load of hides and meat in for Sandy and Charley and was getting ready to go back skinning. He settled up with Black and took his plunder over to the livery stable where his horse was. It was late afternoon, but he went back to the hall to have one last look for her. He bought a drink at the bar and searched the crowd, then stood looking pensively at the stage, drinking slowly, reluctant to leave.

The prospect of another season of skinning was not pleasant, but he had promised — so he had it to do. And he would not feel so bad about it, he thought, if he could see her again — if only for a few minutes.

He was almost ready to leave when a man left the crowd around the faro game, stopped at the bar beside him and ordered two drinks. While he waited, he turned to Jimmy.

"You look down at the mouth, son," he said. "You look as if you'd lost your best gal."

Jimmy smiled but did not answer.

"I see you standin here looking long-faced," the man went on, "and thinks I, maybe we could cheer each other up."

He was a little bleary-eyed man, dressed in a worn but well-pressed suit. As he talked he stood close to Jimmy, breathing in his face an acrid sickly smell. He winked and clapped Jimmy on the shoulder in a friendly, ingratiating way.

Jimmy said nothing. He did not like the stranger — and yet he seemed to mean well.

The bartender brought the two drinks and the man offered one to Jimmy. "Partners in gloom," he said. "Let's drink to better days."

Jimmy accepted the drink, not wanting to hurt the little man's feelings. He sipped it and thought he could taste the acrid bitterness that was on the stranger's breath, then brushed the thought aside as foolish.

"You look as if you'd lost your best gal," the man repeated.

"That's not a bad guess," Jimmy admitted. "What did you lose?"

"A little cash in a crooked faro game."

"You too?"

The stranger went on talking, but Jimmy paid no attention — because he saw her. She had come in the back way and was walking toward the stage, vivid and beautiful beyond all his memory of her.

He finished the drink, feeling lightheaded and needing to yell for pure joy. He was aware vaguely that the stranger was still talking, but he paid no attention, only nodding his head, keeping his eyes on Letty. The music started and she had not yet seen him — or she was pretending. He could not understand the words she sang but her voice was warm and clear, pulsing in him like the beating of his heart. It seemed like he stood a long time waiting for her to look at him; his eyes blurred as if he had kept them open too long, and she seemed to be farther away. Her voice had been strong and clear to him, but that too was growing fainter. He seemed to be floating upward, away from her.

The sensation was odd, suddenly frightening; and he tried to turn his attention inward. But his mind was sluggish; he could not seem to think.

Someone caught his arm and turned him around roughly. He recognized Thimmes standing beside the stranger in the blurry light, though both men seemed far away and indistinct.

Thimmes said, "This buttermilk thinks my game ain't on the square, does he?"

"That's what he says," the stranger replied.

Jimmy drew his hand across his eyes to clear them, and shook his head.

"He's bound to deny it," the stranger said.

He saw Thimmes square off to swing at him; and it seemed like he had plenty of time to move, but he could not. His muscles were slow and weak. The blow caught him on the cheekbone. He felt the impact but there was no pain, only a reddish flash of light; and suddenly he went down. The faces floating above him were hazy and unstable. He got to his feet and saw someone move toward him and there was another flash and he was down again. He still did not feel any pain, but all his muscles were rubbery and unreliable. He kept getting up but he could no longer distinguish objects. Finally he felt nothing but a sense of drifting. Around him moved a fantastic multi-colored play of lights and himself moving weightlessly among them . . .

He awakened gradually to an awareness of pain in his face and all over his body. He tried to open his eyes, but only one of them came open, and that only a little. He was on his back in bed and on the ceiling of the room a yellow, flickering light dimmed and brightened with the throbbing in his head. He shut his eye again and lay quiet trying to remember what had happened, but he could not. He remembered being at the bar and hearing Letty sing — but after that nothing.

He heard a movement, and someone put a cool wet cloth over his face very gently, left it a moment and took it away. He opened his eye again and turned his head, wincing from the soreness of his neck, and saw her hazily in the yellow lamplight, bending over a basin of water.

She was still dressed as he had seen her on the stage in the red-purple and the shiny bunch of flowers in her hair. Her face was flushed and tearful. When she turned toward him, he tried to smile but his lips felt inflexible, thick as rope.

She dropped to her knees beside the bed and put her face close to his, letting her hand fall lightly on his hair. "Jimmy," she said, drawing a long sobbing breath, "I thought you'd never come out of it." She dropped her face into the pillow and wept aloud.

He turned painfully on his side and put his hand on her hair, feeling weak and awkward.

"Aw," he said, "I ain't so bad off. I ain't dead."

She raised her head. "Not so bad off," she said indignantly. "He very nearly killed you, that's all."

"Who did?"

"Tim. Who did you think?"

"I don't remember much about it. Did I get in a fight?"

"A fight!" she said sarcastically. "It wasn't much of a fight. You kept getting up and he kept knocking you down. Damn you, why didn't you stay down? I couldn't help you. I couldn't even get close. You just kept getting up, and your poor face all bloody and surprised-looking. You make me sick," she exploded, and started crying again, burrowing in the pillow.

He sat up in the bed, feeling dizzy and sick, and dropped back weakly, shutting his eyes and gritting his teeth against the nausea.

Her hands came quickly to his face and she was kissing him

moistly and warmly. "You poor kid," she crooned, "Jimmy. Does it hurt so bad?"

"Naw, when you do that I feel fine."

"I don't believe you, you're crazy. Do you want anything?"

"Yes. You."

"I mean anything to eat or drink or something."

"Especially something."

"You stop it. I want to help you, and you act like there was nothing wrong. Stop it."

"I'm all right. I just feel weak and lightheaded . . . " His voice drifted off against his will. He wanted to go on talking to her, but she seemed too far away now, and he slipped off into darkness . . .

When he awakened again there was nothing. Turning his head he saw only blackness; and the thought came to him that he was blind. He sat up in a suffocation of fear, pushing at the darkness with his hands. He heard her beside him then and felt her hand on his shoulder pulling him back. He relaxed slowly and lay down, his heart still pounding.

"Is it dark?" he asked.

"Dark? Of course it's dark. Can't you see?"

"That's it, I can't," he laughed shakily. "I thought I was blind."

He heard her caught breath and felt her hand warm on his face. "You're always making me cry," she said tearfully. "I don't know what it is about you, but I can't help it. You're so kind of heart-breaking. You're so damned innocent," she said angrily into the pillow.

He reached over and touched her hair, lifting it and pressing his hand against the bare warm skin of her neck. She shivered and stopped crying and he could hear her breathing.

"Leave me alone," she said. "It makes me mad just to think about you."

He explored her shoulders, finding them bare; and suddenly he realized she was in bed with him. For a moment the thought took all his breath; his hand paused on her shoulder, warmly, and as if his feelings were pouring into her through his fingertips, she began shivering violently. She was tense and fearful in his arms, and it was a long time before she was wholly his . . .

He slept again, awakening into warm sunlight. He found her

watching him through half-closed eyes, her lips full and parted —
smiling. When she saw him awake she sat up and climbed out of
bed, keeping herself well covered with her night gown.

"Hey," he said in puzzlement, "what the devil! Come on back."

She turned to him, her fingers on her lips. "Be quiet."

"All right. But come on back."

"No. I won't."

"Don't you want to?"

"It isn't that."

"Why then?"

"Because I won't. I can't have a baby."

"Why not? It looks like you got all you need to work with."

"You're mean," she said pouting. "I mean I can't afford to. It
would spoil everything."

He settled back, considering the possibility, and he could not
help smiling.

"Don't you look so smug," she blazed at him.

"I can't help it if I like the idea. I just like it, that's all."

"You . . . " she said, and started to cry.

"Don't you like the idea at all?"

"No."

"I don't believe it."

She looked at him then and came and sat on the bed. "I guess
I like it a little," she admitted. "But I won't. I won't be poor all
my life. I'm making money now, and if I stay with it, I can live
like I want."

"How's that?"

"Oh, nice clothes, a nice home — a lot of things. But you have
to have money."

"I haven't got much money," he admitted. "But maybe I could
make some."

"How?"

"I don't know. Anyhow, you can't starve in this country."

"I guess you'd want me to live with you in a tepee."

"A tepee's nice in summer. And it ain't so bad in winter. But
I'd build you a house, if you'd like."

"A log house with a dirt roof, I suppose," she said bitterly.

"That a good kind. And chink it with cow cuts."

"Cow cuts?"

"Sure. But they got to be fresh. Best way is to catch em in a towel. You hold the four corners like this—" He took her handkerchief to demonstrate. "Then you stand in the middle of the floor, whirl it around your head a few times and turn loose of one corner. That fills up all the cracks," he explained gravely. "A cow can't do that."

She scowled at him, but he could see laughter in her eyes. "That's terrible. I won't."

"All right." He laughed happily. "I'll do it. You can watch— through one of the cracks."

She thrust her lip out in a pout and he pulled her down to him and kissed her. But she shivered and fought against him, scared and frantic, so he let her go.

"What makes you so scared?" he asked. "I can't do anything to you I haven't already done."

"I couldn't help that last night. But I can now. I don't want to hurt you, Jimmy."

"Hurt me!" He sat up in amazement.

"Be quiet," she said, pushing him back down. "Someone'll hear you."

She stood up and walked over to the mirror and studied her face. "I look different, don't I?"

"A little pinker, maybe. And juicy like an apple."

"No, not that. But it's something. Even after worrying about you all night. I look better."

"Sure," he said proudly. "Come on back."

She ignored him, asking later, "How do you feel?"

"All right, except kind of funny in the stomach."

"It serves you right for getting drunk."

"I wasn't drunk. I only had two—I bought one and some guy gave me one."

"Who?"

"A little bleary-eyed guy."

"Of course," she exclaimed. "I should have guessed. They drugged you, poor little simpleton." She came back and kissed him. "I think they almost killed you."

He tried to catch her again, but she avoided him and went into another room to dress. She came back later, completely changed, wearing a dress of dark, stiff material that concealed the roundness of her breasts and flared out falsely at the waist. Her face was paler and her luxuriant hair was done up tightly and covered with a hard little hat.

"I'll bring you something to eat," she told him. "After that I'll be gone the rest of the day. You'd better stay in bed for a while." Her voice was crisp, and when she was not speaking she held her lips together, compressing their fullness.

He shook his head.

"All right, I guess you don't have to. But I wish you'd wait till I've been gone a while before you leave — and try not to let anyone see you." She stopped, then went on to explain. "It's not that I'm worried about my reputation. Everyone thinks I'm just an expensive whore, anyway. But as long as they think I'm expensive enough, I don't care. They'll still pay to look at me."

"You mean I'm too poor?"

She flushed and bit her lip. "Maybe. Mostly I don't want Tim to find out. He might kill you."

He smiled at her and she softened a little. "Do you think I am?"

"What?" He grinned wickedly, "Expensive?"

"No!" She stamped her foot and he thought she would cry.

"I was foolin. I don't think you are. You wouldn't do good in that work. If it so happened I wasn't sort of foolish about you anyway, I think you'd have to pay me."

She stared at him a moment, lips trembling, then flounced out, slamming the door. She brought the food, opening the door quickly and setting the basket on the table, and left without a word.

Jimmy left a while later. At the livery stable he reached for his purse to pay the bill — and the purse was gone, and with it all that was left of his summer's wages.

The stable man laughed at him. "Jesus Christ, boy, is this the first you've noticed it? You look like somebody'd got your money all right, but not just recently. What happened?"

"I don't know," Jimmy said. "And that's the truth. I just don't know."

"Well, no money, no pony."

He borrowed the money from Black.

"I'm sorry you got hurt, Jimmy," Black said. "It's a shame. You're a good kid. But you got a lot to learn."

"How do you mean?"

"You trust everybody — and it ain't smart. To get along in this old world you got to be smart or tough, and you ain't either one, yet."

When he got back to camp there was work waiting for him. Buffalo were plenty and Charley was hunting in all the daylight, sitting up nights loading shells and taking care of his guns. He would not stop to help with the skinning. "Git all you can," he told them. "The hell with the rest. It's better to skin steady and lose a few than for both you guys to be waiting on me."

Woodfoot was way behind on the skinning, working and cussing when Jimmy got there to help. "This guy has gone kill-crazy," Woodfoot told him. "I just hope he sticks to buffalo, that's all."

It was cold, nights. The ones they left out unskinned were frozen stiff by morning. So they tried to skin the fresh kill in the mornings and get the old ones afternoons when the sun had thawed them out. But even with the two of them working they went behind. Some days they could not even get the fresh ones done; and when the older ones started to stink, they let them go.

Jimmy threw himself angrily into the work, taking a bitter pleasure in his own exhaustion, trying to cover with it his disquietude. He was dissatisfied with himself and the way he was living. A nostalgia for his old life with the Indians alternated with a desire to be white, to find his place among these men. And always Letty came into his thoughts. He thought of her now — he did not know why — with anger and resentment, ripping savagely at the hide of the animal he was skinning, or, if he were riding, drawing his pistol and shooting at something. He tried insistently to put her out of his mind, but she always recurred, disturbing even his exhausted sleep at night. It seemed to him that all it meant to be white — all the impossible things he could never be or understand, stood between them; and she beyond mocking him — and loving him too.

He drugged himself with work.

"What's got into you, Jimmy?" Woodfoot wanted to know. "You

go after this like a cat killin snakes. You tryin to work me down?"

"Naw, it ain't you. It's me. I ought to be draggin a log."

"Don't be too hard on yourself," Woodfoot said. "It won't get you a thing. Look what it got Sandy."

It was a week or two before he got the whole story about Sandy. At first Woodfoot was reluctant to say anything, but finally it all came out. "Don't say a word to Charley, though," Woodfoot warned him. "It'd be like throwin a match into a keg of powder."

"How did you find out, if you didn't ask?"

"He told me. He couldn't hold it in then. But I don't believe that about Sandy disappearing. My idea is that Charley killed him and when he went back he was too worked up to find the place."

"Did you take a look?"

"No," Woodfoot admitted. "He didn't let me out of his sight the first few days. By God, he had me spooked. He still has."

Jimmy could not believe Sandy was dead. He made a trip to the Rocks to find out, but turned back without really looking. There was snow on the ground, making a search impossible, and he did not like to go near.

He had not realized before how much he depended on Sandy. Now he felt lost and more alone than he had ever been.

So he worked, withdrawn, hardly aware of Woodfoot but watching Charley when the chance came, more curiously and coldly than he had ever watched a man before.

For a while Charley was touchy and irritable. It seemed impossible to say anything without offending him or to do anything that pleased him. So that after a while neither Woodfoot nor Jimmy would talk to him. At meal time and in the evenings — almost the only times they ever saw him — he would sit morosely apart, wolfing his food and rushing off to hunt or, if it were dark, to load his shells by firelight. And there would be talk only when he was gone.

Gradually he calmed down, but he would not talk — not even when he made a big stand. He would clean his gun and ride off with hardly a second glance, leaving them with fifty or sixty buffalo to skin and maybe three hours of daylight.

Then the two of them would sail into it, cussing the work — and Charley too, if he were not in sight — skinning as long as they could see, and if there was a moon, working at night, too. And like as not Charley would be out shooting again at daylight before Woodfoot and Jimmy even made it into camp. He never offered to help skin nor ever came near the hide grounds. He did not even count the hides to try to figure how much he was making. It seemed as if the only thing important to him was the killing, and he worked at that with absolute concentration.

He was shooting better than ever now — they rarely found an animal with more than one bullet in it — and he had a knack for picking the little bunches in the hills, the ones that were easy to handle. He worked systematically, trying to kill all the animals in each little bunch to keep them from mixing with the other herds — the remaining few in any bunch were always gun shy, and if they mixed with other bunches they would stampede at the first shot, ruining the chances of a stand.

Sometimes Jimmy would see him riding hell-for-leather after two or three buffalo — maybe only a couple of yearlings — and he would keep at it, riding the big bay hard enough to kill an ordinary horse.

"It may look foolish to go to all that trouble for a kip hide," Charley admitted. "But in the end it pays. The rest of the buffalo in this valley are tame as cattle, and that's why."

After a couple of months, he was talking again, but not much. He would explain his methods to Jimmy, telling in detail sometimes how he worked up to some particular kill. But there was an intentness, an inner concentration in his voice that made Jimmy uncomfortable listening. It was like hearing a man talking in his sleep.

And yet, as time went on he became more friendly toward Jimmy. "You got the makins of a good hunter," he would say, "and I can help you. I like you."

But Jimmy could not honestly return the feeling. He was curiously repelled by Charley's advances. But he forced himself to respond, feeling that if once he could understand this man he would know what it meant to be white.

To please Charley he began practicing with his pistol again, shooting from the wagon when they were moving or setting up targets around camp. Charley worked with him sometimes, showing him how to squeeze the trigger and how to move and how to stand — he had every phase of shooting thought out and he was anxious for Jimmy to get it right.

"It's a good thing for a man to know how to shoot," he would say. "He can make a living at it. And by God he can keep his self-respect."

Jimmy came finally to practice in all his spare time, not so much out of a desire to be good with a gun, but because it was an interesting and active distraction that kept his mind off his troubles.

Now, riding down off the divide, remembering, his hands dropped continually to his hip and fell away. He had left his gun at camp.

"You ain't good enough to carry it yet," Charley had told him. "You might get hurt. This is likely to be a rough bunch so you'll be better off without it."

For a long while before they reached the station Jimmy could see the smoke — a thin silver ribbon rising tall in the windless air — and hear shots, coming in little flurries but clear and sharp. Nearer, the smoke separated into three strands above a grove of cottonwoods, and through the trees he saw the building and the chimneys. There were bales of hides stacked outside and a corral full of horses beyond. Between the building and the corral some men were shooting with pistols.

They left the trail, coming out onto a flat that sloped down to the trees and ended beyond in a coulee. The flat was clean and glittering, unmarked except for the trail across it and a few outcroppings of rock that stood out darkly, trailing delicately molded, tapering drifts.

The building was made of freshly cut cottonwood logs, chinked with mud and straw, topped with a dirt roof which, except around the chimneys, was capped clean with snow. It was long and low, with half a dozen undersized windows and a lean-to on one side at the end. The clear area around the building was spotted with the stumps of trees used in the construction. In the middle of the clearing was the two-pronged trunk of a giant cottonwood that had been too big to use. It had been topped and the main branches hacked off fifteen or twenty feet above the ground, leaving the stubs extended upward like arms.

They put their horses in the corral and walked back toward the building, stopping for a while to watch the shooting. There were only two men shooting, the one big and bearded, dressed in buffalo-hide leggings, the other small and white-faced, in a fancy black suit. Coming closer Jimmy recognized the smaller one as Thimmes.

There were two men throwing up cans, putting them up at the same time and to about the same height. The big man was hitting his maybe one out of four, but Thimmes was getting at least half.

Charley watched quietly for a while, then, waiting till the cans went up together, he drew his gun and hit both of them before either of the other men fired. There was an astonished silence while Charley reloaded his gun and walked on toward the building. Some of the men tried to persuade him to come back and shoot some more, but he shook his head grinning.

"No," he said. "That was strictly accidental. I really can't shoot for sour apples."

They went on through the side door into the dim noisy interior of the building, stopping just inside to get used to the dark.

There was a bar across from the door, a double-decked rig of rough plank laid on saw horses with some plates of glass along the top. There were three bartenders, one of whom he recognized as the owner of Ed's Saloon in Sandpoint. Charley and Woodfoot went on over to the bar, but Jimmy stepped aside along the wall and stood there quietly watching.

The building was maybe thirty feet wide and fifty long, with the bar along the far side at the end and a counter extending from the bar almost the full length of the building, loaded with grub and supplies. There were three big funnel-shaped sheet metal stoves spaced out down the middle, each surrounded by a cluster of men drinking and talking. There were half a dozen card tables, all filled, and a faro game on down toward the end. At the far end, just beyond the last stove, two musicians, one with a fiddle and one with an accordion, were sitting up on a platform that was built on the stumps of four trees. They were playing but the music was hardly audible above the noise of the room. There were a few women in the crowd — he could hear, now and then, the high-pitched sound of their voices.

The far end around the platform was decorated with red and

green paper bells and paper streamers and colored ropes. In the middle, high above the platform, hung a shiny silver star.

The hides had all been moved out, but there was still the smell of them mixed with tobacco smoke, the sweet, sickly odor of burning tobacco-juice spit on the stoves and the smell of whiskey. There was the faint, clean, outdoor smell of sagebrush from a few stalks flattened to the ground where the hides had pressed them; and the smell of fresh-cut wood.

There was no floor in the building — the ground was smooth except for a few stumps sawed off close, and a few outcroppings of rock, and here and there a pressed-down stalk of sagebrush.

Looking toward the bar, he saw Woodfoot holding a drink out for him so he went over, just as Black came along the counter to the bar. Black shook hands with Charley.

"How's huntin?" he asked. "You got a few hides for me, I hope."

"Some," Charley said. "How many, Woodfoot?"

"Around three thousand, give or take a few."

"I don't believe it!" Black exclaimed. "Where's Sandy?"

"He ain't here," Charley said tensely. "Me and him ain't together now. He up and disappeared."

Black nodded. "I figgered he'd quit. And you got three thousand yourself and just Woodfoot to skin?"

"And the kid. By God, he's a good skinner."

There were others listening now.

"That's a slew of hides," a big mild-faced man remarked. "You must have a good spot. Where you located?"

"Across the divide on Sand River. A little valley in there. But I don't need any help. The way I hunt, those buffalo are tame as cattle, and that's the way I want em to stay."

"Hell, there ought to be enough for two, anyway. Maybe I'll come over. They're gettin scarce where I am."

"I wouldn't," Charley told him. "Unless you want to fight. And if that's what you want, we can take care of it right here." He was standing with his right hand resting on the bar, his left holding the tin cup of whiskey.

The big man studied him a moment, then his muscles seemed to sag and he turned away along the bar.

Charley laughed harshly and drank his whiskey.

The women were circulating through the crowd giggling and squealing, making quick trips to the lean-to with the men who would follow them. The lean-to, Jimmy thought, must be partitioned off, because they seemed to be running shifts of three.

There was a lot of shouting and swearing going on in the groups around the stove. In one of them the talk suddenly exploded into action. Two men disengaged themselves, whaling away at each other with their fists.

Jimmy saw one of the bartenders — a big slick-haired man with stiff mustaches — come over the goods counter and sidle up close to the fighters and stand there waiting.

For a while it looked like an even match, but suddenly one of them collapsed like a pole-axed steer and stretched out on the ground. The other dropped his hands and stepped back, and the bartender took him a short choppy lick to the side of the head and he went down a little way from the other. The bartender took him by the feet, dragged him out into the snow and came back for the other.

Jimmy left the bar then and moved on down toward the stage, stopping at the edge of the group around the last stove. He could hear the music now, and seeing Thimmes at the faro table he half expected Letty to appear from somewhere and start singing. But she did not. A light-haired, girlish-looking woman stopped plying her trade long enough to sing one song in a loud strident voice. When she finished she jumped down off the platform into the arms of the first comer and disappeared into the lean-to.

The musicians stopped playing to have a drink, then started again. He liked the music but it gave him a lonesome, sad feeling. When it stopped again, above the noise of the crowd he heard someone call his name. Glancing over, he saw Thimmes beckoning with his hand.

"Come here, kid," he called. "Make some easy money."

Jimmy shook his head.

"What's the matter, sonny, you afraid?"

"Naw. I played that before."

"You was just unlucky. Come on and try again."

Jimmy looked away without answering.

"Hey, I'm talkin to you. If I was you I'd answer."

"I ain't playin. I been bit by that snake once and that's enough."

"Meanin it's crooked, sonny?"

"Not meanin anything except I won't play."

"You're a sassy youngster. I got me a notion to take you down a notch."

Jimmy shrugged. "I ain't lookin for trouble. But I ain't playin faro either." He turned away, aware that the men around were watching him.

"You ain't much of a man, are you? Take anything, don't you?"

Jimmy did not answer. Glancing back he saw Thimmes coming toward him so he turned and Thimmes stood facing him.

"You said my game was crooked once before," Thimmes said. "Now you're gonna take it back."

"Naw, I won't."

"You askin for another lickin?"

"If I got one to take, I will," Jimmy told him. "Any time you're ready."

Thimmes hesitated. "You ain't gettin off so easy this time, sonny. You're big enough to fight like a man now." He unbuckled his gun belt and held it out to Jimmy.

Jimmy took the belt and Thimmes went back to the table and borrowed his dealer's belt.

"Don't be a damn fool, Jimmy," Woodfoot said. "Don't put that thing on."

Jimmy did not answer. He was suddenly sure he would be killed, but he would not back down. He would give it a try. He buckled the belt and looked up to see Charley standing at the edge of the crowd smiling.

Thimmes put the belt on and turned, his head cocked like a rooster's.

Charley spoke then, loud. "This might be a fair fight," he said to Thimmes. "But before you start, there's somethin you ought to know. This kid is the best skinner I got. Now if he shoots you, I won't object, but if it's the other way, it's gonna cost me money. And it's gonna cost you a damn sight more than that. Now, go ahead."

"Hell, Charley," Thimmes said. "I didn't know he was a friend of yours." He came over to Jimmy smiling, his eyes expressionless. "Put her there, kid," he said, extending his hand.

Jimmy ignored the hand. He unbuckled the gun belt, letting it drop to the floor, and turned away. He walked over to the stove thinking that maybe he should thank Charley, but feeling that somehow it didn't matter one way or the other; that what Charley had said about losing money had been very close to the truth.

He stopped by the stove, feeling lonesome and withdrawn, hearing no friendly sound in all the talk and laughter, no warmth.

There was a large outcropping of sandstone near the stove. It looked out of place, but somehow a friendly presence in all the strangeness. He sidled up to it now and leaned against it, running his hand over the familiar sandy surface as he listened to the music.

Woodfoot came up and gave him a drink. "Cheer up, for Christ sake, Jimmy. Christmas don't come but once a year."

"Thanks," Jimmy said, smiling.

"That's more like it. You know, I don't understand how such a likable kid as you can get into so much trouble. It beats me, it does now. Like with that damn gambler, what did he want to kill you for? You'll have to watch him from now on out. Keep away from him. I don't understand it."

The musicians hit up a lively tune, shaking the platform with their enthusiasm. The blond girl who had sung came out of the crowd, swinging her hips in time with the music. She passed the stove and seeing Jimmy turned, smiling at him familiarly.

"You're the nervy kid that almost got himself shot just now, ain't you, sweetie?"

She was not a girl, as he had thought, but a woman of maybe forty; and the realization shocked him. Her body was slender with virginal round breasts and slim waist, and she moved lithely and easily as a girl. It was her face that was old — lined and eroded-looking, smoothed over with a dead-white powder. Her eyelids were narrowed, almost concealing her eyes, giving him the odd feeling that she was wearing a mask; that she would remove it now and reveal herself as the young, beautiful girl he had thought her.

She stood waiting for him to answer, her smile fixed and without warmth.

"Can't you talk, sweetie?"

Jimmy nodded in confusion. "I guess it was me all right. I didn't think you'd seen it."

"I see a lot of things besides the ceiling," she laughed. "I think you're kinda cute." She leaned forward and kissed him on the mouth.

Her lips were dry and papery, dusty with powder, and she smelled of flowers and whiskey. She stepped back and stood watching him with the same immovable expression as before, and he dropped his eyes under her gaze, blushing.

"Bashful, too. Never been kissed before. But I think you're a man, anyway, sweetie. Come on."

Jimmy hesitated, but Woodfoot took his cup and gave him a shove. "Go on, damn it," he laughed. "It'll loosen you up a little. Take the stiffness out, so to speak."

She walked ahead of him into the lean-to and into a little cubicle curtained off with buffalo hides, shivering as she left the warm interior of the building.

"What a hell of a place to bring a woman," she complained. "Freezing and dirty and unpleasant. Christ, what a godforsaken country." She caught up a woolen robe off the bed and slipped into it pulling it tight around her, and turned the mask of her face on him, holding her hand out. He gave her ten dollars and she started to give him change but he shook his head. She took a roll of bills out of the pocket of the robe and wrapped the ten around it with a kind of tenderness. She stepped back then, undoing the robe, and tripped on a low stump. She fell backward across the bed and lay there without moving, swearing with a venomous anger that transfigured her face. She spit the words out and her eyes burned, traveling impartially over the rough ceiling, the walls and the buffalo-hide curtains, touching himself finally. Her face was shining and mobile, her eyes and teeth flashing.

She met his eyes and her face gathered itself again into the false smile, the color faded and the light died in her eyes. She sat up and began undressing under the robe.

He turned and went out, glancing back to see her face kindling

again in anger — or surprise. He went back to the stove and Woodfoot gave him his drink.

"Jesus, but that was a quick trip," he observed. "You didn't
hardly get your money's worth, did you?"

"All I wanted," Jimmy said, finishing his drink. He took Woodfoot's cup and his own and went back to the bar for drinks. Waiting, he heard someone shouting above the noise, and saw Ed, the
bartender, on the platform between the musicians, gesturing for
attention. When the noise quieted, he announced something about
a Christmas play and the singing of Christmas songs. He jumped
down and pushed the crowd back, clearing all the space between
the stove and the platform, then climbed back up.

Making his way back to Woodfoot, Jimmy saw two men bring
in a crate full of hay that he supposed was a manger, and set it
down in front of the platform. He found Woodfoot and Charley
together at the edge of the crowd near the stove, and they made
room for him between them.

He saw Ed on the platform paying out a small line that ran up
over a rafter. The star came down till it was just over the manger
and stopped as Ed tied the line. There was a lot of activity around
the lean-to. All the women and a few men had gone inside and
there was a lot of squealing and yelling going on. After a while a
man in a long white robe came through the doorway, leading a
reluctant burro. A woman was riding, sitting precariously sideways,
clutching fearfully at the burro's mane. She was dressed in a long
full dress with a white hood; he recognized her as the woman he
had been with.

The man stopped at the edge of the platform and made as if to
knock on a door. Ed stepped down and the two exchanged some
words that Jimmy did not hear. Then the man came on as far as
the manger, tied the burro to it and helped the woman down.

Three more of the girls and three men came out of the lean-to
then in single file, and lining up in front of the other players, sang.
They filed out again, revealing the woman sitting beside the manger
holding a baby — only he could see it was not a baby but a doll —
and the man standing beside the burro.

Three men in long robes, carrying shepherds' crooks, came in
then, carrying gifts in their arms and singing. They came slowly,

stopping in front of the manger and kneeling. They touched their heads almost to the ground, then still kneeling, held their gifts out toward the woman and child.

As he watched, Jimmy saw movement at the base of the big rock near them by the stove; but looking over he saw nothing. There was a crevice in the rock where he had seen the movement, so he watched it a moment. There was a slow, almost imperceptible movement again, and a dusty-looking snake emerged from the crevice, turning its head around slowly toward the heat from the stove. It moved again sluggishly. And suddenly the nearest of the three shepherds saw it. He dropped his gifts and his voice went way out of tune, then stopped altogether. He knelt there transfixed, his mouth still open.

There was a roar of laughter that drowned out the singing; when it died down the other shepherds had seen the snake and were falling over each other getting away from it. The woman dropped the doll into the manger and screamed; and in all the uproar the burro spooked and headed for the door dragging the manger.

Charley's gun blasted close to Jimmy's ear and the snake's head went to pieces. The body began coiling and writhing slowly in front of the stove, the light-colored belly reflecting the light each time it turned.

The woman stopped screaming when the shot sounded. She ran over and picked up one of the crooks the shepherds had dropped and began beating the squirming body of the snake, her face bright and contorted with rage. The crook broke off close to her hand but she went on swinging the stub end of it.

Jimmy left then, emerging into the cool air and vivid sunlight with a sense of awakening. He caught up his horse and rode out across the flat, breathing hard to get the smell out of his nose. He did not look back.

PART III
SPRING 1883

CHAPTER
2 4

IN THE EAST THE FEATHERY BANK OF CLOUD moved upward off the sun, high and white, into the luminous sky, and the land lay washed in a brilliance of morning light. There was a cleanness of the air, Sandy thought, a limpid quality as of pure water, and the same freshness.

After the slow color of the sunrise the country around him flowered suddenly with white. Standing on the flat top of the highest of the Medicine Rocks, he could see the whole valley — to the west the shiny earthen flow of the river and beyond it the grassy waving hills; south the flat land of the valley sloping up on the east toward the divide, broken on the upslope by outcroppings of rimrock, laced and veined with creeks and coulees; and far on, past the old camp, Twin Buttes clean as glass, shining above the timbered hills. In the low places along the creeks and the river, hawthorn bloomed, and chokecherry, white splashes in the sun like foam. And scattered here and there over the valley were the little pyramids of bones he had gathered, cone-shaped and white as tepees, a strange flowering of the land. The Rocks around him to the west caught the slanted light giving it back a chalky white; and white were the bleached poles of the platform supporting the bundled figure, and the other with the white buffalo robe.

He walked to the southern edge of the rock and looked down, seeing below him the neat plot of the old man's garden, laid out in a square, the rows traced lightly now with green; and, west, the dead-end wash that led down to the creek — the place where Charley had shot him and left him for dead, and where he would have died too, except for the old man.

It was hard to remember that now — not what had happened before he was shot; he could remember that plainly and all the details of how the country was — but how he had felt then and all the hazy time of weakness and pain afterwards.

He did not know how long it had been; he could only remember the time of his illness in flashes, as fitful alternations of light and dark, of unconsciousness and pain, of cold and heat. He had been feverish and delirious at first, in the brief intervals of lucidity cursing the light and wishing only for the darkness — the extinguishment of pain. And over all the flickering unreality of it, the only clarity the old man's face and it as unreal as all the rest, but unforgettable. And that was all, just the face, the skin dark and colorless but the beard and hair white and shining, a frame of light floating above him in the darkness whenever he came to the surface of his pain.

Then one morning he awakened and the fever was gone. He was in a cave and it was filled with light. The door flap was open to the east, and seeing the Rocks and the hills beyond, he knew instantly where he was. The cave he knew must be in a shelf of rocks to be so high; and from the sun he could tell it was on the southeast side of the Rocks.

He knew where he was; it was the snow that startled him. The hills as far as he could see were robed white and stainless, so bright it blinded him to look. Trees, willows, all the little shrubbery along the streams were scaled and glittering with frost. The sun was up clear of the hills, shining on him through the doorway, and the warmth of it on his face was like the touch of hands.

He was tired now and weak, but not in pain, though there was a dull soreness in his chest and hip, sharpening only when he moved. He was bound tightly with bandages around the chest and hips. He closed his eyes against the sharpness of the light and dropped off to sleep, awakening again to see the old man sitting near him, cross-legged, on the floor. He was making a basket of willow switches, weaving deftly with knotted, withered hands. His neck was bent forward above his work, almost at right angles to his shoulders, and there was a scar on it showing livid among the stained, scraggly whiskers.

Sandy remembered him then — the old man he had seen the night he had killed the white buffalo. But he seemed real now and human; the memory was the memory of a dream and the old man another man in another country. As he watched, the old man stopped weaving, as if he felt Sandy's eyes on him. He turned his body slightly at the waist and twisted his head to the side and Sandy saw his eyes were blue and bright.

"Dad gum it," he whispered, "it's time you woke up, man. You ought to make up your mind whether to live or die and not keep a man on tenterhooks like this."

Sandy smiled. "Feels like I'll make it," he said, realizing as he spoke that he was glad to be alive. He felt revived and somehow cleaner than he had felt for a long time.

"Seem like I've seen you before," the old man said. He looked down at the basket, a smile stirring his whiskers, but he did not begin weaving again.

Sandy said nothing, remembering again the night of the white buffalo.

"Ain't you the feller I see shootin all the dead buffalo?" He looked up again, his eyes merry.

Sandy assented, feeling the blood rush to his face.

"How do you feel about it now? You wasn't drunk? No," he answered himself, "you couldn't 've killed all those buffalo drunk."

"Naw," Sandy said, "I wasn't drunk. Not whiskey drunk. I'll tell you the truth, it don't seem like it was me. It's not just that it's past; it's like it was somebody else. And you too — you seem different."

The old man looked up again. "I ain't changed. The same old Joe Parson. Parson Joe I been called mostly — when there was ary one around to call."

"Sandy, I'm called. Sandy MacKenzie. I'm much obliged to you for this."

"If it's worth anything to you, you're welcome. Especially if it's worth anything."

"It is," Sandy declared with conviction. "By God, it is."

Parson smiled, not looking up. "Didn't look like it was when you got hurt, not the way you acted."

"You saw it?" Sandy asked, surprised.

"I see you put somethin under that horse's tail and I see the feller get up after he was throwed and shoot you. No man could be as slow and awkward as you was. That's why I figgered it wasn't worth much."

"It wasn't that exactly. I wasn't tryin to get killed. But I had to stop him from ridin out of there. And I didn't want to shoot him."

"So you let him shoot you?"

"In a way I owed him that much."

"It didn't do him any good. On top of that, it was a danged expensive delay, wasn't it?"

Sandy nodded. "But I'd do it again. Even if I knew I'd live." He grinned wryly. "The only thing is, I'd like to know if it helped or not. Did he catch the horse?"

"He caught him all right. He was back about dark, lookin for you — actin kindy crazy. There was snow by then, though, so he couldn't tell where you'd gone or how. He rode up and down like somethin was after him for a while, then lit out. Next day I see his tracks goin back up the river."

"Alone?"

"Only one horse, anyway."

"It was worth it then," Sandy said, feeling an immense relief. He was sure the woman was all right; he would not have to worry about her any more. He lay quiet for a while taking stock of himself. He felt good. He knew he was not through with his troubles yet, but he would have the strength for anything from now on.

"How did you get me up here that day?" he asked.

"It wasn't easy. Main strength and awkwardness."

"Why? I mean, did you know who I was?"

"I knew you all right. When I see the feller shoot I figgered you was done for — he had the way of a gunman. But then it come to me that you wasn't. I don't know why, it just come to me. So I brought down bandages and done the best I could. Lookin back now, it was the least I could do, seeing that in a way I was the cause of it."

"How do you mean?"

"Because I turned the danged horse loose. I didn't like to see him starve."

"It was a natural thing to do," Sandy said. He was tired now and did not care to talk about it any more.

Parson brought him some bitter tea and some raw liver and he was able to eat for the first time.

He gained strength slowly, lying at the back of the cave, when he could looking out through the doorway at the snow-covered land, hearing often the sound of Charley's gun crashing in the valley, and seeing now and then the dark shapes of buffalo on the far white hills, and more and more often the shadowy-moving packs of wolves.

He saw Jimmy one day riding along the hills to the east. He came toward the Rocks as far as the creek and rode up and down for a while as if looking for something. Sandy, unable to move, called to him, but he did not hear and after a while rode off.

The old man was gone much of the time, coming back evenings with meat that Sandy knew was of Charley's shooting, or with corn or dried roots and vegetables that he had stored somewhere among the rocks. When he was in the cave he was always busy, making baskets or mats, or merely whittling. He was cheerful, though he did not talk much — maybe, Sandy thought, because he could only whisper. Mostly he just listened, questioning now and then, but never volunteering anything about himself. It was a long winter, and at the end of it Sandy had told almost everything about himself, but had learned almost nothing about the old man.

Sandy's wounds healed slowly and painfully and it was late winter before he got outside the cave by himself. The old man made him a crutch and he learned to walk again, though with a limp from the wound in his hip that he knew he would always have. It was not painful but awkward and disconcerting till he got used to it. As he gained strength he ate meat ravenously — till in the spring when the supply was gradually stopped. As the snow melted, the old man went out more often, coming back now with spoiled meat or none. He carried an old muzzle loader, but it seemed like he never shot anything with it.

And finally there was no longer the faraway sound of Charley's rifle and no more buffalo or buffalo meat. The antelope moved out of the valley onto the plains and the elk to higher ground, leaving the valley populous with wolves that filled the night air with howling and the cries of their hunting.

Magpies and crows swarmed thick in the willows along the streams, chattering and cawing continuously on the warm days. Buzzards sailed overhead; and when the wind was in the south, the air was heavy with the stench of rotting meat. Flies blown by the wind settled in the rocks, emerging from the cracks days to buzz thickly and dart through the cave. He had never known the flies so thick, nor the carrion birds.

As the warm days of spring came on, the wolves gradually disappeared, leaving the valley empty of game. Even the rabbits and prairie dogs were gone.

They had no meat now except a scant ration of jerky, and subsisted on dried turnips and berries and a little corn from the old man's stores.

The old man went out, carrying a rawhide sack in which he gathered buffalo chips. Every day Sandy would see him with the sack on his back, bent far forward under the weight of it, walking slowly over the flats picking up chips. When he had the sack full he would come back to the rocks and dump them on an immense pile he had built just below the cave.

As the ground thawed he began working his garden, covering it first with crumbled manure from the bottom of the pile, then spading it up. The ground was ready long before it was warm enough to plant, a little island of richness in the soilless sand around the rocks.

Sandy was almost recovered. At first he tried to help with the garden, but the old man would not allow it. He gave no reason except that he preferred to do it alone. So Sandy was left with nothing to do and a need for activity as his strength increased.

He tried hunting, but there was little game, and it seemed like he had little enthusiasm for it.

In the end he gave it up and just walked around the valley, not thinking or planning; feeling a nameless desire, a need to do something, he could not tell what. And in all his walks he saw no buffalo except the dead. They were gone completely — not a cow and calf or an old bull remained.

But the bones were thick. In nearly all the little swales and coulees were scattered clusters of bones, some that he recognized as his own killing of the year before, but most of them more recent with meat still on them, still stinking, the heads still haired and fleshed.

It was on one of these walks that he saw a party of Indians. He was off to the northwest of the Rocks, walking along the bluff above the flat where Charley had made his first big stand.

The snow was gone except on the north sides of the hills in little gullies near the top, small greyish white strips like the bones scattered in the flat. It was a cold bleak afternoon with a chilly, wet-smelling wind and a haze of rain in the air.

He felt good. The cold kept him moving, quieting the perpetual restlessness he felt these days. But still he was unsatisfied, lonesome in a way he had never been before. He would welcome even Charley for company, he thought.

Thinking of Charley he stopped and looked down at the flat, reconstructing the way the stand had been made. Across from him was a grove of cottonwoods and to the left the mouth of the creek where buffalo had watered; and to the right, north, the trails coming down out of the hills and the main trail along the river.

He was thinking how it must have been, when he saw the Indians coming up onto the hills from a river crossing. There were six of them and maybe twice as many horses, the extras all carrying packs. Two of the ridden ones were rigged with travoises. On some of the packs he could just make out the forms of children.

He was unaccountably pleased and excited at seeing them — as if they were old friends — and possessed by a sudden, strong desire to go down to meet them. But he did not move. Something about the look of the party — he could not tell what — prevented him.

So he sat down among some rocks and waited.

As he waited, he saw a rider leave the party and ride on ahead at a lope.

The rain increased, changing from the haze to a cold steady drizzle obscuring the hills, and the light dimmed. The Indians came on slowly in a blurred group hardly distinguishable, except in movement, from the grey outcroppings of rock along the hills.

Sandy climbed part way down the face of the bluff and sat down under an overhang of sandstone out of the rain, still watching with excited anticipation. The trail passed close below him, so he would get a good look at them. Maybe, he thought, he would get a chance to talk to them if they were Sioux.

The advance rider was in the flat now. He turned off the trail just before he reached Sandy and rode into the grove of cottonwoods by the river. Sandy could not tell what tribe he belonged to. He was dressed in ragged black trousers and coat with a wide-brimmed reservation hat from under which his braids hung. He had a revolver strapped on outside the coat and carried a rifle. He was middle-aged, thin and pale of face, hunched over in the saddle like an old man. His horse was a bony ragged black, splashed with mud on the chest and belly and caved in around the flanks.

He left the horse in the grove and walked out across the flat toward the bluff carrying his rifle, his trousers flapping wetly around his legs. He climbed the bluff maybe fifty yards to the north of Sandy and disappeared over the rim.

Peering cautiously out from under the overhang, Sandy could see him looking back along the trail, his head thrown back. He stayed there till the rest of the party came into the flat, then climbed down and walked back to the grove and, with the others, set about making camp.

There were two more men, three women, one of them old, and four small children. Three of the kids were on pack horses, looking tiny and precarious perched on top of the packs; the fourth was on a travois with just his head sticking out from under the canvas. Half a dozen dogs nosed around among the trees, shaking themselves constantly. The three kids got down off the packs and hung around close to the women, trying to get warmth from them and getting underfoot at every step.

The men unsaddled their horses and began taking the packs off the others. The old woman, after walking slowly around among the clear spaces in the trees, selected two spots for the tents, marked them and began gathering wood. The other two were unpacking the travoises. One of them lifted the kid off the pack and carried him over under a tree, putting him down with his back against the trunk. She covered him with a piece of canvas and went back to the travois.

The kid sat quietly, making no movement except with his head, which he turned constantly from side to side, watching everything with enormous, dark eyes.

Sandy could see his body slipping gradually over against the trunk. Finally he fell over on his side and lay there, still making no movement except with his head; and Sandy realized that he was paralyzed. After a while the woman noticed him and came back over to pick him up.

The men had unpacked the horses. He saw one of them throw a fresh cowhide over a limb out of reach of the dogs. When the women finished with the travoises, the men watered the horses and picketed them in the flat.

The women put up two ragged four-wall tents that sagged and billowed with the breeze. The three kids were huddled around the fire the old woman had built. The crippled one, still by the tree, stared toward the fire, his eyes shiny with the light.

It was not like a camp of Indians at all, Sandy thought. There was no talk or laughter, not even among the kids. The men and women moved slowly and without dignity as if tired beyond endurance. Only the old woman and the chief showed any life, she doing the cooking, keeping the dogs away from the food, moving about constantly; he keeping watch around camp, climbing the bluff often or walking back along the trail, always carrying his rifle.

It was dark now and the rain had stopped. The clouds thinned and moved off, revealing a bright full moon almost directly overhead. It shone whitely on the puddles and the bones in the flat.

Sandy still sat under the ledge, watching, knowing now though, that he would never go down to them and talk. They would not welcome him. The anticipation he had felt was gone — as if their misery had infected him. He was cold and depressed and somehow ashamed to face them. He wanted to help them, but there was nothing he could do, no way he could reach them. He decided to leave, feeling that he was retreating, in some way doing something he should not do.

He stepped out from under the overhang into the moonlight and climbed back up the bluff, moving quietly. He was just reaching the top when one of the dogs in camp barked frenziedly. He stood up on the rim beside a boulder and in the same instant heard the report of a rifle and heard the bullet ricochet off the rock at his side. He ran back from the bluff till he was out of sight of the camp and turned south toward the creek that cut down through the bluff. He reached it and climbed down the cut bank, stopping near the top to look back. In the moonlight he saw the chief appear at the top and stand there looking, his rifle held ready. He did not search, as Sandy had expected, but stood exposed as if trying to draw fire.

Sandy wondered where the other men were and moved out along the creek bank till he could see the campground again. The fire had been put out. The horses were bunched up close to the trees, some of them already saddled, and the Indians were moving about quickly among the shadows. He heard one of the kids cry and heard the sound muffled suddenly. With chagrin, he realized that they were going on. They had not even eaten yet, but they were leaving — and because of him. They were running from someone — he might have known from the way the chief had kept watching the back trail — and had mistaken him for one of the pursuers. And he could not tell them any different now.

He left then, crossing the creek a little way upstream, and went on southeast across the silent moonwashed hills toward the Rocks. In his mind he was seeing the Indians with their mud-splashed, gaunt horses lined out on the trail; hearing the kids whimpering from the cold, the sound of hooves in mud and the muffled wooden sound of the travois poles dragging.

Parson was in bed when he got back to the cave, but there were still the bright coals of a fire in the fireplace. Sandy sat down on his bed without saying anything, and put his head on his hands. There was no use lying down — he would not sleep.

"Dad gum it," Parson said, "you look like you had to go and couldn't. What's got into you?"

"I don't know. I feel useless. But I can't, by God, think of anything to do. And what I do think of always turns out wrong."

"Why, what've you done now?"

"Nothing. And that went wrong too." He told Parson about the Indians.

"Well, it ain't much to worry about; it might even be a favor for em. If somebody's after em, it'll give em that much more of a start."

"It ain't that," Sandy said. "It's just that they looked so damn down and out."

"They wouldn't think so. Anyway, are you responsible for em?"

"No, but I seem to feel that way about it."

"Well, that ain't a thing you can settle with the Indians. You got to settle it with yourself. I don't know how, but maybe it'll come to you."

Sandy could see him dimly in the darkness, lying on his bed smoking a pipe. His robe was drawn over him up to his chin, his head, propped straight upright against a rolled blanket, looking strangely detached.

"Like with me," he went on. "It was simple. The first time I come here — not so many years back — I was tryin to hunt, a damn fool notion and me with my head drawed over till I could hardly sight a gun. I was with a sportsman's outfit, a bunch of greenhorns, and I was sick of it. One day I left camp alone and never went back.

"Our camp was south of here at the Twin Buttes. It was a clear day and even from there I could see the Rocks white and clean as snow. I thought I'd walk down here and see em close up, so I done it. I shot at some antelope waterin at the crick and missed em clean. I come down to where they had watered, stood my gun against a bush and had a drink. I turned around and drew back to look at the Rocks, and it come to me then what I'd do, sudden-like. And I ne'er saw hide nor hair of them greenhorns, nor anyone else except Indians till you fellers come along. But I been easy in my mind since; I've ne'er had regrets."

It was interesting, Sandy thought, but it had nothing to do with his own case. Aloud he said, "It sounds all right, but it depends on what you had to be uneasy about. I don't really take you for a blamed saint. But it's somethin like that."

The old man drew on his pipe and in the thin glow from the bowl Sandy saw his eyes bright and laughing.

"I ain't much like a saint. It was a farmer I set out to be. But I wasn't even that, though I done all right, in a way. I could make a crop as good as any man and I had me some good farms. But some way or other they always petered out on me. I'd make good for a few years, then things'd go bad on me — drought, poor crops, some damn thing — so I'd move on. Altogether I went through half a dozen farms all the way from Pennsylvania to Kansas, before I give it up. Then I only gave it up because I got the call to the gospel.

"Well, I'd never preached a word in my life, but I had a way with talk of makin people see. I could write a good sermon; but I'd have the devil's own time speakin it. Then I found out that with a little drop of whiskey, I could be a regular hell-roarer. So that's the way I worked. I'd write the sermon sober, give it drunk. It worked good. Except that after while I found it hard to stay sober long enough to do the writing. Well, it finally got to where I couldn't. And right there was where the trouble commenced.

"The devil was too familiar, I guess. Anyhow I took to namin him too personally. There was some who took exception to my interpretations; and finally some feller give me an argument I couldn't answer. And the reason I couldn't answer was, he cut my throat. Well, that put an end to preachin, though I got to admit it gave me a prayerful look. I figured it was a visitation from the Lord and quit drinkin for a while.

"But then I thought I was done for. I'd never be able to hold up my head again, I thought. So I had a time of it to keep from takin a gun to that feller, but I didn't. I took to drink again though.

"I'd been somethin of a hunter in my younger days, so by and by when my neck healed up, I hired out to that sportsman, which is how I came to be here." He stopped for a while and Sandy could hear the soft rush of the wind outside and the even, whistling sound of the old man's breathing.

"Well," he went on, "the short of it is, I stayed. And the way it turned out, it looks like that feller that sliced my throat done me a favor — though he sure God never meant to. It set me to lookin at the ground. Which is what I should have done in the first place. It made me see what I had to do. And made it easier for me to do it." He stopped and puffed again, smiling. "Like with the chips. I can't miss em."

Sandy lay down then. He sensed a parallel — he could not put it in words — between himself and Parson. It had worked out all right for the old man; maybe it would for himself. Maybe the worst part was past, the "visitation from the Lord," and something might just come to him.

He was out early next morning, curious whether anyone had passed following the Indians. He walked toward the river, cross-ing the trail to the south of the camp, and saw that no one had. But their tracks were there for anyone to follow, cut sharp in the mud and frozen indelibly. The sky was clear, and there would be no rain or snow to obscure them.

He walked north idly, toward where the Indians had camped, and crossed the creek just below where he had hidden the night before, coming even with the camp just as he saw the riders come down into the flat. Glancing into the trees, he saw that the Indians had forgotten the cowhide in their hurry to leave — it was still slung over the limb. The riders were too close now — he would not have time to hide it.

Instead of turning off the trail, he walked straight on, meeting the riders on the flat just beyond the grove. There were five men in the party, two of them wearing badges. One of these, a big smooth-jowled, heavy-set man, Sandy took to be the sheriff; the other he recognized as a buffalo hunter he had known back in Kansas. Hollis, his name was; he had been known as a gunman in those days and he didn't look as if he had changed much. He had a dark, sharp-cut face, hard and expressionless. The other three looked like ranchers, cattlemen probably.

A couple of mongrel dogs came up from behind and growled around his legs, but he paid them no mind and they went on. Sandy nodded to the men but did not speak, waiting to see what they would ask him.

The sheriff spoke first. "We're lookin for a bunch of Injuns that killed some of these gentlemen's cattle. We been trailin em a couple of days now. You didn't see em go through here, did you?"

Sandy ignored the question. "You after em to take em back to the reservation?"

Hollis laughed. "We didn't bring any pack outfits to haul em back with. Say, ain't I seen you someplace before?"

"How many did they kill?" Sandy asked the sheriff.

"One is all we know about; they probably got more, though."

"It don't make a damn bit of difference," one of the cattlemen put in, crowding to the front, "one or a dozen. We got to put a stop to it. We can't have a bunch of damn redskins livin off our herds. Wolves are bad enough." He was a big, indignant-faced man, but there was nothing vicious about him, Sandy decided.

"How do you know it was this bunch?" he asked.

"Well, Hollis here is a pretty good tracker," the sheriff said, "and he says it is. And we've had a good trail to follow."

"We've got these redskins red-handed," Hollis laughed. "But it don't make much difference, as far as that goes. If they ain't stole some already, they will. So we can't make a mistake."

"We'll know when we find them," the cattleman said. "They've got one hide, anyway, if it's the right bunch."

"I got to find out," the sheriff said apologetically, glancing toward the ranchers. He would give it up, Sandy thought, except for them.

Sandy walked up close to the one who had been talking. "Look," he said, "if you could see those Indians, I don't think you'd feel the way you do. They looked wore out and starved; if they killed your cow, that was the reason."

"Hell, a damned Injun's always starvin," Hollis said. He kept his horse moving and fretting, though the animal was tired.

"They had their women with em," Sandy went on, "and kids —

little tykes, freezin and hungry, and one of em crippled so he couldn't even sit up. Just as sure as you catch em, it's the women and kids you'll hurt — and it's somethin you'll have the rest of your lives to regret."

"You're talkin as if they was people," Hollis said, "which they ain't. They're no better than wolves — the same in fact, only harder on cattle."

"Don't let this gunman drag you into it," Sandy said. "He wants blood, that's all, like oil, to keep him from rustin. But blood won't help you."

"Why you damn Injun lover," Hollis growled, riding up close. "You better watch how you talk."

"Leave him alone," the sheriff said.

Sandy did not take his eyes from the cattleman's face, knowing he had made an impression.

No one said anything for a moment. The dogs were yapping in the grove up ahead. The other two cattlemen had drawn apart, and Sandy heard one of them say, "It looks like prime cattle country through here."

Sandy went on, finally, "If there'd been buffalo, they wouldn't have taken the cow. And it was white men that killed the buffalo. You ought to consider that."

"We never killed any buffalo," the cattleman said. "It ain't our fault they're gone."

"Buffalo or no buffalo," the sheriff said, "they got to live under the law."

"They didn't make the law," Sandy said, "or have any part in makin it. So you got to give em time to get used to it. They've had their own law — and it was different. And they lived on the buffalo, and nothing else. Now it's all changed; a new law they don't understand, and cattle in the place of buffalo. It's hard for em, you got to admit."

The dogs were fighting over something at the campground. Hollis started to ride ahead along the trail, then suddenly turned back, laughing triumphantly. "By God," he said, "no wonder I didn't know you, you ain't got a rifle." He turned to the cattlemen. "Look who's talkin for the starvin redskin, old Sandy McKenzie, one of the best buffalo hunters that ever hit Kansas. How many thousand hides you took, Sandy? You're startin in a little late with your talk, ain't you?"

The cattlemen smiled.

"It's true," Sandy admitted. "I'm no better than the next man. But it don't change the case any."

"What are you doin here without a gun?" Hollis asked.

Sandy did not answer.

"There's already one crazy old coot I've heard about in this place. Now there's another." He wheeled his horse and rode on along the trail toward where the dogs were fighting. Sandy heard him laugh again and knew he had found the hide. He came back with it over his horse's neck, the brand turned out and showing plain in the light-colored hair.

"What I don't understand," Hollis chuckled, "is why you didn't hide it."

"I didn't have time," Sandy said lamely.

"It's my brand," the indignant-faced rancher said. And seeing the anger mount in his face, Sandy knew there was no use talking any more.

They put spurs to their horses then and rode on, forcing Sandy, angry and helpless, back off the trail. At the edge of the grove, Hollis swung his horse sideways and grinned back viciously at Sandy. "Bonepicker," he said contemptuously, and rode on.

Sandy wondered for a minute what he had meant; then glancing down, saw that he was standing by the rib rack of a big carcass. He glanced around the flat at the scattered bones, the anger draining out of him. It was no use. He could not bring back the buffalo or fight for the Indians the battles that were already lost. Parson was right, the way he felt was something he had to settle with himself, not with the Indians.

He kept seeing Hollis, his face a mask of contempt saying, "Bonepicker," and was puzzled by his own lack of rancor. The word and the picture seemed to float just at the surface of his mind, insistent, inexplicable.

He stood a long time in tension, a need sharp and driving as the need for a woman rising out of the turmoil of his feelings. He had to do something.

He was walking now across the flat, tensely, almost running. And suddenly he stopped and picked up a bone and threw it with a vehemence that was yet not anger. Then — as if it came to him through his hands — he knew what it was he had to do.

He began gathering the bones and throwing them together in a heap at the center of the flat . . .

He worked at it every day after that, early and late, finding a satisfaction, a release, that he did not question or try to understand. It would be a good way to get another start, he thought. He could haul the bones in later — it would save him time to have them already stacked. The horns he kept separate, using a leg bone for a mallet to knock them off.

It was hard work with a lot of bending and walking, but his strength was coming back now in a flood of energy and will to work.

The smell was the worst part. The stench was in his nose all day, coming off on his clothes and filling the cave at night. He could not get used to it, but it was something he could stand.

The old man never once asked him what he was doing. If he thought anything he made no comment other than a sly smile.

Sandy finished the lower end of the valley and moved to the old camp for a more central location. The old man gave him some corn and dried berries — for the rest, he lived on fish that he caught along the river, leaving lines set while he worked. It was monotonous, but he stayed with it till he was finished.

He spent the last night before he left for Sandpoint, visiting the old man, but he was up early and on his way before daylight. He walked out toward the river, turning before he crossed the creek for a last look. The Rocks were rimed beautifully with moonlight; in the east beyond, the light was beginning, fading the blue-black sky over the hills, lighting a rolled bank of cloud.

Impulsively he walked back toward the rocks, thinking he would go up and have a look before he left. He had never been up on the high ones. He left his pack at the bottom of the biggest and found a way up, feeling a sharp anticipation as he climbed.

The top was flat and smooth, illumined thinly with moonlight, swept by a clean fresh breeze. On the far side, toward the east, were two frameworks of bleached poles, maybe six feet high with platforms at the top. One of the platforms was flat, covered with shining white; the other, a burial platform, bore a dark, robed figure.

He walked over slowly, knowing before he reached the platforms what he would find. It would be the white buffalo hide — and the young Indian Charley had killed. He recalled the time vividly — the old Indian trying to trade; his own weak fumbling of the situation that had ended with Charley murdering the young Indian for no other reason than that Sandy had riled him.

It was the young Indian, as he had thought — he recognized the battered revolver and the old rifle that lay on the platform. The robe was tattered, caved in to the shape of the bones; the skull lay outside, fleshless, but with some hair still clinging. On the other platform was the white hide, stretched tight and well preserved even after a year's exposure. The hair was still tight, bleached now by the sun to a pure white. For just an instant, he wondered how much money it would bring; then turned and walked away from it to the edge of the rock.

Eastward the morning showed in a growing luminescence of the sky, drilled less brightly now with stars. The light increased, the cloud bank lifted and he stood watching the sunrise with a flooding, a bursting within him — he could not have said what he felt, but saw it rather in the flow of color that revealed the white-flecked land, that the land grew out of, rising up out of darkness and flowing off and away beyond sight . . .

It was full daylight when he left for Sandpoint.

PART IV
FALL 1883

CHAPTER
25

SNOW WAS FALLING WHEN THEY CROSSED THE divide and started down into the valley, little flurries and swirls drifting with the wind surges, thickening and clearing in the air ahead. From the summit the valley was obscured, but farther down the snow thinned and from the high spots Jimmy could see the trees around the old camp small and far down and the river curving past, grey as the sky. On the flats near the trees was a scattering of small dark spots that he knew immediately were animals, though he could not tell what kind.

Charley was on ahead, starting up the next rise, his rifle out of the scabbard, balanced in front of him as if he expected to see buffalo beyond every hill. Since leaving Sandpoint they had not seen a single buffalo — and Charley was in a tension of expectation and disappointment.

For two days now Jimmy had ridden beside the wagon, talking with Woodfoot or amusing himself by shooting at rocks or sage-brush or an occasional rabbit — and Charley coming back every little while to tell him to stop for fear of scaring off the buffalo. But he could not help shooting — it had become a habit with him; and he would be at it again in a little while.

He could tell Charley was worrying about him now, looking back occasionally, but for the most part intent on what was ahead. And with the snow, he was worrying about his rifle — he kept wiping it with his sleeve, though never ceasing to search the country around for sign of buffalo.

He might just as well put the damn thing back in the scabbard, Jimmy thought. He would not see any buffalo.

Coming down the hill the road skirted the top of an old slide. A rock, loosened by the jar of the wagon wheels, rolled down the steep slope, gathering speed quickly and bouncing. He drew his gun and hit the rock twice before it reached bottom, seeing the splinters fly off and hearing the lead sing into the air.

Woodfoot yelled at him and pointed, grinning, toward the top of the next hill. Jimmy looked up in time to see Charley wheel at the top and come plunging back down fit to break his neck. He knew instantly that Charley had seen the animals on the flats and thought they were buffalo. How he himself knew they were not, he could not tell, but he was sure of it.

He reloaded and holstered his gun just as Charley reached the wagon.

"Damn it, Jimmy," Charley yelled, "will you cut out the foolishness! There's buffalo ahead and you'll scare em clear out of the country. Now lay off." He reined around to leave. "I'm goin on ahead now and see if I can get a shot. And I don't want you guys to come blunderin down and spoil it for me." He lit out, spurring the bay to a run up the steep hill.

"You reckon there's really buffalo?" Woodfoot asked.

Jimmy shook his head. "It's something down there on the flats all right — I saw from above. But it ain't buffalo — horses, maybe, or cattle, but not buffalo."

Woodfoot laughed. "A man can't tell that far away, not even you."

Jimmy shrugged. "All right. Wait." Woodfoot's disbelief did not bother him. He was sure of what he had said. And the very sureness made him feel sad. He would feel no triumph at being proved right.

At the top of the hill they paused, seeing Charley far on below, just leaving the trail and cutting slantwise across a sidehill toward a coulee. From above, it was hard to judge the slope of the hill, but Jimmy could tell it was steep by the way the bay moved. Toward the bottom where the hill came together with the coulee, he saw the bay turn straight down and set all four feet and slide, his rump almost touching the ground. He piled up at the bottom in the cloud of dust his hooves had plowed up. Charley was thrown clear, and Jimmy saw him for a second spread-eagled on the sandy bottom of the coulee. But he was on his feet instantly and back in the saddle, without ever having dropped his rifle. He lit out down the coulee at a run, dodging the boulders and bushes with a recklessness that was strange and out of character. On the whole, Jimmy thought, Charley was pretty careful.

He watched Charley till he went out of sight between two hills, then looked down again at the animals on the flats. And suddenly he understood Charley's frenzy. He could see the animals more clearly now — cattle, he knew, though they were all the same dark color as buffalo — all, that is, except one, and that was white, showing dimly against the grey-green earth. Near the shack and partly hidden by the trees he saw a wagon loaded with something white.

Woodfoot could see it now and was laughing. "The crazy son-of-a-bitch is 'stalkin' somebody's work stock. Breakin his fool neck to get a shot at somebody's cows."

"You see the white one?" Jimmy asked.

"No!" Woodfoot choked. "Is there a white one, sure enough? By God, no wonder. The poor bastard." He burst into laughter again, rocking back and forth on the seat like a man in pain.

Watching him, Jimmy was suddenly resentful and angry. It was funny all right, but not that funny. He rode on ahead of the wagon, coming to the top of the next rise in time to catch a glimpse of Charley, far on down, just coming to where the coulee cut out onto the flat. He was not over half a mile from the cattle, but he was still riding fast, not having seen them yet over the banks of the coulee.

A little way out, he stopped, dismounted and crept carefully up the bank, his rifle across his arm. He stopped just an instant at the top, looking, then went slowly back down the bank and sat down.

Jimmy rode on, not caring to watch him any longer.

Where the trail came out onto the flats Charley met them, looking abashed and sore. His face was skinned up from the fall and still covered with dirt, his trousers torn. He sat his horse beside the trail watching them defiantly as they came up, running his hand over a deep scratch in the polished stock of his gun. There was no humor in his face — and Jimmy noticed that Woodfoot was not laughing either.

"If either of you birds got anything funny to say, get it out now," he said petulantly.

For just an instant Jimmy's anger flared, and he had a notion to say something about the white ox; but he knew it would not be funny. All the humor was gone out of the situation. It was only pathetic now — but explosive too. He wondered idly what Charley would do. Either cry, he thought, or start shooting, one.

"We'll stop at the old camp tonight," Charley said. "After we rout out this bird, whoever he is, and his damn cattle. It's our camp, by God, we made it." He put his rifle in the scabbard and rode on ahead.

It was still snowing lightly. The flakes were fine, drifting with the wind like mist, and there was still no sign of whiteness on the ground.

Charley, on ahead, was twisting and turning in the saddle, searching the country as if he were lost; there was a frantic, lost quality in his movements. Following the way his eyes traveled, Jimmy felt suddenly that there was something changed about the place since he had seen it last. It was a while before he could tell what it was: there were no bones. He realized then that he had not seen any since they crossed the divide. And for a moment it struck him as strange and inexplicable — as if there never had been any buffalo here and his memory were playing him tricks. As far as he could see around him on the flats there was no show of white — only the mist of snow driven on the wind, disappearing as it touched the ground. There were chips if you looked for them, and along the trail the grass was high and rich from the droppings of animals that had passed — but untouched now.

He remembered the wagon then, loaded with white, and it came to him. A bonepicker.

But the feeling of strangeness stayed with him, puzzling him. In that instant before the explanation had come, he had known a deep and intimate sympathy for Charley, as if he had looked from within him onto the suddenly changed, inimical land.

As they approached the camp, he rode up beside Charley, seeing a man come out of the shack and walk out to meet them. It was still too far to see his face with the mist of snow moving between — but even then, even though the man walked with a limp, Jimmy knew it was Sandy.

And suddenly he was yelling, spurring his horse ahead into a run, catching through the corner of his eye a glimpse of Charley watching him in open-mouthed surprise. When he reached Sandy he dismounted, feeling unexpectedly shy. Sandy held out his hand smiling, looking at him with grey, steady eyes. "By golly, it's good to see you again, Jimmy. You've changed some, bigger I think."

Jimmy nodded, lowering his eyes as he shook hands. For the life of him he could think of nothing to say. But seeing Sandy moved him deeply, he could not tell why.

Sandy continued to hold his hand strongly till Charley rode up. He turned then, not smiling but with a look of friendliness and warmth that Jimmy could not understand. Watching him, Jimmy sensed a change — Sandy seemed taller now, more square of shoulder; there was a warmth and strength about him beyond Jimmy's memory of him. He was dressed the same as always, in the leathers, and he was clean-shaven, but his face was thinner. He was covered with a fine dust from head to foot, from the bonepicking, Jimmy supposed, and he smelled of old carcasses.

"You ain't the one I see come a-hellin down that coulee a while ago, are you, Charley?" Sandy asked. "If so, you had me guessin."

Charley nodded, taking out his pipe and filling it with nervous hands. He was pale and his eyes seemed glazed and opaque.

"Well, git down, man," Sandy went on, "Don't set there lookin like you'd seen a ghost. By golly, I may be covered with dust, but it ain't from bein buried."

Charley obeyed numbly, his expression frozen, tense. He did not take his eyes off Sandy's face even as he dismounted. Watching him, Jimmy was seized with a sharp uneasiness, a sense of impending danger. He felt like shouting at Charley as if to awaken him.

"I was just fixin to build a fire and rustle up a meal," Sandy said amiably. "You boys are just in time. And Woodfoot too, ain't it?"

Jimmy nodded, hearing the wagon roll up, but he did not take his eyes off Charley. He was tense himself now, fascinated by the way Charley was acting.

Sandy walked toward the wagon, shouting at Woodfoot, and the tension broke. The tense line of Charley's shoulders melted; he turned to his horse and put his hand on the saddle just an instant, then walked toward the shack leading the horse, his pipe, still unlit, clamped between his teeth.

Jimmy was helping Woodfoot unhitch when he heard the sound, and looking south along the river, saw the riders. There were three of them, coming at a run and near enough now that he could hear the sound of hooves. They were maybe half a mile away, bearing off to the east a little toward Sandy's cattle.

Sandy saw them too. He headed for Jimmy's horse, then changed his mind and ran over to the shack. "I'm gonna use your horse a minute, Charley!" he shouted. He mounted and headed out toward his cattle at a run. Jimmy mounted and followed, wondering why Sandy had changed his mind about the horses. Probably, he thought, to keep Charley from helping him.

When the riders saw Sandy they slowed down and changed their course toward him, and Jimmy saw then that they were Indians, Crows. He rode up with Sandy and the Indians reined up beside them.

Two of them were old men, but the third was young, no older than himself. The old ones wore black, ill-fitting trousers and broad-brimmed reservation hats from under which their braids hung. Both wore blankets and carried old muzzle-loader rifles. The young one was dressed in blue pants and a fringed leather coat. He wore a light-colored cowboy hat and high-heeled boots, and his hair was cut. He had a new Remington rifle.

Sandy shook hands with all of them; then with a sly smile, he indicated the cattle. "Whoa-haws," he said. "Not buffalo."

The young Indian laughed loudly. "I told these birds it was cattle," he said. "But they don't see so good any more. They was dead set on buffalo, like all these old-timers."

"It's an easy mistake to make in this kind of weather," Sandy said. "But the odd thing is, someone else just made the same mistake, and he ain't an old-timer. Maybe it's the light."

The young Indian laughed again. "That's a good one — the light. It ain't that. They just can't get it through their heads there ain't any more buffalo, that's all. Next thing, they'll be mistakin jack rabbits for buffalo. It ain't the light."

The two old men listened quietly while the young one talked, watching him with sad eyes. When he stopped, one of them said haltingly. "Bad hunting — no meat, three, four sleeps. No buffalo. Buffalo not come yet." He waved toward the north. "Later, plenty buffalo. Young man not know."

Sandy paused a moment. "I got meat," he said finally.

"Buffalo?" The two old ones watched him eagerly.

He shook his head. "Elk. You're welcome to what I got."

It was getting dark now, and the snow had stopped, having left no traces on the ground. The wind was keening in the leafless cottonwoods around camp, bitterly cold.

Woodfoot had a fire going in front of the shack with a big pot of water heating. He had found a hindquarter of elk and was cutting off pieces, throwing them into the pot. Sandy brought some dried wild turnips and berries and put them in the stew, then rummaged around in the shack, coming out finally with a bottle of whiskey and a dried tongue. He threw the tongue into the pot. "Buffalo," he said. "Last season's."

The two old Indians nodded, impressed.

"The last, maybe," the young one said.

"The last I got," Sandy told him.

They all sat down around the fire, and Sandy passed the whiskey, giving it to the Indians first. They drank gratefully, and one of them handed it to Charley. He hesitated for a second, Jimmy noticed, but he drank.

Woodfoot, watching Charley curiously, smiled as he drank, and turned to Sandy. "You'll have to paint your cattle blue, Sandy," he laughed. "Or lose em in the stampede, one."

"It wouldn't be new," Sandy said. "I lost my cattle in a stampede the first time I pulled in here. But it was a different kind of stampede. It was buffalo. The time me and Charley threw in together."

"By God, there was plenty of buffalo then," Charley said, ignoring the joke. "Late in the season too. But at that not so many as last year. Five thousand hides I got me last season. That was huntin. And they wouldn't get thick like that one year and be gone the next. There's buffalo yet. They're just late by God, that's all. They just ain't come south yet."

The young Indian laughed stridently. "That's a good one — ain't come south yet. And the Crees and Blackfeet sayin they ain't come north yet."

Sandy half rose as the young Indian spoke, his eyes on Charley, but Charley did not move and Sandy settled back.

One of the old ones spoke. "The white man is right. The buffalo are not dead. They are numberless, the buffalo. They cannot all be dead. Even the white man cannot kill them all. Every year they come from the caves. There is no end to them."

"Stories of the old men," the young Indian explained. "They come from the caves under the lakes north somewhere — or south somewhere. No one ever saw them come — but some old men have heard them fighting to get out. It wasn't the sound of the waves," he said ironically.

"It's a big country," Sandy said. "It's likely there's buffalo yet."

"Huh," the young Indian snorted. "Another year and there won't even be the bones."

"It's a big country," Sandy repeated. He passed the bottle and there was no more talk for a while.

When the meat was done, Woodfoot brought some tin plates out of the wagon and Sandy filled four of them with stew. With a pointed stick he fished around in the pot till he found the tongue. He divided it carefully into three pieces, placing one on each of the remaining plates. He handed one to each of the old Indians and to Jimmy's surprise, gave the other to Charley. Both Charley and the young Indian regarded him with surprise, but he made no comment. He sat down with a plate for himself and began eating.

They all slept in the shack, though it was crowded with seven men. The wind had shifted around to the north and increased and it was colder than ever. It howled in the trees and worried and whipped the loose ends of the hides that covered the shack.

Jimmy went to sleep listening to the wind, but it seemed like he had just dropped off when Charley started rolling around groaning and woke him up again. He found Charley in the dark and shook him awake and tried to go back to sleep, but before he dozed off, Charley was at it again. Jimmy could hear him above the wind, breathing hard as if he were running.

It was Sandy who awakened Charley this time. "What's wrong with you, Charley? Damned if you ain't been raisin a hell of a fuss." He lit a match, shielding it with his hands, and Jimmy saw Charley sitting up, looking bewildered. He was still breathing hard.

"What's wrong?" Sandy repeated. "You sick?"

"Naw," Charley said hoarsely. "But I can't breathe. It's too damn close in here."

"With this wind blowin through?" Sandy laughed. "Hell, you could throw a cat through almost anyplace."

"There's plenty of room outside," Woodfoot put in. "And air."

The match went out. Sandy went back to bed and Jimmy did not hear any more from Charley through the night. When he awakened at dawn, Charley was sitting against the wall, wrapped in his robes, dozing uncomfortably.

After breakfast as they were hitching up to leave, Charley took Sandy aside and talked to him earnestly for a while. Jimmy did not hear what was said; but as the two men came toward the wagon afterwards he heard Sandy say, "It's all right, Charley. If you haven't got it don't worry about it."

"I had it all right," Charley said. "But I haven't now. Hell, I got this outfit on credit from Black. I'm not forgettin that I owe it to you though."

They pulled out then. "We might as well keep movin," Charley said. "We'll try it on up the river, and maybe cut over to Yellowstone country if we don't find any. Then we can swing back and they'll be here by that time."

It looked like a long trip ahead, Jimmy thought, and for nothing. He hated to agree with the young Indian, but he was sure there would be no buffalo. Coming in from Miles City a few days before, he had traveled through the buffalo country north of the Yellowstone for three days and had seen not a sign of them, not even an old lone bull. All he had seen was bones. And wolves and hunters aplenty.

He had been just as sure of it when they left Sandpoint, and he had expected Charley to realize it and quit. But he knew now that Charley never would — no more than the two old Indians would ever give them up. Riding along beside the wagon he kept remembering the day before — the cold wind, the mist of snow; Charley and the two old Indians and the young one, a new kind of medicine man, he thought bitterly.

It was odd and ironic, to link Charley and the two old Indians — Charley the old fire eater, the Indian killer, sharing the last buffalo tongue with the old men and sleeping in the same room with them. It was no wonder, Jimmy thought with sudden insight, no wonder he could not breathe.

No amount of hunting would ever convince Charley that the buffalo were gone. And being sure of it himself, Jimmy thought, made it hard to keep on. He had a notion to quit now and be done with it. And yet he knew he would not. He would stay with Charley for a while yet — at least till he resolved his own feelings. There was something about Charley that drew him — or rather compelled him — and he could not understand it. He should never have put in with Charley this last time, he knew now. And in a way he had known it then, yet had done it all the same.

He had spent the summer working for a cattleman down in the Powder River country, and when the job ran out, he headed back for Sandpoint, thinking maybe he would get a job with Black. But the real reason was to look for Letty — as he had looked for her a dozen times before.

When he reached Sandpoint he forced himself to stop in at the store first to speak to Black, and it was there he ran into Charley.

He tried to sneak out, but Charley saw him and latched on.

"Dog it all, Jimmy," he said, "I'm glad to see you. You're just the man I need." He had just talked Black out of an outfit and he was determined to have Jimmy again for a skinner.

Jimmy agreed to go, partly just to get rid of him. But it was no use — Charley stuck with him. He seemed overjoyed at seeing Jimmy, as if he were a long-lost friend, and it made Jimmy uncomfortable. He walked all over town thinking maybe Charley would get tired of following, but he did not.

Jimmy gave it up finally and stopped in at the Hall. He bought Charley a drink, and as always began searching the crowd. He saw Thimmes first and was almost glad to see him, thinking she would not be far away; but thinking also that he would have it out now with Thimmes. He had waited for it a long time — and been a bit worried too — but now that the time had come he was fiercely glad.

And then he remembered: he could never settle anything with Thimmes when Charley was around. He would have to wait again. And the thought galled him out of all proportion. He was angry and resentful but helpless too.

He saw Letty after that, but he could not get close to her. When she was singing she always looked the other way, and when she was free she avoided him. But she was conscious of him he knew. And the thought calmed him. Seeing her again, he knew he would wait. He would have it out with Thimmes some other time, and it would be settled. He left the next day, and he had not yet spoken to her.

Now, riding beside the wagon, he tried to sort out his feelings about Thimmes, but he could not. He would have to kill him, that much was clear. But beyond that he was confused. He had no desire, no need to kill Thimmes. There was no sense to it. If you were going to kill someone you should at least hate him. But he had no violent emotions about Thimmes in spite of the things he had done — only an idle curiosity as to what made him act the way he did. He simply wanted Letty — and to get her he had to shoot Thimmes. But there was no sense to that either.

It was more than that, he realized now. He had come to look on the act as a kind of key, a badge that would prove his manhood and make him acceptable to white men.

Beyond Twin Buttes the bones were plenty. In the little valleys the wagon wheels rolled over them cracking explosively along racked ribs or jarring over the big skulls.

It was a cold trip, the wind always in the north, never easing up. And kind of lonesome and gloomy with no one talking now. All the way to the upper camp they saw no game — not even antelope or elk. He had never known the game to be so scarce nor the country so unfriendly and forbidding.

On the evening of the fourth day, they pulled into the little valley where the upper camp was located. They stopped by the spring below the cave and Jimmy and Woodfoot started unhitching while Charley walked up to the cave.

Jimmy was bending over to unhook a tug when the mules began snorting and trembling. He looked up in time to see Charley jump back from the doorway, drawing his gun in the same motion. A lion shot out of the darkness, turning along the shadowed ledge and making a tremendous leap up the face of it. In the same instant Charley's gun blasted twice in succession. The lion screamed with the echo of the shots, clawed for its footing on the smooth sandstone at the top, and went on over out of sight.

Jimmy left Woodfoot struggling with the scared mules and ran up the slope, finding Charley peering cautiously into the cave, his gun drawn and ready. He went in finally, and Jimmy followed.

Inside it was nearly dark and the air was heavy with the smell of rotten meat and the rank, sour smell of cat. There was the partly eaten carcass of a deer on the floor and another skeleton that was dry now.

"I hate a killin goddamn cat," Charley swore. "We'll never get the stink out of here now." He kicked savagely at the dry carcass, scattering the bones and raising a rotten-smelling dust. "I figured on campin here a few days to get us some meat," he went on. "And a goddamn cat spoils it."

He was breathing through his mouth to avoid the smell and he sounded as if he were smothering, a kind of sobbing sound. He turned suddenly and stumbled back outside and ran down to the wagon. He picked up his rifle and came back up the slope, still running, climbed the ledge and disappeared over the top, the way the cat had gone.

Jimmy unsaddled the horses and helped Woodfoot hobble the mules. They came back, and while Woodfoot brought up his pots and grub, he built a fire in front of the cave. Then he set out to find Charley, following the cat's trail by the blood. In the growing darkness the spatters showed slick and clear on the exposed rocks of the ledge. It had the bright red look of lung blood.

The cat had moved south following the rim, going slowly, he could tell, badly hurt. At one place it had climbed a low shelf of rock, and on the edge of the shelf the blood was smeared where the belly had dragged over it.

He saw Charley then standing at the edge of the overhang, looking down, his rifle ready.

"He's down there in another cave," Charley explained. "And there's no way in the world to get a shot at him except to wait till he comes out. And by God that's what I'll do, if it takes till doomsday."

"It might, at that," Jimmy said. "He's about done for, and he ain't likely to come out." He lay down and looked over the edge seeing, fifteen or twenty feet below him, the ledge the cat had dropped onto and the cave above it. He could hear the cat draw a sighing breath now and then and release it in a long whine. In between he could hear the air kind of chattering in its throat.

"I'll get a rope," he told Charley. "We can climb down onto the ledge and get him."

"And get clawed up?" Charley snorted. "Naw. I'll wait. He's bound to peek out of there sooner or later and I'll nail him. It's gonna be moonlight, good enough to shoot by. I'll wait."

Jimmy shrugged. "All right. But you better go get a bite to eat and a robe. You'll get damn cold up here in the wind."

"No. I'm gonna wait. You go ahead and eat, then you can bring me some if you want. By God, I'm gonna get that cat if it takes a year."

He brought Charley his supper and a robe, then stayed with him a while. It was bright moonlight and the sky was clear except for a few light clouds rushing south high overhead. The wind was sharp and cold, blowing sand along the ledge with a rasping, papery sound, dropping on down to whistle in the trees below. Beyond the trees and the meadow, the choppy metal surface of the river lay bright and cold and in the lulls of the wind he could hear the waves.

Close by a wolf howled, a long tapering wail, hanging in the darkness; then a crazy, mocking yammer of coyotes. The cat was still wheezing and sighing in the cave below.

Charley sat wrapped in the robe with his feet hanging over the ledge. The rifle was across his knees, the polished metal glittering in the moonlight. He sat there, intent on the cave below, not looking up even when Jimmy left.

Woodfoot had the cave cleaned out and a fire going in the fireplace. "A man can get used to the smell," he said, "but not to that damn cold wind."

It was late when they went to bed, but Jimmy could not sleep. He lay awake, hearing in his mind the whining of the lion, seeing Charley alone on the dark ledge, waiting. He lay a long time listening for the shot that would end the tension, but none came.

After a while he got up quietly and went back out, finding Charley just as he had left him.

The lion was making more noise now — low rasping noises in its throat that sounded like talking. Charley did not say anything when Jimmy came up but continued to stare downward hypnotically.

The moon was overhead, throwing a silver light on the shelf below, shading the face of the rock to a complete blackness, so that now the strangely human noises of the cat seemed to come out of the solid rock.

The sounds became louder, till he expected momentarily to see the grey form appear on the whiteness of the shelf below. But suddenly it was quiet. There was a strange, unbreathing silence with only the wind's rushing. Then out of the rock the sound began, thin at first but swelling and rising to a piercing, knifelike scream. It died slowly, and in the same instant the cat appeared, startlingly black against the shelf below. It kicked forward on its belly till its head hung over the side, and stopped. The legs kicked once more and it slid limply out of sight into the darkness. He heard it flopping in the brush below, stirring and crackling the dry leaves, growing weaker till finally it stopped.

He stepped back, his heart still pounding from the shock of the scream.

Charley had not moved when the cat appeared. He sat there

still, the rifle balanced across his knees, staring downward into the darkness.

"You didn't shoot," Jimmy said quietly.

Charley shook his head and stood up. Then, as if awakening, he said sharply, "What the hell difference does it make? He's dead, ain't he?"

On the way back to the cave, Jimmy asked, "Do you want the hide?"

"Hell no. I'm no damn trophy hunter."

Charley would not sleep in the cave. He made his bed outside, building a fire before he lay down which he kept going all night.

Next morning just as they were ready to leave, Woodfoot walked down to take a look at the dead lion. He came back carrying what looked like a piece of its fur. He held it up to Charley, who was on his horse, and Jimmy saw that he had peeled off just the top of the cat's head along with the ears.

"I figured you might want it for a keepsake," he told Charley unsmilingly. "It ain't every guy that's killed a lion with just his pistol."

Charley leaned down to take it, his face pale, but just as he reached out, the bay caught a whiff of it and shied violently, almost losing him. When he got himself righted, he forced the bay back savagely and caught the scalp out of Woodfoot's hand. Standing up in the stirrups, he threw it off into the trees and without a word rode back to where the trail led up out of the valley and went on along it.

Woodfoot grinned mischievously at Jimmy. "He's gettin a little weak at the seams, ain't he?"

Jimmy did not answer. He mounted and rode on ahead of the wagon.

They traveled on up river, in the evening reaching the point where the trail led off southeast to Yellowstone country. They made camp in a little meadow by the river, and while they were eating supper two men with a string of jaded pack mules came along the trail from upriver. Seeing the fire, they turned off and stopped.

One was a big grizzled man of maybe fifty that Jimmy remembered seeing at the Christmas celebration the year before, the other a pasty-faced kid of about Jimmy's age with an old single-shot pistol stuck in his belt.

Both men knew Charley and shook hands with him. "If you fellers got no objections," the old man said, "we'll camp here and chew the fat a little."

"It's all right, Zeke," Charley said. "Did you see any buffalo up the river?"

"Nary a one. And that's just what we was lookin for, me and the kid here. We've traveled a far piece too since we started. We been through the Grand River country and the Moreau and up the Yellowstone a piece, and then over to Sand River and down here. We busted a wagon wheel crossin the Yellowstone so we packed what we could on the mules and kept goin."

"Where to now?" Charley asked.

"North, by God, as far as Sandpoint and then we're done."

"Givin up?"

"Yes, by Jesus. Only a crazy man hunts for somethin that ain't there."

"You figger they're gone all over?"

"I wouldn't say that. There may be some in Canada. They was a big herd went north from Miles City this last spring. Maybe some made it across the line. If they did there may be buffalo yet. But I doubt that you and me'll ever see em."

The two of them went on downstream then to make their camp.

"I guess that's the end of it," Woodfoot said. "We might as well load up with bones and go back."

"Bones," Charley snorted. "Go back just because this blind old windbag can't find em? Hell no, we ain't goin back."

After supper the two men came back and sat around the fire talking. The kid had a bunch of small white bones in which he was drilling holes with an awl.

"I'm gonna string em on my belt," he told Charley. "Finger bones they are."

"The kid found a bunch of em back up the river," Zeke explained. "Some dead injuns, three of em, been there a year or two. The hair was still on em but the bones was clean. A white man must of killed em fer they wasn't scalped."

"The hair was rotten, though," the kid put in. "And not good for anything. I'd of made me a bridle if it was any count. These little bones'll look good on a belt though, and I already got me a quirt of Injun hide. You want to see it?"

Charley shook his head. He looked queer, Jimmy thought, a little peaked.

The old man went on talking, but Charley was not listening, Jimmy could see. He watched the kid for a long time drilling the holes in the bones.

He was particular, the kid was, and skillful too, handling the awl with a nice precision. He had made a little wooden clamp to hold the bones while he worked on them and he held it with his knees. He had two little buckskin sacks beside him, one with the finished bones, the other with the rest.

After a while Charley got up and picked up the two little sacks gingerly, as he would a snake, and dropped them carefully on the fire. The sacks oozed oil, shriveling, then turned black and burst into flame.

The kid sat there watching with his jaw hanging down. When the sacks started burning, he screwed up his face and turned to Charley almost in tears. "What did you do that for?" he quavered. "You didn't have to do that."

Charley did not answer. He stepped back away from the fire and sat down again, his face turned away from the light. He took out his pipe and without filling it, sat passing it rapidly back and forth from one hand to the other, staring off into the night.

Charley was up early the next morning. He saddled his horse and helped Jimmy bring in the mules and harness them — a thing he seldom did — while Woodfoot cooked breakfast. All his movements were fast and jerky and he had a hard time with the mules. They were afraid of him and kept jerking away as he was harnessing. Strangely enough, he did not swear at them or whip them, but kept on doggedly till they were finished.

After breakfast Zeke and the kid rode up, their mules packed and ready to go. He looked tired, Zeke did, defeated, and the mules moved reluctantly, their heads hanging.

It was a grey morning, the wind around in the southwest now and smelling of snow. Thinking of the long trip across to the Yellowstone and of the distance he had come already, Jimmy knew suddenly that he could not go on. He realized that he had come only because he felt sorry for Charley. He still did. But there was no use going on — it would not help any.

"You can't tell," Zeke said to Charley. "You might run on to somethin. Maybe I'm just unlucky."

"You're damn tootin," Charley said. "I'll find em. There's got to be more buffalo, they can't just disappear into thin air. We'll keep after em by God till we find em."

"Well, good luck, anyway," Zeke said. He rode on behind the mules. The kid was off his horse, adjusting his saddle.

Charley untied his horse from the wagon. "I'm goin on ahead," he told Jimmy. "You two can trail along."

Jimmy forced himself to speak then. "I'm goin back, Charley," he said. "You don't need two skinners anyhow."

"The hell I don't," Charley said in surprise. "No, by God, you ain't goin back. Get that out of your head."

"Naw, I ain't goin. It's no use when there ain't any buffalo anyhow. You're just chasin the rainbow."

"Get on your horse, Jimmy," Charley said. "I don't want to hurt you. Now cut out the damn foolishness. Hell, we're just gettin started."

"I ain't goin. The only way you're gonna make me is to put me in a box. And the only way you can do that is to shoot me."

"You think I won't?"

"I think you can't. But you're welcome to try."

He stood there relaxed, ready to shoot if he had to. But watching Charley's eyes, he knew he would not have to. He was sorry then for what he had done, seeing the weariness and hurt in Charley's face. He turned away and walked to his horse. When he looked again Charley was mounted.

"You comin?" he asked Woodfoot.

Woodfoot shook his head. "It's no use, Charley. Here, you want your outfit?"

"No. You can give it back to Black." He swung his horse around and went up out of the meadow and along the trail to the Yellowstone.

Jimmy turned angrily on Woodfoot. "Damn it, you didn't need to quit him just because I did."

Woodfoot looked surprised. "Hell, am I any different from you?"

The kid was staring at Jimmy with open admiration. "You must be pretty good to stand up to Charley like that. Maybe I could get you to show me something about it."

"I'll show you what I just learned," Jimmy said fiercely. He drew his revolver and took out all the shells, then turned and threw the gun into the willows along the river. The kid left his horse, without taking his eyes off the spot where it fell, and started toward the willows.

"No you don't," Jimmy told him. "Come on back here."

"Hell with it," the kid said, pausing. "If you don't want it, I ain't gonna let it go to waste. This damned old thing of mine ain't worth packin and that's a good gun."

"No you don't," Jimmy repeated. "To get that gun you got me to lick."

The kid stopped and turned, his hand on the old single-shot. "Hell," he said. "Like I say, this ain't much count, but it still packs a big slug. And you just threw your gun away."

Jimmy walked toward him slowly and carelessly till there was not ten feet between them. He dropped his hand to the big skinning knife in his belt. "Now," he said quietly.

"What do you mean?"

"Let's see how big a slug it packs."

The kid hesitated. "Hell," he said, his voice trembling. "I was only foolin. What's it gonna hurt you if I get that gun. It won't do you any good."

"It won't do me any good at all," Jimmy agreed. "Or you either. That gun won't make a man out of you any more than the one you got. Now get on out of here."

The kid mounted and rode on after Zeke, looking back. He would likely sneak back and get the gun, Jimmy thought. Well, the hell with it. He would not even pick it up again to throw it some-place else.

On the way back to Sandpoint, they filled the wagon box with horns, so it was over a week later when they got in. Black bought the horns and took back the outfit.

"I heard you was on your way back," he told them. "Old Zeke

Carter was in. Well, it's too bad, but the end was bound to come. It settles the buffalo hunters all right. But it settles the Indians too, you got to look at that." He turned to Jimmy. "I guess I was wrong about you not bein tough, Jimmy, after what I hear about you and Charley. But by heavens that wasn't very smart. Every cheap gunman in the country'll be after your hair now. And Thimmes — you better watch him. He's scared now and he's apt to shoot you in the back."

Jimmy shrugged. "I ain't lookin for Thimmes. Or trouble, either. But, hell, a man can't just disappear."

Outside, he put out his hand to shake with Woodfoot. "I think I'll drift."

"Where to?"

"I don't know, Miles City, maybe."

"Not yet. Let me buy you a drink, anyway. Damned if you ain't a funny kid. Ain't you even gonna give her another try?"

"Who?"

"Why, this gal you been mopin about all this time."

"I changed my mind."

He tied his horse to the rack in front of the hall and they went in. Woodfoot ordered the drinks, and out of habit Jimmy turned to search the crowd and saw her coming toward him, her face flushed. She stopped in front of him, her eyes flashing.

"I suppose you're looking for Tim to kill him, aren't you, you — " she hesitated, "you gunman."

"Me? Do you see any guns on me?"

She seemed to look at him then for the first time, and her eyes were puzzled. "Where is it?"

"What?"

"Your gun."

"I haven't got one. Does it make you feel any better?"

She shook her head. "You must be crazy. You'd better leave."

"Why?"

"Because Tim thinks you're after him and he'll shoot you on sight."

"You mean after he sees I haven't got a gun."

She nodded, looking around, fearfully now. "Go on," she pleaded. "Get out of here."

"Naw. Not for a while anyway."

She left and walked quickly back to the stage and disappeared. She came back in a moment carrying a gun and belt. "Here, put this on, at least till you leave."

He shook his head, but she started crying so he took the belt and put it on. He took all the shells out of the gun, dropped them in his pocket, and put it back in the holster, watching her all the while. He saw her anger begin to rise again; then saw her glance toward the door. And before he looked he knew it was Thimmes. His heart sank as he turned, thinking of Letty and of the empty gun.

Seeing him, Thimmes paused, then came on toward him slowly and carefully. Directly in front of Jimmy he stopped and thrust out his hand. "Let's stop this damn nonsense," he said. "Shake and we'll call it quits."

Jimmy smiled with an immense relief. "I guess we're about even," he said, taking the outstretched hand.

He laid the gun and belt on the bar and ordered drinks. When he turned back Letty was gone. He stayed a while, talking with Thimmes and Woodfoot, then shook hands with them and left.

It was dark outside and snowing, big flakes showing white and feathery in the light of windows, coming down straight through the windless air. It was soft and quiet underfoot — there was not enough yet to pack — but under the noises of the town he could hear it striking his hat with the sound of gentle rain. He brushed it off the saddle with his hat and mounted.

As he rode the clouds broke, the snow stopped. Moonlight came and went over the snow-bright slopes and the dark river as the clouds thinned, and in the blue-black patches of sky the stars were sharp.

Ahead, the plains swept clean and shining; and to the right the badlands, brooding and slashed with darkness, rose upward toward the far, invisible hills.

PART V
WINTER 1883-1884

CHAPTER

26

IT WAS NEARLY DARK WHEN SANDY CAME IN
sight of the fort, and cold, thirty below at least, he thought, but
there was no wind so a man could stand it. There was snow on the
ground, light powdery stuff that puffed out like dust when a hoof
struck it.

The weather had been good for traveling, the air still and the
sky clear. A week now it had been that way, ever since he left
Sand River to start north. If it held another three or four days, he
would reach the Agency and either find her or not and have it over
with.

He had put it off a long time, wanting to have his feelings clear
before he faced her again, to be a whole man, as he had not been in
years; as she had never known him. He had to be sure he was not
going because he felt obliged to her, grateful for the strength she
had given him; or simply because she was an Indian and he therefore
felt responsible.

But he was clear in his mind now and sure. And maybe too late.
It was over a year since he had seen her, the night at Twin Buttes,

and he had no right to expect her to be waiting. But he had to make the trip and be sure.

He was through with bonepicking. He had hauled them in to the railroad and sold them for a fair stake — enough to buy a small freight outfit. But at the last minute he changed his mind and took up a homestead at the old camp on Sand River. He built a cabin and sheds and put his money into stock and equipment.

He was surprised at himself at the time, but glad too. For the first time in his life he felt that he was settled, that he had found the place he would never leave. He would go back there after this trip and start again; and this time he would do all right, he knew. It was a good prospect — if a little late — and he was equal to it. Young, he felt, and strong.

He crossed the river on the ice, coming into the fort just at dark. He left his saddle horse and pack animals at the livery stable and made his way to the little one-story hotel, arriving just as supper was being served. The cook showed him to a little cubbyhole of a room at the back and gave him some water to wash up with. When he came back to the dining room a place was set for him at the long table. As he sat down he nodded to the three other men who were eating, though they hardly noticed him, being involved in an argument that had evidently been going on for some time.

One of the three was an Indian the others called Sammy, a man in his early twenties maybe, dressed as a white man in new expensive clothes, his hair cut short. He spoke good English and in his manner was assured and competent; but under his hard, polished surface Sandy sensed a defiance, a bitterness, a sadness.

Of the other two, Sandy recognized one immediately as a priest of some cut or other, a big strong-bodied man who had yet a softness about him — in the fullness of his lips, the pink delicate skin, the chubby, uncalloused hands.

The other was a medium-sized, grey-haired man, nervous, energetic and harassed-looking. It was cool in the room, but Sandy noticed he was sweating as he ate.

"Don't scourge yourself too heavily, Major," the priest was saying. "It's not for poor mortals to see the whole of God's design — or change it. Look at it this way — you've done all that's humanly possible; to wish to do more than that is no less than sacrilege since it would involve a change of the great design." He wiped his mouth delicately and went on eating.

"Thanks for the reassurance," the Major said wryly. "But what's impossible for one man may not be for another. Maybe I don't have the insight to read the design — but I don't think I'd quit trying to change it, even if I could."

"A human sentiment," the priest said magnanimously, "and for-givable. God works in mysterious ways, as the phrase goes. In try-ing to save these Indians, we work toward our own salvation; in this respect whether we save them or not is immaterial. Their salvation is God's work."

"What you're sayin," the Indian put in, "is that they're gettin what they deserve — God's against em. So it's better not to bust a gut tryin to help for fear of upsettin the old boy's design."

"You misconstrue, Sammy boy. I said no such thing. I too feel sympathy for these heathen. I merely suggest that God may have other plans."

"I'll agree with you this far," Sammy said. "Maybe it's better to let em starve than to prolong the agony. It took a lot of effort to get em where they are — why turn around and undo it?"

"You've a hard heart, Sammy. And toward your own people too."

"Not my people. I'm no more an Indian than I am a white man. I'm alive, that's all. I made my choice. But I'm not proud of actin like a white man."

"This is all froth," the Major said, impatiently. "Here is a people that needs help. We killed their buffalo and took their land. It's our responsibility to help them now. It's that simple."

"Not simple," the priest said. "I deny that. Only our part as Christians is simple — to show charity, to pity the unfortunate."

"They won't thank you for it," Sammy told him. "They think they're better men than you; that the old ways were better; they'd as soon die with the buffalo gone now, and the land."

"The old ones maybe," the Major said. "But what about the young? That's where your argument sticks, Sammy. We've got to help the young."

"I've got to help nobody. Who ever helped me? No one. You get paid to help, Major, as their agent. The priest here don't get paid, but he don't do anything either. His job is savin souls, not Indians. The merchants that furnish the supplies have good assurance the government will pay — and anyway it's only goods they risk for a chance of a big profit. You want me to take a freight outfit in and risk my neck on only a promise. And whoever heard of a white man keepin a promise to an Indian — since that's what you insist I am? No. I'll help when I got the money in my hand."

"A most cynical young man," the priest observed to Sandy. "Not a Christian at all."

"Not a Christian," Sammy agreed. "Just looking out for myself — like the rest of you. Like I said, I ain't proud of it, the way you are."

"I'll try to raise the money," the Major said. "But even if I do, one man won't be enough. You'll have to have help."

"The priest here might help — if he wasn't afraid of wreckin the design."

"I work in my own small way," the priest said. "Unfortunately this isn't my kind of work."

"All right," Sammy laughed. "You make medicine for me."

The priest was not amused.

"I might be able to help," Sandy offered. "I was headin for the Agency, anyhow. I'll tell you what, you dig up the money to pay Sammy here, and I'll throw in with him for the trip."

"Do you know anything about freighting?" the Major asked.

"I've freighted here before. Sandy McKenzie."

"I've heard of you," the Major smiled, extending his hand. "It's a needful thing you're doing, Sandy. These people are starving. They have nothing, not even hope. It was the end of the buffalo that did it," he went on to explain. "No one expected it to come so quick. Up till just this last fall, they were able to get what meat they needed — then suddenly nothing, not a buffalo. They had raised a few cattle and sheep and what with this and the buffalo, the agent — the one before me — had reported them as nearly self-supporting. And then the buffalo failed. The agent left and I came into his place. Some had died of starvation already. I issued what food was left — mainly a stock of condemned bacon — and came here for help. So far I've raised enough for one outfit. But it looked like I wouldn't find the men. The government will probably pay you — but I can't promise."

"It's all right. I was goin in anyway. But what about the government, won't they help?"

"They're sending supplies all right — from Fort Benton. It'll take weeks to get them in."

Sammy was watching Sandy curiously. "What do you get out of it?" he asked.

"What it's worth to me. I ain't a saint either."

They were loaded up and on their way before noon the next day. It was Sammy's outfit, a twelve-mule, jerk-line rig with a wagon and trail wagon and a coaster on behind loaded with grain for the mules and a camp outfit. They had half a dozen extra mules and Sandy's three horses.

"You'll have trouble," the Major said. "It's a bad enough go in summer, but now with this cold and snow, it'll be a wonder if you make it at all."

"We'll make it all right," Sandy told him, "if the weather holds. This cold ain't bad as long as the wind is down. But with just a breeze, she'll drift to beat hell."

They pulled up away from the river, heading northwest, the extra mules strung out behind the coaster wagon and Sammy riding alongside on Sandy's horse, helping to keep the green mules in line. He carried a shot whip, which he wielded with a great show of fierceness and considerable skill. But he left no welts with it, Sandy noticed.

Sandy himself rode the near wheeler, controlling the leaders with a jerk line to the off lead mule. Tied to his saddle and running back to the brakestaff was a line with which he could set the brakes of the lead wagon — not that it would help much in the snow. They would have to rough lock on any kind of grades.

It was a quiet day, grey and cloudy, but cold, the mules' breath freezing on the tips of their hair, giving them a grey-quilled look. The snow was almost axle-deep, but light and not hard to buck. It splashed out from the mules' feet, rolling back like sand behind them. Ahead of the front axle it piled up and spilled out over the hubs between the spokes of the wheels. Looking back on a long curve, he could see the middle dragged smooth and level and along the edges the shallow traces of the wheels.

Ahead the plains stretched toward the grey sky, flat-looking with no shadows to mark their contours. It was impossible to see the dips in the ground except as the mules moved down into them and up again. It was a kind of darkness in light that oppressed a man's vision, Sandy thought, and his hearing too — the far stretch of white, domed under a close sky and themselves the only sign of life. The sounds of the outfit were small and plaintive — the tinkle of the hame bells, the clink of chains and the squeak of leather; the muffled squealing of iron tires on snow, the chucking of the hubs — clear but echoless.

When the way was clear, Sammy rode on ahead, picking the trail more by instinct than by sight. There was nothing on the surface to go by except when they dropped down into the creek bottoms where they could follow the trail through cut willows and trees.

They moved slowly but steadily, covering almost half the distance in the first three days. It was open plains country for the most part, smooth, rolling hills marked occasionally by out-croppings of grey rock — cone-shaped hills or long flat-topped buttes jutting dark and startling against the snow. A few creek beds lined with brush and cottonwoods cut east and south through the hills and in the bottoms there was grass for the stock.

On the morning of the fourth day the wind came up, not a gale — just a moderate wind — but out of the north and cold. The fine powdery snow moved with it like dust, so thick and blinding after a few minutes that Sandy could hardly see his leaders. And Sammy, riding ahead, was lost completely to sight. The mules kept trying to cut off to the side and turn from it and it kept him busy trying to keep them in line.

After a little Sammy came back and rode alongside.

"We might as well turn around and get as far as we can on the way back," he told Sandy. "We'll never make it now."

Sandy shook his head. "I'm not goin back. You help me to the next bottom and you can have my horse to ride back, but I'm stayin with it."

Sammy shrugged and rode up alongside to help keep the mules in line.

Sandy's face was already numb from the cut of the wind. He tied his bandanna around below his eyes, knowing that even in that short time his nose had frozen slightly. Snow, fine as dust, sifted into his clothes and down his neck; his breath moistened the bandanna and in a few minutes it was frozen stiff and, pressed against his face, began freezing to the skin.

Sammy, masked like himself, was riding beside the leaders, lashing them in earnest now, to keep them moving. They flinched under the sting of it but moved more and more slowly, twisting and squirming in the face of the wind. They were on the point of quitting altogether when the road dropped down into a creek bottom. The mules stopped and Sammy rode east into the blind swirl of snow. He was back in a minute. "There's a little stand of cottonwoods and some brush that'll make a good windbreak. The snow's almost too deep already, but we can maybe pull in."

"Naw," Sandy told him. "We'll leave the coaster here and pull the rest of the outfit onto high ground. She'll drift clear out of sight down here."

"It's no damn use. We'll never get anywhere afterwards with the drifts to buck. No use even trying. We'll have to leave em. We'll be lucky to get back with the stock, let alone the wagons."

Sandy uncoupled the coaster and the trail wagon and climbed up again. He yelled at the mules and Sammy helped get them started again. They made it to the top of the next ridge and brought up the trail wagon. Coming back, they pulled the coaster into the shelter of the trees.

Sammy had not said anything about the cattle, and Sandy did not see them till Sammy rode into the bunch, crowding them out of the way of the mules with his horse and flicking them with his whip. Their backs were covered with snow and they stood humped up, rumps to the wind. There were maybe fifty or sixty, Sandy thought.

He pulled the wagon in close to the trees and they unhitched the mules, turning them loose in the lee of the wagon. The wind was not bad among the trees. There was a steep hill to the north of the creek that broke the force of the wind so that snow coming in over the trees floated down in spirals and flurries, settling finally among the trees, waist deep already.

They shoveled off a space among the trees and set up their round Sibley tent and the funnel-shaped stove in it. They brought in the canvas covers off the wagons and stretched them between two cottonwoods to make a shelter for the mules. Among the trees they found some stacks of peeled cottonwood limbs — the leavings of a winter camp of Indians who had wintered their horses on the bark and left the limbs ricked up to dry for future firewood. They built a fire in the stove and hung their bandannas up to thaw the ice out.

"We can bring in the mules and horses two at a time and thaw em out," Sammy suggested. "We can maybe keep them from freezing that way. There ain't much we can do for those goddamn cattle. This is no place to raise cattle without you got shelter for em. The buffalo could hardly stand this, let alone a damn cow."

"You couldn't expect a cattleman to put up buildings on the reservation," Sandy told him. "They're doin good just to get the grass."

"It's a damn shame anyway. This storm is fierce. I never seen it so cold. Maybe the priest was right. Maybe the old boy's got it in for em after all — and us too." He laughed as he said it, but there was worry in his face.

They brought in a couple of mules then. The fine snow had sifted into the hair, melted a little and frozen again, so that their hides were caked with a solid layer of ice and snow. Ice hanging from their bellies began to drip in the heat.

They kept them in till the ice melted and rubbed them down with dry cloths before taking them out again.

After that they were busy hauling in wood and working with the mules, hardly stopping even to eat. They had to lay poles across between some trees to keep the cattle from crowding the mules out of the shelter and to keep them from knocking the tent over.

By evening the cattle were hardly visible for the snow that had drifted over them. They were crowded together solid, not moving much any more, but just enduring. Some at the edges were already freezing — he saw one, forced outward by a movement from the center, try to take a step and fall forward on its knees when the frozen legs refused to stir. It stayed that way for a moment, head buried in the snow, then keeled over, struggled a little and lay still.

It grew steadily colder with darkness. They were still taking the mules into the tent in pairs, but it was not enough. They built a fire in front of the shelter and kept it going.

Late in the night, the cattle, attracted by the heat, broke the fence. A big steer at the edge was forced backward till his hind quarters were in the fire, but he did not seem to feel it. The fire sizzled in the ice on his legs and Sandy caught the smell of burning hair. Before they could get him out he collapsed full in the fire and started bawling and struggling. Sandy shot him then, but they had to let the fire go out and build a new fence closer to the shelter — they couldn't budge the cattle.

They worked in the dark, running back and forth to the tent every few minutes to keep from freezing. By the time they finished the fence and got the fire going again, it was nearly morning. The wind showed no signs of easing up, though it was still not hard. The air was still full of fine snow that moved like spray, glittering in the firelight.

Near the shelter a tree exploded with a deep, jarring report that seemed to come out of the ground. Now and then, over the crackling of the fire and the steady stream of the wind, Sandy would hear the sharp hollow crack of a cow's horn bursting as the core froze and expanded.

During the day they took turns and managed to get a little sleep, though the storm did not ease up. They had to grain the mules to keep them from freezing, cutting heavily into their supply. The next day they started bringing in green cottonwood limbs for the mules to gnaw on, when they had time peeling bark off with their knives for the mules that did not know what to do with the limbs.

The storm kept on day after day. The light at midday, with the sun obscured by snow, was no more than twilight. Working out in the storm bringing fire wood and limbs for the mules, their faces were continually frostbitten, even with the protection of their bandannas, so that the skin became inflamed and watery, soaking the cloth so it froze even quicker.

They ran out of grain for the mules and the supply of green cottonwood ran low. Finally they had to spend a day breaking a trail out to the freight wagon, and start feeding the flour they were carrying.

Sammy was visibly worried about the storm. He did not joke about it now but worked harder and more grimly; and he did not talk about quitting any more. It was not fear for his own safety that worried him, either, Sandy knew. The two of them were all right — surrounded by meat and firewood, they could last out a year of the storm. It was something else, Sandy thought. Gradually Sammy became quieter, and when he talked his speech was slower and less precise. He would not sleep and spent most of his time working with the animals, coming in to thaw out when he had to, standing by the stove and staring at the flapping canvas, abstracted and gloomy.

Once, making a trip into the trees for limbs, Sandy came on him in the shelter of a big cottonwood, burning some kind of grass on a little fire and singing. Sandy watched him a moment and stepped back into the trees, unnoticed.

Finally the wind let up. The sun rose far to the south, and for a while the sky cleared. From the ridge they could see the Rockies, patched white and glassy blue beyond the blinding white of prairie.

They had saved the mules, but most of the flour was gone. Nearly all of the cattle were dead, many of them still standing, frozen solid, with snow drifted tight around them. Toward the center of the bunch the melting snow showed that some few were still alive. But they were not moving. Their necks and legs were frozen and as they thawed out, they began folding up and falling. Sandy walked out over the backs of the frozen cattle and shot the fallen ones.

"We'll skin out what we can," he told Sammy, "and load up with meat to make up for the flour we've used. The way it looks now, these mules'll have to learn to eat meat before we're through. You still want to go back?"

Sammy shook his head. "I changed my mind. This sunshine makes things look better, don't it?"

The sun was brilliant now, the light blinding, but there was no warmth to it. As they skinned, the hide fell away stiff from the knife. They built little fires among the unskinned carcasses to keep them from freezing.

They worked feverishly all day, skinning and quartering out the meat. By evening they had enough to replace the flour and a load for the coaster wagon. They pulled the joints out in bunches with a long line and a pair of mules, dragging them over the tops of the frozen cattle and along the trail they had broken to the wagons. Loading it, they left the rest of the flour on top to feed the mules.

The wolves had showed up early in the day. They trotted around the edges of the frozen cattle, slavering at the smell of the warm meat, keeping the mules in a constant fret. They gnawed at the frozen carcasses at the edge of the bunch, but the meat was frozen too hard for their teeth to cut.

Around noon the mist began to form, obscuring the shining mountains. It did not drift like cloud or seem to move at all; it was just there, filling the whole sky with a luminous, brilliant white that darkened gradually as it thickened.

And with the mist, Sammy's gloom returned. His face darkened and he worked harder, stopping only once to disappear into the trees — Sandy caught the smell of his incense fire again and heard him singing.

That night they kept the fire going in front of the shelter to keep the wolves away from the mules, taking turns getting up to replenish it. The wolves cleaned up what was left from the butchering during the night and in the morning were gone.

Both men were up before daylight getting ready to leave. As they were walking to the shelter to feed and harness the mules, a big snowshoe rabbit that had been picking up feed around the mules hopped away ahead of them blending into the mist. It had almost reached the corner of a clump of willows when the blurred shape of a bird — no more than a shadow — dropped soundlessly from above, catching the rabbit in the middle of a jump. The rabbit squealed shrilly and the shadow rose white and insubstantial, beating upward over the trees and disappearing, wraith-like. The rabbit was still squealing and the sound seemed to come from above as if the bird had circled overhead. Then suddenly the sound stopped and there was nothing.

Except for the first sight of the rabbit, and the squeal, the whole incident might have been something imagined, Sandy thought, a freak movement of the mist — the sight of the bird had been no more substantial than that.

Sammy was standing transfixed, his eyes staring and glassy, with a look not of terror but of awe — and humility. He came to life then, and seeing Sandy watching him, turned away in embarrassment.

"An arctic owl," Sandy observed. "I never seen one this far south before."

"Was it?" Sammy asked indifferently. He had his own idea, Sandy thought, but he would not argue.

Sandy helped harness the mules, and while Sammy filled the nosebags with flour, he walked back into the trees for more firewood to cook breakfast with. It took him a while to dig it up from under the snow, and he had just loaded up to start back when he heard a strange horse whinny. He put the wood down and made his way quietly back, keeping out of sight behind the shelter. He could hear the squeak of saddle leather now and knew there were riders in camp.

"You just step over here close where I can watch you, Sammy," he heard a voice say. "You're damn lucky I didn't shoot you on sight, like I'd shoot any damned Injun stealin my cattle. Where's your partner?"

"He quit on me," Sammy said. "He lit out for the Fort when the storm hit."

"He may be tellin the truth," the voice said. "But he's pretty smart for an Injun — he ain't got much guts though. We better keep our eyes peeled. If anybody shows up first thing I'm gonna do is pull the trigger. You want to change your story?"

"No," Sammy said.

"We heard shootin over here yesterday," the voice went on. "But we was snowed in. Anyhow it looks like we got here in time. You made quite a killin on my cattle, Sammy. You know — I got a perfect right to shoot you for that."

"The ones I killed would've died anyway. I just put em out of their misery. I took some meat because I had to feed up the flour I was takin in to the Agency . . . But it's no loss to you. I was leavin the hides, and that's all you would've saved anyhow. And I saved you the work of skinning."

"See, I told you he was smart," the voice said. "That's a good story, Sammy, and it may be right. But the way it is, I got you where the hair is short. You should've let em die and not put those bullet holes in em. So you see, I got you. But what I was thinkin, you bein a pretty smart Injun, maybe we can make a deal — not that I got any objection to shootin you. But if you was to give me part of those supplies, we'd just forget the whole thing."

"No, I can't do it. Those people are starvin. I can't give it away."

It was hard to move in the deep snow without making a racket, but Sandy made it up close behind the shelter without being heard. Through a slit between the canvases he could see the man who was talking, a big, thick-chested man with a dark beard. There were two other riders, each with two pack horses, but he could not see their faces. The bearded man had his gun on Sammy all the time he was talking, and Sandy, waist-deep in snow, was afraid to move for fear of being heard. He could shoot the one now but the others would get Sammy. He would have to wait.

"Now that ain't like you, Sammy," the bearded man said. "You've always showed good sense when it come to business dealings — not a real Injun at all. I'll tell you what, I'll trade you the hides, to make it more like a business proposition."

Sammy shook his head, and Sandy could see his face, set and proud.

"Maybe you don't understand, Sammy. I can kill you and take the supplies anyway. But I'd rather have it more honest and businesslike. Maybe you need a little persuadin."

He put his horse over close, and hit Sammy alongside the head with his gun barrel, knocking him down, out of the line of Sandy's sight. The horse reared and turned toward the horses of the other two riders, and in that instant Sandy moved into the open, his gun leveled. The two riders facing him saw the situation immediately and kept their hands up in sight.

"If you turn your horse," Sandy said to the other, "you're mighty reckless."

The big man stiffened and made the suggestion of a motion to turn, then dropped his gun.

The big man turned then sputtering. "By God," he said, "it just goes to show you can never trust a damned Injun. I would've sworn this one didn't have the guts to take a lickin, and that was what fooled me."

Sammy was up now, the side of his face bleeding, but clear-eyed. He picked the man's gun out of the snow and stepped around beside the other two riders and took their revolvers.

"What he told you," Sandy said, "was the truth except about my own part — I shot the few cattle we skinned, though they were all but dead anyway — you can see that. So you've got no grievance. The hides are yours, already off, and it's a good deal you're makin, considering you're on the reservation illegally and stealin the graze."

"Steal the graze be damned. They don't use it, do they? And they never will. By God, it belongs to the man that uses it."

"That's a flexible enough standard even for your purposes," Sandy remarked. "It allows your conscience plenty of rein, don't it?"

"Conscience. You got plenty of room to talk about that, killin my cattle and stealin the meat."

"You wouldn't use it," Sandy laughed. "It belongs to the man that uses it, don't it?"

The man ignored him. "And it ain't only that. You're stealin it to feed the damned Injuns so they can steal more."

"It's no use to argue," Sandy said. "But we thank you for the meat — and pay you with the hides. And I've been thinkin too that as a kind of courtesy, you might help us for a while. I figured on lettin you go on a promise to leave us alone, but I see you can't be trusted. We'll do it this way: you're ridin good fresh horses; you can break trail for us for a day or two — so you don't go back to your camp for more guns. We'll start now and you can help Sammy while I sort of ride herd."

It worked out all right. They hooked on four of the extra mules, then put the cattlemen and the extra stock out ahead of the wagon to break trail.

On the ridges and out on the level the going was easy. It was on the south sides of the slopes and in the creek bottoms where they had trouble — bucking snow up to a horse's back, coupling and uncoupling the wagons, taking them through one at a time. It was miserable work fighting chains and eveners, floundering in snow all day, at night peeling cottonwood for the stock; and all the time keeping an eye on the three men. They worked hard, though unwillingly, and after the second day the big man was ready to call it quits.

"By God," he said, "I wouldn't come this far to haul this stuff back if you gave it to me, let alone fight for it. And as for gettin even with you, I can't think of any better punishment than this you're gettin. You turn us loose now, we won't bother you."

He let them go, returning their guns but keeping their shells.

They went slower after that. The mules were weakening on the slim ration of flour and the little dab of cottonwood bark they had saved. Then they ran out of that. They were keeping to the ridges as much as possible where the snow had blown off, and there was a little grass, but not enough to help much. So now they had to stop, leave the wagons, and hunt for cottonwood to peel. And when they found the trees, it was hard to get any feed ahead. Some of the mules and Sandy's horse would gnaw the bark holding the limb with a front foot. But the rest had to be fed and it was nearly all the two men could do to keep up with them, let alone get any ahead. But they kept at it, finally saving up a wagonbox full.

They started out on the last stretch then. At night they would hang three or four quarters of beef over a fire and roast them, cutting off the meat when it cooled and feeding it with the bark. It was a strange kind of mule feed, but it kept them going.

Sandy was dog-tired, frostbitten in hands and feet, dead-headed from lack of sleep, but finding in himself reserves of strength he wouldn't have thought he possessed. And he was amazed and strangely relieved at the way Sammy had thrown himself into the collar. Since the storm he had worked even harder than Sandy, and yet he seemed vigorous and strong. There was a quietness in him now of strength and dignity; a humility, Sandy thought, that was new in him. He felt the change vividly, in the way Sammy acted, and within himself too, as if the weight of his own responsibility were lessened by Sammy's assumption.

There was a constant fall of frost, tiny dry crystals that glittered with a cold light and lay powdery and weightless on the snow. The sun came up far to the south, glowing palely beyond the mist, rising shadowless to the mid-sky and setting colorless and almost imperceptible. Daytime was hardly more than twilight, and the white owls hunted at all hours along the creek bottoms.

The falling frost and mist closed in his vision till he had the odd sensation of traveling always in one place in spite of all his effort and striving. So that, topping a hill that overlooked a creek bottom and a little flat, he was surprised and shocked to see the Agency.

There was a rough square of buildings in the middle of the flat, snow-covered, their sides showing almost black through the fall of frost. Pitched in a rough circle around the square and almost covering the flat were the light-colored lodges. There was little sign of life except the barely visible smoke hanging over part of the lodges and one building of the quadrangle. It was the silence that struck him; he missed the usual clamor of dogs. Gone for food, he supposed, and there were no horses. He had a chilling, startling perception of death, as if it hung like the mist over the village.

He jerked the brake line, setting the wheels of the lead wagon and they moved down onto the flat.

There were people appearing now, slow-moving and sad-faced, with a hopeless look of starvation. They walked alongside the wagons or fell in behind, floundering in the snow, old men and women falling in their attempts to hurry and getting up to fall again.

He saw a wolf emerge from one of the smokeless lodges and leap away toward the trees. A young woman walked beside the teams carrying a baby. She stumbled in the deep snow and fell, dropping the baby as she went down. It fell headfirst into the snow and came to rest with its legs thrust stiffly upward, motionless.

They pulled into the quadrangle and stopped. Indians swarmed over the wagons, opening sacks and boxes, eating whatever came to hand. They engulfed the wagons completely, and more kept coming, streaming into the quadrangle from the lodges. In a matter of minutes the wagons were unloaded. There was nothing left and still they kept coming to search hopefully through the empty wagons, then stand around in the bitter cold staring hungrily at the mules while the two men unharnessed them. When they finished, Sammy climbed up on the wagon and spoke briefly. The Indians crowded in around the animals then and began leading them away, leaving only Sandy's three horses.

"You're not likely to get paid for that," Sandy said.

"I don't expect," Sammy admitted, showing a sudden embarrassment. "But hell, those mules couldn't make it back to the fort in the shape they're in. And there's damn little feed for em around here."

"How'll you get back yourself?"

"I guess I'll stick around a while."

"Thanks," Sandy said. He put out his hand then and Sammy took it. They stood looking at each other a moment, both deeply moved but unable to speak further. Sammy turned first and went out of the quadrangle toward the lodges, walking strongly and purposefully, as if he knew where he was going.

Sandy led his horses to the Agency stable and found some hay for them. He felt lightheaded and in spite of his fatigue his step was springy.

All the buildings in the square were closed except the carpentry shop through the window of which he could see someone moving and a flickering of light. There were coffins stacked up in front of it like cordwood, smelling of fresh pine. From within came the industrious sound of a hammer.

He looked in at the door and saw a little wrinkled, grey-bearded man working quickly and mechanically, nailing together a coffin. There was a stack of boxes along the right hand wall, and from beyond the stack a play of light, from a fireplace he supposed, threw wavering shadows on the walls and ceiling. There was a small Indian boy handing nails to the carpenter as he needed them. Seeing Sandy, the carpenter nodded but did not stop his work.

Walking out of the quadrangle Sandy began searching reluctantly, afraid of what he would find. He followed the trails through the deep snow from one lodge to another, keeping his mind from the hope, from the living ahead. It was almost dark, the only light a faint luminosity of the mist and a thin shine of the frost falling. Beyond the last ring of lodges he could see the shadowy movements of wolves and coyotes and hear them yipping and howling along the creek. He could hear the murmur of talk through the village, but no laughter and singing, and now and then above the murmur the cry of a woman keening for someone dead, the sound not loud but piercing and lonesome in the cold night.

There were fires in most of the lodges, magnifying on the lodge skins the shadows of the people within; but some were dark. He looked in one of these and saw the wolf-torn bodies of a woman and child; he did not look in any more of the unlighted ones.

There were coffins outside nearly all the lodges, standing fresh and clean-looking in the snow, capped white with frost. He passed a medicine man's painted tepee, seeing a man sitting in front facing east, hands extended on his knees. On the ground before him was the black, frosted mark of a fire. Coming closer Sandy saw he was dead.

It was hard to go on — everywhere he looked were the signs of death. Yet he would not stop till he had looked in every lighted lodge, seeing the suffering with deep compassion.

He did not find her.

He would have returned to look in all the unlighted lodges, but it was too dark — he would try again tomorrow.

Hardly noticing what he was doing he walked back to the carpentry shop and went in. The carpenter nodded at him again and went on working.

There was a kerosene light on the stack of coffins now, and beyond it Sandy saw the fireplace. There was a bright fire of aspen wood burning clearly and without smoke, mobilizing the room with pale shadows. Playing before it among the wood scraps and curled shavings that covered the floor, were half a dozen small children, all Indian. The boy he had noticed before was still holding nails for the carpenter, giving them to him one at a time as he needed them. A little girl sitting next to the fire had tied some spiraled shavings in her dark hair and they hung down over her shoulders white and curled.

"You come in with the freight outfit?" the carpenter asked.

Sandy nodded.

"I Jacks," the carpenter said, pushing a coffin toward Sandy, "you look plumb tuckered. Set for a while. I ain't gonna stop, fer I got a passel of these boxes to make yet."

He went on hammering and Sandy sat down. The children had stopped playing and were watching him, their backs turned to the fire, their dark eyes round and bright in the pallor of their faces.

"I been havin a hell of a run of these things lately — little ones especially," the carpenter continued. "They been dyin like flies — consumption it is mostly, and starvation. And they been askin for boxes. It's kindy strange too. Usually I make a few every month — it's orders from Washington — and maybe they get used and maybe they don't. (I ain't got any orders yet about fillin em.) Mostly they don't get used in the usual way. These Injuns don't believe in ground burial. They don't like the idea of the spirit locked up down there in the dark. So mostly they throw the lid away and hang em in a tree, open to the sun. They're people of the sun, these Injuns, mistrustful of the dark. It's heathen, maybe," he said, shaking his head, "but a way of believin. They been puttin the lids on lately, though they can't bury em now with the ground froze. So I don't know, maybe it's just to keep the wolves out till spring. But it's strange all the same. They could hang em up frost or no frost, but they ain't doin it. I don't know. Maybe they just gave up. Maybe it's the buffalo bein gone or the mist hidin the sun. I Jacks, it is damned odd weather, ain't it? These owls now, it ain't often they come this far south. If it don't clear up before too long, the whole damn kaboodle of em'll up and die." He finished the box he was on and began laying out the ends for another.

For the first time Sandy noticed a little boy of maybe two peering at him from inside one of the coffins. He could only see the eyes and the top of the head — but there was something familiar — and suddenly he knew.

"The kids," he asked, "whose are they?"

"Orphans mostly. They hang around here by the fire, and they like to play in the shavins — like any kids. I throw em a shovelful of beans or whatever I can spare now and then, and it keeps em alive. The Injuns help em too — but they ain't got anything themselves now. I Jacks, they're tough though. You can't kill em all."

"This one in the box," Sandy said, shakily, "what about him?"

"What about him? He's a little shy, that's all. I ain't fixin to put the lid on him. Kids, now," he chuckled, "ain't much different, Injun or white."

"I mean, is he an orphan, too?"

"No, he's got a ma. She leaves him here when she's out scoutin for food. That's why he's so shy. He ain't here all the time. She'll be along here directly, with maybe some old dry berries or old bones to boil or some scrapins from the inside of tree bark — somethin. And she'll offer me some and take the kid away. You watch now. You can't kill people like that."

Sandy went over to the coffin, his spirits lifting. He dropped to his knees beside it, smiling, and picked up a thin shaving. Holding it to his lips he made a squeaky little whistle. The child's face broke into a smile and he came slowly along the box toward Sandy, holding out his hand for the shaving.

Sandy was just lifting him out of the coffin when he heard her voice and turned to see her smiling at him from the doorway.

They left the next day. Riding out of the square, they passed the painted tepee with the frozen figure sitting in front. The head was dropped forward and the hands were lying palm upward on the knees. On one of them, frozen to the flesh, glittering and quilled with frost, was the brass gear of a watch, a cold and perfect image of the sun.

PART VI
FALL 1885

CHAPTER
2 7

IN THE EVENING OF A COLD CLEAR DAY THEY CAME
in sight of Sandpoint. Woodfoot had dropped back from the main
bunch of cowboys to ride with Charley, not trying to talk but feeling a little sorry for him. Most all day Charley had ridden apart from
the others, fighting the big bay to keep him back, looking woebe-
gone and sorrowful — and for no good reason except that the other
cowboys took a delight in tormenting him. Not enough to make
him mad but enough to set him apart from them. He had no sense
of humor, Charley, no way of answering them except to withdraw,
and when he did that Woodfoot somehow felt responsible for him.

It was odd, he thought, the way he had stuck with Charley. Not
that he especially liked him — he had even disliked him at first
and been a little afraid of him too. But if you knew a man well
enough you got so you could handle him and it became sort of
comfortable to be around him. You could always predict him even
when you couldn't control him. It was a strange companionship —
but easy and at times interesting, too.

Riding along now toward Sandpoint, tired after the roundup,

looking forward to a spree, he felt a certain affection for Charley
— the kind a man felt for an animal that was out of its element and
helpless.

That was odd, too, that he should think of Charley that way.
He was potentially a strong man, Charley was, intelligent and
capable in almost anything he did. But there was something lack-
ing in him — a fire that had gone out with the end of the buffalo.
He was still lightning with a gun and all the young punchers knew
it and were careful accordingly; but they seemed to sense — as
Woodfoot knew — that he would never fight again. In his thirties
Charley was an old man, living backward, back to the days he had
been strong, his days as a hunter, talking about it till no one would
listen any more, then withdrawing to long periods of morose silence
— as now.

It was two years now they had worked for the cattle outfits that
were moving into the country. This past summer they had worked
on a roundup crew in the Sand River country, himself as cook and
Charley as a cowhand. It had been an interesting season — most
of the men were youngsters, full of devilment — and the whole
time had been a succession of practical jokes and good-humored
exchanges. But for the same reasons Woodfoot liked it, Charley
did not.

Charley did not fit in as a cowboy — he was as good a rider as
any in the camp and the best with a rope, but somehow he was not
good with cattle. He had no enthusiasm and little recklessness.
So he had been assigned to camp part of the time to help Woodfoot;
and that was hard on his self-respect. And he did not like jokes.
He had come close to killing a cowboy who put a snake in his
bed — so there were no more pranks like that. But still the jokes
went on.

It had been a pleasant season, Woodfoot thought again. And he
was through now, with money to spend and nothing to do for a
while — nothing but get drunk and maybe find a woman. Then
figure out a grubstake job for the winter.

They left their horses at the livery stable and followed the bunch
of cowboys to Ed's saloon. Charley had to check his gun at the
door, along with the others, and without it he looked naked and
lost. He had had his teeth pulled and his face was hollowed and

gaunt, puckered around the mouth; and there was something lost and hurt about his eyes.

Old Bill Brady, the taxidermist, was working at the other end of the bar, hanging up the head of a big buffalo bull. He had a block and tackle strung from the ceiling to raise and lower it with.

Charley walked down the bar past the other punchers and stood looking at the head. One of the cowboys, a little cocky one by the name of Chuck, called to Brady, "Hey Bill, let that thing down and throw a blanket over it, will you?"

"Why?"

"Well, it's like to strike a chord with Charley there, and start him to singin."

The others laughed. Charley reddened but said nothing.

Woodfoot ordered drinks for himself and Charley, and looked around at the collection of heads that covered the walls — most of them new since he had been in.

Seeing his interest, Ed, the bartender, said, "Old Bill is gonna get me a head of every game animal around here. Only thing I can't get him to mount is an Injun — to stuff, that is." He grinned. "He's mounted a few, I reckon, but never stuffed any that I know of. It'd be just the thing to go along with that buffalo head."

"It seems like he had one in the window a few years back," one of the cowboys recalled. "A Cheyenne, it was. How come you didn't stuff that one, Bill?"

"You hit a touchy point there," Ed laughed. "Anyway it would've been hard to fix. The head was all shot up. And on top of that, for a while it looked like he wasn't gonna die, didn't it Bill? The head is what you'd need though, alongside that buffalo."

"And a buffalo hunter to put between em," Chuck said. "Like Charley here, he'd be a good one — easy to mount. You wouldn't have to skin him, just let out the air and poke the stuffin in."

"Hell," Ed said, "Charley ain't windy. He ain't said a word yet."

"He ain't had a drink yet either," Chuck laughed.

"Charley's all right," Woodfoot put in. "He's been rode, but he's seldom been mounted. And if I ain't a long ways wrong, they ain't anyone around here about to climb him, either."

"Oh, I don't know," Chuck bristled. "But I'll tell you what, Woodfoot. You let us pick our own fights."

"That way," Woodfoot laughed at him, "you can tie on accordin to the size of your rope. Fair enough."

Chuck had been riding Charley for a long time now — and somehow it riled Woodfoot. He was afraid Charley was going to knuckle under, and he hated to see it. But there was nothing he could do. If he stayed he would have to watch it — or make it worse with his talk, one.

He finished his drink and went out. Walking idly along the street, he stopped in at the store to say hello to Black.

"There's someone looking for you," Black told him. "You and Charley. Remember old Stevens, the professor? Well, he got word somehow that there's a few buffalo left in the butte country up on the Antelope divide, and he's out to get em for the museum. He needs a hunter and he won't consider anyone but Charley. He don't like Charley, but he saw him shoot and he can't forget it. So he's been waitin. I expect him back in a little while if you'll wait."

Woodfoot nodded. "I read about it in the paper. The army furnishin supplies and the railroads free transportation — as a public service. They give it quite a send-off."

Stevens came in, smiling as he saw Woodfoot. Ladlaw was with him, looking more like a man now, not quite so cocky. Stevens explained his proposition. "We need a camp man and a man to do the shooting. You and Charley fill the bill — if you'd care to take it."

"We'll take it," Woodfoot said. "Both of us out of a job. When do you want us?"

"Right away. But where's Charley? I'd better talk to him."

"He'll come all right," Woodfoot assured him. "I'll see to that."

"I'll have to see him. Where is he?"

"Over at Ed's. We can mosey over if you'd like. No hurry, though. He ain't likely to leave. What I want to know is, what makes you think there's any more buffalo?"

"I have reliable information. And it looks like the last chance to preserve specimens for the future."

"Old *Bison americanus*." Woodfoot shook his head. "His goose is cooked now for sure, ain't it? We'll save em for the future if we have to kill the last jack one of em, won't we?"

Stevens took the bait. "The senseless hunters and the savages will kill them anyway, and leave no record for posterity."

"They sure will. And the army and railroads backin em down to the last buffalo. Seems like I read somethin about that." He grinned mischievously at Stevens' indignation. "The only thing out of place, though, is you. Last time I talked to you, you was worried about extinction. Now, by golly, it's you and Charley for the last buffalo."

Stevens did not answer, realizing now that he was being jollied.

Charley was still at the bar when they came in. Part of the cow-boys had gone upstairs. The others were fooling with a couple of young women who had come down, and the lot of them were pestering Charley. As he came in the door, Woodfoot saw one of the girls step up to Charley, rub herself suggestively against him and step back shrieking with laughter at his embarrassment.

He looked so pitiful and inadequate, Charley did, that Woodfoot was afraid Stevens would see it and change his mind. He stopped in the middle of the room and pointed to the heads.

"This ought to be right in your line," he said. "Stuffed for posterity."

"They're nice heads," Stevens admitted. "But what I have in mind is something more complete."

"Not just the heads," Woodfoot filled in, "but the posteriors, too. Posteriors for posterity — eyes and assholes, too. Well, this is the way we do it out west. Stuff one end and mount the other — but you got to go upstairs for that."

Stevens looked bewildered, but he smiled halfheartedly.

"Stuffed heads and mounted posteriors," Woodfoot went on, laughing at his own joke. "It's what we got the most of around here. You don't see much evidence of that last — if you did I guess you'd call it posterity. But the stuffed heads are stickin out all over."

Charley had seen Stevens but he just stood there looking guilty and did not come over. Stevens went along the bar and shook hands with him.

"I need a buffalo hunter," he told Charley, "and you're the best I ever saw. So I've been waiting."

"There ain't any buffalo," Charley said gloomily.

"There's a few," Stevens assured him. "And I want them for the museum."

A smile came slowly over Charley's face and he seemed to expand.

The cowboys had stopped talking and were listening. "Stand back boys," Chuck said, "and give him room. He'll make a ride now sure."

Stevens looked around questioningly.

"Don't mind these coyotes," Charley said with dignity. "They make a racket but they don't bite. I'll do it," he went on. "And if there's buffalo, we'll git em, sure. It's a good thing you waited. These coyotes around here don't know what huntin means. I'll get me a new rifle."

"Do you need money?"

"Naw, I got me a stake. When do we leave?"

"Tomorrow, if possible. I have an outfit lined up."

Ladlaw had been hanging back. Charley went over to him, and Ladlaw shook hands but with a standoffish, hostile look. Remembering how Charley had served him before, though, Woodfoot did not blame him. Ladlaw was likely to even it up this trip, he thought.

The two men left then, and Charley went back to the bar and called for another drink. There was a brightness in his eyes, a feverish look, like he had when he hunted.

The cowboys went on with their fooling, ignoring Charley now. They would not bother him any more, Woodfoot thought.

Charley drank his whiskey and poured another and downed it. Then, setting his glass down with a crash, he stood up and walked straight into the group of cowboys, elbowing the first ones aside. He caught the girl — the one who had rubbed him — by the arms just below the shoulders, and forcing her back against the bar, held a long kiss on her lips.

Chuck tried to pull him off, but he was not strong enough; and when Charley finished he turned and, brushing the little puncher aside as he would a child, went up the stairs, the girl following.

"By golly, Ed," Woodfoot laughed. "You mighty like to had the other kind of trophy to hang up, one of those posteriors of Stevens'. I ain't speakin of Chuck here, either. He wouldn't be so damn different from what you already got."

Chuck spluttered fiercely, but Woodfoot laughed at him.

"You just been gelded, Chuck," he said, "only you ain't found it out yet. You'll simmer down. You're lucky you didn't get used for stuffin.'"

Woodfoot ordered another drink and settled down to enjoy it. He felt good, and things were looking up . . .

They were over a week on the way out. The old buffalo country they traveled through was cattle range now; the bones were gone and the only traces of the big herds the deep-cut trails, used now by cattle, but filling in for all that. The old camps of Indians and after them the buffalo hunters were now line camps for cowboys. He had seen the same change in Kansas — even more abrupt and spectacular — but without the finality, the sharp sense of termination.

The last buffalo hunt, he thought, for Stevens and Charley — or anyone — and there was a sadness about it, but an irony too. They would kill the last buffalo, if they could, and stuff the hide for curious people to stare at, giving it, as Stevens said, the immortality of a museum. A piece of a continent would be gone, and with it a people and the life they lived. But you couldn't put a country in a museum, or a people, or the way they lived. And what would a stuffed hide have to tell of that? How would the loss be felt and by whom? The hunt was over now, the game gone, and what of the hunter?

That was it, he thought smiling, what of the hunter? What of Charley and Sandy and even himself, and now this most curious and inexplicable of all, Stevens?

At the top of the divide on the way to the old camp on Sand River, they left the trail and turned south into the rough butte country. The buttes were tall and flat-topped for the most part, capped with a scant growth of jack pine and scrub cedar, curving in a chain off to the southwest toward the highest part of the divide, a small plateau. He could see it now beyond the last butte, flat and sharp in the clean winter light, its sides raked and lined with gulleys and ravines. Far off to the right and down he could see the thin grey line of Sand River and he thought he could make out the little grove of trees where the old camp had been.

It was a rough, scarred country on the divide, chiseled and gouged with stream beds, most of them dry now, showing little growth except sagebrush and greasewood and little patches of thin curly buffalo grass. On down the slope on either side were badlands, devastated, lifeless.

It was hard country to travel with a wagon, and they moved slowly and laboriously. But it was here they began to see buffalo signs.

All the way out Charley had been boiling over with a feverish, exuberant vitality that surprised Woodfoot. Stevens was collecting specimens of all the animal life in the region, so Charley was in his element — shooting everything he came across. He had a new Winchester-Hotchkiss repeating rifle which he used for larger game, and Stevens furnished him a small shotgun for birds. He was at it continuously, at all hours, riding the big bay far beyond the endurance of any ordinary horse.

Now, with the first signs of buffalo, he quieted down and became almost comically serious. He scouted far on ahead of the wagons, finally, when they were almost to the high plateau, coming on his first buffalo, a crippled bull, and killing it. And he was more foolishly and irrepressibly elated than he had been after his biggest stands.

They made camp in one of the ravines coming off the plateau where there was a spring and some grass for the stock. The next day the four of them crossed the plateau to scout the country to the west. In the afternoon, as they were riding down a hogback between two ravines, Charley sighted buffalo. He was riding in the lead when suddenly he wheeled his horse and crowded the others down off the north side of the ridge. He dismounted, pale with excitement, and when he spoke his voice was hoarse and unnatural.

"They ain't likely to see us," he told Stevens. "A buffalo don't depend much on his eyesight. And the wind is right, but no use taking any chances. They're down at the mouth of the ravine on a little flat by a water hole, maybe a dozen of em." He drew a map on the ground with his toe. "They're bedded down, so they probably just had a drink, and their noses are pointed into the wind away from us. It's a good situation for a stand if I can work down

within range. What we want to do is work down the north side
of the ridge and be ready to follow em in case they run. They're
gonna take out across that flat into the wind, if they go at all."

Stevens assented but Ladlaw hesitated. "Suppose they come back
up the ravine? You could never follow them in there — but from
up here you'd stand a chance to cut them off."

"I just explained to you," Charley said with irritation. "They'll
go the other way. A buffalo don't like the brush. On top of that
he runs into the wind nine times out of ten, especially if it's open
country that way. He's a prairie animal, the buffalo is, made for
open country."

"It may be," Ladlaw admitted. "But if I were a buffalo, I'd head
for cover. And these ravines are where we've found the most signs.
So I'll just play my own hand and stay here. The rest of you can
go on."

Charley shrugged and rode off along the side of the ridge; Woodfoot and Stevens followed, but Ladlaw stayed where he was, his
jaw set.

"It may be just as well," Charley laughed. "He won't get tangled
up with any buffalo up here. But he's apt to break his neck if he
rides down that hill."

They moved on down the ridge, keeping out of sight till they
were almost to the flat before Charley took another look. He
peeked over the ridge, then rode back down to them and dismounted. "Go on down almost to the point," he whispered. "You
can see em from there. And if they run, take out after em. It's a
long shot from the top of the ridge — but I'll have to take it."

Woodfoot and Stevens rode on. Looking back, Woodfoot saw
Charley fiddling with his sights. Near the end of the ridge where
it sloped out onto the flat, they left their horses and moved cautiously up for a look.

Woodfoot saw the buffalo at a glance, to the southeast of them
now, on the flat, not over a quarter of a mile away. There were
half a dozen bulls and four cows, two with late spring calves, all
bedded down except one old bull grazing off to one side. The
mouth of the ravine was maybe a half a mile beyond, showing a
dense growth of scrubby pine and brush.

The ridge they had come down curved a little to the south, so that looking back up it now Woodfoot caught sight of Charley. He had expected to see him right at the top; instead he was crawling slowly down the south side toward a little projection of sandstone. If he made it, Woodfoot thought, he would be within good rifle range, though shooting down. He had it figured right.

The old bull was beginning to look around, as if he sensed danger. He hooked another bull lying at the edge of the herd, bringing him up, and the two of them walked through the bunch.

Charley had reached the rock. He cut loose with the first shot, and Woodfoot saw the bullet kick up dirt beyond the herd. The sound crashed through the silence; and before the clatter of echoes stopped the buffalo were up and gone, scattering wide on the flat, heading for the ravine.

Charley emptied his rifle at the running animals, missing clean as far as Woodfoot could tell.

"It's that damn new rifle," Woodfoot told Stevens as they ran for their horses. "By golly, it's the first time I ever seen old Charley miss." He could hardly believe it. Something must have gone wrong.

Stevens did not answer, but he looked disgusted and annoyed.

They climbed the ridge and took out across the flat — but Woodfoot knew there was no chance of catching the buffalo. He saw Charley bring the bay up over the ridge and down, riding fit to break his fool neck. The horse came down in stiff-legged jumps, sliding a few feet every time he hit, winding up at the bottom in a cloud of dust but still running. Woodfoot and Stevens were both laying on leather, but Charley passed them before they reached the ravine, going into the brush full tilt and out of sight. They slowed down when they reached the brush, and Woodfoot caught a glimpse of Charley crossing a little open spot on ahead, still going strong.

They heard shots then — but not the Winchester — and Woodfoot knew that Ladlaw had intercepted the herd. They found him a little later, standing happily by a big bull he had killed. Woodfoot thought he could still hear Charley crashing through the brush on up the ravine.

"He can still ride," Stevens snorted, "even if he can't shoot."

Ladlaw and Stevens set to work on the bull, making a lot of

careful measurements first, then skinning with painstaking care. Ladlaw was pleased with himself, Woodfoot could see, but he had the sense to be quiet about it. He would do his talking when Charley was around.

Darkness came early in the ravine. Clouds that had come up earlier in the day closed over solid above the ridges, shutting off the light. It was too late now to make it back to camp. So Woodfoot staked out the horses, dug what food they had brought out of the saddlebags and fixed a meal, roasting some of the hump meat off the old bull.

Charley did not get back till long after dark. Woodfoot was already in bed, but he got up and gave Charley some food he had left by the fire to keep warm.

"I lost em up on the plateau," Charley said. "It got dark on me. And now I'll be damned if it don't look like snow. By God, it looks like when things start goin wrong a man might as well quit. If it snows we'll never pick up their trail."

"What happened to you, Charley?" Woodfoot asked. "I never seen you shoot like that before. Must be the gun, ain't it?"

Charley shook his head. "It's a good gun. I just got buck fever," he admitted. "I never had it before — when it came time to shoot I always steadied down. I don't know, seems like everything's goin back on me. Did you see how those buffalo acted? Like deer, by God, or elk. They ain't the same as the ones we used to hunt. It looks like if we get any of these we'll have to run em. At least I got me a horse to do it with, if he don't up and break a leg. That's one thing that ain't gone back on me."

It snowed two or three inches during the night, then cleared off the next day, cold but with no wind. Woodfoot went back for the wagon, finding Charley waiting for him when he returned.

"Stevens and Ladlaw ran onto a couple of cows below here and got em," he said. "I never saw a thing. They sent me to tell you," he ended feebly.

"You sick, Charley?" Woodfoot asked. "You look bad."

Charley shook his head and turned away. He told Woodfoot where to find the two cows, then started out to hunt again, riding at a gallop.

It went on that way for a week, Stevens and Ladlaw hunting together, seeing the only buffalo, and getting some too, and Charley alone, not finding a thing. He hunted early and late, stopping only when it was too dark to see. And still his bad luck held.

He was shaky now and bleary-eyed, worn out, but he would not quit. Even the big bay began to show the strain — he gaunted up and his big bones showed clear through his shaggy winter coat, but he was still full of go. All the men had extra horses, but Charley refused to use his. "When I come on buffalo," he explained, "I want a horse under me, not one of these crowbaits."

"You'll kill him off," Ladlaw said. "He's not a machine, you know."

Charley did not answer. His eyes went blank and he withdrew as completely as if he had walked away. He did not talk now and always sat apart from the others.

A few days later, right after they left camp, the three men struck the fresh tracks of a small herd of buffalo. Charley came back to tell Woodfoot how to find the trail so he could bring the wagon, then lit out again.

The cold had not let up and the snow was the same as it had fallen, dry and powdery. So there was no mud or ice to fight and it made the trail easy to follow. In the creek bottoms hoofed-up clay and sand mixed with the snow, dry and clean.

The trail climbed the plateau, crossed it to the west, and went down steeply through a brushy ravine out onto a flat. It was hard going on both sides of the plateau, so that he made it only to the flat the first day and had to camp for the night. He was out early the next morning following the trail through rolling, barren hill country. Around noon he came on the mangled carcasses of two buffalo calves in the bottom of a hollow. Scattered along the hollow, all within fifty yards of the calves, were half a dozen big wolves, frozen hard as stone. He had not known that Stevens carried strychnine.

He loaded the wolves and went on, meeting Stevens a little later, riding back to meet him. Stevens looked relieved when he saw Woodfoot.

"I poisoned those carcasses," he said. "The wolves had killed them — the only calves in the bunch. Ordinarily I don't use strychnine, but I was so damned mad. They didn't eat much — just killed them for sport. So I just thought I'd try poison. Then later I began thinking that you might try to use some of the meat — so I came back. I already shot a magnificent bull," he bragged. "The biggest one yet. Charley didn't get a one."

He was pleased now, Stevens was, and not so mad about the wolves.

"We lost the herd in some badlands to the south and the other two are trying to pick them up again." He changed his saddle to a fresh horse and mounted again. "I hate to miss out on the chase," he said guiltily. "So I'll go on ahead."

Woodfoot smiled to himself. He hated buffalo hunters, Stevens did, and now he had the fever himself. It was strange, he thought, the way hunting could change a man.

It was evening when he reached the place where Stevens had killed the bull. He saw the smoke of a campfire first, then saw Stevens there waiting for him.

Stevens walked out to meet the wagon and Woodfoot saw that he was quivering with rage. He had a hard time getting started but finally it came out.

"Some thieving Indians stole my buffalo — hide, meat, everything. And what they didn't take they spoiled."

He was indignant, old Stevens was. He walked over to the campfire and kicked a pile of splintered marrow bones, then bent over and tried to pick up the big head, but it was too heavy. He dropped it and wiped his hands in disgust.

The head was splashed with red and yellow paint and there was a red rag tied around one horn.

"The damned coyotes," Stevens burst out again. "Too lazy to skin the head, but they had to spoil it anyway, smearing it with their stupid paint. And the tongue — " He rolled the head over to show where the tongue had been taken out through the lower jaw.

"That paint," Woodfoot commented, "it's probably got some religious meaning. A charm, maybe, to bring buffalo. A herd's apt to stampede through here any minute."

Stevens paid him no heed, but went on with his complaint.

"I was all for trailing them down and making them pay — and

so was Ladlaw — but your precious Charley was afraid. 'I ain't lost
no Indians,' he says. 'It's buffalo I'm lookin for.' A precious lot he's
found. I've done better myself."

Woodfoot grinned mischievously. "You'll likely be remembered
as the last, best buffalo hunter," he said. "But you got to keep
tryin. There's a few left yet."

The sky had clouded over and Woodfoot could smell snow in the
air. Stevens sensed it too, and he was nervous as a cat.

"It's a long way back to camp," he kept saying. "We'd better
get started back."

"We wouldn't get far tonight," Woodfoot said. "We might as
well wait for Charley and Ladlaw. We'll make it back. Hell, it
won't snow that hard."

"All the same, I'd hate to get snowbound here. This country is
fearful."

It was a bleak country all right, Woodfoot thought, enough to
bother anyone not used to it. They were in a little flat that
stretched off to the south like a pass through a maze of badlands;
but it was not a pass. The level beyond was cut with clean, steep-
sided washes that were not visible from a distance, but they made
it impassable for a wagon. It was a dead end, for all the smooth
look of the flat ahead. On both sides the badlands lay jumbled,
steep hills and jagged washes. On some of the hills, usually tilted
at odd angles, were slabs of rust-colored rock, and on all surfaces
flat enough to hold it, clean caps of snow. On some of the larger
hills an occasional vine cedar clung tenaciously and here and there a
spear of sagebrush or greasewood. There was no other growing
thing.

Ladlaw came in about dark. "We got a glimpse of them," he
said, "but lost them again. They went up a sidehill a goat couldn't
climb, much less a horse. Charley was still trying to get that old
bay up it when I left. They'd get up part way and then come
sliding down. It was comical, but it's a wonder he doesn't get hurt.
He wouldn't quit, though. He just kept cursing the poor horse
and trying again. He's about half crazy, do you know it?"

"We had him sized up wrong," Stevens said. "He's no hunter.
And I begin to doubt that he ever was one. When the buffalo were
thick any fool could do it."

"He was good all right," Woodfoot said. "You got cause to re-member that, both of you. But he's like the buffalo — he's changed. He's about to hit bottom, Charley is."

"By heavens," Ladlaw snickered, "he can't hit anything else. You know, the first time I met him he reminded me of a rattle-snake. He still does — but with his poison dried up."

"He ain't as dangerous as he was," Woodfoot admitted.

It was almost midnight when Charley got in. There was still a fire going and food beside it, but he would not eat. He left his horse tied to the wagon, still saddled, and rolled out his robes under the wagon, falling into them without even taking off his gun belt. He was snoring a minute later.

Woodfoot got up and unsaddled the bay. He gave him a feed of grain and threw a blanket over him. The old horse was wet with sweat, already shivering from chill. Woodfoot heard him heaving and coughing for a long time before he went back to sleep.

It was snowing at daylight, big feathery flakes coming down so thick and steady it was hard to see anything more than twenty feet away.

Woodfoot rolled out to build a fire and start breakfast. He had to throw a couple of the wolves off the wagon to get at some of his supplies. He left them lay, a little way from Charley's head, and went on with his work.

Later, after Stevens and Ladlaw were up, he called Charley but got no answer. He went over to the wagon and shook him and Charley stopped snoring and stirred. Woodfoot started back to the fire, then seeing the wolves lying there, eyes open, teeth showing, he stopped and stood them up in the snow near Charley's head, pulling their stiff legs apart to prop them. He stepped back to call, but Ladlaw, who had been watching, stopped him. He climbed into the wagon, threw out the rest of the wolves, and stood them up in a semicircle around Charley. Then he dragged the painted head over, making room for it in front of the wolves. Woodfoot noticed that Stevens was smiling too.

Through the thick fall of snow, the wolves looked startlingly alive and fierce. It would scare any man to awaken suddenly and see them.

Woodfoot had a notion to go back and kick them down; but suddenly Ladlaw let out a terrific yell that ended in a kind of wolf howl.

Charley came up under the wagon like a spring, bumping his head. Seeing the wolves, he froze. He just sat there, completely immobilized, even his face, only his eyes alive and they stricken with terror.

Woodfoot found himself tense and breathless, watching. Charley had to wake up soon, he thought. He could not stay there in terror forever.

But Charley did not move. Woodfoot looked over to see Ladlaw holding his sides suppressing his laughter — but fascinated too. Stevens was grinning, but he was beginning to look guilty.

Woodfoot could stand it no longer. He called, "Charley," and stepped forward through the fall of snow.

Charley moved — suddenly. Woodfoot saw the gun come up and tried to call, and saw the spit of flame; he did not hear the sound. He fell backward numbed, seeing the grey-white fall of snow changing to black . . .

CHAPTER
28

WITH THE SOUND OF A SHOT THE TENSION broke; his vision cleared and through the lacy falling snow Charley saw a man throw up his hands and fall backward. And in that instant he saw that the wolves were not real — not alive. He seemed to awaken — and yet he had seen the wolves as clearly before the shot as now; he had been afraid then too — his mind struggled feebly, trying to define the point at which he had awakened, to separate the waking from the dream. But his thinking was unclear, curtained off, as with the fall of snow that obscured his vision.

He shut his eyes against the dizzying swirl of white, against the sudden weakness that seized him, opening them again — he could not tell how much later — to find nothing changed. But dimly, beyond the frozen, grinning wolves he could see two men standing motionless; and in a flash of clarity he knew they were Stevens and Ladlaw. It must have been Woodfoot who fell; and suddenly his heart was leaping in his chest in a tumult of fear and dread. He came out from under the wagon and walked slowly among the wolves toward the fallen figure, afraid of what he would see but unable to stop.

Woodfoot lay spread-eagled on the snow, his unblinking eyes fixed upward, the laughter gone out of them. Snow had melted in the creases of his leathery face and shone there now like tears. There was a red stain spreading on his grey shirt in the middle of the V made by the opening of his coat.

Ladlaw and Stevens were standing motionless, not ten feet away. He looked at them, from one to the other, expecting some explanation, finding in their wide staring eyes a terror that matched his own of a moment before. They seemed to be staring at something behind him. Fear struck him again, whirling him around to face whatever it was that threatened; but he saw nothing — nothing but blown whorls of snow and the wolves motionless, lifelike, covered now with unmelting white. He turned back and found the two men still staring at him; and in another flash of clarity, knew it was himself they feared. He looked from one to the other and saw them wince as his eyes moved. Looking down he saw the gun in his hand and realized he had been pointing it wherever he looked. He put it in the holster, feeling an unbearable weakness in his muscles.

"It was an accident, Charley," he heard Stevens say. "I swear it wasn't your fault. He was more to blame than you. And the rest of us too."

Charley did not answer. He turned and looked once more at Woodfoot and knew that he was dead. He started for the wagon, reaching forward with his hands for support, and saw the wolves and was struck by an overpowering revulsion. The strength and will left him and he fell forward, shutting his eyes against the whiteness of the snow, feeling it sharply cold against his face . . .

What seemed a long time later he was sitting by the fire, not knowing how he had got there, holding a plate of food on his knees. Automatically he started to eat, then set the plate on the ground and looked around him into the whirling snow. The fire was almost out; the wolves were gone; the buffalo head was covered with snow, only the jet-tipped horns still visible.

Ladlaw and Stevens had harnessed the mules and were preparing hurriedly to leave.

"You'd better try to eat something, Charley," Stevens said, coming over to him. "At least drink this coffee." He handed Charley a cup that had been sitting on a rock by the fire. Charley sat holding the cup, not caring to drink but not knowing what to do with it.

"Climb into the wagon," Stevens said. "We have to get out of here or we'll be trapped."

"You go ahead," Charley told him, trying desperately to keep the shaking out of his voice. "Just leave me my horse and saddle. I don't feel like movin right now."

"We won't go without you," Stevens objected. "Besides, we'd never find our way back through all this snow without you to show us."

Charley stood up, his spirits rising; but he knew inside that Stevens was exaggerating. Still, he looked worried, so maybe it was partly true, maybe they did need him. He walked unsteadily to the wagon, finding that Ladlaw had already saddled the bay.

He found his rifle and rode on ahead into the storm, hearing Ladlaw hollering at the mules to get them started and the muffled squeak of wheels in the fresh snow. It was colder now, the wind coming in shifting gusts, clearing brief avenues of sight through the grey streaked snow. The bay turned sideways against the gusts, but he moved steadily and in the right direction, so that Charley finally gave him his head and stopped thinking about the trail.

His face became numb from the wind and snow and he felt that way inside — unfeeling and unremembering. He rode in a vortex of descending snow that closed him in, opening now and then on brief glimpses of country he did not recognize, except that he could tell they were coming to the end of the badlands and into the hills.

Where the trail turned east he stopped to wait for the wagon; and it was then he saw the buffalo. At first he did not believe his eyes, thinking it only a configuration of rocks against the slope off to the left. But when the snow cleared again he saw the head turn toward him and the fluttering of the long frontlet — an enormous bull plastered on back and sides with snow but head and under parts showing dark and shaggy.

The gun was heavy and slow as he brought it up and held it tight to his shoulder to wait for a break in the snow. He was drawn up to a single, breathless point of concentration, and when he saw again — just the outline — fired quick and blind. The snow cleared and he saw the bull drop out of sight and knew he had hit. He kicked the bay to a run, reaching the spot where the bull had disappeared and finding in front of him a steep-cut wash. He forced the bay over the bank without a pause, and saw the bull disappear around a bend in the gulley. Dimly, he heard Stevens and Ladlaw calling him but only for an instant; then he rounded the bend and there was nothing but the wind in his ears and the pound of hooves under him. The banks of the gulley flashed by with incredible speed; the bay dodged and twisted past boulders and cave-ins, running hard with his nose stuck way out ahead as if he were running by scent. And Charley urged him on, giving himself up without thought or fear to the danger, intent only on the buffalo. He leaned forward with his hat pulled far down over his eyes, straining for a glimpse of the bull he knew was there, not far in the lead.

Snow flicked cold against his open eyes, caught in his eyelashes, melted and then froze, giving his lids a stiff, mechanical feel when he blinked. For a long time he rode, the bay running strong and steady, but he did not see the bull. He thought he could hear sometimes the sound of running hooves, but he was not sure.

Then suddenly he saw the bull — directly ahead — saw him hesitate, and turn off sharply to the right. Charley tried to stop, knowing instinctively there was a drop-off ahead. But it was too late; he reined the bay to the right and plowed into the buffalo. He felt himself falling then and pushed clear of the saddle, throwing the rifle.

He lit on his back on soft ground with a jar that knocked his wind out and sent lights flashing in his head. He caught a brief, hazy glimpse of the horse lying across the buffalo at the foot of the cut bank. He saw the bull struggle for footing and raise up his shoulders under the weight of the horse; saw the horse try for his own footing and slide off the bull's shoulders and go down again.

Charley came to his feet, the breath still out of him, and searched blindly for the rifle. He saw the buffalo not thirty feet away running again, and drew his pistol and fired, seeing snow jump on the bull's hide as the bullet struck, and fired again. But the bull did not falter. Charley turned and found the bay on his feet. He gave up the rifle and mounted, only now getting his breath back, hearing it sobbing in his throat as if it were someone else, not himself.

The bay was running with a jerky, unbalanced stride and Charley knew he had been hurt in the fall. But the bull was not far ahead, hurt too, barely keeping his lead. Charley kept pushing the bay; he could not stop now, so near the end of the run.

He moved with dreamlike slowness, the big bull just ahead, beyond the curtain of snow, appearing and disappearing with each flurry but keeping the same lead. Since the drop-off — he could not tell how long — he had been traveling in unbroken hills, the ground soft under the snow, absorbing the sound of hooves. All he could hear now above the wind was the bay's gasping breath and the squeak of saddle leather. The bull moved silently before him, shadowlike, seeming large beyond reality in the brief intervals of sight. And Charley followed, straining forward in the saddle, despairing bitterly of ever catching up.

Then the horse slowed and the bull was before him, starting up a steep incline. He found the middle of the back just ahead of the hip joint and fired, hardly hearing the sound or feeling the jump of the pistol. The bull collapsed and rolled back down the bank, coming up on his forelegs to face Charley as he reached bottom.

Charley fired twice at the forehead and the bull went down and began kicking, his hind feet plowing a big arc in the snow.

Even stretched out on the snow in death the bull seemed tremendous; but Charley felt no joy, no elation — nothing — nothing but the sickness of despair that had gripped him at the end of the ride and a deep and utter weariness.

He stood for a long time, numb, bewildered, moved finally by a vague uneasiness. The feeling became insistent in him that he had lost or forgotten something — he could not tell what — becoming finally a kind of panic. His efforts to think increased his confusion till he felt like falling down and weeping.

The wind had increased and was shoving at him in big surges, easing up suddenly so that he rocked back and forth drunkenly.

The noise it made was tumultuous and fierce.

He thought of skinning the bull but he was too distracted to know how to begin. He gave it up and went back to his horse.

The bay was standing where he had stopped, his feet spread wide apart, his head down.

Charley mounted and started to ride away; and it struck him shockingly that he had no idea of where he was. There were no landmarks he could see through the tangled confusion of snow, and he had lost all sense of direction. He pondered a long time before it came to him that he might be able to backtrack.

He found the tracks and rode along them, aware dimly that the bay was barely moving, dragging one hind foot. He would not move faster, though Charley urged him, knowing that the tracks would soon be filled with snow.

He was still in the hill country when the trail disappeared; he dismounted thinking to follow on foot, but he could not. The tracks were gone completely, smoothed out by the drift-snow that slid in a haze along the surface. He stood for a while in uncertainty, aware that he was getting too cold. He thought of making a fire but remembered that there was no wood. He would have to keep going.

He moved with difficulty to mount, pulling himself up with his arms and throwing his weight awkwardly into the saddle. The horse swayed weakly, sidestepped and went down, catching Charley's leg under him as he fell. He struggled feebly to get up but he could not.

Charley worked his leg free. As he stood up the bay dropped his head onto the snow, kicking with one hind foot, furrowing the snow as the bull had done. Charley knew then that he would never get up. And seeing the big ugly head, stretched out helpless for the first time, he was swept by anger and bitterness — but sadness too, and loneliness. He bent over and almost stroked the dark muzzle; then straightened up and put a bullet through the head, and turned quickly away.

The thought of his own danger stirred him. He would freeze soon, he knew, if he did not keep moving. Automatically he started back along the trail toward the buffalo, finding the bay's tracks still plain, though partly filled with drift.

It was hard walking though the wind was behind him, pushing him along. He felt stiff and awkward; his feet sank unevenly in the snow and sand, making him stagger and weave. Yet he seemed to move headlong, the snow streaming by him.

The tracks were smoothed over before he got back to the buffalo, but he kept on, finding the carcass almost covered with snow.

He kicked away some of the snow and began skinning, slowly but methodically. He had to think about every move he made — all his energy was gone and only his will kept him going. He girdled the legs and the neck, then ripped open the belly and the insides of the legs. He peeled the upper side and after a long struggle was able to roll the carcass over and do the other.

He spread the hide out, fur side up, and with his hands brushed off all the snow he could. Then he lay down on one side of it and rolled himself up, burying his face in the damp musky fur.

He did not sleep but lay cold and unthinking for a long time, hearing the wind sweep over him and the whisper of driven snow. Sensation came slowly into his hands and feet, tingling like the pricking of a thousand pins and he realized he was warm again.

With the thought his mind cleared and he was possessed again by the feeling of uneasiness, of having lost something or forgotten it. He was lying on his right side. The arm under him was cramped and he tried to turn onto his back. But he could not stir. For just an instant he thought he had lost control of his muscles and tried again, violently. He knew then it was the hide, pressed close around him and frozen stiff as iron. He could move his fingers and hands a little but not his arms and legs. He tried to squirm upward; but the hide was draped down over his shoulder, pressed tight to the side of his face. He could not even turn his head. In the face of his rising terror he forced himself to lie quiet a moment longer. Methodically he tried first one leg and then the other, then his arms, prying out with all his strength to find a soft place, a spot in the hide that might give to his pressure. But there was no give; he was completely restrained, locked in as if his very skin had turned to stone. Snow had drifted over the opening he had left for air — he could tell by the greyness of the light — and he could not even hear the wind. His heart contracted and he was fighting in a dark violence of horror . . .

He became aware first of a sound, thin and far away, that grew louder as if he were approaching it, moving downward, dropping toward it, till suddenly he was enclosed with it; and the sound was himself, his own gasping, sobbing wails of terror.

It was a long time before he could stop it and lie quiet, holding his mind steeled against all thought.

His right hand was turning numb from the pressure on his arm; he pressed his body upward to relieve it, and stretched his fingers. He felt a smooth cold surface just at the tips of his fingers and with a sudden flash of hope, knew it as the grip of his pistol. If he could turn the barrel inward —

He strained his arm downward, feeling the curve of the handle just beyond the grip of his fingers. He could press it between his thumb and fingers but not enough to exert a pull. He worked at it till he was completely exhausted, his arm weak and aching.

When his strength returned he tried the belt, and with a feeling of triumph, worked it up till he could grip the pistol. He pulled it up with his wrist and fingers, trying to work it up between his belly and the hide; but there was not room. The barrel would not come clear of the holster. He had to give it up after a while. And after the little hope, his despair was greater than before. Even the gun, he thought, even the goddamn gun.

The darkness was complete now. There was not a glimmer of light. He had heard something as he worked with the gun but in his concentration had ignored it. He heard it again, the thinnest sliver of sound, drawn out and dying. He steeled himself, holding his breath till he heard it again — the thin, piercing howl of a wolf. His hand found the grip of his pistol; he stiffened against the expected sound, the rip of the bullet in his leg; but there was nothing but the hollow click of the hammer. He snapped it again, counting, five times before he gave way to the frenzy . . .

He awakened in darkness after what seemed like a long sleep, feeling nothing but hearing near him a steady metallic clicking. He listened carefully, concluding finally that it was the snapping of a pistol. It was his own, he knew, though he could not feel the movement of his hand. He willed the finger to stop, but the sound went on steadily.

It was odd, he thought, lucidly. He would not have believed it possible — that his mind should be so clear, yet so apart from him.

He tried to send his will along his arm, through his wrist into his fingers; and thought he heard a slowing of the rhythm. He kept trying till the sound stopped, and he found the power to draw his fingers away from the grip.

He felt better then. Cutting his eyes upward toward the snowed-over opening, he thought he could see light, only the faintest glow, a vaporous shining, and knew he had passed through a night and imagined the sun rising in the cold sky.

He was looking down from far up, seeing the hills in a brilliance of light, folded clean and stainless under snow. He could see the creeks that veined the slopes joining and growing as they moved down, and far off the dark shining thread of the river. Of himself and the buffalo there were no traces. Nothing moved. There was no sound nor any color.

But strangely he was not afraid. He felt at peace and there was nothing fearful or hostile to him in all the white, silent land . . .

He was in darkness again, staring upward at the vaporous light, rapt, unmoving. There was no sensation in all his body; he was weightless, insubstantial, and there was nothing now except the light.